Quilted Lilies

a novel by

Ann Hazelwood

C&T PUBLISHING
Another Maker Inspired!

Text © 2014 by Ann Hazelwood
Artwork © 2014 by C&T Publishing, Inc.

Executive Book Editor: Elaine H. Brelsford

Proofreader: Adriana Fitch

Graphic Design: Sarah Bozone

Cover Design: Michael Buckingham

Photography: Charles R. Lynch

Published by C&T Publishing, Inc., P.O. Box 1456, Lafayette, CA 94549

Library of Congress Cataloging-in-Publication Data

Hazelwood, Ann Watkins.
   Quilted lilies / By Ann Hazelwood.
      pages ; cm. -- (Colebridge Community series ; 6)
   ISBN 978-1-60460-182-4 (softcover : acid-free paper)
   1. Quilting--Missouri--Fiction. I. Title.
   PS3608.A98846Q55 2015
   813'.6--dc23
                        2014045283

POD Edition

"I fell in love with Anne's characters! I would love to see the Taylor House, plus I love flowers, gardens, and gazebos! I am wishing I had the next book to read."

—Marianne Rudisel, Terre Haute, Indiana

"Considering the fact that I'm not a 'reader,' I've become so involved with the Colebridge characters that I have to pace myself so I don't read each book too fast."

—Terry Doyle, Rantoul, Illinois

"I moved to Colebridge! I have become Anne Brown! If only I could step over to Grandmother Davis's position to advise Anne before the next page turns. Ann Hazelwood has captured me into the beloved Colebridge series."

—Jackie Reeves, Angels Camp, California

The pattern for this block is available at:
https://tinyurl.com/16469-patterns-download

With Appreciation

One does not fulfill one's success without the help of family and friends. I would like to acknowledge and thank the following:

First and utmost, my heartfelt thanks to my husband, Keith Hazelwood, and my sons, Joel and Jason Watkins, who continue to give me love and support. I love you!

My writer's group, The Wee Writers—Jan, Mary, Janet, Hallye, Ann, and Lilah. Their talent and friendship are such an inspiration to me.

My friends and former employees of my former business, Patches etc., who continue to cheer me on and occasionally share my travels.

Last, but certainly not least, is the C&T Publishing staff, Meredith Schroeder, who believed in this fiction series, and my patient editor, Elaine Brelsford, whose wisdom makes me a better writer. I feel they are on this journey with me and I hope to make them proud.

Dedication

Throughout my Colebridge series, I had the good fortune to have resources like Parkview Gardens and Greenhouses in St. Charles, Missouri. Their willingness to promote my books and provide fresh white lilies on many occasions, was very much appreciated. The atmosphere and friendly staff were an inspiration to each novel.

It is with great gratitude I dedicate *Quilted Lilies* to Holly Gillette and her team at Parkview Gardens.

CHAPTER 1

Stop! This is crazy! How am I supposed to write with the pounding of hammers, whirring of saws, and voices coming from the room next door and outside of our house at 333 Lincoln? I thought my little spot nicknamed "the waiting room" was safe from the outside world.

This previous sitting room, off our master bedroom, was called the waiting room because everyone was waiting for something special to take place there. Most thought it was waiting to be used as a nursery for a child I might have with my husband, Sam, but I felt it was waiting for when I had time to write my book about the Taylors, the former owners of 333 Lincoln. Sam took advantage of the small, handy room by using it as a waiting room for his next trip. It was a perfect place for his luggage and things he needed quickly when packing to go away on business.

If or when Sam and I would need a nursery, I felt it should

be across the hall, where the cheery smaller-sized bedroom called for someone special to inhabit it. It appeared I wasn't going to win with my writing room remaining in the waiting room. Sam insisted we remodel the bedroom next door to accommodate a home office for me. It wouldn't be as cozy or handy, but I didn't want Sam to think I didn't appreciate his concern for me. He was probably thinking I would eventually work from home as I took care of little Dicksons running around the house. That was not going to happen, but it was best left unsaid.

The sound of the workmen putting in shelves and wainscoting told me this was indeed happening soon! Sam seldom traveled anymore since being named president of Martingale, and as the historic purist that he was, he insisted the small room be what it was intended to be—a sitting room for our gorgeous bedroom.

The activity outdoors was created by Kip, our handyman and gardener, who was building a beautiful arbor and patio room off our sunporch. We had neglected the rear of our historic home because of our love for the south porch that faced the circle driveway to our house. It's previous owners, Albert and Marion Taylor, spent many hours drinking lemonade cocktails, according to the letters we discovered from Mr. Taylor. I enhanced the pretty spot by having a gazebo built in this special area of the property. It was a surprise for one of Sam's birthdays. Our beautiful yard was like having our own park. It had a rose and lily garden as well as a sizable herb garden. The hedges, trees, and bushes were all unique, thanks to the Taylors' love for beauty.

The best feature was a charming potting shed. When Sam and I first looked at the run down house, I dismissed the idea of ever living there until I discovered the potting shed. It took my breath away, for I loved watching flowers and plants grow. I never had the opportunity to garden when I lived with my widowed mother on Melrose Street, so this was perfect. The overgrown vines and dirt covering the inside of the potting shed couldn't hide the shed's history. I could see there had been an active gardener at some point in time that worked out of this tiny shack.

My repairs to the space were minimal. I fixed the broken windows and cleaned up the debris. The raised flower bed in the corner, an old potting counter, and the shelves on the wall all remained as before. I told Mother that if I'd had access to this place while growing up, I'd have hidden and played there every day. Sam offered to modernize and expand it to fit my needs, but I insisted it remain intact or the charm and history would disappear, which were the very things I loved about it.

Early spring was the perfect time to enhance the yard. It was my favorite time of year. So many redbud and dogwood trees on the grounds were enough to cheer anyone. The early lime-green trees gave us hope of a great summer to come on the top of this hill. Kip planted many bulbs the year before and said the surprise blooms would make me happy. Kip was a godsend to us, for his talents were many. He was a cute, single guy that loved the outdoors. He had needed a job, and his timing in coming to us was perfect. He also helped Kevin at my shop with deliveries when needed. He was the gardener that 333 Lincoln needed, despite how much I wanted to do it all myself.

The past winter had been challenging, to say the least. Besides harsh weather that closed my shop on several occasions, the business owners on the street took the risk of an outdoor quilt show. The Ghostly Quilts on Main Quilt Show not only brought a surprise of success to the local shop owners, it also was the day of the unexpected arrival of twins for my best friend, Nancy, who was helping us in the flower shop at the time! It was a day I will never forget.

Life had not been dull ever since I married Sam. We always had the ongoing challenge of my Grandmother Davis's spirit that haunted us at any given moment. She made her presence known at my mother's home, but when I moved to 333 Lincoln, we discovered she was the ghost the whole community was whispering about on the top of this hill. We discovered from letters written by Albert Taylor, that my grandmother had been his mistress. She'd worked for Mr. Taylor as a young woman, but when she became pregnant, he ignored her and stayed married to his wife, Marion, here at 333 Lincoln. My grandmother named her daughter Mary and gave up her up for adoption.

Mary never gave up finding her roots, but thanks to her conscientious daughter, Amanda, she connected with us and the Taylor house. Amanda had a brother named William. The reunion of an aunt and cousins who were new to us was amazing and we were thankful for the unraveling of information that led them to us.

Shortly before Mary passed away, she met her half sisters Sylvia (my mother), Aunt Julia, and her half brother, Uncle Ken. Unfortunately, another sister, Aunt Marie, had recently died. Heart disease had taken her as it did Mary as well. When I think of the health pattern, it was not a surprise when my cousin Sue told me Uncle Ken had been in poor health due to heart disease. I hoped and prayed that it would not strike my mother.

CHAPTER 2

The last few months had been stressful for me as I balanced my expanded business, social engagements, writing, home decorating, and Sam's own history of heart problems. I found myself doing things for others and getting away from what I really loved. I knew if I didn't make changes, I would become burnt out and start taking out my frustrations on the people I loved. So far, my new plan was working, but it was difficult. I had a manager, Sally, who was now only going to concentrate on the bridal business at the shop instead of day-to-day operations and designing. I put Jean, our sweet employee from England, in charge of scheduling, which she was thrilled to do. Abbey, the newest employee, was the most creative person on the staff, so she got to take over the ordering, for which she seemed to have a clever knack.

In a small shop like mine, customers wanted to see the owner. They valued my opinion, and because I was a native of Colebridge, they wanted to share their happiest and saddest moments in life with me. I valued that greatly and it was part of the reward I received. As my shop had grown and employees were added, I found I missed doing the floral designing and wanted interactions with the clientele that I had worked so hard to build.

I loved the historic area of Colebridge along the Missouri River. That is where the heart of the city lived, and when I envisioned opening a shop on Main Street, I could picture myself belonging there. I could look out my front door and see the river between the shops across the street. The historic main street was a community within itself. I wanted to do my share of belonging there, but learned that I had to impose limitations in my involvement.

"Would you like me to fix you a bit of lunch, Anne, while I am here?" asked Ella, peeking into my little room. She had become more than a cleaning lady. She had become family. Unlike my previous cleaning lady, she and my ghostly grandmother seemed to get along.

"Oh, that might be a good idea. The time has gotten away from me," I said, grateful for her suggestion. "You might offer something to Kip as well. He's been here working since early this morning."

"Sure will," she happily answered. "I already took him some lemonade."

I shut down my laptop realizing I hadn't written a great deal, but had made notes as to what I wanted to enter the next time I sat down to write. I was collecting bits and pieces about our house and its previous family, but the more I wrote, the more I inserted my own observations and feelings. I had no deadline for my book, so I just continued to journal as I found information.

When I went downstairs, Kip was already at the kitchen table eagerly taking advantage of the generous turkey sandwich Ella had made for him.

"How's it going out there today?" I asked Kip between his bites.

"Wait until you see," he responded with a big smile. "With this great weather, I am really making progress. If there's no rain, I'll be able to start painting the arbor next week. I'm putting in the fire pit today. What a great spot that will be next fall when the first chill comes along."

"It was a great idea. It's like building an outdoor room to the house. I'll have to start looking for just the right furniture to make it look like an indoor living space. I have seen some great examples in magazines."

"I'll be going then, Anne, unless you can think of anything else," Ella said, gathering her things. "I brought a plate of oatmeal cookies that's on the counter if you all need dessert."

"Thanks, Miss Ella," Kip quickly said. "Oatmeal is my favorite, so I don't mind if I do."

"You are wonderful, Ella. Thank you so much," I chimed in. "I'll be sure Sam gets some before Kip eats them all!"

We laughed and I gave her a quick hug before she left.

As I started my sandwich, I realized that I was letting Ella become my 'mother' like when I was single and living at home. She was taking a personal interest in our lives here at 333 Lincoln and I took advantage of her services, just as I did with my biological mother. The only difference was that this was my choice and I was paying her. I had never and would likely never have any interest in cooking or cleaning, so my choices were made accordingly.

"I heard on the radio that the river is really rising again," announced Kip, going for the cookies. "They don't expect it to crest for a week or more."

"I know shop owners are already concerned," I added. "Most of them were on the street when we had that really bad flood in 1993. It got too close for comfort, but the worst part was that the publicity really hurt business. Why the media has to make things so dramatic beats me. It's worse for the folks on the river side of the street because the first place the water goes is in their basements. Luckily, we are on the other side."

"Better get back to work before that mean boss of mine gets after me," Kip kidded.

I nodded with a big grin. "I'll be out shortly to check on things when I do some watering," I said as I still savored the good sandwich in front of me.

CHAPTER 3

Kip went back to work while I cleaned up our luncheon plates. My cell phone went off.

"Hey, sweetie," Sam said, his sexy voice sending tingles down my spine. "Are you enjoying your day off?"

"I am," I cheerfully responded. "Is everything okay there?"

"Well, we'll see," he said with hesitation. "One of our clients wants to meet up for dinner to discuss some of the problems we're having, so several of us need to go. I'm sorry, but I have no choice here."

"Oh, Sam, I'm sorry," I responded. "You hardly slept last night. I suppose I can give Mother a call to join me for dinner since I haven't talked with her in some time."

"Good idea, and give her my love," he said kindly. "Tell her it's time we have some more of that pot roast of hers."

"Okay, I will, but try to get home at a decent hour,

okay?" I pleaded.

"I hear you, Mrs. Dickson," he teased. "I love you, baby!"

Another night of work, I lamented. *How could anyone put up with working so many hours and still be so sweet and loving?*

Sam's health history and a recent heart attack were always in the back of my mind as he piled on more work in his new role as president of the company. It was an achievement he had worked hard to attain and I was proud of him. His widowed mother and I worried greatly about him.

It was difficult for me to balance my concerns without sounding like a nagging wife. He wasn't the only one who struggled with overload. He frequently lectured me prior to my decision to expand my flower shop.

I walked out the back door to see Kip on his knees laying brick around the circular fire pit. He was in deep concentration with country music playing in the background, so I didn't disturb him.

I headed to the potting shed, making a note that stepping stones should be leading directly to the shed instead of going through the grass or coming from the other side of the house. I wanted to pull out the potted ferns that had been hibernating through the winter. They had brown leaves scattered everywhere on the brick floor of the shed, but the green leaves were still healthy and seemed to be begging to get out of doors. I wanted to place them around the new patio, but for now, they could camp out near the shed to take a deep breath of fresh spring air.

I frequently lost all track of time when I entered this little slice of heaven. Each visit triggered memories of how I found a crazy quilt wrapped around an ornate vase hidden under the potting bench. It belonged to Marion Taylor, as we later discovered. After I rescued the quilt, we found cut-up letters from her husband when he was in Europe. They revealed accusations that Albert had fathered a child with a former employee named Martha Abbot. That woman turned out to be my grandmother, who became Martha Davis when she later married. This scenario backed up why her spirit remained to annoy and bother anyone at 333 Lincoln, where Albert had lived with his wife. Everyone in town told us of a ghost that existed up here on the hill in this house, but no one knew who she was. She was indeed unhappy, just as she apparently had been in real life. Aunt Julia never had good things to say about her, however, like my mother, the other siblings remained kind. I knew Grandmother approved of me in many ways.

Thank goodness she took a liking to Sam and me living in the Taylors' house. She wanted her say in many situations, but she wasn't cruel. Well, maybe once. She didn't like us going in the attic. She once gave a scare to Nora, our cleaning lady, and then a slight push to Ella, our current housekeeper, which resulted in a trip to the hospital. Ella set her straight, refusing to give in to her nonsense, and all has been well ever since.

We all identified with Grandmother's ill will, because she had to give up her child, Mary, for adoption. That had to be difficult in any day and time. Mary grew up, married, and went about her life with many unanswered questions looming. Thankfully, she was reunited with us before she died. I had promised Aunt Mary on her deathbed that I would include my cousins Amanda and William in our family gatherings. It is nice to know our extended family, even if they don't live close by.

After I swept up the dry leaves, I realized that time had once again gotten away from me. That was the effect this potting shed had. I wanted spring to turn everything green and colorful immediately.

My shop, with all its vibrant colors and life, sustained me through the rest of the year, which helped. Every little plant was like a life that was waiting to burst with success, bringing joy to folks like me.

In my shop, I quickly learned that everyone had a favorite flower. Mine had always been red roses. Anything red was always a favorite. Grandmother Davis loved lilies and it was obvious in everything she did. She wanted to make sure we all knew it! For years, she had placed live, unexplained lilies on her lover Albert's grave until their daughter Mary died. It all made crazy sense.

CHAPTER 4

Mother and I connected about having dinner and she said she needed to stop by Harry's before she came over. She said she had made vegetable soup and would be glad to bring some. It sounded good, but now every conversation I had with her included Harry in some way. They had books in common, as she was a former librarian and he worked at Pointer's Book Store. They became closer when Mother started working part time there. However, it wasn't long until Mother had to leave the job due to her aching knees. Lifting boxes and books proved to be too difficult health wise for her to continue working there.

Harry had been a history teacher earlier in his career and the whole town knew him to be charming. I sure was off the mark when I expected Mother to be lonely after I left the house. She, like me, had never lived alone before, so she jumped in immediately by redoing the house, spicing up her wardrobe, cutting her hair, and taking on a part-time job. She was financially comfortable and didn't need to work, but she found it enjoyable. After she quit the bookstore, she still loved being connected to it by writing reviews for their newsletter.

"What a lovely evening! Don't you love it?" Mother asked cheerfully upon her arrival.

"I do love it, so why don't we enjoy a drink here on the porch while the soup warms up?" I suggested.

"I brought some cornbread, too," she added as she made herself at home on the porch chair. "I dropped some off for Harry as well. He's having friends over for cards tonight." She seemed to light up when she brought up his name.

I went in to prepare dinner for us on the sunporch so she could see the latest handiwork from Kip. I never knew how much to ask her about Harry. I felt if she wanted me to know something, she'd tell me.

"So, what's new, Mother?" I asked casually as I rejoined her.

"Oh, just staying busy," she said as she took a sip of her drink. "Harry and I have looked into going on a guided tour as a getaway. I can't remember where they said we would go, but it sure sounds nice. Harry does not like driving much at night and my knees can't take a lot of walking, so I think we may try it. I know I used to wonder why on earth anyone would want to go on one of those tours, but here I am, thinking about it."

We chuckled.

"It sounds just perfect for the two of you," I agreed. "We don't see as many tours on our street as we used to.

So many of the tourists just get off the bus and find the closest bench. They really don't want to shop. They don't need another thing to drag home, and who wants to bring packages on the bus?"

"Well, that won't be Harry and me," she said with a smile. "So, Sam is still working tonight?"

I nodded. "Yes, he is working more than ever with his new title and responsibilities. He doesn't travel nearly as much, so that's a good thing. He isn't sleeping well, so I'm not sure what that's all about."

Mother shook her head like she was sad to hear it.

We went inside, and as I brought in the soup, Mother admired the progress on the patio.

"This is quite large, Anne. Do you really think you'll use it? Is the arbor going to be covered with something?"

"Yes, we're just not sure with what," I answered as I tasted my soup. "I've seen different ideas, so we'll see. This soup is delicious, Mother. No one can make soup like you do!"

She blushed. "Before I forget, I told Donna we would have a small bridal luncheon for Amanda in a few weeks, so I hope that's still okay with you." Mother's statement served as a gentle reminder. "I called Amanda and she'll be bringing three friends that will be in her wedding. She said the wedding will be small and will take place at a hotel."

"Oh, that'll be nice. Aunt Mary would be thrilled that we are helping. What should we give her for a wedding present?"

"I'm not really sure, but we still have plenty of quilts to give out that belonged to my mother. We also have some from your Aunt Marie. You surely could take some more of those, Anne, with all the bedrooms you have here."

"I will," I said agreeably, putting butter on my cornbread. "I know there's still another white on white one that I would like to see again. I took the one that I have in our bedroom. Has Aunt Julia taken some?"

"She doesn't have much interest in older quilts," Mother said, frowning. "I told her to be thinking of Sarah. We have lots of photos to go through as well. I don't like having to store all this. I need to be downsizing some."

"Oh, Mother, stop it," I teased. "If you really mean it, we have plenty of room here. The attic is cleaned out now and there are plenty of empty closets."

"I will take you up on that, my dear," she said, grinning.

"I am curious about Grandmother's photos since we know now that she had an early affair with Albert Taylor. I hope there are some of her when she was younger."

"I'm sure there will be," Mother affirmed. "You haven't mentioned anything lately about the little Barrister twins. Have you seen them?"

"Nancy constantly shares pictures with me and they are absolutely the cutest!" I replied. "They really do look alike and are growing so quickly. Nancy is so happy."

"Well, that should be a good sign of encouragement for you, my dear," Mother said, not missing a chance to gently tease me about having a baby. "This big house needs a big family. You just can't imagine the amount of joy children can bring."

I shook my head, but gave her a kind smile. "I'm thinking about it and you can rest assured it will happen someday," I said, giving her a wink. "I couldn't even say that six months ago."

Mother's response was a kind of surprised smile. "I need to get going, Anne," she said as we cleared the last crumbs from the table. "You and Sam finish the rest of the soup."

"Sam will love finding the leftovers when he gets home, so thank you!" I gave her a kiss on the cheek.

As I saw her out the door, I was especially thankful to have such a happy and contented mother. I sure was lucky there!

I was ready for an early evening, so I set the house alarm before I went up the stairs. Just as I began to undress, the land phone rang at my bedside table.

"Hey, still up?" It was Sue, my cousin.

"Sure, what's up with you?" I asked as I continued pulling off my clothes.

"Mia's asleep and I'm sitting here alone like most nights, feeling sorry for myself."

"What brought this on?" I asked, feeling concerned about the tone in her voice.

"Well, I've been thinking," she began. "Sometimes, even with the two of us, it feels lonely, like our family isn't complete." She paused as I waited to hear more. "I know you are going to think I'm nuts, but I am considering adopting another baby. You and I both grew up as the only children in our families and I think we both wish we had siblings. I want to do that for Mia."

I remained quiet as I tried to absorb this new information.

"I want her to have a little brother."

This was surprising! "I certainly can relate, Sue, and you seemed to enjoy the process of the adoption and taking care of Mia," I said, being very careful in my choice of words. "How far have you taken this idea?"

"Not far, just thinking, thinking, and thinking right now," she answered. "My mom and dad will have a fit, I know. They already worry way too much about us right now. If I went through with this, I'd have to find a job with different hours, but frankly, I'm ready for that change as well."

"Well, you *have* really been thinking, haven't you?" I said in a positive voice. "You are a big girl and know what's involved, so I say you should go with your heart and gut. You only have one life and you should create it as you see fit, especially the things you have control of." I could hear her snicker in the background.

"I sure asked the right person, that's for sure."

I could hear a change of mood in her voice.

"I knew you would understand if anyone would. Thanks, Anne, you are a gem. I think I have some planning to do!"

We hung up shortly after I calmed her fears about adding more change to her personal and work life. I knew the feeling of wanting more as I dismissed feelings of guilt. It made me feel good to console her and encourage her to pursue her dreams.

Good for her, I thought, as I found my way to bed.

CHAPTER 5

I didn't hear a peep from Sam until he rose early the next morning. He never slept in and always started his day earlier than me. That usually meant I would find him drinking coffee at the kitchen table with the newspaper or with his laptop propped open. I put on my robe, wanting to see him before he left for work.

"Hey, sleepy eyes," he said, smiling when he heard me enter the kitchen. "Are you taking a walk on this gorgeous day?"

"Yes, hope to," I returned his good mood, leaning over to kiss him on the cheek. "I missed you last night. What time did you get home?"

"Around eleven. You were fast asleep and I decided not to wake you. Did you have dinner with your mother?"

"Yes, she brought over vegetable soup and we had a nice time catching up, I guess you could say." I poured myself a cup of coffee. "So, what's on your plate today?"

"Busy, busy as usual," he said while buttering his toast. "Oh, just so you know, I am going to put an offer in on the Brody property next door today. I hope you're on board with that. I figure we have got to protect this property here on the hill or who knows what might develop? The asking price is high, but I'll lowball it as best I can."

"I see your point," I agreed, nodding. "It's just so sad when I think about it all. I remember when Mrs. Brody told me how Mr. Taylor kept trying to buy her property from her and she refused to sell. I hope she would approve of us, Sam."

He grinned. "Remember that she is the lady who brought a blackberry pie over to us on our wedding day. I don't think those on-and-off deliveries of flowers from you hurt our relationship any. She definitely liked you, Annie. You gave her respect and attention."

"I guess her nephew will get all the proceeds from the sale," I mused, thinking about him coming and going up the hill. "That's the only family she ever mentioned."

"Let me handle it, sweetie," Sam said, kissing me on the forehead. "I've got to run. Are you planning to be home tonight? Isn't this book club night?"

"No, it's tomorrow. I think we need to have dinner together."

"Fine," he said, a broad smile stretching across his handsome face. "It may even be a celebration if my offer on the property is promptly accepted. I promise to make dinner with you happen somehow. Do you want me to cook?"

"No, I'll prepare something like spaghetti and salad. How's that?" I quickly suggested. It was something I knew I couldn't screw up and Sam seemed to enjoy it.

"Perfect. You haven't done that in a while." Sam was nearing the door. "Get some of Nick's garlic bread if you can get over there. I can make a meal off of that and something good to drink. See you, baby!"

What he was saying was, if I screwed up the spaghetti, there would be good wine and bread. As I made my way up the stairs, I couldn't help but worry what this extra land purchase would mean for Sam. He never complained but seemed to just take on more and more. That all added up to more stress.

On my quick walk down the hill, around our block, and back up the hill, I stopped for a minute to assess Mrs. Brody's property. The yellow jonquils were popping up all over despite the long, unattended grass and overgrown bushes. It had been her home all her life, I remembered her telling me. I should have visited with her more before she died. I'll bet she could have shed a lot more light on the life of the Taylor family.

When I got to the shop that morning, Sally was consulting with a bridal customer. I was amazed at how well she managed to deal with mothers and daughters who didn't always see eye to eye. When she talked me into expanding my shop to accommodate large weddings, she got her wish. It kept her busy full time. She already had coffee made for her appointment, and when I poured myself another cup, Kevin came in the back door.

"Man, that river is coming up faster than I've ever seen it!" he announced. "My brother's place is getting it bad down by the river road. We sandbagged last night, but tomorrow, I need to help him move out. Do you think you can call Kip to come in?"

"Oh, Kevin, that's terrible," I consoled him. "Of course. I'll call Kip soon. Does your brother have a family?"

"He has a wife, plus their dog, Patches," he said, getting himself a cup of coffee.

"Cute name for a dog," I commented.

Kevin agreed and then said, "They're sandbagging farther down on Main Street, I noticed this morning. I'm glad we're on this side of the street, even though it's never gotten as high as Main Street."

"Top of the morning to you both," Jean announced in her English accent as she entered the shop. "It's a beautiful sight out there, despite that bloody river they keep talking about on the telly. I wish they would put a sock in it."

"I don't think a sock will do it," Kevin teased.

We all chuckled.

"I'm going to water the flower boxes out front, Jean. Would you get going first thing on the Kendall order?" I headed to the front door. "She always comes in early to pick up her order. Kevin, I think everything's in good shape so you can leave, and don't worry about tomorrow. If I can do anything to help, let me know."

Jean looked puzzled about the comment, but went right to the cooler to get started on her arrangements for Mrs. Kendall.

CHAPTER 6

I loved watering my plants, especially in the spring. I felt like their caregiver when they arrived at my shop and I certainly saw myself as their mother at 333 Lincoln. It was my goal for them to thrive, and it made me feel wonderful when I observed that happening. Kevin did a fine job putting geraniums in our flower boxes in front of the shop each year, along with ivy and a few white nasturtiums. Main Street shop owners were getting more creative with their outdoor plantings and I offered a discount if they needed anything from my shop.

Gayle, from Glass Works next door, came out to say hello as she often did when she saw me outside watering my beloved plants.

"How do you like my plants this year, Anne?" she asked with obvious pride.

"You did very well, Gayle," I responded as I looked at the two flowering pots flanking her front door. "Do you want me to give them a drink?"

"No thanks. I did earlier. I've wanted to talk with you, Anne. Do you have a minute? You are always rushed, it seems."

She had me pegged correctly. "Sure. What's up?" I put down my watering can. It appeared that this could be a serious matter.

"It's my mother," she began. "You know she lives in Alabama. I need to visit again and find her some sort of senior living arrangement. Perhaps it will be more of a nursing home. She can't live alone any longer. Frankly, don't know how I am going to manage it all."

"Gayle, I'm so sorry." We sat on the bench outside her shop. "You have such good employees, so surely they will be fine."

"You're right, but they don't work for free, Anne," she lamented. "I've already been gone so much and business has been so slow with all this flooding publicity. I'm truly struggling and my lease is up this summer. I don't know what to do. I feel so guilty not being there with her, and then if she goes into a facility, there is her house to deal with."

I was at a loss for words regarding her unfortunate situation. I thought for a moment before I spoke. "You have to make her your priority," I said, just thinking of my own mother having me primarily to depend upon. "Maybe you could cut your shop hours when you are gone to help with the expenses. The flooding issue will calm down when the river crests. Right now, we may as well all be under water."

"I don't want to leave Main Street," she said, nearly in tears. "I've been here eight years now, and feel I'm really established in this location. God has thrown me this zinger from out of the blue and I don't feel I have many choices but to move to

Alabama and straighten things out."

Oh, this is serious, I thought to myself.

"Perhaps God has given you an opportunity instead of a problem, Gayle," I said, trying to lift her spirits. "You don't want to go into more debt and commit to a lease right now. Do you think the landlord would work with you by allowing you to rent month to month?"

Gayle shook her head.

"I'll bet they love stained glass in Alabama! What if you moved into your mother's house and opened a business there after you got settled?"

"I have thought of all of those options, but didn't know if I was just fooling myself into thinking everything could work out," she confessed.

"Of course it can if you take it one step at a time," I encouraged her, sounding confident. "I'm sure there will be a charming little street or neighborhood that would love to have a cute shop like yours. You would be able to stay in your mother's house for free, right? That would be a big help."

She nodded. "We'll have to see about her finances first, I suppose." Gayle stood to follow a customer that was approaching her shop. "Don't say anything just yet, but thanks for helping me think this through. I knew you would understand, being an only child like me." She met her customer with a cheerful greeting.

I remained seated, looking at the beautiful street that I would never want to say good-bye to. I also knew I would do anything for my mother. I was so lucky she was here with me and still in reasonably good health.

"Your cell phone is ringing on your desk, Anne, just so you know," said Sally from the front door. Her client was leaving as

I came in the door and it appeared as though she'd successfully booked the wedding. I went to my phone and it had been Kip calling, so I rang him back.

"Had a question on the stepping stones before I go any further," Kip explained. "I can't do much more here today until you look at some things, so I wanted you to know I'm leaving."

"Oh sure," I quickly answered. "By the way, could you possibly fill in for Kevin tomorrow with deliveries? He has a brother that has to move because of the flooding."

"Sure, I'll give him a call to see if I can help in some other way," Kip offered.

The retail room was filling with bustling voices, so I knew I was needed out front. Mrs. Kendall was paying for her order and wanted to engage me in small talk as I helped a young man pick out a birthday bouquet for his girlfriend. Jean was politely explaining to an older lady that she could not return a floral centerpiece if her husband didn't like it. Her charm worked as it always did. Out of the corner of my eye I spotted a young, attractive girl selecting a small floral arrangement of roses and baby's breath from the refrigerated case. Where everyone was coming from all at one time, I wasn't sure, but we needed to pick up these walk-in sales anytime we could get them.

CHAPTER 7

"Can I help you with that?" I asked as the young girl handed me the arrangement. "These baby roses will keep on blooming with this soil and grass base. It's what I like most about them."

"It is a sweet arrangement, and just the size I was looking for," she said, getting her wallet out of her purse. "I expected there to be floodwater near your shop, so I called before I came. I needed to get some spices from across the street, so I thought I'd take care of this errand as well."

"I'm so glad you did," I responded. "We certainly like having that shop across the street." We laughed and made small talk about our favorite spices there.

"You're Mrs. Dickson, the owner, right?" she asked, quite out of the blue. "You live on top of that hill on Lincoln Street, if I'm correct."

I nodded, smiling. "Why yes, how do you know that?"

"Well, my Grandma Tilley used to tell us stories about working up on that hill when she was a young girl."

"Are you kidding me? I want to hear more. What did she do there?"

"I guess a little of everything, but mostly cooked. If I remember, my mom said Grandma Tilley lived there during the week and came home on the weekends, unless the owner's wife was having a party."

"That would have been Marion Taylor, right?" I asked, making sure her story was correct.

"Yes ma'am," she said nodding.

"What was your grandmother's name?" I asked, hoping to get as much information as I could.

"Samantha Tilley. She died a good while back. My mom said she loved Mrs. Taylor, but she didn't like it when Mr. Taylor was around. She was always glad when he was gone."

"This is the kind of information I have wanted to learn. I'm sorry. I didn't get your name," I said, feeling foolish.

"Beverly." She stated it and did not offer her last name.

"Would you like to visit 333 Lincoln and see the room where I think your grandmother lived?" I asked, feeling excitement growing within me. "I really would like to hear more. Is your mother still living, Beverly?"

"No, she died of breast cancer last year," she said, sadness evident in her response. "I would love to see the top of the hill sometime, Mrs. Dickson."

"Well, let's do that soon," I suggested. "You can take one of our business cards."

She placed her check on the countertop.

"We won't need your check, Beverly," I said with a smile. "You have just given me something much more valuable.

I would so like to hear more. I have been accumulating information about the house, and I'll bet you'll be very helpful. Give me your number and I will call you."

"Thank you so much, Mrs. Dickson," she said shyly. "I don't know how much help I can be, but I would like to see where she worked and all." She recited her telephone number and I wrote it on a nearby notepad.

She left as I held on tightly to numbers I had written down. I couldn't believe this stroke of luck! Everyone was intrigued with the Lincoln hill. I only hoped her secondhand information would be useful and interesting. I would call her soon.

When I arrived home that evening with my crunchy Italian bread in hand, I couldn't wait to tell Sam about meeting the granddaughter of the Taylors' cook.

Oh, please don't let him call and say he will be late tonight.

Sam was my best friend, so I always wanted him on hand for every little bit of news I wanted to share.

I wasn't a very creative cook, or much of a cook at all, but Sam liked the spaghetti sauce that I managed to enhance from plain store-bought sauce. He loved my red wine salad with mandarin oranges, sliced roasted almonds, and touches of bleu cheese. I put on a red checked apron that I kept handy and started to mix up the sauce.

With daylight still lingering outdoors, lighting our new patio, it would be fun for the two of us to have a view of it while enjoying our dinner. I covered the glass-top table with a red checkered tablecloth and created a cozy Italian themed place for us to have dinner. I went to the cupboard that had a multitude of candlesticks to choose from and brought a pair to the table for that romantic touch. Placing the wine glasses on the table made me think of a blue empty wine bottle I had saved. I pulled a few pretty greens from the garden and used them as my centerpiece. Ah, now for the music. In my quest to create just the right atmosphere for our dinner, I nearly forgot that I had sauce bubbling on the stove. As I filled a pan of water to boil for the spaghetti, I felt like I was playing house with the man I so dearly loved. How lucky could a girl be?

CHAPTER 8

"What's this?" asked a familiar voice coming in the kitchen. It was Sam and he was on time! "Who is the pretty lady in an apron? Is she slaving away for some handsome guest that she hopes walks in the door?" He grinned as he gave me a kiss on the cheek. I blushed, hoping I didn't look too forlorn from my cooking efforts.

"I'm so glad to see you!" I greeted him, wiping my hands on the apron. "Your timing is perfect, honey."

"Can I do something—like pour the drinks?" he asked, looking around to get a read on the progress of the meal.

"Yes, as a matter of fact, you can. There is a little café around the corner just waiting for the server to arrive. If we allow a few minutes for the bread to heat, we'll make our reservation just in time."

He looked at me with confusion until he saw my setting in the next room. He turned to give me a big grin.

I removed my apron and brought our salad and bread to the table. Sam pulled my chair out for me and started admiring my creative table.

"I'm glad I dressed for dinner. I wouldn't want to miss this date for anything."

We settled down and Sam made a toast to his beautiful bride. It was a sweet moment, because I loved to surprise him and appreciated that he noticed the effort I had put into our dinner.

"First, I want to know if we are the new owners of the Brody property," I asked, not sure if I really wanted to know.

"I'm afraid we are one of several who are interested, so the broker said it would be a few days before a decision would be made." Sam's voice held a somber tone. "I don't know who they are, of course, which is unsettling. I really thought we would have been the first and maybe only buyer to show interest."

"Maybe we will still have a chance," I offered, trying to give him hope.

"Unfortunately, since we invested so much into our property, it makes their place much more desirable," he explained as he was eating and enjoying my culinary efforts.

"What would we do with it if we did get it, Sam?" I asked, passing him the bread.

"Most of it is wooded, which I'd like to keep it that way," Sam shared, talking between bites. "We want to keep our privacy up here as much as possible. There's a total of twenty acres. You may want to create a nursery of sorts or a few greenhouses. How about that?"

Did I hear him correctly? "You would actually consider that, Sam?" I questioned, wanting more clarification on this new disclosure. "Don't tease me like that. You know that is too big of a carrot to dangle in front of my nose."

He laughed. "I think Mrs. Brody would approve of that and we could remodel her little house into an office or guest house," he proposed. "It would be better than someone else living there. The ground is good and it would require little clearing."

"Sam, this is too much," I gushed. "How come you didn't tell me any of this sooner?"

"I had to have time to think if it's the best use, and from the agricultural approach, it can save us some taxes and make my wife very happy," he shared, taking my hand. "I'll bet Kip would be the perfect guy to help us with all of that. I think you have your hands pretty busy right now. You seem calmer lately, as if you have things in place, am I right?"

"You know me so well, Sam." I looked at him fondly. "I thought I was going to have a breakdown until I reorganized my priorities. Oh Sam, I can just see all of this. What a wonderful idea. This has to work out financially, of course." I had to calm myself down. This news was over the top but the whole purchase might not happen.

"That is a true statement, my dear." Sam was nodding at me. "Let's find out what we'll have to pay or if they will let us have it at all."

My mind was going crazy considering rows of greenhouses on that property!

"So, what else went on today?" he asked, taking a second helping of salad.

What else could matter now? I thought. "I do have some pretty exciting news of my own to share, I suppose. In the shop today, I met the granddaughter of a maid named

Samantha Tilley that used to work for the Taylors! She has secondhand information, but she is curious about the house, as you can imagine, so I invited her to come visit. She is a darling young African American girl named Beverly, but I didn't get her last name. She did give me her phone number."

"That is pretty significant for your research, isn't it?"

"Would you like to be here when she comes?" I enthusiastically wanted to include him.

"Sure, if I'm available, but most of this research I am leaving up to you, Anne," he reminded me. "You might ask her to bring any old photos that she might have."

"Good idea, honey!" I exclaimed, beaming at him. "She did say her grandmother was very fond of Marion, but not Albert."

"That's not the first time we've heard that," Sam said, laughing under his breath.

"I also haven't had a chance to tell you that Sue is thinking about a second adoption," I shared with a smile. "She doesn't want Mia to be an only child like her and she feels her family is not complete. She's thinking about adopting a little boy this time."

"That is good news, and I'm sure it'll be easier for her the second time. We should support her in any way we can. That little Mia is quite a sweetie pie!"

"I thought you only had one sweetie," I teased, smiling at him.

"No question that you are my main sweetie," he returned, kissing my hand. "I'd like to ask the waiter if there's any dessert. Have you seen him?"

I laughed. "Sorry, I think they are sold out." I looked around as if looking for the waiter.

"Well then, my sweet Mrs. Dickson, your Mr. Dickson should be able to come up with something sweet." He tenderly kissed my hand. "I think we should blow out the candles, close this place down, and be on our way."

I knew what he was leading up to, but how was I to concentrate on Mr. Dickson when I was planning my greenhouses!

CHAPTER 9

After dreaming of acres of lily fields, I awoke with renewed energy to start my day. I knew if I wanted to attend the Jane Austen Literary Club that evening, I would have to stay focused on the schedule we had planned at the shop. Sally had booked a wedding for tomorrow, so we had our hands full. I also scheduled Abbey to come in to help. She loved living in an apartment on Main Street and being close by to help me out at times like this. She'd certainly been a big help to us with the outdoor quilt show.

I skipped my morning walk, and sure enough, everyone was busy working when I arrived. Abbey was thrilled to have the extra hours. She was my most creative designer. Coming from New York, I sometimes had to watch her out-of-the box designs for this conservative Midwest clientele.

Sally scheduled all of our wedding business and also took control of producing the product for it, which delighted me. Thanks to her pushing for the shop expansion so we could take on large weddings, our bottom line had increased significantly, just as she predicted. I was more than happy to pass most of it onto her salary. She was single and had some interest in a guy named Tim. He didn't know she was alive most of the time, although he did seem to value her friendship. I kept encouraging her to hang in there and be happy with their great friendship.

Jean, my English employee, started a Jane Austen Literary Club here in Colebridge because she was a *Janeite*, a term given to anyone who adores Jane Austen. She belonged to a similar club when she lived in England. Because of her hospitality, she had no problem gaining members as we enjoyed her English tea and homemade scones.

I picked Mother up on time, which pleased her. She loved those pockets of time when we had an opportunity to visit a bit. I was dying to share the news of us putting in an offer on the Brody property, but was afraid it was too premature. I did quickly tell her I had met Beverly, who could perhaps shed more light on the Taylor family's history.

"This Sunday is the bridal luncheon for Amanda. Don't forget." Mother often reminded me of the family's social obligations. "I can't believe it, but Joyce said she really wants to drive in for it if Ken is feeling okay. Frankly, I think she wants to spend some time with that little granddaughter Mia and I don't blame her."

"Oh, what a nice day that will be for them." I pictured their reunion in my mind. "I hope she does! Sue will enjoy having her here. Mia doesn't really know her grandmother with Aunt Joyce living so far away."

"While I think of it, Anne, I have all the boxes of photos

from Aunt Marie and also the ones she kept of Mothers as well," she revealed. "They are all together. I really wish you would keep them at your house. I am trying hard to clean out and organize. I also put all the quilts in your old bedroom for everyone to choose from. I'm sure Joyce will take a couple when she comes."

I tried to envision the sight in my old room.

We were standing in front of Jean's front porch when Sue arrived.

"So what's the big powwow all about?" Sue kidded.

"I was reminding Anne about the luncheon this weekend, and that your mother said she may drive here for that!" Mother told Sue. "I know that Amanda would be thrilled."

"Yeah, it looks like it," Sue nodded. "Dad really wants her to come, so I'm counting on it. Mia will love it, of course."

"That's great, Sue. Let me know if I can do anything," I said excitedly. "We'd better go in before they start without us."

The group appeared smaller tonight, and when I went to find a chair, Abbey motioned for me to sit next to her.

"Sit here, Anne," she whispered. "I brought some cookies tonight, so I got here a little earlier." She lowered her voice even more. "I'm afraid I walked into a fight between Al and Jean." I looked at her strangely, hoping no one could hear in spite of Abbey's lowered tone. "Jean was in tears and refused to tell me what was wrong. Do you know what's going on? She always teases that he is such a stinker, but what does that mean?"

Sadness now took hold of me. I didn't want to hear that. I also knew it was not a marriage made in heaven, but I never wanted to ask personal questions of my employees, unless they brought it up.

Jean appeared to be her happy self as she tried to get everyone's attention. She began by thanking Abbey for her delicious cookies that we all knew came from Nick's Bakery.

"Tonight's report will be about meals and manners in Jane's time," Jean began.

This should be interesting, I thought.

"I shall be reading some notes and hope you will pop in with your observations from reading her books," Jean began. "Let's begin with breakfast, which was described to be much later in the morning then we would perhaps enjoy. A light breakfast of toast and tea might be enjoyed after they did some letter writing, shopping, or walking. If you recall, in earlier times, heavier foods like cheese, bread, and meat were eaten on pewter plates and mugs. To my delight, in Jane's world, they always used china tea cups, as I always do. All the better to enjoy the liquid refreshments, do you not think?"

We all agreed with her.

"Unlike my practice, hot drinks were usually not enjoyed during a cold day, just in the mornings and evenings. I collect that this diet would certainly be a healthier one."

Many nodded in agreement and whispered among themselves.

"The word luncheon was only mentioned once that I could find, and I gather that invitations to a lunch just didn't happen. If guests happened to be present during the day, they were, of course, offered something like tea cakes or scones. Jane did write that Elizabeth Bennet in *Pride and Prejudice* experienced cold meat and hothouse fruit at Pemberley."

Everyone listened intently as they tried to remember

reading that part.

"Dinner, as we know it, was at a much later hour, which was considered to be very fashionable at the time. In 1808, Jane wrote, "We never dine now till five." Frankly, that's an early hour for us because we are just getting home from our workday. Right, Miss Anne?"

I smiled and nodded.

"Dinner was the most elaborate meal of the day." Jean paused.

"I remember Jane writing about Mrs. Bennet in *Pride and Prejudice* bragging about serving at least three courses," Sally chimed in.

"Right, Miss Sally," Jean continued. "A course would be a multitude of meats, fish, vegetables, and perhaps one or two puddings. Their dessert would be nuts, fruit, and lots of wine!"

Everyone applauded.

"After the dessert was served, I learned that's when the servants disappeared."

"That's when the men and women separated, isn't it?" Aunt Julia asked.

"Yes ma'am, that's when the ladies left the room and the men stayed to smoke, have more to drink, and talk politics," Jean explained. It was evident that she loved feeling she had our complete attention and that we appreciated her leadership in our club.

"Can you imagine what those old geezers talked about back then?" Aunt Julia teased.

Everyone roared with laughter.

"What I found particularly odd in my notes is that a tea would happen an hour or so after dinner," Jean continued.

"The men would sometimes join them again, but sometimes, it would be a whole new set of guests. It was perfectly acceptable to be invited to an after-dinner tea and not be invited to the dinner!"

"It is odd, Jean," agreed Mother. "I read that supper was the meal after the ball before the guests would drive home. Did you find that to be the case, Jean?"

"Indeed, Miss Sylvia," she nodded. "I noticed in the south, you see references to supper clubs in this country. I am sorry to report that you all will not be served any supper before your journey home."

Everyone clapped and laughed.

"This was all was so interesting, Jean," I said, stretching my legs and preparing to leave. "Thank you so much." In spite of Jean having such a bad start to the evening, she certainly came through with flying colors. Jean was one of the sweetest, most generous people I knew. As Mother and I said our good-byes, she reminded Aunt Julia and Sue of Amanda's luncheon on Sunday.

On the way home, Mother said how she missed our quilting in her basement as we had done so regularly for a while. The last quilt we worked on was for Isabella, the owner of the local quilt shop.

"Well, it sounds like this family has plenty of quilts, but if we add another baby to the family, there will be a good excuse to make a new one," I teased.

"Anne, are you trying to tell me something?" Mother gasped.

"No, no, not me," I assured her. "I'm sorry. I was thinking of Sue. She is tossing the idea around about adopting a little boy!"

"Oh my, gracious be!" Mother said with joy. "That would be so wonderful! It isn't as wonderful as having my first grandchild, but it is still pretty wonderful!"

I laughed. "Patience, Mother, patience," I said, kissing her on the cheek when I dropped her off.

CHAPTER 10

Fridays were always extra busy, especially if Sally had booked a wedding on the weekend. Kevin was now putting more hours in and delivering more than usual. I always hoped that my Friday nights would be date nights with Sam. We were trying harder now to make that happen.

Around three that afternoon, Sam called to see if I had any interest in joining him for dinner with one of his clients. I had done that now and then, but I was the third wheel in most cases and typically found myself sitting there thinking about how I could make better use of my time. I didn't want to say it, but it wouldn't exactly be a date night. I told him we had a wedding scheduled and that most of us would not likely leave the shop until after six. He understood that I could not join him on this occasion.

The day flew by and the schedule was tight. As we were sweeping up for the day, Sally said she wondered if I could join her at Charley's tonight.

"That sounds like a great idea, since Sam won't be coming home for dinner," I responded as I went into my office.

"When Jean comes back in from taking the trash to the alley, I'll see if she'd like to join us," Sally suggested.

I wondered what Jean's response would be. It didn't take long for me to overhear the conversation between them.

"If I go, Al will be like a mad man in the street," Jean said emphatically. "I have my hands full now with the old codger. We'd have blarney for sure. Don't know why he'd give a lump. All he does is sit in front of the telly."

"What's blarney?" asked Sally, trying not to laugh.

"Don't ask, Miss Sally," Jean advised, shaking her head in disgust. "I've been a bit shattered today, but you are a sweetheart to ask. Have a jolly night, my friends. Ta ta!" Out of the door she went.

"What's up with them?" Sally asked, coming into my office.

"I'm not sure, but I don't think it's good. Abbey said she walked in on a fight between them when she arrived early at the literary club."

"Man, I hate to hear that," Sally said, shaking her head. "I hope she has someone to talk to. I don't think she wants to discuss much about that around here, do you?"

"No, and that's good and bad," I agreed, getting my purse to leave. "I have little tolerance for men's poor behaviors, as you may know, so let's get out of here before I have blarney!"

Sally laughed.

Brad, the bartender, was glad to see me. It had been a while since I had been down the street to everyone's favorite watering hole and eatery. It was half a block away, which made it very handy. Brad remembered my choice of beverage and Sally ordered for herself.

The place was pretty empty, which was unusual. I was glad Ted Collins, my former boyfriend, wasn't sitting at the bar, as he had been on many previous occasions. I started our conversation by asking Sally for an update on her wannabe boyfriend, Tim.

"He's great, as always," She replied, giving me a big smile. "We went to a baseball game last week and had a great time. I'm his best buddy right now!"

"Hang in there, Sally," I said, trying to encourage her. "One day, he will take another look at you. Perhaps you should shake things up a bit and see if he notices."

"What are you talking about?" she said, sounding defensive.

"Well, you could start with a different hairstyle or show a little more skin in some of your outfits." I thought she was going to throw her drink at me.

"What is that supposed to mean?"

"Hey, don't take it the wrong way, but what you're doing now isn't working. I know when I dated Ted, I was almost invisible to myself. I dressed the same old way because I wasn't concerned about impressing him. When I met Sam, it was like my senses became alive again. I chose clothes that showed off my figure and took more care with my makeup. It did more for me than it probably did for him. I felt more feminine and sexy. He had to pick up on those vibes. Do you see what I mean?"

"Gotcha."

I could see that she was cooling down as she absorbed

what I had just shared.

"Why are you so darn smart?" she said, giving me a big grin. "No wonder you can run a business and do all you do." We laughed.

"I'm just sayin'," I teased back. "Hey, how about we share an artichoke dip and order the French dip that we always crave?"

"Sure, what's a couple more pounds just when I decide to look sexier?"

"You just missed Ted," Brad announced, knowing I could take teasing that came from him.

"Well, my timing is improving then," I shot back, smiling. "How is he doing?"

"He's on the wagon right now, so I hope it continues," Brad said, switching quickly to a serious tone of voice. "He always asks if I've seen you."

"That's great, but if he is truly on the wagon, why would he come here to tempt himself?"

"Habit—and probably hoping he'll run into you!" Brad said with a wink.

Sally looked at me strangely.

Sally and I continued our conversation, mixing business with pleasure, just as my husband was doing right now. On my way home, I couldn't help but think about Ted. I knew in the back of my mind that I was not his only disappointment in life, but that he was likely still grieving over his mother's death, which was rumored to be a suicide.

To my surprise, Sam had arrived home before me. He was in the study pouring over his laptop. He seemed to be intent on whatever he was reading, so I gave him a soft peck on the back of his neck.

"How was your dinner?" I asked, tugging at his earlobe.

"Great, sweetie!" he answered, not looking up from the screen. "How was your evening?"

"Sally and I grabbed a bite at Charley's. It was a long day!"

He shut off his laptop and turned toward me. "I got some disappointing news today."

I waited for him to continue.

"Our offer was rejected on the property."

The news was so opposite from what I wanted to hear. "So, whose offer was accepted?" I asked, not sure I was ready to know.

"I'm told that they did not accept any of the offers, so I guess that's good news," he said, shaking his head. "The realtor said the other buyers dropped out completely after giving their best offer. This property is not zoned commercial, so it's a hefty price for any other use."

"So, it's just going to sit there as is?" I asked hearing frustration attaching itself to my voice.

"No, not for long," Sam said, perking up. "I'm going to counter offer tomorrow."

I was taken by surprise.

"This property belongs to us, Anne."

I looked at him in disbelief. "Really?"

"Really," Sam confirmed as he took me into his arms.

CHAPTER 11

Sunday's weather was perfect for a bridal luncheon. We gathered on the patio of Donna's Tea Room until everyone had arrived. Aunt Joyce did make the trip, taking a taxi from the airport to save anyone from having to pick her up. She looked great, and we couldn't have been happier to see her.

Amanda looked slim and gorgeous in a simple white cotton dress, as if she were getting married this afternoon. Her friends Kelly, Bridgett, and Harriet were darling and excited to be there with us.

Walking into the tearoom was like entering a fairyland. Donna had chosen to use the Havilland china pattern called Esther from her own collection. It was a dainty, pink, floral design with heavy gold trim. Donna loved pink, which was evident in so many of her pretty things, but it was also the color Amanda was using, along with black, for her wedding. For the arrangements at each table, Abbey had used delicate, pink roses and baby's breath. There was also a matching corsage for the bride-to-be.

Between the lunch and opening gifts, Amanda shared that her brother, William, was very happy with his job and was going to give her away at her wedding some months away.

Watching the glow of happiness from Amanda reminded me of myself sitting here some time back. The memory hit strongest when she opened a very large gift that had no card attached to it. Aunt Julia and I looked at each other with that oh-not-that-again look on our faces. It was a sparkling set of crystal goblets with matching wine glasses, fit for a queen. Amanda was delighted with the lovely gift. Donna once again said she had no idea who may have delivered the package or whom it was from. We told her not to worry, as we would find out where it came from.

When it would be a good time to share with Amanda that it was from deceased Grandmother Davis, we did not know. Maybe this time it was from Amanda's deceased mother and not Grandmother. How many of them could there be?

"I really wish you, Julia, and Sarah would stop by the house afterwards to take a look at some things, Anne," Mother pleaded as she got ready to leave.

I looked at Aunt Julia.

"Sure, but we can't stay long." Aunt Julia accepted the invitation but had some other commitments to attend to later that day.

"No problem, Mother. I just want to grab a couple of these cupcakes for Sam before I leave."

Amanda's tears of joy when saying good-bye were all

we needed to know that we had spent yet another memorable day together. Aunt Mary would be pleased that we had so easily added Amanda and her brother to our family.

When we arrived at my childhood home, there were boxes sitting in the foyer.

"What's this all about, Mother?" I asked, hoping they weren't all meant for me.

"Be careful. Don't trip. They are all ready for Goodwill to pick up tomorrow morning," she explained.

"Is there anything I would want?" asked Sarah with curiosity.

"No, honey, I'm afraid not," Mother said laughing. "Come on up to Anne's bedroom."

Well, at least I still claimed a bedroom here!

"Oh my, you weren't kidding when you said to come look at quilts," Aunt Julia gasped in amazement.

"Aunt Sylvia, how did you get so many?" asked Sarah.

Mother laughed. "Just have a seat, and I'll try to tell you what little I know about each one," she said in preparation. She held up the first one. "This pieced quilt is one that I remember Marie made because she not only did it in pink and white, but also in blue and white. It's called a Double Irish Chain. She did a crib-sized one for somebody as well. Some of these have notes attached by either Marie or Mother."

"Mom, that pink one would be cool in my room," volunteered Sarah as she looked at Aunt Julia.

"Sure, if no one else wants it," answered Aunt Julia.

"It's yours, Sarah," Mother announced as she began folding it up. "These all have to find homes."

"This one is called Periwinkle on the note, but it doesn't say who made it," Mother was gathering information from the small piece of paper. "It looks like Mother's handwriting."

No one made an offer. It was a quilt of many colors that someone had made from a bag full of scraps, most likely. She put it aside.

"This one looks really old," I commented to Mother.

"Yes, remember this, Julia? It was usually spread across the end of Mother's bed. The note says it's called Pineapple.

"Pineapple?" asked Sarah in disbelief. "It looks nothing like a pineapple."

We all laughed in agreement.

"I'll pass on that one," said Aunt Julia, who never seemed to want any of her mother's things or anything that looked antique.

"I'll take it for one of the extra bedrooms," I offered. "With all the satin and silk fabric, this shouldn't really be used. I can see it at the end of a bed, on a quilt rack, or even on the wall. It's very graphic. I know Sam would love this one."

"I can remember resting on her bed and feeling those fabrics," Mother said fondly. "Who knows if history dictated these pattern names or if the quilters gave them their own names? Joyce said she'd drop by before she would go home to take some also. I know she wants this Bow Tie quilt that I have folded and put on that loveseat. She said Ken spoke of that quilt often, so that one has a home!"

"This one looks like Christmas with all this green and red!" I said in admiration.

Mother picked up the corner to read the paper pinned to the quilt.

"It's called Carolina Lily and this note is in Mother's handwriting. You know her love for lilies!"

"It's got your name all over it," Aunt Julia teased, looking at me. "I am not going there, plus that does not go with anything else in my house."

"I love it, but then I love lilies, too," I said, pulling the quilt closer to me. "I don't think this one has been used. The handwork is beautiful."

"So many of these are like brand new," Mother agreed. "Our mother put many things away, saving them for good."

Funny, but Mother has said that to me a time or two herself.

"I may hang this on the wall in one of the bedrooms I'm planning," I said as I pictured the room in my mind. "The walls are dark green in there, which would pick up on this green. You know which room I mean, Mother?"

"Yes, I do," she said smiling. "I think it would be perfect."

Julia took the next two quilts to be a bit more accommodating. One was a simple Nine Patch design of multicolors, whose maker we did not know. The other one was a cross-stitch kit quilt in lavenders and blues that Aunt Marie had constructed. We still had more to see, but Aunt Julia said she needed to get home. She had told Sarah she could go see a movie that evening.

I found myself sitting on the floor admiring the delicate workmanship of the red and green quilt while Mother went downstairs to see Sarah and Aunt Julia to the door.

CHAPTER 12

I could not believe all the work that went into these quilts. When Mother returned, she unfolded the next one. I eagerly announced that it was a Double Wedding Ring. In spite of my limited knowledge of quilts, I at least had the name of that pattern in my memory. I passed on that one, as it was a multitude of pastel colors, which was not my taste. I came with a note in Aunt Marie's handwriting and read that this quilt was was from Fred's side of the family. She'd been married to Fred, but he had died some years earlier.

Putting that one aside, I noticed the next one was all white, and white quilts always tended to be some of my favorites. I had already taken one from Aunt Marie after she died and kept it in our master bedroom.

"I knew you would love this one. Mother made it, and I remember it has a paper attached somewhere on one of the corners. I hope it's still here. It has been a while since I looked at all of these quilts."

I quickly stood up so I could open up the carefully-stitched quilt. It had scalloped edges, which only added to its delicate beauty.

"Here's something." I pulled one corner that had a note safety pinned to it like her others. The paper was yellowed and crunched, but Grandmother's writing remained clear. "It says, 'Under these lilies, I weep to sleep.'"

"Well, that's strange," Mother came over to look at the note. "That's definitely her writing, and I remember seeing this quilt as I grew up. I don't think she really used it much."

"Of course it's Grandmother's. Look at this." I spread the whole quilt on the nearby bed. "It's all quilted lilies, her favorite. It couldn't be anyone else's, and think about what this note says. It was under this quilt that she shed her tears. Her tears were for Albert and her absent daughter. She was rather poetic, Mother. Did you ever pick up on that?" I was about to tear up myself, recalling her personal anguish.

"Oh, Anne, I think you're making too much of this." Mother had averted her gaze from the quilt to the floor, and I could see tears glistening in her eyes. "Well, maybe she had a talent of sorts. She was always writing letters. She wouldn't have had much time to do anything else with the big family we had."

"Letters? Are there any of her letters around? For her to write this simple description attached to this quilt says something about her. She wanted someone besides herself to know this, don't you think?"

Mother ignored me.

"Would you say that she was a romantic?"

Mother shook her head.

Perhaps most people don't think of their parents that way. I suppose her children are the wrong ones to ask.

Mother began slowly, "If anything, she didn't have much time or patience for that kind of silliness, as you can imagine with all of us girls in the family. She may have been a different person when she was very young and foolish with Albert, but as she raised us, she was the stern one and my father was the more sensitive one. Mother's favorite was Ken and Father cherished his little girls. I think that's the way it goes, sometimes."

I had never heard my Mother talk like this before.

"Well, this quilt is mine, Mother," I said, holding it close. "It goes to 333 Lincoln, where I think she would like the quilt to live."

"Sure, it's yours, Anne," Mother agreed. "Just don't read too much into this. It is a beauty, isn't it? I wonder where she got all these lily designs. I think you're right about one thing. As long as it takes to make one of these quilts, there are lots of feelings that go into them. Mother would have a quilt in a frame most of the time. Father would fuss about that sometimes, because it took up so much space in our living room. Those stitches were made on good and bad days, I suppose. I've experienced that myself since we've had quilts in the basement downstairs. Sometimes the stitches flow with joy and other times, the worries get stitched in, too."

I could relate to her observations, which made the quilt even more special.

"Remember when Ted and I broke up? I came downstairs to the quilt frame and cried," I reminded Mother. "I fell asleep. Remember me getting makeup on the quilt and not knowing what to do?"

She remembered alright, but she never accepted that when the stains were gone the next morning that it was due to Grandmother.

"Yes, honey, but let's not give Grandmother too much credit." She smiled.

"Whatever, but that quilt was a comfort to all of us at the time," I insisted. "You do remember that much, don't you?"

"Yes, you're right," she finally said. "I came down one night when I couldn't sleep recently. I guess I was thinking too much about Harry and felt guilty about thinking of someone else besides your father."

Oh my. This was news to me.

"I quilted for a while on Isabella's quilt and I felt better, just thinking as I stitched."

"That's special, Mother," I said, reaching over to touch her arm. "I love you, and I will love Grandmother's quilt!"

"Good." She turned away to straighten the other quilts.

I stayed a little longer looking at Carpenter's Wheel, Dresden Plate, Broken Dishes, Monkey Wrench, Snail's Trail, and Card Trick-patterned quilts, which were mostly scrappy colors with such crazy names! There were more, and I assured Mother that as my bedroom plans evolved, I would take another look at the quilts that remained. She wanted Joyce, Sue, and Amanda to make some of the choices as well. We were lucky to have so many quilts. Mother said when Grandmother finished a quilt, it usually went straight to the cedar chest where it was saved "for good."

Besides bringing home cupcakes for Sam, I drove home with a bag of quilts that were going to be used in my home.

But more than that, I was taking home the history of my family. It was like re-purposing their existence and loving them all over again.

CHAPTER 13

I walked in the door with goodie bag in hand and found Sam wrestling with papers on the glass table in the sunporch.

"Hey, mister, what's all this about?" I inquired, announcing my arrival.

He barely looked up at me. "Hi, sweetie, how was the lunch?"

"Great! I brought you some dessert."

He wasn't listening.

"Is everything okay? What's up with all these papers?"

"I wish I knew," he said, sounding puzzled. "I thought if I printed all this out, I could visualize it better than scrolling down through pages on the computer."

"What are you looking for?"

"It's complicated."

I couldn't miss the worried expression fixed on his face.

"Something's not adding up." He started stacking some

of the papers.

I paused before speaking. "Is all this what's keeping you up nights?"

He took a deep breath. "I suppose. It's nothing for you to worry about. It's like a puzzle that has a missing piece and I can't find it."

I knew I certainly couldn't help there, but he seemed so worried. "Are you hungry?" I asked, thinking that would surely get a reaction.

"No, not really." He began to clean up his papers.

"I'm going to have some iced tea," he said suddenly. "How about we sit on the porch for a while? I have something to tell you." He nodded like I should proceed.

I topped off our cold tall glasses with a slice of lemon and headed for the front porch. I knew Sam was worried about something, but perhaps a relaxing moment and talking about something else would be helpful. When he joined me, I handed him his drink and put my feet up on a wicker stool.

"This breeze is wonderful. It's a good place to clear your head!"

"I wish," Sam said tensely, taking his first sip. "Very refreshing."

"Since I have no suggestions to help you with your problem, I may as well tell you about what happened today at the shower. The whole event was lovely, especially since Aunt Joyce flew in to be there with us. Amanda is very happy and she also received an anonymous gift, as I did at my shower. It was more crystal, of course!"

Sam kept quiet as if I had mentioned a family secret.

"So anyway, the really cool part of the afternoon was going by Mother's on the way home."

"Why?" He finally began to show some interest in what I was sharing.

"Well, Aunt Julia, Sarah and I went over to look at the quilts that are at Mother's house," I explained. "She has them from Grandmother and Aunt Marie. There were stacks of them! Most of them had a piece of paper attached to them telling the pattern and so on. I ended up coming home with three of them. Aunt Julia took some home, but she really doesn't appreciate antique quilts, so the rest of the family needs to take them off Mother's hands."

By now he was no longer listening again, however, I felt compelled to carry on with my story.

"She is trying to unload things. She has boxes and boxes going to Goodwill tomorrow. Anyway, one of the quilts I brought home is all white with beautiful quilted lilies all over it. It had an old wrinkled note on it in Grandmother's handwriting that says, 'Under these lilies I weep to sleep.' Isn't that special, Sam? You know what she was referring to. What I never knew about her was that she was rather poetic, wouldn't you say?"

He simply nodded and I could tell he was not overly impressed.

"I'll get it. You have to see this." I jumped out of my chair to go in to get the quilt. When I returned, Sam's head was between his hands as if he were thinking really hard. I walked toward him and opened up the quilt as much as I could.

He lifted his head and looked blankly at the quilt. "It is very pretty, Anne. She loved lilies, so it's no surprise, right?"

"That's true, but I think when she made this, she was very sad, as you can interpret from this note. Look at this." I held out the corner with the note. "I feel the love and sadness in this quilt. It belongs here in our house, Sam. I know she would have loved for me to have this quilt. None of her daughters want to realize that part of her life with Albert. I live in his house and with her, I might add, so it belongs here."

Again, he looked at me strangely, like he didn't know what the fuss was all about. "I understand and I'm glad it makes you happy to have it," he said, clearly out of kindness to me.

I wanted him to be more excited, but frankly, it was abundantly clear that he had his mind on other things.

"I guess I'll put it on a quilt rack until it works in one of the other bedrooms," I kept explaining. "I took one for the green bedroom and then there is a smaller antique one that I may put on the wall in the upstairs hall."

"Great, honey," he quietly said as he got up to go into the house. "I have a little more emailing to do. If you want to fix a snack for us, it's all I'll need for now. I want to get to bed early tonight. I have an early meeting to be ready for tomorrow."

"Sure, let's go in." I gave up on my exciting news. "Those cupcakes were really good that I brought home."

"I have all the sweetness I need with you around, Annie." He kissed me on the cheek before going inside.

The rest of the short evening was quiet and worrisome. It was not like Sam to be acting like this. It was obvious that something was wrong at work and he didn't know how to fix it. I didn't want to make matters worse with all my questions. I knew now that my new quilt, iced tea, and even a delicious cupcake were not going to fix whatever was on Sam's mind.

CHAPTER 14

Sam tossed and turned the whole night, but it didn't stop him from getting up early just as he had planned. I dressed for my walk, thinking today would be a good day to check the river water levels and walk on the trail. Sam was on the computer when I came downstairs and I suggested he might want to go to the gym sometime today to relieve some of his stress. He looked at me like a child that had been scolded.

"Come here," he said, pulling me close to him. "Have I told you lately that I love you?"

"No, and I was beginning to worry," I teased, giving him a quick kiss. "I was just trying to remind you about the talk we had a while back about stressing ourselves out so much."

"What I'm dealing with right now is part of my job," he said, looking straight into my eyes. "It's not something I can make go away. I appreciate your concern. You have a nice walk and I'll let you know later about my schedule."

"Yes, I hear you." I walked toward the door to leave. "Love you!" I called, blowing him a kiss.

As I drove toward the river, I had to trust that Sam had it all under control or it would drive me crazy. The river had gone down a bit, which was good news. There were still areas blocked on the trail where water still stood. The taller Queen Anne's lace were still clinging for survival while standing in the water.

There was still so much to be thankful for today, despite the river causing havoc with downtown commerce and Sam having serious business issues. Why on earth would he want to add more responsibility to our lives by making another offer on the Brody property? I walked fairly briskly for about half an hour when my cell phone rang. It was mother.

"Good morning!" My greeting had a distinctly breathless quality due to my walking pace.

"Did I catch you at a bad time, Anne?"

"I'm just finishing my walk. You're calling early. Is everything alright?"

"Yes, I was just wondering if you and Sam had any plans for dinner tonight."

The question caught me off guard and I had to think for a minute. "There are no plans that I know of as yet," I answered. "Sam told me later he'd have to let me know. Something is bugging him at work. I don't know what it's all about, but he's not been sleeping as a result. Why do you want to know?"

"Harry is coming over and I'm making the pot roast that both he and Sam enjoy so much. Do you think you could come? It would mean a lot to us both if you could join us."

"Well, that's sweet of you," I told her. "I will certainly be there, but I can't answer for Sam until I hear from him later today."

"Good. How about six o'clock?" she suggested quickly. "Maybe I can talk you into taking a couple more quilts with you. Joyce stopped by later to take two off my hands. I want to send the box of photographs with you tonight, so when you have time, you can look through them. You mentioned your curiosity regarding letters, so I will put them in the box as well."

"Okay, that's fine, but there's no hurry."

"See you for dinner then, honey," she quipped and then hung up.

She sure is anxious to get rid of stuff!

In a way, she was like me in that once she had made up her mind to do something, she couldn't let it go until it was done. I didn't know if the enticement of Mother's pot roast would lure Sam to dinner or not.

When I got out of the shower and dressed, I called Sam at work to tell him of our dinner invitation. I had to leave a message, of course, but he was great at returning my calls.

Funeral orders dominated our day at the shop, with some more urgent than others. Sally already had our flower cart out front filled with perky petunias and small pots of bright tulips. I didn't know who could refuse them as they walked by. Abbey had done a darling Easter display in the window. Our Beatrix Potter flower pots were so precious and they looked irresistible among the green plants and tulips.

When we finally got a break to share a sub sandwich for lunch, I told them about the quilts I had brought home. Again, I spoke particularly of the lily quilt.

"You should truly value that, Miss Anne," Jean

64

responded. "I cannot devise her sentiment, poor soul. I would venture that she knew you would own it one day, do you not?"

"I suppose," I answered with reservation in my voice. "I just think her writing conveys she was rather poetic. I can't wait to see if there were any letters saved from her. Her daughters don't seem to think there was that side of her. They said she was closest to Uncle Ken and that their father was more sensitive to the girls."

"That's normal," chimed in Sally. "What are you going to do with the lily quilt?"

"Just put it somewhere where I can see and enjoy it," I explained. "I'll have to think of a way to preserve that note from her. I can't just keep it pinned to the quilt. It's already in poor condition."

"I just hope you'll not discover bits of letters inside some of the quilts like we did with the poor potting shed quilt," Jean said with a laugh. "That was a doozy, if you get my meaning!"

"That's a good word for it!" laughed Sally.

The workday was nearly over when I realized I had not heard from Sam regarding dinner. After Jean and Sally left, I gave him a call.

"Sorry, Anne, I meant to call you sooner," he explained. "I'll be there as soon as I can. I'm not going to miss the pot roast."

"Wonderful, I'll see you there then." Hearing his voice and knowing that he would be with us at dinner caused me to begin to feel more relaxed, like things might be okay.

CHAPTER 15

Harry was setting the table when I walked into Mother's home. It turned out that he came early to help with dinner. It smelled heavenly when I joined her in the kitchen. She had this menu down pat as one of her favorites.

"This is a real treat, Mother. What can I do to be helpful?"

"Is Sam coming, Anne?" Mother asked, sounding worried.

"He'll be here, but I can't say when," I explained as I got a drink for myself.

"Oh, good!" She seemed elated. "I have a good-sized box for you to take home, full of photos. Do you want to go ahead and put them in your car? You may forget when you get ready to leave."

"My goodness, Mother. What is the hurry with getting rid of everything?"

"You have the room, honey, and I have accumulated too much stuff from Mother and Marie, plus your stuff and my stuff! There's just too much stuff!"

Harry was chuckling in the background.

"Give this pitcher to Harry and have him pour the water, if you would," she ordered.

As always, I did as I was told. I had a feeling that Harry was trained to do the same.

We had just taken a seat in the living room with our drinks when Sam arrived. After Mother got a big hug from him, she brought him a drink and he joined us. Sam looked to be in a good mood as he relished the thought of a delicious meal. Before he took a seat, he helped himself to a veggie tray Mother had on the coffee table.

"I'm so glad you could join us in spite of your busy schedules and all, but we were anxious to have you both together to share some news," she said, clearly nervous.

My heart raced. I should have known that there was a reason for this dinner.

"What is it?" I asked, expecting bad news.

"Anne, if I may have the floor here," said Harry in a soft tone. "We wanted both of you here to tell you that your mother and I have decided to get married and we would like to have your blessing."

I thought I was going to faint. I looked at Sam as if I didn't hear Harry correctly, but Sam was sitting there with a big smile on his face. If this was to be a wonderful Kodak moment for Mother, I didn't want to ruin it.

"Surely this is not a shock, is it, Anne?" Mother said in a sweet voice.

I couldn't answer. I had to find some words.

"We are at a place in our relationship where we would like to be together more. We feel very fortunate to have found each other and have talked about the idea for some time."

"Your mother is a special lady, Anne," Harry said, picking up the conversation. "My life has been renewed since we found each other and I know she feels the same. Sylvia would like me to move in here and we both have been trying to clear things out, as you may know, so this just seemed right."

I still couldn't speak. Why was this shocking to me?

Sam remained silent with that smile on his face.

"So, Anne, what do you think?" Mother finally asked her dumbfounded daughter.

Think before you speak, I warned myself.

"I guess congratulations are in order," I finally said with a smile. "I have to say that you surprised me, but if that's what the two of you want, I certainly want to support you."

Mother came over to give me a hug. Her eyes held the glisten of tears, but I wasn't emotionally there yet.

"Thanks, Anne," Harry said. "I told Sylvia you would want her to be happy. I promise to try my best to make that happen."

They looked at each other as if the weight of the world had just been lifted from them.

"That is wonderful news," Sam finally said. "You both deserve happiness. When is the big day?"

I couldn't believe he asked that.

"We'd like it to be soon, with just family and maybe a few friends," Mother answered, smiling. "I'd like your help, Anne, even though you are so busy."

This is just what I need.

"It wasn't that long ago when you took me by surprise when you told me that Sam was the one, and that you wanted to marry him, remember?"

Not fair, I thought.

"Sure, I'll do what I can," I finally said, giving her a smile.

"Well, Sylvia, I'll bet that pot roast is more than ready for us, am I right?" Harry said, walking toward the kitchen.

"I'm ready," said Sam, joining him.

I got up, still feeling strange and thinking of Father. What would he think?

Mother reacted as if she had just gotten permission from her parents to attend her first dance and cheerfully attended to getting dinner on the table. When we were seated, Sam lifted his glass to make a toast to the newly engaged couple.

"Here's to health and happiness for two wonderful people," Sam announced.

"Here, here," I said along with the others. So far, I gave myself an A-plus for not messing anything up. Mother probably knew me well enough to know I really was in shock.

The rest of the evening was a blur as everyone chattered away at the table enjoying all the food. I could hardly eat anything, but tried to behave as if it was a typical meal we were sharing together. As the evening progressed, it was heartwarming to see Mother so happy. How could I deny her that? She never denied me my choices, which were sometimes questionable. We said our good-byes with hugs, knowing we left two people very relieved and happy. I was quiet on the way home. Sam knew I needed time to digest this new situation.

The more I stayed awake that night thinking about my

father, I had to admit that he would not want Mother to be alone any longer. I should feel the same. Sam held me closely, seeming to know his love would sooth my worries.

CHAPTER 16

I walked along the trail the next morning and realized I'd probably appeared insensitive to Mother's announcement. I hadn't asked about any details, but I'm sure they were to come. I still couldn't believe she hadn't dropped any hints about their plans—or had she? Maybe I just hadn't been paying close enough attention.

When I got in my car to drive home, Sue called me.

"Good morning to you!" She sounded very cheerful.

"Hey, Sue!" I responded.

"I just wanted you to know that I got my application in at the adoption agency!" Sue announced.

"Wow, good move! What did they tell you?"

"Well, it helps having my previous record, of course, and she told me if I wanted a boy, I had a better chance if I was willing to take one that's a little older. I told her I preferred one that is no older than four years old. Baby boys are more in demand, it seems."

Images of little boys waiting for homes flitted through my mind.

"I told her I would consider nearly any scenario except adopting a handicapped child. As a single parent, I couldn't handle that alone. I certainly admire anyone who can. When I think of the little tykes that get passed by, it makes me sad. Those early years are so important. Just imagining the children left behind in those institutions makes me crazy. I'm also open to adopting another girl, of course. The adoption caseworker confirmed it is still easier to find a little girl."

"Sounds like you are a mommy that is ready to go."

"Now that I have made up my mind, I really am. Hey, any word on what's happening for Easter this year?"

"I assume we'll do brunch at Donna's as we always have before, but neither Aunt Julia nor Mother has said anything. There may be another event in addition to Easter this year."

"Like what?"

"Mother and Harry had Sam and I over for dinner last night and announced that they are getting married."

"Seriously?" Sue said, astonished. "I had no idea they were at that point. Good for them! How did you handle that?"

"Like a good daughter is supposed to!" I bragged. "It's no wonder she has been clearing out her place. Harry is going to move into the house. I brought home quilts, and last night I inherited a huge box of pictures from Grandmother and Aunt Marie."

"So, what are the details?"

"I really don't know, but she said soon." I tried to picture a ceremony with my mother as a bride. "You may want to act innocent when she calls to tell you. I have got to get home.

Congratulations on your next pregnancy, I guess I should say!"

As I was showering and getting dressed, I couldn't help but admire Sue for taking charge of her life and family. I came downstairs to enjoy some of the coffee Sam had made. I was pouring it into my travel thermos when Mother called.

"Hey, my dear, is there any way you can stop by for a little while to talk this morning?" Her voice sounded like she was very concerned about something.

"Not today, Mother." I was sad to have to give her that answer. "We have such a hectic schedule before the first delivery and Jean left a message saying she can't be in until about noon, so it will have to be another time."

"I just wanted to discuss the wedding with you," she said nervously. "I knew I threw you for a loop last night and wanted to know how you really feel about this. I want to include you in my plans, so I hope we can talk soon."

"Sure, Mother, don't worry," I assured her, trying to make her feel better. "If you are happy, then I am happy. If Sam calls and has to work late, I'll try to stop by after work. How about that?"

"Great," she responded. "I was tickled that he could come last night despite his schedule."

"I was too! I sure wonder what is going on at work that has him so stressed." Looking at the clock reminded me that this should not be a long conversation. "It was sweet of you to call, Mother." We confirmed tonight's plans and hung up.

I felt better than I had before not hearing from her. If I had to have a step-father, no one would be better than Harry. He already seemed to be part of the family.

CHAPTER 17

Sally and I worked diligently all morning on the orders that Kevin was to deliver.

"Brought you bits of scones, Miss Anne, to make up for my tardiness today," Jean said as she came in the door.

"Great! Glad you're here!" I shouted. "If you can get started on the Trinity church order right away, that would be very helpful!"

"Right," she said heading straight to the design room. She didn't seem her cheery self for some reason.

Out of concern, I followed her to the design room. "Is everything okay, Jean?"

She nodded, but a second look at her made me notice a bandage on her cheek.

"What happened to you?" I eased closer to her to get a better look.

"Bumping the wrong way, I'm afraid," she said, turning

away from me.

The phone began to ring, so I went to the front counter and picked up the receiver.

"Is Jean available?" a familiar voice asked. I recognized Al's voice immediately.

"Sure, I'll go get her. Hang on." I told Jean it was Al on the phone.

She looked up from her work and asked if I could tell him that she had to run an errand on the street.

I now knew that Al was the problem. The expression on her face was unlike her usual good nature. Clearly, something out of the ordinary had happened between them recently.

I returned to the counter. "Sorry, Al, she just went to get us coffee on the street," I falsely answered. "I'll have her call you."

He hung up without a good-bye or thank you.

Having seen the entire scene play out, Sally came up to me and whispered, "What are we going to do?"

I shrugged.

We both walked into the room to console Jean. "For heaven's sake, Jean. What is going on here? Did Al do this to you?"

She started to cry.

"I want to help you. You are like family to me, and I'm sure whatever problems you and Al are having, he shouldn't be hurting you like this."

"You cannot help me, Miss Anne," she mumbled. "I no longer make him happy."

"What is making him upset, Jean?" I asked, touching her hand.

"Everything!" Jean blurted out. "He's always hitting the

bottle lately. He thinks I'm stupid, ugly, and an English drag."
She was shaking.

"Oh my gosh."

Sally was fuming.

Just then, the UPS driver came in the door and needed
someone to sign for packages so Sally went to accept the
deliveries.

"Listen to me, Jean," I said, looking into her eyes.
"Are you listening? Look at me. You are the sweetest and
most loving person I know. You are talented beyond belief
and pretty sharp looking if you want my opinion. Al has a
problem and he's taking it out on you. Has he hit you before?"

She nodded.

"It's the liquor talking, Miss Anne," she sniffed. "He
doesn't mean it. He says he's sorry."

"They all say that, Jean," I said, anger welling up inside
me. "You are in a very dangerous situation and you need to
get out of that environment before he really hurts you. Does
he want to stop drinking?"

She waited to answer. Finally, she shook her head.

"You are not going back in that house," I insisted. I felt
so sorry for her.

"You can come home with me, Jean," Sally offered,
coming back into the room. "You need a break and he needs
to figure this all out. Does he realize he will lose you with
this behavior?"

Jean didn't respond. Trying to pull herself together,
Jean blew her nose, blinked, and assured us that it was not
our problem. "He'll throw a tizzy if I don't come home, Miss
Anne," she said. "I appreciate your offer, Sally, but it will just
make my situation worse."

"How long has this been going on, Jean?" I questioned her.

She shrugged.

"Please don't go back until he says he will get help for his drinking. Do you realize you could call the police for this kind of behavior? You could put him in jail. Does he realize that?"

"I wouldn't do that," she said, turning her attention back to the arrangement she was working on.

Sally and I looked at one another, sharing a look of frustration and exasperation.

"Do you think you have to put up with this because you love him?" I asked, trying to look her in the eye.

"I do love my Al so, but not when he gets like this," she admitted through her sniffles.

"That's admirable, Jean, but you must take care of yourself," I insisted. "Please stay with Sally or me until he decides to get help."

The phone was ringing again, so Sally left to answer it.

"Please let me finish my day for you, Miss Anne, or I will feel worse," she begged. "You don't have to compensate me for my time today. I've not been efficient."

"That's nonsense, Jean," I told her. "I will pay you for a full day after what you've been through."

She seemed to be able to compose herself and I felt I had to leave her alone to think about the things we had told her. I didn't know how I could sleep knowing she would be going home to someone who would hurt her.

An hour or so later, Sally was leaving and Jean finished her piece as if nothing were wrong.

"Will you promise to call me if you need me?" I asked

her as she got her purse. "You call the police if he lays one hand on you, do you hear?"

She nodded. "I'll see you first thing on the morrow, Miss Anne," she said, pulling the shop door closed behind her.

CHAPTER 18

Concern about Sam and Jean consumed most of my thoughts. Several days passed before I called Mother to ask her to lunch so we could discuss her wedding plans. I picked her up and told her I wanted her to try Rascino's, the popular new restaurant in Colebridge that she had only heard about. She felt at ease when she saw two friends from her card club having lunch in one of the booths.

"This is quite lovely, Anne," she said, looking around. "It's not the charm we love at Donna's, but I can see the attraction here."

"There's no place like our favorite tearoom, but they have a following by offering all natural local ingredients in their menu selections. I think you would enjoy one of their salads, Mother."

After we gave our order to the waiter, Mother pulled out a little book which I assumed contained her notes about the wedding.

"I'd like to go over our list of people to invite, Anne. It's very short. It will be under fifty people. We will get married at the church, of course, but I'm at a loss as to where to have the reception." She paused, skimming her list. "I wanted to be sure to ask you today if you would give me away just as I did for you." We both smiled, knowing the answer.

"Of course I will," I responded with a loving smile. "I was hoping you'd ask."

"That will make me so happy." She drew in a deep breath. "I already have asked Julia to stand up for me and Harry's brother, David, will stand up for him. The ceremony will be at two, with a reception directly following. I just want light refreshments. We are planning a honeymoon. Harry has been looking through tons of brochures. I think he's enjoying that almost as much as he will enjoy the trip itself!" She lit up as she talked about him. She was giving a lot of thought to this wedding and it was great to see her so excited.

"I have the perfect solution to your reception!" I announced.

"Really?"

"I think 333 Lincoln would be perfect."

Her eyes widened in surprise.

"We can certainly hold over fifty people in that house, and if we have nice weather, we can overflow into our new patio room. It's about finished and it should be very beautiful."

"Oh, Anne, I think I am going to cry right here in front of everyone!" She really did look as if she would! "I am so touched. Have you said anything to Sam?"

"No, I haven't, but he will be totally delighted," I

assured her. "That was one of the reasons we got our big house. He'd like it filled with little Dicksons, but it can serve many purposes, really. Do you think Harry will approve? Remember what you told me when I got married, Mother? It's just not about me anymore."

Our laughter was immediate and hearty.

"He'll be thrilled," she said with a glow on her face. "You must let me pay for any expense involved, Anne."

"I think I am going to need an idea for a wedding gift, so this just may do it!" I said, getting excited about the possibilities.

Mother shook her head as if she couldn't believe it was all happening.

"Now, what are you going to do about a dress, Mrs. Sylvia Stone?"

She blushed. "It's all taken care of. I was at Miss Michele's last week looking at some things and I saw this light yellow silk suit on the rack. It's understated, which I liked, and when I tried it on, it fit like a glove. They'd just gotten it in and I knew it was perfect for our little wedding."

"Great. You didn't show it to Harry, did you?"

"Oh my goodness no, but he'll like it," she assured me.

We continued chatting like schoolgirls planning a party as we enjoyed our lunch.

When I dropped her off, I realized that my own mother was going to be a June bride. That would be a Kodak moment repeated in her life!

Sam arrived home that evening, exhausted as always. I told him I had some good news to share with him. We both changed clothes and sat on the south porch enjoying one another's company while my taco casserole heated up.

"How about I set us up in the gazebo, Sam?" I suggested, eager for a change.

"Not necessary, Anne," he said without hesitation. "How about we fill our plates and just come back here on the porch? I need to quickly get back to some work I bought home."

I gave him a look of disappointment. "Not before you hear my news."

He looked up and gave me his attention. I was happy to see a grin from him. "The floor is yours, sweet Annie."

"We are going to have a wedding reception at 333 Lincoln on June 26th!"

He looked puzzled.

"I offered our house for a small wedding reception for Mother and Harry. Is that okay?"

He hesitated and then smiled. "I think it's fabulous! Was that your idea?"

"Yes, and I told her you would love the idea." I winked at him. "It's such a small group, and it may be a perfect time to show off our new patio room. They are not having a meal, just light refreshments. She has everything pretty well planned. She just needed a place. The news gets better! She asked me to give her away! How about that?"

"That is pretty special! I'm sure Ella can be a big help with everything."

"I am counting on that. I know where we can get gorgeous flowers, and if we have a caterer, we're all set!"

Sam took my arm and brought me closer to him. He knew this made me very happy.

CHAPTER 19

To our surprise, Aunt Julia invited us to Easter brunch at her house. It was a nice change, plus she had done some decorating that most of us had not seen. Sarah was pleased to show off her newly painted room in orange and purple, but she was upset that her latest boyfriend had told her that he preferred to just be friends. She had never been heartbroken before, so she was at the height of drama. Amanda and Allen attended, so we wanted to hear about their developing wedding plans. Aunt Julia seemed to be thrilled leading the single life and was quite honored when Mother asked her to be in the ceremony. Mother said that a wedding shower for her was out of the question. We decided a private lunch with her the day before the ceremony would be more meaningful. Of course, Aunt Julia couldn't resist teasing her about getting unexpected crystal from their mother as a wedding present.

It was good seeing Sam enjoy the day and putting aside

his worries for this short while. Sue announced at the dinner table that her application for a new little brother or sister for Mia was in. Meanwhile, Mia continued to be the center of attention at our family gatherings. She did have a special fondness for Sam, which made me wish she had her own daddy to snuggle up with.

As we were getting ready to leave, Mother asked if I had found a moment to look at any of the pictures or letters in the boxes.

"There's been no time, but if Sam intends to work the rest of this evening, perhaps I will take a peek later on," I shared. "I am most anxious to look through them and I can't tell you how thrilled I am about the lily quilt, Mother."

"I know, and I'm thrilled you have it," she said, giving me a little hug good-bye.

"Thanks for the lovely centerpiece, Anne," Aunt Julia said. "I love a colorful spring mixture like that."

"You are most welcome," I responded. "I love your new changes. They are so you!"

With that, we were off, having enjoyed another wonderful day together as a family.

The thought of having the whole evening to myself sounded really enticing. We certainly wouldn't need any more food. Aunt Julia sent us home with a little package of leftover ham in case we wanted sandwiches the next day. Sam was quiet going home, most likely thinking of his game plan for the evening.

"So, are things getting better with this giant problem you have at work, Sam?" My words seemed to break into the silence that spread between us. "I hate to keep asking, but surely there is some progress, right?"

He paused as if he were trying to choose his words carefully. "I suppose you could say there is, but it's turning out to be a bigger and more complicated problem than I thought it would be."

"Can you give me any hints about the nature of the problem?" I was reluctant to drop the subject now that Sam seemed willing to talk.

"I probably should, but you must keep this between us," he cautioned. "Remember how quickly Mr. Martingale decided to retire? It certainly caught me by surprise. I didn't think it would be for another year or so. Well, there have been some unexplained financial transactions that keep going back to Martingale. No one ever bothered to question any of his transactions until I came along."

This was indeed sounding bad.

"I have been trying to keep my investigation under wraps until I have more details. I certainly don't need to alarm the rest of the board at this point, but it's not looking good. So far, it appears that some form of embezzlement has been taking place for many years."

"Oh Sam, that's horrible," I said, shocked. "Does anyone else know you've been working on this problem?"

"There wasn't anyone for some time, but Tony, our CPA, was starting to figure out some things on his own and has come to me looking for answers. I have shared some things with him without incriminating anyone, but time will tell. I've asked him to be completely confidential regarding this matter, so Anne, you must do the same."

I realized I knew more than I really wanted to know. "No wonder you have been so stressed. I worry that you are paying a heavy price as you work through all of this. Nothing is worth another heart attack, I hope you know."

He silently squeezed my hand as we walked in the front door of 333 Lincoln.

I wanted to run upstairs, get on my knees, and quickly ask God to take away Sam's terrible problem. He was such an honest person himself. What if he was right and there was an internal thief? Would Sam's safety be at risk if he were to reveal something? Would Sam be able to pursue the necessary channels without it affecting his health? Would I be strong enough if this scandal caused a long season of turmoil in our lives?

CHAPTER 20

Quietness overtook our home. Our minds were too absorbed with our individual thoughts to speak. We both changed our clothes and Sam went immediately to the study and opened his laptop. I knew I could not help him with this problem, but I could certainly look out for his wellbeing.

I walked into my new office, which still felt foreign to me. I liked my little waiting room where I'd been cozily tucked away. My current office space had a new area rug along with my small desk and chair. In the corner were the two boxes of photos from home. The closet held my Taylor suitcase and potting shed quilt. I needed to think of a way to make this a space where I felt I could be creative and productive.

I sat down on the rug by the boxes, noticing the contents just seemed to be thrown in. There was no particular order. I felt the best way to approach this task would be to separate everything into piles on the floor divided by subject matter. The box I inherited of Grandmother's had older black-and-white photographs. This box was where I wanted to start because I might find earlier pictures of my grandmother. It would be a good distraction from my troubled husband downstairs.

I pulled out a few packages of letters grouped together with a faded ribbon. I assumed they must relate to the same topic or person. I was hoping there would be more, but nonetheless, I was pleased. This project was going to take me forever, but I approached it as I did many other tasks and broke it down into smaller segments.

I saw a framed photo and I pulled it out to see who it was. It was Grandmother and Grandfather Davis. It was later than a wedding photo and done by a professional photographer, so it was quite well done. I put it aside on my desk. This would be displayed somewhere in our home. I wondered if Grandmother had ever shared with him that she had entered into an affair with Albert Taylor.

I couldn't identify anyone in the next group of pictures, so I put those aside to ask Mother or Aunt Julia about. I could see there would be many piles on the floor. Luckily, there was plenty of room. There was a photograph of a little girl playing in a sandbox and I knew immediately that it was Mother. What a little doll she was! I could visualize this in a small frame as well, so I put it on the pile of other pieces that would need frames. There was one of Aunt Marie and Aunt Julia standing in front of a large lilac bush holding Easter baskets.

I definitely need to give that to Aunt Julia. I'm sure she would cherish it.

A photo of Uncle Ken and Aunt Joyce holding a sweet little blonde girl caused me to remember that Sue had been adopted. This made me think of Sue expanding her own family by adoption. I wondered if she had seen this photo. It made me wonder how much Sue had tried to find her biological family. It must feel strange to look at other family members and not see resemblances like I could. Who would our children look like, I wondered? Sam's dark hair and my blonde hair would make an interesting combination. Would that make a redhead? I put Sue's family photograph with the picture I intended to give to Aunt Julia. That officially started a pile of pictures to give to others. I turned my attention back to the remaining pieces.

"Are you having fun in there?" Sam asked, peeking in the door.

I jumped, surprised. "I am making a big mess, but don't know how else to approach this," I said between yawns. "It's no wonder Mother didn't want to deal with this!"

He smiled. "Are you ready for bed?" Sam asked as he stretched.

"Yes, I sure am. I have a busy day tomorrow. So far, I have only found one picture that is framed of my Grandmother and Grandfather." I pointed to my desk.

Sam moved in closer to get a better look. "I can't imagine all the photos my mother has," he reflected, looking around the room. "Who knows? We may inherit those as well!"

"Yikes," I responded, not wanting to think about it. "Okay, pull me up." I reached out my hand. "I'm off to bed. This is overwhelming."

He nodded and pulled me up into a warm embrace.

Once in bed, Sam immediately fell asleep. How he could always do this was beyond me. His worries seemed to surface in the middle of the night, however, and then he would get up. My problem was getting to sleep before my worries book would come open.

I thought of Jean. Was she safe over the holiday weekend? Was my mother going to be happy in her new marriage, or was she making a mistake? Would Sam uncover something that would put him in danger? Stop! Turn the page!

CHAPTER 21

Before I left to take my walk the next morning, Ella arrived to clean our home.

"So, Anne, what did you think about the wedding news?" Ella asked as she put her purse away. "Did it take you by surprise?"

"Yes and no," I answered with an approving smile. "I'm really happy for them. Their reception will be here at our house if Harry approves, so I'd like some help, Ella."

"You don't say," she responded. "That is mighty nice of you, Anne. You know I'll do whatever I can for all of you. I'm very happy for them."

"Well, don't panic about the task, as we'll have plenty of other help," I continued. "I'll see to it that there are plenty of flowers, you'll have the place presentable, and Mother has a good caterer in mind."

She nodded and smiled.

"It gets me off the hook trying to think of the right wedding present."

She nodded once more. "I will be losing one of my paying clients, which is the only downside to this," Ella complained. "I suppose I can muster up another client somewhere."

"Are things still that tight for you financially, Ella?"

She shrugged her shoulders and began getting her cleaning equipment.

"You know Sam and I are willing to help in any way we can. You have put up with so much here."

"You gave me a generous raise, Anne, so you have done quite enough," she said politely. "My landlord has a cruel plan to eliminate tenants that have been there for a long time by continuing to raise the rent until we move on. He then has an opportunity to significantly raise the rent for the new tenant."

"That's terrible, Ella," I said sympathetically. "I knew they did this in the city but didn't know they did it here in Colebridge. I'd better be on my way. It's getting late." I had gone out the door and started down the hill when my cell phone rang.

"Are you up and about, Anne?" Sue's voice asked.

"Yes, I just started my walk," I said, speaking between heavy breaths.

"I just couldn't wait one more minute to call you," Sue announced excitedly.

"You have news from the agency already?"

"No, but it's definitely the next best thing!"

"What, what?" I asked, wanting to know everything she knew.

"Yesterday, Nancy called and said she and Richard were

talking about expanding the grief services department and asked me if I would be interested in a position there."

I refrained from interrupting with a jillion questions.

"She said they have been touched by my sensitivity and volunteerism with the baby quilts. She also said my secretarial skills would be an asset for the company. In other words, I would be creating my own job description with my own hours, which is perfect for my future plans."

"Oh my goodness, Sue, this is good news!" I was elated. "Leave it to Nancy to observe all that."

"The salary is a little better and it's even closer to my house."

"It's perfect! When do you start?"

"As soon as I can!" she said with certainty. "I'll give them a two-week notice here and I hope to do that at the end of the day."

"Wow, this will be a life change for you!"

"Speaking of good news, Aunt Sylvia's engagement to Harry is certainly wonderful!"

"Yes, I'm still trying to absorb it all. I've got to get going, Sue. Please keep us posted on everything and congratulations to you!" I couldn't have been happier for Sue who was trying to carve her own slice of life without a significant other or husband. She certainly was a great mother, so there was no stopping her now. Perhaps Mr. Right would notice this amazing person one day.

On my phone, I noticed I had missed a call from Amanda. I clicked to hear her long message.

"You don't have to call me right back, Anne, but I wondered if you would be so kind as to attend the guest book at my wedding. I meant to ask you at the shower but things got so hectic. I also wanted to ask if you ever heard who the person was that sent the crystal. I certainly want to send a thank you note. Hope to hear from you soon. Love you!"

Yes, there never was a dull moment, that was for sure. Of course I would take on the guest book task. After all, it was an honor to be asked and she was family.

I showered and dressed for the day and had so many things on my mind. I walked past my office and saw the lily quilt draped over my writing chair. I went in the room to look at it more closely and run my fingers across the very tiny quilting stitches. The words "Under these lilies I weep to sleep" ran through my mind again. I didn't want to just use this quilt in one of the bedrooms that may or not be used. I wanted this quilt near me so I could touch and admire it. I took the quilt and went back into our master bedroom. I picked up the previous white quilt that I had placed at the bottom of our bed and replaced it with the lily quilt. I wanted to see it when I woke up and went to sleep. Somehow, it was a comforting maneuver for me. I took the other white quilt and put it in the red and white guest room where a quilt rack had an empty place to hold one more quilt.

There is a place and time for every quilt, I thought.

CHAPTER 22

I parked in front of the shop and saw our flower cart was already placed on the sidewalk. All of the spring colors were beautiful, as were my two flower boxes in front of the shop. No one would have any doubt that this was a flower shop! The first time my flower cart came out, the preservationists on the street went into a tizzy because they just knew it wasn't historic and felt it would encourage others to junk up the street. I had done my homework and proved to them that flower carts had been used throughout history. Of course, it didn't make me any friends with the tight-knit group.

I went straight to my office to look at emails. The first one was from Ted's office inviting me to a ribbon cutting at his new office expansion. Since it wasn't a personal invitation, I did not respond. If I decided to go, it would be a nice gesture on my part, since the last few times I saw him I was clearly rude to him. Perhaps I could take Sally with me if I attended.

"Your mother is on the phone, Anne," Sally announced as she walked by my door.

"Well, how is the soon-to-be Mrs. Sylvia Stone?" I teased.

"Don't rush it, sweetie," she teased back. "I just called your house by mistake and Ella answered."

"Yes, it's her day to clean."

"She told me Sam was not feeling well and that he came home from work to rest. What's going on with him, Anne?"

I felt a bit dumbfounded. What could have happened?

"I don't know anything about him not feeling well today. I'll call him and see if he's okay."

"I meant to call to ask if you and Sam wanted to go with Harry and me to Amanda's wedding."

"Sure, but we'll talk about that later, okay?" I hung up quickly so that I could call home.

I first tried calling Sam's cell phone, which went immediately to voice mail. I then tried the house, and after ringing a good while, it went to voice mail also. Maybe he had left and returned to work.

"Miss Anne, I brought us some tea sandwiches today for a bite of lunch," Jean said as she peeked in my office.

"Oh, Jean, how nice," I replied, getting out of my chair. "I'll be happy to have a bite when I return from an errand."

"Jolly good," she responded, going back to the design room.

I took my purse and headed toward the door while telling Sally I needed to do something. She was with a customer and I wasn't sure she even heard me leave. Was

I overreacting? There would be no way I could continue working at the shop not knowing what was going on with Sam.

When I arrived at our driveway, I saw Sam's car parked in front. I walked into a very quiet house. I thought I might find him in the study on the computer, but he wasn't there. I checked in the kitchen before heading up to our bedroom. There, I found Sam sound asleep and still wearing his work clothes. He didn't hear me at all, which was strange. I couldn't remember Sam ever taking a nap on a work day.

I softly nudged him on the shoulder, making him jump in surprise. "Honey, are you okay?" I whispered.

He rolled over in my direction and gave me a quizzical look. "I'm fine, just fine."

"What brought you home?"

He sighed like a little boy getting caught at something. "Don't worry, Anne," he reassured me as he began to wake up. "I took the stairs at work thinking I needed the exercise. I was going faster than I typically do and got out of breath and had to rest. I started breaking out in a cold sweat and that scared me."

I sat down on the bed next to him.

"So, I just went to get some fresh air and decided to knock it off for awhile."

"How do you feel now?"

"Pretty good, but I'd feel better if some good-looking gal hadn't woke me up," he joked, giving me a big grin. "What are you doing home?"

I knew I couldn't give him the chain of events because he'd be upset. "I forgot something and was shocked to see your car here," I replied, thinking quickly. "Can I fix you some lunch or do anything for you? Did you take your meds today?"

"Of course," he answered with slight aggravation. "I may just stay here and work on the computer. You need to get back to work, honey. I'll be fine."

"Are you sure you don't want me to stay?"

"I'll call you if I need anything, okay? Good-bye, sweet Annie." He turned away from me, clearly planning to go back to sleep.

I came downstairs feeling relieved and yet still very concerned. Sam's condition would always be a worry for both of us.

Jean and Sally were working at the front counter when I returned. Sally was trying to appease Mrs. Thomas who was giving details on another one of her many arrangements she frequently ordered. She was a good customer, but we wondered where on earth she was putting all of her silk arrangements. I said hello and kept walking to the back of the shop where I grabbed one of Jean's tea sandwiches before going into my office. I closed the door. As I sat at my desk, I broke down in tears. My emotions were swift in coming to the surface as I thought about Sam and his heart problems. I had to believe he would be fine. He was my wonderful Sam. He just *had* to be fine.

CHAPTER 23

I was preoccupied thinking about Sam, so much so that I did not think about asking Jean how things were going for her at home. Later in the day, Sally mentioned that Jean seemed to be her normal self, so I decided to wait and not bring anything up about Al. I was about to leave the shop early when Gayle called and asked me to go to lunch with her the next day. I knew she probably wanted to talk about her shop dilemma.

"Check with me in the morning, Gayle," I told her. "I have a few things going on and I don't know my plans yet."

"Oh sure," she replied. "I have someone working at my shop tomorrow, so I thought it would be a good time to visit with you."

Having arranged that and finished up some other business, I left the shop for Sally and Jean to close. Driving home, I realized this weekend was Amanda's wedding.

Would Sam be well enough to go with me? Perhaps I should go with Mother and Harry and leave Sam at home to rest.

I walked in the house feeling a bit nervous and found Sam on the computer in the study, which made me relax. I breathed in a wonderful aroma coming from the kitchen.

"What's cookin', good lookin'?" I said with a twang in my voice as I kissed him on the cheek.

"Beef stroganoff. Remember when I made that for you when I still lived in the loft?"

"Do I ever, Sam," I said, recalling how delicious it was. "It was great! In fact, the whole evening was pretty great, if I recall correctly." I paused to reflect for a moment, remembering that romantic evening when we were first getting to know one another. "I take it that your energy is back?"

"Yes, I feel fine. It was a nice, quiet afternoon."

We had a leisurely dinner on the sunporch while we admired Kip's latest handiwork on the patio room. It appeared to be nearly finished. Sam would not commit to attending Amanda's wedding. He avoided the big elephant in the room, which was talking about his company's finances. I didn't want to create any more pressure on him, so I kept the conversation light.

After dinner, Sam went back to the computer and I cleaned up the kitchen. I was mentally exhausted from the day's worry, but thought I'd go to my office and attempt to write or look through more pictures. I sat on the floor, gazing at the neat piles I had made previously while sorting out the photographs. I was still in the box of older photos which came from Grandmother's house. I was hoping there would be something about her life before she became Mrs.

Davis. Did she ever love my grandfather, or did she just settle in, wanting to get married?

I grabbed a few photos of folks I didn't know and put them on the appropriate pile. I saw an envelope that wasn't addressed, but that had a piece of paper that looked similar to a grocery list. I opened it up and read the word *trousseau* at the top. It listed the items as follows: 3 sets of pillowcases, 6 tea towels, my lily quilt, 2 doilies, Mother's rose china, 6 salts and spoons, my love pillow, 2 candlesticks, and the lavender quilt.

She was saving these items for her marriage, I guessed. The lily quilt no doubt was made or was being made. I would have to ask Mother what lavender quilt she was talking about. Did she list a love pillow? That was weird. It was her handwriting. Was she already engaged to my grandfather, or was this when she was still having an affair with Albert Taylor? I put the list with her other letters. I continued with more interest and found another envelope with a photo of my grandmother with her mother holding the lily quilt. This gave me chills. Did her mother help her make this? I turned the photo over and saw some writing that said *Martha's lily quilt.* Underneath it was printed *L for Love, I for innocence, L for longevity, and Y for yearning for more.*

Again, it appeared to be Grandmother's handwriting. It was kind of corny, so she was probably pretty young. She was proud of the quilt. The photo had yellowed, but I had already decided to get it enlarged and framed. I stared and stared at it. Grandmother was beautiful, but I couldn't say the same for her stout mother. I put the photo and envelope on the framing pile. This made my evening as I felt her presence.

CHAPTER 24

The next morning began with the most comfortable temperatures, so it was no surprise to find Sam sitting out on our new patio reading the paper while enjoying his morning coffee. I had to take time to join him, feeling jealous that he was the one breaking in this beautiful new addition to 333 Lincoln.

"It's nice to see you so relaxed, honey." I sat down next to him.

He winked at me as he continued to read.

"The rest of the new patio furniture should be in this week."

He nodded.

"Well, tomorrow Amanda Anderson will be Mrs. Allen Richards. I sure wish her mother could be here."

"I'm sure, like the rest of the family, that she will be there in spirit," he jested. "Didn't you say William is giving her away?"

"Yes, and I'm the infamous guest book attendant."

He laughed as he poured himself another cup of coffee. "Would you be terribly upset if I didn't take time to go to the wedding, Anne?"

I wasn't prepared for the question and really didn't know how I was supposed to take it. "Why wouldn't you take the time, Sam?"

"We have auditors coming from Chicago this afternoon, and I'm sure they are staying over a day or two," he explained. "I really need to be there. I'm the one that insisted we do this, so I feel I need to be available."

"This is what you are so worried about, isn't it?"

He nodded.

"I understand. I want you to get to the bottom of this problem. I can go with Mother or Aunt Julia." I could tell he was relieved.

I kissed him good-bye for the day and began my walk deep in thought. I remembered I had a lunch scheduled with Gayle, so I could not take too much time. I still had a lot to accomplish at the shop today.

The tourists loved the perfect weather as well and activity on the street reflected it. Sally called in Abbey to help with a wedding scheduled for the weekend, so getting away for a short lunch would work out after all. I was glad I had declined Amanda's request to do her wedding flowers. I had felt the distance would be inconvenient and I wanted her to be able to relax and not have to worry about any complications on her special day. I felt a local florist could manage the event with more ease.

The morning went by quickly and Gayle was exactly

on time when she appeared in the shop to walk to lunch. We decided to go to the Water Wheel so we could sit outdoors by the creek. As we walked, she reminisced about how she loved the shop and the street. This told me that she had made the decision to move closer to her mother. After we placed our order, she took a deep breath and began her explanation. Her eyes watered as she told me that her mother's condition had worsened and that she felt the need to move more quickly in making her decision.

"I gave my notice to the landlord this week, Anne," she began as she looked away from me. "My lease is not up for several months, and he reminded me of that."

"Oh, Gayle, how hard for you," I said sympathetically. "Surely he won't charge you under these circumstances."

"You know Bill," she said, shaking her head in disgust. "He said if either of us found someone to rent the place sooner, he'd let me off, but otherwise, he would need the rent. I have movers coming in two weeks. I will be going to Mother's house for now. I have to give some notice to my customers. I owe them that."

"Oh, how sad this all is for you. What can I do to help?"

She started to respond, but the waitress was busy placing our food in front of us.

"I don't know why I ordered this." Gayle pushed her food aside. "I'll take it to go. I'm just too upset to eat."

"I still say to look at this as a future opportunity to open a shop at a new location, minus you having to pay for housing," I encouraged.

"That is if I can sell my condo in a short time, which I doubt." she explained. "So, the bottom line is that I can only hope the shop gets rented in a timely manner. If you know anyone, please have them contact me or Bill."

"I will. Word gets out quickly on the street. You know that."

As we nibbled at our lunch, I couldn't help but put myself in her shoes. The street had a way of engulfing all your thoughts and energy. Once a street person, always a street person, was a saying I had heard so often. I tried to cheer her up as best I could, but we both walked away feeling like we were saying good-bye forever.

The street's activity soon distracted me from Gayle's problems as she quickly returned to her shop. As soon as I walked in the door of my shop, I began helping an elderly gentleman who was choosing a bouquet for his wife. At the counter, I heard a familiar voice ask for me. It was Beverly, whose grandmother worked as a cook for the Taylors. I felt terrible that I had not called her to visit, but there hadn't been time. I walked over to her and gave her my apologies.

"That's alright, Mrs. Dickson. I just came back to pick up that cute lady flower pot in the window." She pointed it out. "It's my friend's birthday and it looks like her."

"Wonderful," I said, retrieving the flowerpot. "Let me check out this gentleman and then I'll put a bow on it. A pretty yellow one would look great!"

When I finally had a chance to visit with her, I suggested that next week would be perfect for her to visit 333 Lincoln. She was delighted and said she might bring her sister with her.

There were so many questions I wanted to ask her, in hopes that her grandmother would have told her things about the Taylors. I also told her to look for any photographs from her family that may have to do with the Taylor family.

The end of the workday left me feeling somewhat sad as I thought of Sam having to meet with his auditors and Gayle giving up her glass shop that she had worked so hard for. As my staff and customers left for the day, I sat at my desk and tried to think how I could be of help to these two dear people who meant so much to me.

CHAPTER 25

Amanda and Allen's wedding was on a picture-perfect day. Harry and Mother were happy to have me accompany them for the occasion. Sue and Mia came with Aunt Julia and Sarah, so we had a nice representation from Amanda's mother's side of the family. It was very pleasant meeting Allen's family and some folks from Amanda's father's side of the family as well.

Because of the small number of guests, we were seated in a small room that opened up to a reception area. It was hard to sit through the ceremony as my mind was distracted by thoughts of Sam. I missed him not being at my side, plus the thought of his discomfort right now was even more difficult to bear. I wondered if he could handle what might be ahead of him. I glanced at Mother who was watching this ceremony and possibly thinking of her own wedding plans. Would hearing these vows repeated give her second thoughts? Aunt Julia always pretended to be so content with her new single life, but would this romantic ceremony make her sad and lonely? Having Sam in my life added contentment like I had never known could be possible. Hearing vows spoken again only made me miss him more.

The newly married couple made their way down the aisle with big smiles and lots of kisses. I looked over at Mother who had tears in her eyes as she comfortably linked her arm with Harry's and prepared to exit our row.

We joined Sue who was holding back the energized Mia, who had sat still long enough and was ready to make circles around the tables. Dressed in white, she could have been a flower girl. She was turning into an adorable child with a personality that naturally drew others to her. It was no wonder Sam melted when she was around. The possibility of having a little Mia of our own was at least flitting through my thoughts every now and then.

"I don't know how Mia will handle any competition if or when she gets a brother or sister," Sue said as she was wiping Mia's nose.

"Are we getting closer to any news?' I asked, hopeful for a quick adoption placement for Sue.

"They tell me I am, but I really don't know what that means," she replied. Still holding a wiggling Mia's hand, Sue added, "I don't think we'll stay long. Mia still takes a nap and Aunt Julia said Sarah want to get back early for something."

"Well, my duties are done, so perhaps I'll ride back with you and let Mother and Harry enjoy themselves in private," I suggested.

"Oh sure, that would be great," Sue said with a big smile.

Mother understood my departure after I told her I was worried about Sam. I could tell they wanted to meet more of the family and to be able to take their time visiting with others at the reception. We said our good-byes to the delightful couple and knew that Amanda and her groom were off to happy and successful lives.

On the way home, I told them all about my plans to meet with Beverly the following week. They had to agree that it was a unique introduction to the Taylors that was more than a coincidence.

"I don't know if I should say anything, Anne, but Sally indicated that Jean and Al were having problems," Sue announced. "Is everything alright?"

"Oh dear, I hate for any gossip to start about that, but no, I don't think things are okay."

"Oh no, not poor Jean," Aunt Julia said, astonished.

"Without going into detail, I have to say that I suspect his drinking is causing some abuse and we're trying to convince her that she does not have to endure any of it," I explained emphatically.

"Talk all you want to her, but I know from this girl at work in a similar position and until they decide they have had enough, no change will happen," claimed Sue.

"On another subject, Sue, when do you start at Barrister's?" I asked, mostly to avoid dirty details about Jean.

"Next week. I just have one more week at my current job. I will be counting the days."

I added, "Sue is making a good move in many ways. I'll bet they treat their employees very well, plus you will be creating your own job description."

"That is pretty awesome when you think about it Sue," Aunt Julia said in agreement.

"I keep thinking I should be taking on a new adventure," Aunt Julia shared. "I told Sarah the other day that we should do something together that we both enjoy."

Sarah grinned but had no comment.

"What would you like to do?" I asked, curious.

"I know it sounds crazy, but at times I envy you, Anne, working on Main Street," Aunt Julia remarked. "I know it's hard work, but as I observe how much you love what you do, so it doesn't seem to be work. Am I right?"

I laughed. "You are right in some ways. I can't imagine not being around flowers and not doing something creative. I'm lucky to be able to do that. I was lucky to be able to have the proper capital to do it as well. Most business people don't have that luxury."

She nodded.

"I told Mom that as much as she decorates, she should do it for other people," Sarah said.

"I am not a decorator. I do like pretty things like art, paper products, and coffee table books." She laughed and we agreed that they all fit together. "No one sees the beauty in paper like I do, I'm afraid. I don't want a bookstore, that's for sure, but I see art in beautiful papers, and I don't mean scrapbooking necessarily. That's cute, but trendy. I see a classier venue for paper."

"Wow, you have been thinking!" I said. "I love paper too and I agree with your description completely."

We now arrived at 333 Lincoln and Sam's car was in the driveway. I said my thanks and good-byes quickly, eager to greet Sam inside the house.

CHAPTER 26

I couldn't get into the house fast enough. I called Sam's name but got no response. As I walked toward the kitchen, I could see Sam sitting outdoors in the back patio. His body was bent forward as if he were deep in thought. I don't think he heard me call his name.

"Sam, honey, when did you get home?"

"Hey, Annie," he said, turning my way. "I left when the auditors left. None of the staff was there today but me."

"How did it go?" I asked, joining him on a chair nearby.

"It's not looking good," he said as he shook his head in disgust.

I stared at him, waiting for more information.

"They've agreed with everything I've shown them so far. In other words, they share my concerns and raised even more questions than answers. I think they may be here for a while."

"What does all this mean, Sam?"

"My worst nightmare is embezzlement. I didn't want to say the word, but it's looking like it more and more. It could lead to a criminal investigation if this is going where I think it is."

I began to feel physically ill. "What? You can't be serious, Sam. How could anything like this happen?"

"That's what this audit is all about!" he answered impatiently. "You must keep this between us, Anne. They are experts at this, and with some luck, they will find some explanations. I am trying hard to be optimistic here." He got up and I thought for a moment he was going to break down and cry. This was much more serious than I ever imagined. "I have not involved our financial officer at this point in case he may have played a role in this. I am furious that I did not insist upon an audit when I took over. The board kept reassuring me everything was fine and that it would only delay Mr. Martingale's retirement."

"Well, what was the big hurry?" I felt my anger growing in defense of poor Sam. "That wasn't fair to you!"

"All good comments, Annie, but sooner or later we will get to the bottom of this. I just hope the damage isn't so severe that it puts the whole company in jeopardy."

The thought of it all horrified me, but I had to be positive for Sam's sake. "None of this is your fault, Sam," I insisted. "You must remember that. I worry about how this is affecting your health. Remember how we both said nothing is worth the risk of another heart attack."

He nodded. "I'm sorry to involve you, Annie, but we've not kept any secrets between us and this truly has been the big elephant in the room, as you have often referred to it. I will deal with this."

"Do the other employees know?" I hoped they did not.

"They will tomorrow," Sam said, shaking his head sadly. "I'm sure most will just think of it as a normal procedure. Aaron is not going to be happy, that's for sure. He will have a lot of questions to answer."

"I take it that he is your CFO?"

"Yes."

"I need something to drink." I had an uncomfortable feeling of helplessness. "Can I get you anything?" I got no answer. "Did you eat anything today?"

"Not really."

"Well, I think we need a pizza at a time like this, so I am going to call one in. I barely ate a thing at the wedding. I got a ride home with Aunt Julia so Mother and Harry could spend as much time there as they wanted."

"I'm sorry, honey. I forgot to ask you about the wedding. How was it?"

"It was very beautiful and romantic. I could have used someone there to hold my hand like Harry and Mother were doing."

He grinned. "Pizza actually sounds pretty good right now."

I blew him a kiss and went in to call Pete's Pizza.

We managed to continue small talk about the wedding as we picked at our pizza. There was no way to completely erase what was on our minds. Sam wanted to catch up on his emails so he finished his dinner and went into the study. I was exhausted and wanted a hot shower that would wash away all my worries. I went upstairs to our bedroom.

I got into my white cotton gown and sat down on the

edge of the bed to pray. There was no one else in this world to help us. I prayed that God would keep Sam well and assist him through this turmoil. Sam was a good man. What if he was blamed or accused of something through all this?

Please, please, I begged.

I could no longer hold back the tears that had been welling up inside. I grabbed the lily quilt and pulled it up around me for comfort as I leaned back on the bed. I pulled it over my face. I didn't want Sam to hear me cry. That would only add to his distress. Is this how Grandmother felt when she wrote *Under these lilies I weep to sleep?* How could I possibly sleep?

CHAPTER 27

I woke from the bright sunlight coming in from the window and discovered I was still wrapped up in the lily quilt on top of the bed. Sam's side of the bed was not slept in. I got up and grabbed my robe to head downstairs. There was no answer when I called his name nor was there the smell of coffee that I had come to expect each morning.

I went to the kitchen table to get my cell phone when I noticed a note addressed to me from Sam. It read: *Annie, Left early for work. Try to have a good day. Love, Sam*

Relieved to know where he was, I decided not to call him. I sat down to gather my thoughts, check my phone for calls, and review the schedule for the day. I would grab a Starbucks and stop by the bank. I wasn't in the mood for my walk. The quicker I became busy, the quicker I could forget about Sam's problems.

I walked in the shop with muffins for everyone. Sally was delighted to see the treats and reported that Kevin would not have to come in until noon for deliveries. Jean was stripping stems for an arrangement as I walked by her while on my way to my office.

"I brought a treat for you, Jean," I happily announced.

"Thank you, Miss Anne," she said with a sad ring in her voice.

This was not my Jean talking.

I kept going and started reading my emails and looking over the order sheet for the day when I heard a loud crash. I rushed out, hearing Jean shriek in surprise at the mishap. I looked down to see a broken vase and water spreading across the floor. Sally was not far behind me.

"Oh, I am so, so sorry," she said, tears falling down her face. "I don't know how that happened."

"It's no big deal, Jean. Did you cut yourself? Come into to my office and take a break."

"I'll clean it up in a jiffy, Jean," offered Sally. "I've done this before myself."

Jean came right in and I noticed she was shaking terribly.

I closed the door behind us, not knowing quite where to start the conversation. "What's going on, Jean?" I said softly as she put her head in her hands. "Is it Al? Did you get any sleep last night?"

She shook her head.

I waited for some verbal response.

"The nutter had too much bevvy," she finally muttered.

"Did he hurt you?"

She didn't answer the question. "I thought he had taken leave, but to my misfortune, he returned." Her voice now elevated. "I can tell you straight away that I will have to go back to Bath to escape him. In vain I have struggled to get on, but now

I cannot devise what he will do next."

"Oh, Jean, no one should put up with this," I said firmly. "Have you ever called the police?"

"Calling a copper would not keep me out of harm's way, Miss Anne. I know now I must take leave from him."

"Yes, we can agree on that point," I reassured her while putting my arm around her. "Do you have any plan at all, Jean?"

Jean remained thoughtful for a moment. "I'll ring my sister, Ellen, and leave when I can," she revealed as she got up to pace the room.

"Ellen lives in Bath?"

She nodded.

"Do you really want to go back there, or do you just want to escape Al?"

She again was silent.

"You can stay with Sam and me, you know!"

"You always have such openness of heart, Miss Anne, but Sally's flat would be unknown to Al so I may have to oblige her offer."

"Perfect," I stated before she changed her mind. "We will all help you, Jean, so just say when. The sooner you leave, the better for your own safety. Alcoholism is a terrible disease, Jean. From what I know of Al though, he loves you."

She looked at me strangely. "Anne, I'm afraid he's a bit of a skirt chaser too, which breaks my very soul." She was about to cry all over again.

"I am so, so sorry for you, Jean," I managed to say. "Please drink some of this coffee. I'll bring Sally in here so you two can discuss plans. I'll keep an eye out front."

I went to the front counter where Sally was just finishing up a pick-up order.

"Go back and talk to her, Sally. I think she's ready to take you up on your offer. We need to do something quickly before he really hurts her. Take your time, I'll take over."

Sally had a tremendous look of concern and sadness on her face as she left to go to my office.

What else could go wrong today? I was getting myself more coffee when Phil, another merchant from the street, walked in the front door.

"Hey, Dickson girl, where have you been keeping yourself?" Phil teasingly asked. "You missed another merchants' meeting last week."

"Oh, I know. I have been very busy, Phil. So, what's going on?"

"Well, I thought you'd find it interesting that they want to do another outdoor quilt show next fall," he announced with a smile.

"Oh boy, did you agree to chair that again?"

He laughed and nodded.

"Please don't look at me to help, Phil. I have my hands full."

"Luckily, you have given us the one and only Abbey who is a great worker and who has agreed to help us again this year," he happily bragged.

"That's great," I said, giving him a thumbs-up sign. "I am so happy she is involved. Moving here has made her very happy. I think she has found a main street family."

"Hey, I am sorry to hear we are losing Gayle on the street," Phil mentioned.

"You and me both. I worry who Bill may rent her space to. I wish I had known that a year ago. I would have expanded in that direction. Do you know anyone that's looking for a space?"

"No, but this block never has a vacancy, so he may already

have numbers to call," Phil reminded me. "I'd better get going. I just wanted to say hi." Phil exited quickly because my telephone began to ring.

It was Ella, returning a call that I had made to her earlier. "Thanks for calling back, Ella," I began. "I need you to come tomorrow instead of Wednesday if you can. They are delivering our outdoor furniture in the morning. Is that okay?"

"Sure," she said with a sniffle in her voice. "I have a bit of a sinus condition, so I don't know how my energy will hold out, but I can be there."

After I thanked her, I reminded myself of her hardships and how much she was becoming like family. I didn't want to take advantage of her, but she was easy to do that with.

Sally and Jean came from my office and Sally began describing a bouquet she wanted Jean to arrange. It seemed that things were normal again. When Sally joined me at the front counter, I wanted to change the subject from Jean, so I asked her about Tim.

"Tim who?" she said grinning. "No progress there, Anne, so I am moving on. He called to go to a baseball game this past weekend, but I didn't feel like being his pity person, so I turned him down. I think I'm beginning to see why Paige was not interested in him. There has to be more to a guy than good looks and sports."

I laughed. "Well, good for you, Sally! We'll see if he misses his buddy, right?"

"Right!" she said, winking.

CHAPTER 28

Before I locked the door for the day, I called Sam to find out if I would see him for dinner. He finally picked up his cell phone after several rings and told me he needed to stay late along with a few other co-workers. I didn't want to keep him from his work, so I quickly gave him my love and hung up. I visualized God having his arms around Sam to help him through this process.

It was indeed a stressful day, so I decided to pick up something from Charley's to take home for dinner. I was pleased to see the bar was nearly empty. I placed my order for a chicken quesadilla. While I waited, I sat at the counter and glanced through a newspaper that had been left by a previous customer.

I heard a small commotion near the front door. It was Richard and Nancy pushing their double stroller into the waiting area. I immediately ran over to greet them and kissed the two little darlings on their cheeks. They were now about six months old and were the definition of cute. They both drooled from teething but their smiles revealed traits from each of their parents. I explained that Sam was unavailable for dinner and that I was waiting on my to-go order. They wanted me to join them.

"I have had a horrendous day and I just need to get food and get home," I explained. "Sam is working late and the cupboard is bare."

They laughed.

"Let's try to get together real soon before the summer is gone!"

They agreed and off they went to their table. As I watched everyone they encountered make such a fuss over them, I reflected on how this had been Nancy's goal in life and how her family was more than picture perfect.

I took my dinner to the car and almost dropped my bag when a horrible thought entered my mind. I had not taken my birth control pill this morning! My routine had been turned upside down when I didn't discover Sam in my bed. Part of me felt it would not matter, but it was not like me to be so careless. As I drove home, I convinced myself that Sam's attention had been diverted lately, so I wouldn't have anything to worry about.

I went right up to change into my jeans and T-shirt and then went to the kitchen. I reheated the quesadilla and sat at the kitchen table to decide how to spend the rest of my short evening. It was still daylight and the potting shed was calling my name. I knew watering had to be done there. I went to the back patio to plan where I wanted the new furniture placed. It was already a favorite spot of Sam's, but my favorite place to relax would always be the south porch where the Taylors had enjoyed sitting so many years ago.

As I walked to the potting shed, I could tell Kip's handiwork was keeping things beautiful and alive. When I opened the door I noticed my cacti needed a drink and some spider webs had wasted no time in finding their favorite spots once again. It was so hot, even with leaving the door ajar so some air could come through. We hadn't had any rain for some time now and it was starting to show. Outside once again, I walked around the herb garden that always seemed to bring such calmness to me with its array of different shades of green. It was one of the first things I constructed when I came to 333 Lincoln. I tore of some sprigs of mint to put in my ice tea later on this evening.

I walked along deadheading flowers where I could, especially the geraniums in the gazebo flower boxes. The soil was dry, so I unrolled a hose and began to water them. There was a part of me that turned into a little farmer's wife when I tended my plants. I was careful not to touch the leaves as I gazed at the rich red color of the flower. Every home should have geraniums. They are a sign of warmth and hospitality, as far as I was concerned. They could add charm to a rickety log cabin if they had to.

I sat briefly on the south porch and reminded myself that Mother's wedding reception would be here in no time. Mother was working out floral details with Sally for the ceremony and reception. Tomorrow, I would go over things with Ella to make the house elegant, clean, and festive. It felt good to think of happy moments ahead instead of Sam's work and Jean's abusive husband.

It was beginning to get dark and my eyes were feeling

heavy. Crawling into bed with a good book sounded better than trying to write something tonight.

I went up to bed and came out of the shower in time to hear Sam coming up the stairs. I looked at my birth control pills on the shelf. I wasn't going to tell Sam. It was a conversation we had entertained too many times, and he had his mind on more serious things.

"Sam, honey, are you okay?"

He didn't answer, but smiled at me. "You look so sweet and beautiful in that pretty white gown," he said softly as he began to remove his tie. "You are such a pleasant sight when I come home each day. I hope you know that." He looked exhausted.

I went over to him. "Oh Sam, I love you so much. How did things go today? Is there progress one way or another?"

"More and more things are surfacing, which is not good, Annie," he said, backing away from me to get undressed. "Aaron is furious with me for starting this process. I'm afraid he is taking it very personally."

"It's not making him look good, in other words?"

"Right." He went in to brush his teeth as I sat there speechless.

When he came to bed, he pulled the covers back and collapsed on the white sheets. Fully reclined, he gently lifted my left hand, brushed his lips to the back of my hand, and was asleep in seconds. I looked at this very handsome, successful man that seemed to have it all. He was too good and honest. I loved him so much and it made me feel I had a purpose in this marriage. I would be there for him...no matter what!

CHAPTER 29

I felt better after Ella and I went over every detail of Mother's wedding reception. I assured Ella I would give her a bonus for all her help on the event. There was part of me that wished I had her at my side every day. She took great care to please us, along with a few other clients that she had. I also told her she had a room here any time she would need it in case she wanted to rest or stay over. She knew I was also pleased that Grandmother had accepted her and left her alone.

The completion of the patio room outside of our sunporch was just as I planned it. The comfortable couches and chairs in shades of green complemented the white and brown wicker trim and tables. Lots of green plants made it feel like a tropical setting somewhere far south of Colebridge. The center fireplace will be a tempting spot when the weather turns cool this fall. The décor reminded me of something one would see at a southern plantation. Sam was especially pleased because it was designed with comfort in mind.

I stopped by Mother's home to make sure we were on the same page for her big day. The house looked great with freshly-painted rooms and some rearrangement of furniture to make room for Harry. This was a new chapter in her life and I found myself getting caught up in the excitement.

"I think we are in great shape, Anne," Mother said, clearly exuberant.

"Everything is ready at 333 Lincoln except the flowers that will be delivered," I reported. "The house looks great, Mother. How is Harry doing?"

"Really well, but he is more excited about the honeymoon. He has been planning and planning. He won't tell me where we're going and I don't care as long as it is warm and sunny!"

It reminded me of Sam's planned secret honeymoon. "I think that is a guy thing, Mother," I teased.

"Don't forget, when we return, I'd like you to have that Ginny Lyn bed in the back bedroom," she reminded. "I repainted in there, and Harry plans to use it for an office."

Things really were changing. "I'll be happy to and I have a room just waiting for it," I assured her. "Oh, Mother, I just hope I don't cry at the wedding. I am so happy for you, but I keep getting so emotional."

"I know that, Anne, because it is very emotional for me, too," she said, putting her arm around me. "Your wedding was the same way. I didn't know what to expect. I am so proud of how you have accepted Harry. I couldn't ask for a better daughter and now a better husband. Harry has been so good to me and we want to be together for the rest of our lives!" Her eyes glistened with tears. An obvious sign of her endearing happiness.

"Oh Mother, I *am* so happy for you!" I chased the thought out of my mind, wondering if she ever had these same happy moments with my father.

"See, honey, we are getting this all out of the way so we can enjoy the wedding!"

We both broke into laughter.

"Ella has been such a help with all this," I confessed. "I couldn't have done this without her."

"I feel bad that she'll be losing a job after this. I know she needs every penny."

"I hated when her rent went up. She did mention how unexpected that was."

"Have you ever thought of asking her to move in at your place, Anne?" Mother asked, catching me off guard. "You seem to need her more than any of us. I do think she'd need a little more room than that maid's quarters you showed me. You could possibly set up a bartering arrangement together."

"Oh, no, I haven't thought of that. I don't know what Sam would think about that. He is the king of the 333 Lincoln castle on the hill. He is so proud of it."

"Well, and so are you! As you are learning, with a big estate like yours and it possibly doubling in size with gaining the neighboring property, it takes a cleaning lady, a gardener, and even a cook. You will own the whole hill before you know it. You both are busy and cannot do it all. No wonder you don't want to have children. You'd have to add a nanny to the staff!"

I gave her a strange look. "Mother, stop it," I said, smiling. "I have to get going." I walked toward the door. "I will introduce the thought to Sam, but right now, he has a lot on his plate and we have a wedding on our hands. I will meet you at the church. How many are coming again?"

"We are at about thirty-five if everyone shows up," she said, grinning.

"Good-bye until your wedding day!" I blew her a kiss. "I can't wait to see you come down that aisle. I love you!"

When I got back to the shop, Sally, Abbey, and Jean were all working on flowers for Mother and Harry's wedding. They knew everything had to be extra beautiful for this occasion. When I got Sally alone, I asked her if Jean had moved in. She said the plan was for her to be picked up to go to the wedding and that she would not return. That sounded safe to me.

"She has been walking on eggshells all week around him," Sally said in a quiet voice. "She has been taking things out slowly so he won't notice. I don't think he suspects anything, but he will throw a fit when he finds out. I have Abbey working for her Monday because he will be coming here looking for her. You'd better have the police on speed dial."

"Oh dear," I said, hating to think the worst. "Is he still drinking?"

"Oh sure, but he tells her he is not, of course," she said, noticing Jean come our way. "How is Sam doing with his work crisis?"

"He's been very quiet about it," I reported. "He is trying not to upset me, of course, with the wedding and all. He goes in early and comes home late. I keep praying."

Sally nodded with a smile.

"Hey, where's Kevin today?" Abbey asked as she joined us.

"He had to help his brother today so Kip will be in

soon," I said. "What's going on these days with the two of you?"

"Not much," she said, tilting her head. "We went to a party together last weekend and had a great time. He's supposed to help me put some shelving up so I thought about asking him to come over tonight."

"That sounds like a married couple," Sally teased.

We laughed.

"Kevin turns red every time I bring up her name. I think they've got a thing going on!" Sally was enjoying herself entirely at Abbey's expense.

Abbey blushed.

"You both are pretty cool people, so I hope it works out for you guys!" I said affectionately.

Jean was listening with a smile on her face. She had so much on her mind. I worried that she would have more than her safety to worry about when this was all said and done. She would need some financial assistance. Perhaps at the right time, I could be helpful.

CHAPTER 30

Sam inspected what I had chosen to wear to the wedding. It was a formfitting dress of raspberry silk. He gave me a whistle as he fastened my diamond necklace, once owned by Grandmother Davis. This was a day I could also wear the fabulous large diamond ring Mother had given me on my birthday.

"You look like a million bucks, sweet Annie," Sam said with admiration.

"I actually am wearing nearly a million bucks today as a matter of fact, so I'd better look like it!" I teased.

"I personally love your pearls better, but today, it's all about my mother-in-law and Harry Stone."

I nodded in agreement.

We arrived at the church just before Mother and Harry's arrival. Mother was made up to the hilt and her yellow silk suit was perfect for the occasion. She was truly a beautiful woman. Aunt Julia was as lovely as ever standing beside

Mother. Harry looked especially handsome in his tuxedo, as did his best man David Stone, his brother who flew in from California to stand up for him. He and his beautiful wife, Olivia, made a stunning couple. David was younger than Harry, but they were very close. David told Mother they were very happy that Harry had found someone special to love.

The ceremony was short, which was just what Mother wanted. In the end, I was able to keep my emotions in check. Seeing Mother and Harry exchange vows with such undeniable joy tested me in my quest not to cry. After the ceremony, another touching moment was seeing the brothers' tearful embrace. The strength of the bond of family was so evident between them.

Ella hurried from the ceremony to join the caterers. Valet parking was arranged, putting some vehicles into the mowed fields nearby. This was a new experience at 333 Lincoln. I wondered if the Taylors had such grand gatherings and what would Mrs. Brody think about all this, if she were still alive?

The gorgeous white floral and ivy garland draped on the staircase was the first thing I noticed. It was close to being as beautiful as the large Christmas tree we had each year. On my large, round center table in the entryway, I had a large white bouquet and the guestbook. Of course, white lilies were mixed in with every arrangement. Grandmother must be enjoying them all. The dining room sparkled with lit candles and floral arrangements that complemented the attractively presented food.

"Anne, Anne, this is all too much," Mother gushed. "Did I really order all this?"

"You cannot afford all of this, Mother," I teased. "This

is what you have me for, Mrs. Stone."

"You are the first to call me Mrs. Stone," Mother said sentimentally.

"Do you like it?"

"I love it, don't you?" she giggled.

"All the Brown girls are married now," I said, hoping I wouldn't upset her.

Harry came over to join us. He put his arm around me and showered me with compliments. "I don't know how to thank you," he said sincerely. "David and Olivia love the house and can't wait for a tour."

"Please make them feel at home, Harry. They are a delightful couple."

Sam came over, making it a comfortable foursome.

"Harry, have you noticed the new patio room outside the sunporch?" I asked.

"It's another magnificent touch from that daughter of yours, Sylvia," Sam bragged. "May I show it off to you both?"

"My, yes," Mother said with excitement.

I watched them walk off together. It was a touching sight as I reminded myself that our family had added another member today. I looked around the room, seeing the newly-married Allen and Amanda as well as William. I walked over to Sally and Jean who were standing near the punch bowl.

"The flowers are exceptional, Sally. Did you ever think about going into the floral and bridal business?"

She gave me a sarcastic look.

"I am in a bit of heaven, Miss Anne," Jean said as she looked around. "Miss Sylvia is so happy!"

I knew what Jean must be thinking. Today, a happy couple was starting their life together and one unhappy couple was ending theirs.

Mia had already introduced herself to nearly everyone. She was wearing a ruffled pink polka dot dress with a matching headband. Pink was her favorite color and she would let you know it. She seemed to follow Sam around and, of course, he freely gave her a cookie whenever she asked. He truly was fond of her. Somehow, I could picture Sam more easily with a daughter than a son.

Aunt Julia and Sue joined me as I helped myself to one of the petit fours.

"Who is going to be the next one between the two of you?" I asked, winking as they laughed off the comment. "Are you okay with Uncle Jim being here?"

"Of course, Anne. He has always loved Sylvia. Plus, it was nice to have Sarah here so they could spend some time together," she responded. "When I see Sarah with Jim, she looks like a sophisticated grown woman, doesn't she? Where has the time gone?"

"She does look very beautiful today," I commented. "I love her hair like that."

"Oh Ella, please come here and visit with us," I invited as she walked closer to us. "Ella is priceless around here. I couldn't have done this without her. Ella, I want to make sure you meet everyone. Between us girls, Grandmother loves her too."

Ella blushed.

"Speaking of Mother, Anne, has Sylvia received any mysterious gifts from her?" asked Aunt Julia in jest.

"Ella, you didn't hear that," I said, ignoring the question.

Ella knew to move on in the conversation. "I have heard so much about all of you, especially that darling little girl that has captured Sam's attention," Ella said. "I can't wait until we have more little ones running around here."

"We can't either, Ella," chimed in Sue.

We were interrupted by David Stone who was the first to give a wedding toast to the bride and groom. More toasts followed, accompanied by much laughter. I kept silent as I stood next to Mother, giving her some loving support. Sam was the last to speak and he did so eloquently, as he so often did. The way Sam acted today, you would never know he had a care in the world. He then thanked all the guests for coming to our home and mentioned there were more refreshments to enjoy.

After a while, Mother approached me about them needing to leave. She thanked me again for everything and said she would call me as soon as they arrived at their destination. She gave me a big hug and we were then joined by Harry and Sam. We walked them to the car, along with the guests who were still remaining.

"Oh no, who tied the cans to the car?" asked Harry, laughing.

"Turnabout is fair play," said David's voice from behind me. "There's a just-married sign on the back seat if you want to use it." Everyone was getting a real kick out of it. They left the cans attached as we watched them drive off in Harry's gray Mercedes. It was a sight to behold. I knew Mother was probably crying as she looked back at her Kodak moment.

Sam held me tighter, knowing this was emotional for me to watch, and I was certainly trying hard to hold back the tears.

"You'll have plenty of time later to reflect, honey," he whispered in my ear. "I love you! You gave your mother the most perfect wedding! Let's go in and be happy!"

CHAPTER 31

Mother and Harry called as planned from a hotel in Tucson, Arizona, where Harry had lived for a short while in his younger years. Mother had not been out west much to speak of, so Harry wanted her to have a grand tour. They no doubt were having a good time and could not tell me when they might return. In the meantime, we received word that our offer on the Brody property had been accepted! While we were excited, we were also so tired from the wedding and so distracted by Sam's stressful work situation that we seemed to just move on to the next items on our ever-growing list of responsibilities.

July 4th was this coming weekend. The shop owners on Main Street were busy preparing for one of the city's biggest parties. Sam had warned me for weeks that he was not up for the usual picnic on the fourth that was historically his birthday party. He had too much on his mind and a quiet dinner somewhere with his wife would suffice.

The week following the fourth was going to be the last day for Gayle's Glass Works next door. The merchants were planning a little party for her at her shop to say good-bye. There was an insecure feeling that wanted to creep into me as I watched her exit Main Street. I couldn't imagine ever doing so myself and her departure made me just a little uneasy.

When the morning of Sam's birthday arrived, I put on my best face for the day at hand, not really knowing what to expect. I only prayed Sam would not receive bad news on this day in particular. When I came down to the breakfast table as usual, Sam told me he had made early reservations at Rascino's. He was taking a liking to its healthy menu choices. It seemed weird to me that he was the one making the plans for his birthday, but I didn't question things too much these days.

"You don't feel too well today do you, Sam?" I asked as sweetly as I knew how.

He didn't answer. "I'm afraid that the press is going to pick up on this story any day now and it might be today," he reported with a serious tone. "If anyone asks you any questions, I'd advise you not to answer and absolutely do not get involved."

"Of course, Sam," I acknowledged. "I'm sorry all this is happening. I want this day to be so nice for you. Remember our saying, 'Do not worry, say your prayers, and be thankful?'"

He grinned. "I sure do and it certainly fits today's agenda. Lying awake last night, I kept wondering if buying the Brody property was such a good idea. What if Martingale goes under with all of this?"

"Stop, stop right now," I insisted, kissing him on the cheek. "I think it may be what saves us if there should be any financial difficulty. Land is always a good investment. The security of being able to rent it or—better yet—grow things, makes me feel pretty good."

He gave me that grin that I was after. "Good point Annie," he noted. "Do you mind meeting me at Rascino's? It will save me time."

"Sure, birthday boy," I teased. "You'd just better show up!"

He blew me a kiss as he went out the door.

After he left, I decided to take twenty minutes to walk our hill. On the way back up the hill, I wanted to check the empty Brody house to make sure vandals had not discovered the secluded location. As I did just that, huffing and puffing, I saw the many new weeds appearing that were taking advantage of the unattended land. I was sorry for the appearance, hoping we would beautify it as soon as we could. I would talk to Kip to see if he couldn't make it more presentable with some mowing.

When I got to work, Sally and Jean came into my office to discuss a sizable order that had come in overnight.

"Jean, do you think it's odd we have not heard from Al here at the shop?" I asked delicately.

"Very odd, Miss Anne," she answered sadly. "I think he knows I am here working, which he may find comforting, or he just may not give a care."

"I worry about your comings and goings, Jean," said Sally, clearly concerned.

"He's probably drinking most of the time and may even be somewhat relieved he has you out of the house," I said, getting angry. "Have you thought about what the next step will be, Jean?"

She smiled, which took me by surprise. "Staying with Miss Sally here has been a real treat and salvation," she said, looking at Sally. "I have never felt so free and without any fear! It is mighty clear, I must file for divorce and never return to such a state. I love it here in Colebridge, I must say. I hated not having our Austen literary meeting last week. I did enjoy that so! If I still want to go back to England after my unfinished business, then I shall."

"It all makes good sense, Jean," I concluded. "Thank you so much, Sally, for all you are doing."

"We've been having a bit of fun, have we not, Miss Sally?" Jean said, snickering.

"Oh boy, well good for you guys," I said with satisfaction. "So, are we ready for the big weekend?"

They nodded and got back to work. Gayle came in the front door.

"I see you're having sales, Gayle. How is that all going?" I asked.

"Quite good. I may not have much left to move. I did send some supplies on ahead that I might be using at some point in time."

"Any word on who the new tenant might be?"

"Bill said no one has inquired that he would be happy with," she said. "He wants to paint and put new carpet down, so I don't think he is in any hurry."

That actually sounded smart to me.

"You will keep in touch with us, won't you?"

"If it's not too painful," she admitted. "I know I am going to be homesick for the street, I'm afraid."

"Not when you meet those new faces and customers!" I said with a reassuring tone. "That may be where Mr. Right is also located."

She blushed. The girls agreed with me. She left feeling like she had things to look forward to in spite of what she was leaving behind. That's what we all would have to do for Jean. We would have to be happy for what could be in her future, but we certainly would miss her!

The day was getting away from me. I had lots to do before Sam's dinner tonight. I tried not to think about what his day may actually be like at Martingale.

CHAPTER 32

I arrived at Rascino's right on time with no Sam in sight. I decided to wait for him at the bar, carrying only a simple birthday card instead of a wrapped gift. I ordered a drink and noticed my friend, Barb, from the Button Shop on the street. Since she only sat a few barstools away from me, it was convenient to make small talk about business. My cell phone rang. I dreaded it might be Sam needing to cancel. I hustled to retrieve the phone from my purse.

"Hey, Anne, this is Sue. Am I calling at a bad time?"

"Oh no, not at all. I am at Rascino's waiting for Sam to arrive for his birthday dinner."

"Well, that's one of the reasons I'm calling, of course," she explained. "Please wish him a happy birthday for me. I am getting terrible about sending cards, I'm afraid. However, you can tell him that my birthday present to him is a new six-month-old nephew that I'll be picking up next month!"

I almost fell off the barstool. "What? Are you serious, Sue? This is so quick compared to last time. He is still a baby! I thought they might have you take an older child, judging by the way they talked. Is he from Honduras like Mia?"

"Yes he is, and the adoption is with the same agency. The same lawyer agreed to go with me again, which makes me so happy."

"Oh, I can't wait to tell Mother when she gets back."

"Have you heard from them, Anne?"

"Yes, they are out west traveling, but they wouldn't tell me when they will return," I reported. "I think they are having a wonderful time. What did your mom and dad say about the new baby? I assume you already told them."

She laughed. "They are quite amused that I'm having this little family without a husband. I'm going to call Aunt Julia as soon as I hang up from talking with you. I'm hoping she'll take care of Mia while I'm gone!"

"Speaking of Mia, when do you plan to tell her?" I asked.

"In time, but not just yet. I definitely will tell her before I leave so she knows I went to get her a baby brother!"

We ended the conversation just as I saw Sam rushing in the door.

"Sorry I'm late, honey," he said, out of breath. "The traffic was just awful coming across the bridge. I came from a meeting I had late this afternoon."

"Well, I'm just glad you're here, birthday boy!" I teased, giving him a kiss on the cheek. "Let's just relax here for a few minutes before we order dinner. I have some exciting news to share with you."

When Sam had a chance to catch his breath, I told him Sue called to wish him happy birthday and that she would have a new baby nephew for him soon. He was so happy. Whatever cares he brought with him from work certainly had disappeared.

"So, did she say what she was going to name him?"

"In all the excitement, I forgot to ask her!" I answered, feeling foolish. "I also wonder if she has a photo of him like she did with Mia's adoption."

"There is only one thing that would make me happier right now and that would be an announcement from you saying we're pregnant!"

"You are so wonderful, Sam," I said, looking at the hopeful and happy expression on his face that I had not seen for some time. "It will happen for us someday!" This was the time to get out the birthday card so I could change the subject. I placed it in front of him.

"No gift this year as you instructed, Mr. Dickson," I joked. "I'm not sure I will have the same willpower on my birthday!"

"That is good news, honey. I'm sure I'll love the card."

"Before I left the shop, I decided to write you a little corny poem on the back. The card just didn't say it quite well enough."

Laughing, he opened it up and read it aloud to me.

A birthday for you is a gift to me.
Each day's surprise I'm happy to see.
Keep in your heart my love from me.
If ever you need it, you have the key.
Happy Birthday,
Love,
Annie

Oh, it sounded so stupid. How could he read it so sweetly? I thought.

"Do I have the key?" he joked.

"Of course! Plus, key was the only word I could think of to rhyme with the word me! Don't make fun, now. That's what you get when you request no gifts."

He laughed again, which was music to my ears after the somberness he had displayed these last few weeks.

We went to our table in a very good mood. After we ordered our food, I thought Sam would fill me in on his day at work, but he didn't. I reported about Jean's plans and he sadly said, "Are you sure they don't have a chance to get back together?"

"Anything's possible, I suppose. If Al would just get some help with his drinking, I think she would consider it. Jean has a heart of gold."

We continued to make small talk after we arrived at home. It wasn't until he joined me in the bedroom that he opened up about his day.

"I'm being interviewed tomorrow by a reporter who has gotten wind of the investigation," he revealed as he began to undress. "There's no sense avoiding it any longer. I'm sure it will be on the local news then."

"Oh Sam, how awful."

"The sooner this all gets resolved, the better," he said, sitting next to me. "It appears as though Mr. Martingale had been helping himself to the till for some time. It's still speculation at this time, plus others may be involved, I'm afraid."

"Where does this leave you, Sam?"

"So far, I'm in the clear, but they are all giving me flack

for bringing this forward," he reported sadly. "Jim got word of it and called me today."

"Maybe he just wanted to wish you a happy birthday!" I said, making light of it.

He shook his head, doubtful.

"Who is implicated so far?"

"I don't want to say, Annie," he said, looking into my eyes. "Right now, I just want to unlock all that love from my wife. She said it was there for me."

I laughed and fell into his arms.

CHAPTER 33

When I arrived at the shop the next morning, I saw on my calendar that I was to meet with Beverly in the afternoon. How I was going to concentrate on anything but Sam's situation was beyond me. I would just have to trust that his innocence would see him through this.

Just as I got myself settled in front of my computer, I heard Aunt Julia's voice greeting Jean and Sally in the front room. I went to greet her, knowing she would want to talk about Sue's good news.

"How about sweet Sue's news?" she asked when she saw me. "It's terribly exciting, isn't it? I have to say, this girl goes after what she wants! I can't believe she's had results so soon. We'd better begin planning another baby shower because we sure don't have any little boy things in this family!"

"Did she tell you if she had chosen a name or what his name is?" I remembered to ask.

"I did ask her that, but she said she wouldn't decide which of the names she had in mind until she saw him in person," she answered.

"That makes sense to me."

"Not to bring up any bad news right now, Anne, but Jim told me what's been going on over at Martingale," she said in a quiet voice so the others couldn't hear.

I motioned for us to talk in my office. "Jim called to tell you that?"

"Oh no, he mentioned it when he dropped off Sarah. He wondered if I knew anything. I told him you had not discussed it with me, which is understandable. Sam is wise to keep this quiet."

I didn't know how to take what she had just said. I took a deep breath. "Believe me, he has been looking into this for a long time," I said, shaking my head. "I'm mostly worried about how this is going to affect his heart. He has spent many sleepless nights over this!" I thought I was going to cry.

"Oh, Anne, the last thing I want to do is upset you," she said apologetically. "It is none of my business."

"Well, he's managing to hold up surprisingly well," I reported. "He's supposed to be interviewed by one of the television stations today, so you can see for yourself tonight on the news, I suppose."

"Good heavens!" she said, surprised.

"Sam told me to stay out of it and not comment on anything," I said, taking another deep breath.

"Let me know if I can do anything, Anne," she said, touching my shoulder. "It will all be fine. Have you heard anything from the honeymooners?"

"Just that they are in Arizona having a great time," I

said as I walked her to the door. The thought of that actually cheered me up.

"Good for them," Aunt Julia commented as she opened the door. "I'm going over to Gayle's to look around and tell her good-bye. I sure hate to see her go."

"I hate to see her go, too. I hope I get a neighbor as nice as her!"

It was nearly afternoon when Sam called to report on his interview.

"They fished for implications and accusations but I didn't give them any concrete information. It's supposed to be on the news at six tonight. I was told that Mr. Martingale was unavailable for comment. I'm sure his lawyer has him holed up somewhere."

"I am glad that part is over for you, Sam. Will you be home for dinner?"

"I will be home in time to see the report, but don't bother fixing me anything, Anne. I don't think I am going to be very hungry."

"I have Beverly coming over to the house in an hour, so I'll be leaving here shortly," I said, knowing he wasn't listening.

After we said good-bye, I told the staff I would be gone for the day. They didn't ask any questions, but they knew something was up.

Beverly was right on schedule. She drove up in a little blue Volkswagen and I greeted her on the south porch. When she got out of the car, it seemed that she couldn't visually take in the place fast enough.

"This is beautiful up here, Mrs. Dickson," she said with admiration.

"Please call me Anne," I said, opening the front door for

her. She was carrying a manila envelope in her hand.

"Come on in," I said, welcoming the air-conditioning. "It sure is a hot one today! How about I get you a cold glass of lemonade?"

Please don't spoil it, Grandmother, I thought to myself as I walked toward the kitchen. She may decide not to be nice to Mrs. Taylor's cook's granddaughter.

"That sounds great," she said as she looked around the large entryway. "This is so beautiful! To think that my granny worked in such a beautiful place is amazing to me."

I showed her the first floor and where I thought the cook's small room might have been. She stared at it for a long time as if she were expecting a sign of some kind. We then went up the stairs where I showed her a picture of a framed newspaper clipping. There was one of Mr. Taylor by himself that she looked at more closely.

"He sure isn't that handsome for being known as such a ladies' man," she quipped.

I had to chuckle in agreement. "That seemed to be his reputation, Beverly," I said sadly.

When I showed her my new office, I told her about finding a suitcase with Miranda Taylor's baby clothes.

"Did your grandmother ever mention a child and what she may have died from?" I asked with hope in my voice.

"I don't remember her saying much about anything like that, but I do recall she said the child had some kind of a fever one time," she recalled. "She always said how sorry she felt for Mrs. Taylor having to care for their little girl alone. It left me with the impression that Mr. Taylor was hardly ever home."

We walked back down the stairs and sat at the kitchen table to drink our lemonade.

"So, did you bring something for me to look at?" I anxiously asked.

"Not much, but I might be able to find more." She pulled out a few yellowed photographs. "Here's the best one with Granny and Mrs. Taylor. It looks like it might have been taken on the front porch out there. They are both working on a quilt, or perhaps just looking at one. I'm not sure."

I took it in my hands and could not believe what I saw. It was the crazy quilt that Mrs. Taylor had made that we found in the potting shed!

"Beverly, this is the quilt I found in the potting shed when we moved in here!" I said with excitement.

"In the potting shed?" she said in disbelief. "What was it doing there?"

"I have this quilt upstairs and have learned a great deal from it," I said, not wanting to go into the entire story. "I'll be happy to show it to you. You never heard your granny say that Mrs. Taylor hid things or anything like that did you?"

"No, but Granny sure did! We found some dollar bills rolled up in one of her quilt edgings. She had some in the mattress, too. It wasn't much, but we continue to find letters and keepsakes here and there!"

"Oh, how interesting."

The next picture was of her granny standing next to another African American man that was likely the gardener.

"I'm sorry. I don't know his name, but by mother told me once that they were good friends," she shared.

I looked closer and recognized the big lilac bush they were standing by. It wasn't that far from the potting shed.

"It is so nice of you to bring this," I said, giving her a smile. "I am still hoping to get photos from the Taylor family."

"Would you like to have the one of the quilt, Anne?" she sweetly asked.

"I absolutely would!" I said, gratefully taking it out of her hand.

"I must get going," Beverly said as she got up from the chair. "I will be sure to let you know if I find anything else. Thank you so much for the lemonade. You have an amazing place here."

As I walked her to the door, I thanked her profusely. It wasn't much, but it was something. When she drove away, I went back to the quilt photograph. No wonder Mrs. Taylor was clever to hide her letters in the quilt. She may have learned a trick or two from Granny!

CHAPTER 34

I was feeling exhausted from my day, so I went upstairs to put the photograph away for safekeeping. I made a mental note to have it enlarged and framed.

Sam wasn't due home for a while, so I went to change into some shorts and a T-shirt. As I thought about checking on the plants in the potting shed, I instead reclined on our bed to think about Beverly's visit. How could I record this in my Taylor book?

Unconsciously, I ran my fingers over Grandmother's lily quilt. The closeness of her little stitches was so soothing to the touch. The lilies, leaves, and vines were so closely quilted together. It must have taken her many hours. I loved any quilt that had scalloped edges as this one did.

As I looked at the narrow binding, I noticed what looked like letters quilted in the curve of the corner scallop. I wasn't sure if I was seeing things, so I took it to the window for better light. There, in beautiful letters, it read, *For my dear Mary.* I was stunned. Mother certainly didn't know this was here! So Grandmother's thoughts were focused on her daughter, Mary, who had been given away for adoption. As she quilted this and thought of Mary, there had probably been more tears shed as she had described in her note. Grandmother must have been wondering where Mary was or what had happened to her. Sadly, this quilt had ended up at my Aunt Marie's house. Marie had no children and now it is on a bed at 333 Lincoln where Grandmother had hoped to live. She had to be looking down at me with much pleasure. In all fairness, however, this quilt should go to Amanda or William. After all, it was meant for their mother.

I still had Grandmother's pineapple quilt on the wall in the upstairs hallway and the Carolina lily in the green guest room. I had the white wholecloth quilt that Aunt Marie had made, so if I had to give up the lily quilt, I supposed I would.

I jumped when I heard Sam coming in the front door. I went into the hallway and called, "I'm up here, honey."

"I'll be up in a minute," he responded.

I put the quilt back in its place.

"Between this heat and the heat at work, I think I need this!" He pointed to the iced tea in his hand. He then sat in his big wing-back chair that I had given him one previous birthday.

"Just relax for a minute and tell me the latest," I said, wanting to hug him and make everything go away.

"I was told today that subpoenas will be going out soon. There will be at least six of them."

I just stayed quiet and listened.

"Has anyone asked you about it all?"

"Not really. Aunt Julia told me that Uncle Jim had asked her what she knew."

"Yeah, he's called me several times, but it's just best I don't discuss anything with him right now," he said as he took another sip of tea. "I'm sure anyone who has worked there will also be wondering if they will be questioned. He'll see the news tonight and will understand why I haven't called him back."

"Are you hungry?" I asked to lighten the conversation.

"Not at all," he answered with certainty. He tilted his head back and closed his eyes. I told him briefly about Beverly's visit and then about the writing on the lily quilt.

"So we have a quilt that doesn't belong to us," he answered with his eyes remaining shut.

"Well, it had to end up with Marie since she didn't know where Mary was," I explained. "I really love this quilt, but I will have to pass it on to Amanda, I think. Grandmother would take satisfaction in knowing it ended up in this house, at least."

Sam opened his eyes and looked at me sternly. "Annie, you're being a bit crazy about all of this," he said, somewhat agitated. "This was Albert and Marion's house, not Martha Davis' house."

Ouch! I got the message.

"I'm going down to get a bite to eat and then water the plants in the potting shed," I said, leaving him to rest. "You'll be down to watch the news in a little bit, right?"

"Yeah, in a minute," he said, closing his eyes again.

Sam was drained mentally. I felt he wasn't himself and he had to be worried sick about this major problem at Martingale. Why did I have to bring up Beverly and the whole thing about Grandmother's quilt? He'd had his fill of my fantasy into the past. That message was loud and clear!

CHAPTER 35

My stomach was churning as the news hour arrived. I knew I was dreading seeing the report because I suspected it would be negative. I was curled up on the study couch when Sam came down to join me.

"I can't believe I fell into a deep sleep!" he shared with a pleasant grin.

"Good! I know you have to be exhausted."

The news began listing the headline stories. One read, *Longtime Colebridge Company Under Investigation for Embezzlement. Stay tuned for more on this breaking story.*

"That should get everyone's attention," Sam said with a sarcastic tone.

I felt sick thinking about what information might be exposed to all of our family members, friends, and Martingale employees.

When the story finally began, it was surprisingly brief.

"Locally owned Martingale and Company is now under federal investigation for what appears to be embezzlement over a period of many years. Newly-appointed president, Sam Dickson, has been fully cooperative in providing helpful information. Louis Martingale, founder and previous president of the company, was not available for comment. Stay tuned to KZYM as we follow the story."

"Oh Sam, this was not as horrible as I thought it might be."

Sam continued to stare at the TV in silence.

"At least they said something nice about you."

"I'm going to bed," he said curtly. "This can of worms is now open and nothing good can come of it." He walked out of the room as if he were personally wounded.

I sat still, realizing Sam's pride and reputation was hurt, despite him being innocent of any wrongdoing. He was the one to open that can of worms. He was too good of a person to ignore any company violations. He thought the world of Mr. Martingale and the feeling had been mutual. He knew that relationship would now be over, and if Mr. Martingale had been embezzling, it would get even uglier and more painful for both men.

I heard my cell phone ring from the kitchen table where I had left it. It made sense that the phone calls would start coming. How Sam and I reacted to it would be judged by many. I couldn't get myself to go and pick it up to see who was calling, nor did I want to. I put my head in my hands and asked God to protect my Sam from hurt and to bring justice quickly so we could get on with our lives. Our home telephone began to ring and I saw that it was Mother. Did she know about this news report even though she was out of town? I quickly picked it up so Sam wouldn't be disturbed.

"Hey, it's your mother, Mrs. Stone, calling," she said with a giggle in her voice. "How are you?"

I took a deep breath. "Oh, fine," I decided to make everything sound as normal as possible. "What's up with the two of you? Where are you now?"

"We're in the little town of Oakley, Kansas," she said like she may not be sure. "We are on our way home and we may be there as soon as tomorrow evening."

"That's great! I can't wait to hear all about your trip!"

"I talked to Aunt Julia yesterday and she told me that Sue is going to get a little boy!"

"Yes, isn't that great?" It felt good to talk about some good news for a change.

"We'll need another baby quilt and another shower, I suppose," she said with excitement.

"That's for sure!" I responded. It was obvious that she had not heard about the Martingale news. "You two be safe and call me when you get home."

We said good-bye and I felt that at least part of my world was normal and happy. She would find out about our troubles soon enough.

I left my cell phone downstairs to go up and check on Sam. He was sound asleep on the bed with a book in his hands. I was grateful that he could sleep through all of this. I took the lily quilt from the end of the bed and covered him up.

"Under these lilies I weep to sleep," I whispered from the note Grandmother had written. My suspicions were that many tears had been shed under this quilt. Perhaps it would offer Sam comfort in some magical way.

I undressed and quietly slid under the covers next to this wonderful man. I'm sure I had no real sense of the enormity of the burden he was enduring.

CHAPTER 36

My heavy sleep made me unaware of Sam's early rising. As I arrived in the kitchen, I saw a note on the table that informed me he had a busy day ahead of him and that he loved his sweet Annie. He was in enough of a hurry to not make his usual pot of coffee. I walked over to our new patio room outside the sunporch and realized that with the summer's heat and our daily stresses of life, we hadn't had much of a chance to enjoy it.

I took my morning walk on the trail along the river. Much of it was shaded and it had a nice breeze, providing respite from the morning heat. I observed many dry plants, but as usual, the weeds had a way of surviving. During my morning prayers, I requested some rain for Colebridge. Rain had a way of washing away troubles and bringing fresh life at the same time.

I was at the end of my walk and approaching my car to

drive home when Nancy called.

"What are you doing up at this hour?"

"I have two little tykes that can't wait to start their day, remember?" she answered, sounding sleepy. "I just had to call and say you have friends that love and support you right now. Whatever this mess is with Martingale, it will pass. Knowing Sam, he has it all under control."

"He does, but it is extremely stressful, Nancy," I admitted. "I'm so worried about him. It's hurtful to both of us to have this all come out in public."

"Well, we thought a barbeque at the Barristers might be just the thing to get your mind off of your troubles. How about it?" she asked optimistically.

"Oh thanks, Nancy. Sam is not very social right now, but I will ask him. It sounds great to me. I'll get back with you. I know I could use some normal activity! Also, Mother will be home any day, so she wants us to quilt something for Sue's new baby boy. I am so excited for Sue. She said she loves her new job, Nancy, but now she'll be gone for a while. Are you handling that okay?"

"Oh, sure. There is someone who helps her out and she'll be taking over while Sue is out. Sue is cut out for this job, though. She can time the grief meetings to her liking and even bring the children for some of them. Richard said perhaps it's time we have child care facilities on the premises for our employees."

"What a great idea, Nancy. So even Andrew and Amy could come sometimes," I teased.

"Exactly!" she said laughing. "Hey, we are all concerned about our Jean. I miss the book club. Is she okay?"

"She said she's getting a divorce, and she and Sally

seem to have worked out living arrangements for now. I have so many issues of my own that I haven't paid too much attention lately."

We chatted for a few more minutes before the twins needed Nancy's full attention. I no sooner hung up from that call when Aunt Julia called.

"I know you have other things on your mind right now, but I wondered if I could stop by this morning to get your advice on something." There was no pretense of small talk and she sounded quite serious.

"Well, that's a first, but it can't take long. I don't know what our commitments are for the day. I am just going home now to shower."

"Great, I'll see you around ten. It won't take long, I promise."

I hurried home to get ready for the day and then went to the shop. There, I saw Jean in the design room by herself, working on a casket spray.

"That's beautiful. How are things going for you, Jean?"

"You left early yesterday, so I didn't have a chance to tell you that Al posted a letter to me here at the shop," she said with a smile.

A smile? That surprised me. "So what was that all about, if you don't mind me asking."

"It was very endearing, Miss Anne," she began. "He wants me to return home because he has started going to Alcoholics Anonymous. A neighbor of ours encouraged him to attend. I am in shock, and I feel he is most earnest. I am in a quandary of sorts, as you can imagine." The strain of the relationship had begun to show on Jean's face, but there was a look of hope in her eyes.

"Do you still love him, Jean?"

"Al is a special sort of a 'gent', as my mother used to say," she said thoughtfully. "He's always had a kind heart, which is why I couldn't understand why I made him so angry as to hit me. Joining AA and admitting he is an alcoholic is a huge, humble step for my Al."

"You're right, because this disease stays with you forever," I said sadly. "You need to understand that you did *nothing* to provoke this, Jean. You must keep yourself safe. None of his behavior is your fault. However, I will say that if you feel you can trust him at this point, perhaps you should give him another chance."

She nodded. "I shall ponder that a bit," she said, going back to the arrangement. "Thank you for not being too hard on the old chap. As you know yourself, he has a blessed side."

The morning flew by. It was ten, and sure enough, Aunt Julia was asking for me. She brought a plate of brownies to the crew, which Kevin spotted immediately.

"What kind of bribe is this, Aunt Julia?" I asked walking toward my office.

"Sarah made these last night and it was her suggestion that I bring them today." She knew how happily they would be received by the entire staff.

We went to my office and she joined me at my desk.

"I just came from seeing Bill at the print shop."

"What on earth for?"

"To rent his shop. What else would I be there for?"

I tried to take in her information and simply could not guess where this conversation was going. "What are you talking about?"

"Sarah and I have been brainstorming about an idea

we've had for some time."

I detected a defensive tone in this last statement. Quickly assessing my options, I chose to keep quiet and let her talk.

"I am ready for a change and a challenge of some kind. I can only do so much charity work and go to so many charity lunches. I also want to include Sarah in whatever I do. She is so artistic and does calligraphy, by the way."

I held on to my silent approach and waited for more information.

"So, we want to open a classy paper and gift shop. I love beautiful stationery, pens, photo albums, and picture frames. We would carry some light electronic gadgets, too."

I felt confused by what she was clearly very excited about. Being a shop owner is hard work. It takes time—lots of personal time. Then, words just seemed to spill out of my mouth. "Do you not live in this current world of technology, Aunt Julia? All the things you just mentioned have all but disappeared from general use! When is the last time you received a handwritten thank you note or letter from someone? It's sad, but I don't think most people are even framing their photographs. We have them stored in our computers and cell phones. Are you following me?" The words had raced out of my mouth.

"I knew you'd say all that, but I think that if presented well, these things will come back," she said, unabashed by my warnings. "Do you know my teenage daughter wants me to buy her a typewriter? She was delighted when I told her I had one on the basement shelf downstairs. We thought we could do handwritten services like wedding invitations. I want to make handmade greeting cards that people will want to give.

I have looked into all this, Anne, and if you can believe it, I even called Jim to get his opinion since it involves Sarah."

"The type of shop you've described would be a dream for someone like me who loves to write, but timing is everything, Aunt Julia. I don't want you to fail. It honestly is a lot of work having a shop. What did Uncle Jim have to say?"

"He seemed to be excited for me, as long as I wasn't expecting financial assistance from him, of course," she said sarcastically. "He was thrilled that Sarah would play a role."

"I give you credit for thinking up a novel idea and wanting to forge ahead despite the obstacles. What will you call the business?"

"You will love it," she said proudly. "It will be called The Written Word."

The idea was settling in. It was a charming title for such a shop. "I love it." And I really did. "Who wouldn't be curious about such a shop, Aunt Julia?"

Curiously, in spite of my own objections, I found myself visualizing a cute little shop with beautiful writing papers, artfully crafted cards, and carefully selected gift items. I think Aunt Julia and Sarah were perhaps ready for an adventure of their own!

CHAPTER 37

On my way over to welcome home the newlyweds, I called Nancy to apologize for not responding to their barbecue invitation. She understood when I told her that Sam was becoming more distant from me as well as others since he currently had so much on his mind.

Now that this was Mr. and Mrs. Stone's home, I couldn't just let myself in the door as I was accustomed to doing. I rang the bell instead. It felt strange until Harry answered the door with a big smile and a hug. It was obvious that they had enjoyed a wonderful trip. Sitting at the table and drinking coffee together was a wonderful way to catch up on their experiences. Mother excitedly showed me two beautiful large flowerpots she had purchased from a high-end pottery shop in one of the tourist areas they visited. She told me to choose one for my new patio. I gave them each a thank-you hug.

After listening to them for a bit, they asked about what

had been going on with Sam and me while they were away. I began giving them an update on the Martingale situation. Their faces changed from happiness to that of alarm. Mother immediately wanted to know if it was affecting Sam's heart condition.

"We'll just have to ride this out, Mother," I replied slowly, hoping to keep myself calm. "I do what I can to listen and try to help, but he can hardly avoid this situation."

After a while, Mother asked about Jean and said she hoped Jean and Al would have a successful reunion.

"Oh, I almost forgot to tell you that I found two wonderful crib quilt tops at a shop in Kansas," she revealed. She went to the dining room to get them, producing a large shopping bag. She pulled them out of the bag. "There is one called Sunbonnet Sue and then a matching one called Overall Sam," she said with excitement. "The appliqué is wonderful. None of us could make these in a reasonable amount of time."

"But Mother, she's not having twins. She's just going to get a little boy."

"Well, I just couldn't separate them," she said. "I'm sure it will come in handy one day."

I wasn't going to question her on that subject. "Harry, you do realize that the basement here turns into quite a quilting party every now and then?" I said, reflecting on some fond memories.

"I know, and it makes your mother very happy," he said, looking flirtatiously at Mother.

"And when I'm happy, you're happy. Right, Harry?" she teased.

I sensed my cue. "Good to have you back," I said, walking toward the door with my flowerpot. "I have errands to run."

When I got to my car, my cell phone rang and Helen Dickson's name was on the screen.

"Hello, Anne," she began. "I'm so glad I could reach you because Sam is not returning my calls. Is he alright? Elaine has been telling me things about his company being investigated for embezzlement. How in the world did that happen? I hate to think about what that is like for Sam."

"It is a worry, Helen, and Sam would not want to upset you," I consoled her. "He is very hurt and humiliated and you know how he doesn't want to be babied!"

"Oh yes, but what can I do to help, Anne?" she asked helplessly.

I felt so bad for her. I knew that no matter what ages your children may be, a parent never stops worrying about them.

"I will tell him you called and that you stand by him and love him very much," I stated. "That's all I have been able to do myself."

"He is in the clear, Anne, is he not?"

"Of course, Helen," I assured her. "He was the one to discover all of this irregularity, so he's not very popular right now. His biggest worry is whether the company will survive after all this is over. You know how dedicated he has been to Martingale!"

"Oh my, yes," she agreed. "I am just so grateful he has you, dear."

The days passed along, one dreary day after another, in the devilish heat. We had said our good-byes to Gayle, and in no time, Aunt Julia and Sarah had brought in painters and carpenters to get started on their new shop. I found it all so strange. To have additional family members right here on the street would be an adjustment for me.

I drove Sue to the airport where she met up with her lawyer. Her excitement was a joy to see, however, I drove away feeling an emptiness I had never experienced before. Everyone, but me, had new plans and were exceedingly happy. Sam was in a dark space and was shutting me out. I felt guilty feeling any joy that came my way.

After changing into shorts and a T-shirt when I got home, I checked on the potting shed and then poured myself some cold iced tea. I chose to sit on the south porch where I found the most comfort. I glanced toward the Brody property, and for the first time, felt regret that we had purchased the additional acreage. Any plans for it would have to wait. The dream of putting greenhouses all over it was now a frivolous adventure. Did my life with Sam have too much too soon? Were we losing control of the things we loved so much? Hmmm...

CHAPTER 38

Mother was determined to quilt on the baby quilt while Sue was out of town. She managed to get commitments from Jean, Isabella, and Nancy to come on Sunday afternoon. Aunt Julia and Sarah were busy working on their shop, but promised to stop by and put a few stitches in the quilt. I told Mother I wouldn't be coming if Sam was going to spend the day at home.

Sam and I both got up at the same time on Saturday morning. I was feeling like we were now an old married couple who had no time for much affection in the midst of our stressful lives. We went down to share our coffee and Sam quickly went to the front porch to get the newspaper. It didn't take long for him to tell me about an article written about Martingale in the paper. It suggested that Sam may have unknowingly covered up important information when he took over as president of the company. Sam made no extra commentary as he continued to read on in silence.

I breathed a deep sigh and decided to speak up. "Sam, honey, I think it would be good for both of us to get away for the day tomorrow," I suggested, feeling braver as I continued. "You need a break from all the publicity and we need time to be together. It's been too long."

He looked at me strangely. "Funny that you suggest that," he blushed. "Jim is being pretty insistent that I play golf with him tomorrow. I was thinking of accepting. It would help me clear my head a bit and Jim may be helpful, given his history with the company. He's been genuinely concerned and I have been ignoring him."

"Sam, that's great!" I said, perking up at the thought. "I think you need your best friend right now."

He smiled. "You don't mind then?" he said as he looked for more reassurance. "I hate to leave you alone again."

"You won't," I said immediately. "There happens to be a group gathering over at Mother's to start quilting on Sue's baby quilt. I will help and then try to throw together some kind of dinner for us when you get home. How about that?"

He nodded in agreement.

I breathed a deep sigh of relief and went for my walk down the Dickson hill, as I now referred to it. I told myself that this all would pass and I should make the most of each day.

I walked around the Brody property to make sure everything was secure. This secluded empty house could easily be tampered with by someone. I knew this place was the last thing Sam had on his mind these days. I walked farther back behind the house where I knew there was a slightly cleared path. It was where Sarah and I had picked blackberries one day, and I could barely drive my car to the area. However, this could be a road someday leading to greenhouses here and there. I could imagine the many baby geraniums and poinsettias all lined up, waiting in the greenhouses for the season ahead. The charming empty barn that hadn't been used in decades could be stabilized to store equipment.

I was getting hotter and hotter from the sun. I should have taken a water bottle with me because I was beginning to feel light-headed. I made it back to the house and Sam was already gone. The sky became dark, and suddenly, a heavy shower began. I stood on the circle drive and let the water cool me down.

"Let it rain, let it rain," I said aloud. "Thank you, God. Please wash away any pain and bring life to those who thirst."

On Sunday afternoon, Mother was quite surprised to see me and even more surprised when I told her Sam had joined Uncle Jim for golf. I had stopped on the way and purchased an ice cream cake for something summery and she was delighted. When I came downstairs to join the others, Sarah insisted we have refreshments early, in case she and Aunt Julia left before refreshment time. They were in awe of the Overall Sam quilt. His outfit was different in each block and surrounded with a blue border that Isabella referred to as sashing. Isabella raved at the small appliqué stitches and told us how to outline quilt around each little boy.

"Maybe you can have the little girl quilt someday for you, Anne," Sarah teased.

"Oh no, don't go there," I quipped. "I think a little girl quilt with the name of Sue needs to belong to someone we know named Sue."

They all agreed that Sue should have the other top.

"Are you all missing our Miss Jane Austen?" Jean asked out of the blue. "I'm sorry I've had to put her aside for my misfortune, ladies. If things work out with my Al, perhaps we can start anew."

"You made it so special, Jean," Mother complimented her. "We miss the wonderful tea, but it was also a time when we all put our daily thoughts aside and just thought about Jane's world and how we could learn from her."

"Well put, Mother," I said as I thought about it.

Mother then gave us a quick report on their honeymoon travels and we watched her beam as she spoke. She could talk freely because Harry was at the library, which is something she said he often did on Sunday afternoons.

Aunt Julia also caught us up in the anticipation of her shop opening in another month. She and Sarah had a trip planned to Kansas City where there was a wholesale gift mart.

"Abbey has approached me about working at our shop on Sundays, since the flower shop is closed," Aunt Julia revealed. "How would you feel about that?"

"She would love it, I'm sure, and she is always anxious to earn extra money," I said, approving. It's been such a convenience having her live on the street. She's become quite active in the merchants' group, too."

"Good. Then I'll tell her it's okay," Aunt Julia said. "Is she still seeing Kevin?"

"I haven't seen or heard too much about that relationship lately, so I really don't know," I reported.

"Sylvia, did you give away all the quilts that you intended to?" Aunt Julia asked.

"No, there's still some I'd like to move on," Mother answered.

"I have a confession to make about the lily quilt, Mother," I shyly said. "I happen to notice that the quilting in one of the curved corners read, *For my dear Mary.*"

They were all ears, as some didn't know what I was talking about.

"I really love that quilt, but now it's only fair that I pass it on to Aunt Mary's daughter, Amanda, right?"

They still were all silent, except Mother.

"Well, I'll be," she said, rather puzzled.

"You are referring to the adopted Mary, right Miss Anne?" Jean was putting it all together.

"Any message like that cannot be ignored," added Isabella.

"Well, Anne, Mary has passed, and if you love it so much, I'm sure she'd want you to have it," Aunt Julia said firmly.

"This is the quilt that had a wrinkled yellow note attached that said *Under these lilies I weep to sleep,*" I told them. "She wept so many years for her daughter, Mary, and her lover, Albert. I can just feel her sadness when I put that quilt around me. I will give it to Amanda one day. It's the right thing to do."

"When will that woman ever stop trying to mess with you, Anne?" Aunt Julia said, frustrated. "I don't know why she has such a hold on you!"

Mother looked embarrassed and didn't know what to say in front of the others.

"I say to keep the quilt," Aunt Julia insisted.

The others started moving about and Sarah wanted to leave, so it was then that I announced that I, Anne Dickson, was going to prepare dinner for my husband that evening. They began to tease me about my domestic talents. Mother insisted I take home the rest of the ice cream cake for Sam. As I started for home, I realized it was another one of those quiltings that got us all thinking in every direction.

CHAPTER 39

The answer to my prayer for rain had finally come that afternoon, which brought about much cooler temperatures for August. It made me think of having a pleasant dinner on our new patio, so when the rain stopped, I got a towel and began wiping down the furniture. I would light candles when the sun went down and I began to think about what I could use for a table centerpiece. The flowers were not the best from the summer's heat, so I cut some of the herbs and lamb's ears to make a low arrangement for the table. It was looking romantic and quite beautiful for Sam, who had taken quite a liking to the patio.

Pork tenderloin was in the oven and my dish of new potatoes and onions was ready to put in the oven soon. When Sam got home, I could easily put his favorite salad together. No doubt, he would love the ice cream cake for dessert.

The longer Sam was gone, the happier I felt that he must be having a good time. I went upstairs to freshen up and check my emails. A message from Ted caught my eye immediately, and I quickly clicked on his name. It was brief. *I am thinking of you through these stressful times. Here for you always, Ted*

It made me shiver with disgust. He had no idea what I was going through, and I felt it most inappropriate for him to contact me. Did he really think I would go crying to him in my misery? He had a lot of nerve!

I clicked on a message from Amanda. She was giving me the address of their new home. As I clicked to reply to thank her, I realized I had the perfect opportunity to tell her about the lily quilt, but I couldn't. She would love it for their new home, I'm sure. I just couldn't put those words into the computer. I knew it had to go to her, but not just yet. Hmmm...

I heard the front door close and went down the stairs to see Sam putting his golf clubs in the corner of the entryway. He gave me a big smile as he came up to me.

"Welcome home! How was your game?"

"I shot an eighty, which is not bad since I haven't played in months. Jim played great, as always, but he gets to the course quite often. Something smells very good!"

"Yes, as promised, we'll have a nice dinner," I assured him, going toward the kitchen. "I decided to have dinner on the patio since it's so nice."

"Terrific," he said, heading toward the stairs. "I am going up to shower and change!" He blew me a kiss. "Did you enjoy your afternoon?"

"I did."

I started the salad, feeling excited about enjoying dinner with Sam. When I finished, I turned on some music and sat down on one of the lounge chairs to relax. It was such a relief to have Sam behaving more normally.

He soon joined me, bringing us both a drink. "Shouldn't you be slaving away in the kitchen?" he teased.

"I've done my share of slaving away, don't worry." I retorted, winking at him.

"I would have been home a little sooner, but Jim and I stopped by the club after the game."

As I started bringing food to the table, I mentioned our quilting party. I was pleased he didn't ask me if I was questioned about the Martingale investigation. I assured him that the visit was pleasant, making it sound like we mostly heard about Mother and Harry's trip.

"I ran into Ted Collins at the club today, and he looked quite surprised to see me," Sam shared.

I cringed at the thought.

"He was with Gordon Moore, who we've done business with."

"Did he come over and speak with you?" I asked, not really sure I wanted to know.

"Oh sure," he said with a laugh. "I got plenty of insincere sympathy, I'm afraid. Gordon at least had a little more class about it. Jim tells me that Ted still hasn't gotten over you and that he seldom dates since he broke up with Wendy."

"That's crazy, Sam," I said, aggravated. "I'm sorry he was rude. You don't need that right now."

"If running into Ted is the worst thing that happens in all of this, I'll be happy. Besides Anne, I would have trouble getting over you as well."

The meal turned out quite good as I watched Sam take second helpings. When I brought out dessert, Sam was stretched out on one of the lounge chairs with his eyes closed.

"Are you up for some of this delicious dessert?" I queried,

putting the cake on the table.

"It depends on what kind of dessert you're offering, sweet Annie," he teased. He pulled me close to him and I settled in on the lounge next to him. "I haven't been a very good husband lately, I'm afraid. I feel badly about that."

"This will pass, Sam, and I certainly haven't felt neglected," I said, looking into his dreamy eyes. "I do worry about you, though."

"I'll have to be honest with you, Anne. It's not looking good," he said, sitting up. "With the debt we'll likely be talking about when this is all said and done, bankruptcy may not be an option and the company may go under. Mr. Martingale may end up in jail before this is all over, which is the real tragic story here."

I felt sick at the thought of it all. "This is horrific, Sam," I said, shaking my head. "I can't believe it will all end this way!"

"I can only control so much, but I'm giving you the worst scenario."

"What will this mean for us, Sam, now that we're straddled with the Brody property, too?"

"I'm trying to evaluate all that, but it's too soon to know what changes will have to be made. The name of Martingale is already ruined. Starting over with a completely new company may be my only choice, if I'm lucky enough to have the capital I'm counting on."

"I'm so, so sorry, Sam. You have worked too hard for this company to see it crumble like this!"

"Hey, I think that ice cream is melting over there!" he exclaimed, changing the subject. "It looks pretty good. Let's indulge ourselves in as many ways as we can. What do you say?"

Sam meant every word as we turned in early and found

ourselves entwined in one another's arms. No one could take away the intense love we shared with each other.

CHAPTER 40

Monday morning, Ella showed up as scheduled. I found myself looking forward to her visits and stayed home until she arrived. She had a habit of bringing homemade goodies, and today, it was gooey butter cake, one of Sam's favorites.

"You spoil him, Ella," I teased. "He's not eating much of anything these days, but I'm sure he will love this!"

"It's good that you are still here, Anne, because I have wanted to talk to you about something," she said with a serious tone.

Oh no, is she going to quit?

"This idea of mine has finally given me the courage to ask you to think about something."

"Sure, have a seat," I offered, pointing to the other kitchen chair at the table. "Would you like some coffee?"

"No, thanks," she said, looking at the floor shyly. "I have

a financial dilemma, you might say. My lease is up very soon, and I've been thinking of what options I may have."

"Oh, Ella, if you need some money, you know Sam and I will help you," I interrupted.

"I couldn't do that, Anne, but your Mother made a suggestion some time back that I have not been able to get out of my mind." She paused and I was dying of curiosity. "If you and Sam could provide me a room here at your home, I could not only clean for you at no cost, but I could also fix your meals. You are both so busy, it may be helpful and may also take away some of your stresses, especially for you, Anne. I would certainly respect your privacy and would make myself scarce in my room when you are at home."

This caught me off guard and I wasn't sure what expression I had on my face. "Mother did suggest this to me as well, Ella. It would certainly be a big help, but I'm not sure how Sam would feel about it."

"Of course," she said with a nod. "A man's home is his castle and I know he'd like to fill it with little Dicksons someday."

"You're right, Ella, but we have our hands full," I said in agreement. "You are already like family and I don't know what we would do without you. Regardless of what Sam thinks about the living arrangement, we will find a way to help you."

"Thanks so much, Anne," she said sincerely. "I sure didn't think that at my age I would be in this predicament. Secretarial work is out of the question since I didn't keep up my technical skills. It is such a privilege to work in this beautiful home. Just in case those little Dicksons do arrive, I think I would be a pretty good babysitter."

I laughed and waved my hand like it was nonsense. "Now you're scaring me, Ella," I said, blushing. "I will talk to Sam tonight if he comes home at a decent hour. Before I forget to tell you, the carpenters finished up in my office, so there is still sawdust here and there that they missed."

"Oh, I'll bet you are enjoying that fine space of yours, Anne," she said as she pulled out her cleaning supplies.

"I'm sure I will someday. Right now, it's turning into a catch-all place for things I want to do."

As the day progressed, Mother called to tell me she had heard from Sue in Honduras. She reported that Sue had met her little boy and that he had a fuller face than Mia and wasn't as underdeveloped. Sue also said she would be there longer than expected because of additional paperwork they were not expecting, so she was glad she had her lawyer with her.

"So, did she name him?" I asked, eager to know what she had decided upon.

"Oh, she did! His name is Eli Kenneth Davis. Isn't that lovely?"

"Yes, it is," I repeated. "Uncle Ken will be thrilled, I'm sure! It will be such fun to have a little boy around."

"Julia said she would have a shower for her when she returned, remember?" Mother reminded me. "I think Sue has everything she needs for the nursery but does not have any boy clothes."

"No problem there!" I said, excited. "There is a new children's shop on the street called Little La La's. Their window displays are so cute! By the way, Mother, this morning while I was talking with Ella, she proposed her moving in with us."

"I wasn't sure she would, but I think that she is definitely interested in doing that," Mother said.

"I don't know if Sam will go for that."

"I know, but all you can do is ask," she suggested. "You and Sam may have some unknown finances of your own someday, Anne, so this could be a win win for all of you."

"Good point as always, Mother." Hmmm…

CHAPTER 41

Sam didn't arrive until eight that evening. When he came home, he said he had to fly to Cincinnati the next morning to see a client that they were trying to retain in spite of all the turmoil. He would be gone for a couple of nights, which was not unusual since he became president. He turned in early, so I didn't dare discuss Ella's request with him. The more I thought about her living with us, the more the idea grew on me. If she moved into the empty bedroom at the end of the hall, she would have her own bathroom. It was a sizable room and she would be close to the back staircase, which would take her directly into the kitchen. Sam and I were gone so much that she could have free use of the whole house. Was I jumping the gun here? Was I reverting to the lifestyle I left on Melrose Street? I would be giving up some independence that I wanted here at 333 Lincoln. Is that really what I wanted?

After seeing Sam off the next morning and taking my

morning walk, I stopped by Little La La's to pick out some clothes for Eli. After much internal debate, I decided to take two everyday outfits and a darling, warm snowsuit for the coming winter. I was shocked at the prices of such small items of clothing, but he was worth it and Sue certainly needed the help. When I got back in the car, I felt almost guilty about the money I had spent. Mother's words of caution came back to me.

I was surprised to find Abbey working instead of Jean when I arrived at the shop.

"Jean is taking the day off to move back home," Sally informed me. "She wanted to do it while Al was at work."

"Well, I suppose we should be happy," I said with some hesitation.

"He'd better not lay a hand on her, that's all I can say," threatened Sally. "Keeping him sober will not be as easy as she thinks it is going to be."

"You were a great friend to help her," Abbey said.

"Jean is genuine and sweet," Sally added. "It was good having her there, especially since Paige moved away."

"What do you hear from her, Sally?" I asked, curious.

"Not much, but she did say she has some job prospects."

"Hey, look out the window!" shouted Abbey from the front room. "They're putting up The Written Word sign. It's beautiful. It must have cost a fortune."

I looked out the window. "Wow, it is beautiful," I said staring at it. "I wonder how she got that approved so quickly. I hope she saves enough money for her inventory!"

"When is she planning to open?" Sally asked, still peering out the window.

"Not until next month," I reported. "She was telling me

that her deliveries were slow, which was starting to worry her."

"Wow, I wish I could have my own shop," said Abbey as she added a vase of flowers to the display case.

"Really?" I asked "What kind of shop would you have, Abbey?"

"I am very fond of everything Christmas, but I think I would love a shop that had one of a kind items of everything from jewelry, clothing, and artwork," she said without hesitation. "There are so many artists that create and sell that way. I would call it the One-of-a-Kind Shop."

I could envision it myself!

"I really like that, Abbey," I said, catching her excitement. "I would go in a shop like that right away. I really like the idea of owning something I knew no one else had. That's not easy to do!"

"I'd shop there too," said Sally. "So, what's stopping you?"

Abbey looked at Sally like she was crazy. "It's a small thing they call capital," she said, going back to her work. "By the way, Anne, I'm glad you're okay with me helping Julia out on Sundays at her shop."

"You don't need my approval, and all that experience will really help you someday when you have your own shop. As much as you love Main Street, I can see why you have that dream."

"You're the best, Anne," Abbey said, practically dancing around the shop. "Kevin said you'd be one to tell me to go for it!"

I smiled to myself.

Why would I not encourage a dream like that? I always had one dream in my hands, one in the works, and one in my head.

CHAPTER 42

It had been a while since I had been home alone overnight. I actually loved the independent feeling it gave me. I was never afraid of most things growing up and cherished my time alone.

Ella had cleaned my office to perfection. It did beg for my attention. I sat down at my writing desk. I think the last time I wrote something here was my poem about the ghosts on Main Street. I was tempted to open my laptop, but that would mean a distraction of existing emails and work. Instead, I picked up my red pen and journal that Sam had brought me from one of his trips. I was thrilled because it was a small gesture that signified he approved of my writing. I opened it to a blank page and asked myself what inspired me. Without hesitation, I thought of the lily quilt and my strange obsession with it.

I walked into our bedroom where it continued to beautifully grace the end of our bed. I sat down on the bed so I could once again feel the texture of the stitches as I ran my hand across the quilt. How could such a plain white quilt mean so much? Without hesitation, my pen started moving.

The Lily Quilt
When I touch your Lily quilt, I somehow feel your pain.
But then I see the beauty of the lilies that you claim.
I also feel the comfort that this quilt seems to bare.
It's loving, pure white softness is like you're really there.
I found your quilted message, For Dear Mary, it truly read.
I promise to do as you wish, just like the message said.
Please leave us as you should, and join the heavens above.
You no longer will weep to sleep, with God's eternal love.

When my fingers stopped, I read it to her aloud. I was hoping this would give her the peace she needed to move on. She had been quiet of late, as if she felt sorry for us and our recent stresses. All of a sudden, the lights flickered on and off as they had done many times before. I smiled, knowing she had gotten the message. I grabbed the lily quilt in the dark, as if it were something I should run to. When the lights came back on, I felt an overwhelming sense of comfort and peace.

My cell phone was ringing in my office, so I tried to regroup my thoughts and move to answer it.

"Hey, Annie, is everything okay?" Sam said when I answered. "What took you so long to answer the phone?"

"Sorry, honey. I was in another part of the house," I responded, somewhat out of breath. "You arrived safely?"

"Yes, thank goodness. It was a rocky flight. We went through a terrible thunderstorm, but now we're here, safe and sound."

"We? Did someone else go with you, Sam?"

"Yes, I asked Brenda to come with me on this trip. This is really her client, but I felt it was a serious enough situation that I needed to come to reassure them as well. I wanted them to sense that everything would be fine when this is over."

I wanted to faint at the thought of Sam and Brenda together. Brenda had been the main reason for my Uncle Jim and Aunt Julia's divorce. As they traveled for Martingale through the years, Uncle Jim and Brenda had an affair.

Sam kept talking, as if mentioning her name was no big deal. I couldn't dare show my jealousy at a time like this in his life. Some time ago, when Sam told me that Brenda had been promoted to take his position as vice president when he became president, I threw somewhat of a tantrum that I didn't want to repeat. Sam was a good and honest man. He was going to pick the best person for the job, which he did, I suppose. His sweet voice was hard to ignore. He loved me more than anything and his good night message gave me peace.

I walked back to our bedroom to get ready to turn in for the night. I wanted to return to the warm feeling I had when I left this room. When I came to bed, I grabbed the lily quilt to say my prayers. I was a very fortunate person and grateful for it. I prayed for Sam's company to survive and for God to keep him healthy. I also asked God to bring Sue and Eli safely home and to make sure that Jean and Al would live happily ever after. I put the quilt beside me in Sam's place on the bed. Somehow, I felt this quilt had a purpose in my life, therefore, I could not return it just yet. Not just yet.

CHAPTER 43

When Sam returned home, he seemed like his old self. The meetings had gone well. Sam said they got as good of a response as they could have hoped. I filled him in on Sue's homecoming, the baby boy's name, and how having a little boy in the family was going to be quite fun. He appreciated the update and said we would provide what we could to help Sue educate her little family in the future.

When Sam suggested we meet at Charley's for dinner, I agreed, thinking this would be a good time to present Ella's idea of moving in with us to Sam.

When I got out of my car on Main Street, I went inside Aunt Julia's new shop to say hello. She was in painting clothes, mixing paint.

"Wow, this is beautiful," I exclaimed as I looked at the great color scheme. "I love the way you have the different sayings painted on the walls."

"I do, too," she bragged. "After all, we are all about the written word! I'm dedicating this little alcove over here to Jane Austen. One of her sayings about books will go on this wall, and I found some really clever Austen-related gift items. Sarah picked out most of the items. They have a Jane Austen pen that you absolutely have to have, Anne."

"Please save me one, will you? You were smart thinking of all of Janeites. They will be your best customers. Sarah is really taking this seriously, isn't she?"

"She really is," she agreed. "She now says she is going to major in journalism next year, which is sure better than one of the art degrees she has had her eye on. She can work here in the summer and pick up extra money for school."

"Our little Sarah going to college. I can hardly believe it!" I said, shaking my head in disbelief. "So, when do you think you'll have Sue's shower?"

"Next week, if it's okay with her," she said, washing her hands. "I have a caterer all lined up to bring us lunch and Sarah said she would do some decorating. I told Sue before she left I would buy her a new bed for Mia. She has plenty of things for the baby except clothes."

"That's good thinking on your part, and I took care of some of the clothes," I reported. "I recently picked up some things at that new little children's shop on the street."

"By the way, there's another Martingale story in today's paper. Did you see it?"

"I stopped looking," I responded as I walked toward the door. "Sam is handling things pretty well and that's all I care about."

"That's right. Here's a real shocker for you. Jim is coming over to the shop tonight to put some shelving together for us.

He's excited for us."

"Of course he would be," I said, smiling. "Tell him hello and thank him for taking Sam golfing."

She nodded as she went back to her paintbrush and paint.

Jean and Sally were both working on centerpieces for the Humane Society dinner that was taking place tonight.

I told them how adorable the centerpieces were turning out. "Did you get moved back home, Jean?" I asked, interrupting their steady work habits.

"Jolly good, since Al was not about," she answered positively. "I told him I'm giving it a go and for us both to suck it up."

We laughed, not sure what it all meant, but I knew she meant business. We both told her to be safe and to use good judgment about what she puts up with. Sally told her how everyone was asking if the Jane Austen Literary Club would be starting again. That pleased her, but she made no promises.

Jean went to answer the shop phone. "Miss Anne, you have a special phone call," she announced.

"I'm at the airport waiting for our next plane to leave," Sue said on the other line. "All is well and we should make it home later tonight. Eli has been sleeping most of the time. I have a couple little toys for him to hold. He looks at me like he doesn't know what he's supposed to do with them. He's so cute, and I get a smile out of him now and then."

"Oh, we cannot wait to meet him, Sue. We love his name, and I'm sure Uncle Ken is thrilled. Call Aunt Julia as soon as you can. She has shower plans for you and there will be things for you that you will need, I'm sure."

"Oh, how sweet!" she responded. "My first concern is

introducing Mia to Eli. That will be most interesting, even though I told her about him."

I was so happy for this single mother who was taking matters into her own hands. She had a new job and a new baby in just a matter of months. On my way to meet Sam down the street, I thought about the new adventures ahead for her and Aunt Julia.

"Hey, beautiful, I'm in here," came a voice from the downstairs seating area. He had a drink waiting for me.

"Glad to see you are drinking tea," I greeted, giving him a kiss on the cheek. "You're here early!"

"Yeah, I came from home. I wasn't feeling well this afternoon and I didn't have any appointments, so I decided to go home and rest a bit."

I couldn't believe I was hearing this. "Really? Are you okay?" I quickly responded without getting too animated.

"Absolutely," he nodded with a smile. "Let's order. I'm starved."

I found myself staring at him as we ate. Was he telling me everything? When we finished and he ordered a cup of coffee, I decided to tell him about Ella's request. As I explained it to him, I wasn't getting any kind of a reaction.

"I can certainly see advantages and disadvantages, Sam," I stated. "I didn't give her an answer, of course. I know I felt I wanted to do something to help her financially, and when she presented this, I thought it might be a win for both of us."

He finally spoke. "We certainly have the room. We'll have to work out her hours. We can't expect her to be at our disposal around the clock, plus we will want our privacy. Is she in good enough health, Anne? We are too busy to be taking care of her, if you know what I mean."

It sounded cruel, but he was right to introduce the subject.

"I think so, except for a few aches and pains, I suppose," I replied, thinking about it. "We'll have to address our concerns with her, and I'm sure she will have some, too."

"She is a sweetheart, and if this doesn't work out, we will try to help her," he finally said before we got ready to leave.

"That sounds good, honey," I agreed, squeezing his hand. Sam's big heart was revealing itself once again.

CHAPTER 44

I was waiting for Aunt Julia and Mother to pick me up to visit Sue when I received a phone call on my cell phone from Dr. Wesley's office. I was taken back, wondering why they were not calling Sam.

"Mrs. Dickson, we are calling to see if you know why Mr. Dickson has not shown up for his last two appointments," said a nurse.

I didn't know what to say.

"He's just been very busy and distracted, so I'm sure he just forgot," I responded. When I hung up, I felt anger spread over my entire body. Without hesitation, I called Sam's number. With frustration, I had to leave a message, telling him to call Dr. Wesley's office right away. What was he trying to prove by ignoring the importance of these appointments?

Aunt Julia and Mother were in a great mood and were anxious to meet Eli. I put my worries aside, not telling them about my phone call. I had to trust that Sam knew what he was doing. It was his body, after all.

As soon as we arrived, Mia went wild, desiring our attention. Mother had thought ahead and brought Mia some new books from Pointer's Book Store. Eli was taking a nap, so we quietly peeked in on him. He was a cute, dark-skinned baby boy with lots of black hair. He was a much healthier-looking baby than Mia had been. We commented about how he really did look like he could be a biological little brother to Mia.

We sat down to enjoy coffee and cinnamon rolls as we talked about the upcoming shower at Aunt Julia's. Sue told us her parents would be visiting in a couple of weeks.

I arrived back at the shop around lunchtime. Abbey was helping Sally with orders for a weekend wedding and Jean was helping a customer on the phone. I was about to go back to my office when Ted came in the front door. After an awkward hello, he told me he was there to pick up a floral order for his secretary who was having a birthday.

"Are you holding up okay, Anne?" he asked quietly as I wrote up his ticket.

"Sure, it'll be fine." I wanted to be brief. "Thanks for your email. I appreciate your concern."

"My father said he wasn't surprised when he heard of the accusations against Mr. Martingale," Ted said, hoping for a reaction from me.

"Well, we'll see how it turns out," I said, keeping myself busy so I wouldn't have to look him in the eyes. "I hope she likes the flowers." I made a point to not encourage more conversation.

"I'm sure she will," he stammered as if he wanted to say more. "Take care now, Anne."

I turned away and went back to my office. The girls looked

at me as if I was going to respond to them in some way. There was really nothing to say, and after all, he was a customer.

Ella was due to come by for dinner, so I left the shop early to pick up some things at the IGA grocery store. The more I thought about Sam's missed appointments, the more aggravated I became.

Thankfully, Sam arrived before Ella that evening, so I could confront him. "Did you reach Dr. Wesley's office, Sam?" I asked, risking a negative response.

"I did," he said as he poured himself a glass of tea. "It's no big deal. I've just been too busy to take the time right now. I'm fine, Anne. I'm seeing him next week."

I didn't respond as I mixed the salad. I didn't want to nag him to make the matter worse. Just as I put the rolls in the oven, Ella arrived.

"I brought you a cherry pie that just came right out of the oven!" She held it out to me. It was snugly wrapped in a towel. She was in a good mood.

"My wife is cooking tonight, Ella," Sam teased as he looked at me for a response. "She can do anything she puts her mind to, so I'm sure it will all be delicious. Thanks for remembering how much I love that cherry pie of yours!"

Sam and Ella continued with their small talk until we sat down in the dining room to eat.

"Ella, Sam and I decided that we would be open to you moving in with us if we all agree to a few guidelines," I announced with a happy tone. I was careful not to use the word "rules."

"Oh, that's wonderful!" she said without hesitation.

Sam took over the conversation from there. He sounded firm in our expectations and she nodded and told us she had considered some of the same issues. She was very pleased that we had chosen the empty back bedroom because she had some of her own furniture that she wanted to bring with her.

"Anne is very busy and I am gone a lot," he said, employing serious tone. "I like knowing you will be here for her. It's not just concerning the household chores, but having you here for moral support as well."

She nodded.

What did he mean by moral support? I thought Sam was my moral support.

She was agreeable to our suggested hours and agreed to move in the first part of September.

"You kids will soon have another anniversary," she reminded us.

"The best years of my life, Ella," Sam said with a big grin. "You want to go back to the Quarry House again, Anne?"

"Yes, I think I do," I said. I had such fond memories of the place.

"I'll call them tomorrow then," he said as he started clearing the table.

Ella started to help but Sam reminded her that she was our guest for the evening. He told both of us to take our coffee out to the patio room because it was such a pleasant evening. We left Sam to abide by his offer and went outdoors, where I lit a few candles. I filled her in on our trip to Sue's to see little Eli. She seemed to take a great deal of interest in how Mia was accepting him.

We talked about many things that evening. They say you really don't know someone until you live with them, so I guess we will soon find out about our dear friend Ella!

CHAPTER 45

When I came down to breakfast, Sam shared that he had already called the Quarry House and had successfully made our reservations.

"I only scheduled three nights," he informed me. "I don't think I can take off any longer than that."

"That's perfect because I can't be gone much longer myself," I said, half awake.

I hadn't slept well the night before because Sam constantly tossed and turned. I started questioning whether it was a good idea for Ella to move in. I hadn't expected Sam to be so agreeable to the whole idea. When Sam offered me his toast, I had no interest.

"It looks like a great morning for a walk, Anne," he said as he looked out onto the sunporch.

A walk was not on my radar screen right now.

"Will you be home for dinner tonight?" I asked, sitting

down at the table where open pages of the morning newspaper were spread out.

"Probably not, Anne," he said, joining me at the table. "We have a meeting at four that will go into the dinner hour, most likely." He saw me looking at the newspaper article.

The headline read, *Martingale's Future Looks Doubtful.* The article went on to say, *Inside sources tell us there will likely be changes resulting from the IRS investigation of alleged embezzlement charges. Employees are skeptical about keeping their jobs.* I couldn't read on. It was too disturbing.

Sam looked at me with pain in his eyes. "We're not there yet, Annie," he said, hurt evident on his face. "The press is only dealing with the negative as they try to keep this story going. I've tried to reassure the employees, but they know that however things turn out, our company will not be the same. There is no reason to sugarcoat it."

I stood, stretched my arms around his waist, and hugged him tightly. I pressed my face to his and could feel the warmth of this man I loved so much.

He returned the embrace without saying a word.

"You deserve so much better, Sam," I said softly. I straightened slowly, standing up near him.

"This is not just about me, Anne," he said with a hint of anger. "None of the two hundred-plus employees deserve this, not to mention what their families are going through. I'm glad now that Jim left when he did. He seems to be doing pretty well these days."

I nodded in agreement.

There was silence for a few moments with both of us realizing there was nothing more to say at this point.

"Maybe I'll call Mother to have dinner with me tonight,"

I said as I folded up the newspaper, quietly eager to remove this bit of news from our kitchen table.

"Don't forget about Harry," Sam said, teasing me.

"No, I think I will just invite her," I decided as I thought about it. "I miss seeing her and I'm sure she's worried about me dealing with all of this publicity."

"As any mother would be," Sam said as he was gathering his things to leave. He looked at his watch, and a look of concern covered his face as he faced his day ahead.

"Go take your walk, Anne," he said coming over to put his hands on my shoulders. "Our lives have to go on as normally as possible or this situation will eat us up. We will be fine. I've told you that. I feel good that I have done the right thing, despite it becoming ugly. You go to that beautiful shop of yours and smell those roses! We have a lot to be thankful for."

"I know, I know," I said, as I brought his face to mine. "You always know what to say and when to say it. I love you so much, Sam. I don't know what I'd do without you!"

"I love you too, sweet Annie," he returned, giving me another hug. "You tell that mother-in-law of mine I could use some of her comfort food sometime soon!"

"She'll love that," I said, walking him toward the door.

He opened the door and blew me a kiss as he so often did.

I now had more of my energy back. The time had passed for a walk, so I picked up the phone to call Mother.

"Good morning, sweetie," she said in that familiar voice I loved.

"How are you doing this morning?" I asked in my cheeriest voice.

"I'm still at the kitchen table, but Harry is already off to the barber shop to get a haircut and then to meet his cronies for coffee. Every Thursday morning, they meet at Diane's Diner."

"Oh, I forget that it's still there!" I recalled. "They were written up in the paper once for serving a thirteen-egg omelet!"

"That's the place," she said laughing.

"Would you be free to go to dinner tonight with me, Mother?" I quickly asked. "Sam will be late again, and I thought maybe we could catch up. How about we go to Donna's? I was thinking about it just being you and me. Do you think Harry would mind?"

"Oh my goodness, no," she casually said. "Is there any special occasion?"

"No, but if we need one, you have a birthday coming soon," I reminded her. "I am just alone so many nights recently, plus I wanted to tell you what we have arranged with Ella. I think we're going to give it a try!"

"We do have a lot to catch up on."

"How about I pick you up around six?" I suggested. We agreed and I felt as if I had something to look forward to..

When I finally walked into the shop, Sally motioned for me to come over to a corner near the flower case.

"What's up? I asked as she looked around.

"Tim finally asked me out on a real date!" she said, blushing.

"Terrific!" I patted her on the back. "How do you know it's a real date?"

"Well, I have been putting some distance between us and only saying yes to his invitations occasionally, but then yesterday he said, 'What's going on, Sally? I miss you! How about we have a nice dinner and then check out that new club at Westport?'"

"Oh my goodness," I responded, happy surprise clear in my tone.

"I nearly fell over!" she went on to say. "His voice was even different!"

I had to laugh. "Oh, Sally, that is special," I exclaimed, sharing her happiness. "I can't wait to hear how that goes!"

I went back to my office with a smile for a change. I had all the shop girls happy. Jean was back with her Al, Abbey and Kevin were progressing well, and now Sally finally had her dream date with Tim. Life was good at Brown's Botanicals!

CHAPTER 46

As the afternoon dragged along, the highlight was Nancy stopping by with her double stroller carrying Andrew and Amy. They were adorable and growing up so fast. Andrew was fair and favored Nancy's beauty while Amy definitely favored Richard's side of the family. Nancy had just come from visiting Sue and got to see baby Eli for the first time. Nancy commented about how the three children would probably go to the same school and play together and how wonderful that would be.

Nancy was ready to give another report as well. "When I got out of my car just now, Julia saw me and gave me a tour of her new shop. It is so cute and quite artistic. She has added so many personal touches! I think she's onto something, Anne. Sarah was as busy as can be unpacking merchandise. The two of them are beyond excited about it all."

"I know what you mean. It's so cool that they are

sharing this together. Jim is even lending them a hand, which is really amazing. Knowing Aunt Julia, I thought she'd be determined to do it all herself."

"Well, is he seeing anyone?" Nancy fished for any recent relationship details.

"No, I don't think so, but I don't think they will ever get back together again. She is way too happy now!" We both had to laugh.

The twins entertained all of us for a while as we acted silly and talked baby talk. Nancy told us that she gave Sue time off work with full pay as a means of helping her financially. I knew that was huge for Sue, who was always worried about making ends meet. I knew all of her savings and investments went to travel expenses for the adoptions.

By late afternoon, the orders were caught up and Kevin had returned from his last delivery. I was struggling on the computer trying to make some changes to our website. My frustration over mastering technology continued to plague me. Except for Kevin, the staff had gone and the front door was locked. I called Kevin in to help me on the computer. It was a piece of cake for him and, to his credit, he always had patience when I asked him questions about the computer. He took over my seat and knew exactly what needed to be changed.

The shop line kept ringing instead of going to voice mail, so I left Kevin to go to the phone by the front counter. I picked it up and answered in our usual shop fashion. "Brown's Botanicals. How can I help you?" I said, feeling somewhat frustrated.

"Mrs. Dickson, is that you?" asked an unfamiliar voice.

"Yes, who is this?"

"This is Cora Blessing from your husband's office," she began. "We haven't met, but I have some alarming news to tell you."

My heart stopped.

"We have just sent your husband away in an ambulance to St. Joseph Hospital. He didn't show up for our meeting at four and didn't answer his phone, so I went to his office to check on him. I found him slumped over his desk. I'm afraid he was unconscious, Mrs. Dickson. He should be at the hospital by the time you get there. I am so sorry."

I dropped the phone receiver. This was the call I feared. He may be dead. Oh God!

"Kevin!" I yelled as loud as I could. "Kevin! Kevin! It's Sam!" I screamed. "They took him to the hospital in an ambulance. "Help me, Kevin. I have to get to the hospital!" I wanted to cry, but I was too frightened. Maybe this all wasn't real.

Kevin emerged from my office, eyes wide with alarm. "I'll drive you," he said hanging up the receiver. "We'll be there in a flash, Anne. Let's get your purse and go. He's had a close call before, so don't worry." He guided me toward my office where he grabbed my purse on the desk. We headed out the back door and into the shop van. I was beginning to shake.

"Stay calm, Anne."

"Pray, Kevin, pray. There's nothing else we can do." I kept a solid grip on my purse, feeling fear and panic set in.

In no time, Kevin pulled up to the emergency room door. He got out of the van and headed to my side of the vehicle. Opening the door, he took me by the arm and steered me into the building. Kevin told the woman at the front desk that we were here to see Sam Dickson, who had been brought in by ambulance. She instructed us to follow her. My legs felt so weak that I could hardly walk.

This just had to be a bad dream, I told myself.

They took us to an empty room to wait. After a while, I had an overwhelming urge to see Sam, rather than waiting politely in this unfamiliar room. I was about to protest when a nurse and what looked to be a doctor came into the room. There was also a man that I knew worked with Sam, but I didn't remember his name.

"Anne, I'm Scott Williams from Martingale," he said, clearly shaken up. "I followed the ambulance here."

"I'm Dr. Feltz, Mrs. Dickson," the other man said softly.

"Where is my husband? I need to see him." I stood and moved toward the door.

"Mrs. Dickson," Dr. Feltz said.

Something unsettling about his warm but careful demeanor stopped me in mid step. I turned to face him.

"I'm afraid he died instantly from a very severe heart attack." He paused. "He was gone before he got to the hospital."

All eyes were on me.

"No, you're wrong!" I objected. "He was fine this morning. No, no, no! This can't be!"

Kevin stepped forward and pulled me close. I started beating on his chest in pure terror.

"Sam would never leave me!" Tears stung my eyes. "Why couldn't you do something to save him?" I was sobbing, gasping for air, and feeling my world spin completely out of control.

"Anne, Anne," Scott finally said. "We are pretty sure he

was dead at his desk for some time. There was no struggle. Whatever the pain, it was quick and over. He just fell forward on his desk."

I couldn't picture the dreadful scene he had described. My legs went weak and I fell to the floor, feeling cloudiness engulf me. They laid me on the couch in the room and I could hear voices. I heard Kevin say he would call my mother. There was movement in the room and the nurse tried to get me to drink some water.

"Sam, Sam, Sam," I mumbled.

Kevin was telling me he had taken my cell phone out of my purse to make a phone call. I started to sit up.

"I want to see him," I begged. "I have a right to see him. Where is he?" I struggled to stand and regain my sense of balance.

"You certainly can, but let's get you steady on your feet first," the doctor said. "You have had a big shock, so just take your time. We are so sorry."

"Anne, please know that everyone at Martingale will do anything they can to help you." Scott added in a sympathetic voice.

"You all killed him! You killed him!" I managed to spit back. "Are all of you happy now?"

By now, I was in complete hysterics, but I meant what I said. All of this time with Sam worrying about the company. Nights spent awake trying to figure out what was happening financially in the company he had trusted. Evening after evening going over records, reviewing reports, and waiting for the nightly news to report on the latest bits of scandal they dug up.

I leveled my gaze at Scott Williams and said evenly,

"You killed him."

Scott Williams, shocked by my outburst, turned and left the room.

CHAPTER 47

It was Kevin who stepped up to help me. He held me and comforted me, assuring me that Mother and Harry would arrive soon. He kept telling me to take deep breaths and to drink a little more water.

There were so many questions I wanted to ask. Somehow, I couldn't believe he was really dead unless I saw him for myself.

Finally, Mother and Harry joined us. They were both crying and at a loss for words. The doctor told them he suspected that Sam had died quite suddenly. Mother held me tightly, like she had when I was a little girl. Harry held onto both of us in disbelief.

"Anne, look at me," Mother finally said. "Sam is no longer in pain and is in God's hands. He's probably looking down on you right now with all his love. He'd want you to be strong through all this. You did everything you could to add happiness to his life. That's all we can really do for one another."

"I want to go see him now."

"Are you steady enough to be on your feet?" the doctor asked.

"I'll be okay. Just take me to him."

"Okay, then follow me."

"Honey, do you want me to come with you?" Mother asked.

"No, I want to see him alone."

Dr. Feltz and I walked down a long corridor. We stopped at a room. The doctor said he'd be right outside the door if I needed him. Then he asked if I was ready. I took a slow, deep breath to steady myself.

I walked in and there he was like he was waiting for me. He almost had the beginning of a smile on his face. I went closer. He looked like he was only asleep. I wanted to call out his name to wake him up. I kept taking deep breaths so I could keep myself from losing total control. I finally regained my composure.

"Sam, honey, if you can hear me or see me, I'm so, so sorry," I said aloud, tears falling unchecked down my cheeks. I rested my head on his chest and told him over and over that I loved him. I touched his hand, which was no longer warm. I couldn't imagine never being able to touch his body again.

"How could you leave me?" I asked as I tried to imagine my life without him. "It was stubborn of you to not see your doctor. You might still be here with me if you had! Sam! How can I possibly survive without you? We were a perfectly matched team."

There was so much more I wanted to tell him but he

remained there in silence. I stared at the most handsome face I had ever seen. He was perfect inside and out, yet could not survive. The longer I stayed, the more I realized he was gone from his perfect physical body. I didn't want to leave him, but I realized had he left me and was gone. He was really gone.

I turned to walk toward the door. Again, my entire being seemed to be on overload and my legs failed to cooperate. I woke to find myself reclining again with voices all around me. I felt someone's hand rubbing over my hands telling me that I was in shock, but that everything would be alright. As I became more aware of my surroundings, it was Mother soothing me. I started to sit up and felt nauseous. Mother urged me to rest for a few minutes. Needing to gain permission, the doctor asked if I wanted an autopsy done on Sam to know the details of his death.

"No, I don't want him disturbed," I said with certainty. "We knew of his heart condition and we know it killed him."

He nodded and then had me sign a few papers, which I was able to do.

"Anne, you come home with us tonight," Mother instructed.

I nodded. I couldn't talk. I just wanted to be alone and curl into a ball. I couldn't think. I was too weak to do anything.

When we got in the car, Mother said, "I called Helen, Anne. She needed to know right away so she could make plans."

"Oh my God. Helen," I said, starting to cry all over again. "How could I not think of his mother? Is she okay?"

"I think she took it the best she could," Mother said

with sadness in her voice.

We walked into my old home on Melrose Street.

"Let's get you to bed, Anne. You have had a great shock and need to rest."

As I got undressed and crawled into bed, I realized that I hadn't slept here since the night before I married Sam. How did I ever end up back here? Where was he? I couldn't stop the tears and pain as I settled into this once-familiar room.

"Harry and I will call the family," Mother said, sitting by my bedside. "You just rest, honey. I love you and know how much you are hurting right now. I lost a husband once, too. Sam loved you as much as he possibly could. Just embrace that thought as you go to sleep." She kissed me on the cheek and closed my bedroom door.

CHAPTER 48

I finally awoke the next morning from a very restless night's sleep. I didn't want to stay in bed and think, so I got dressed quickly in last night's clothes. I made my way downstairs.

Harry greeted me with a hug as Mother hung up from a phone call with her brother, Ken.

"Your uncle and aunt send you their deepest sympathies, Anne. Here's a cup of coffee. It will help you. I am so glad you were able to get some sleep."

I nodded in silence.

"I want to go home, Mother," I said, feeling tears rise to the surface again.

"Of course you do, honey," she said, embracing me. "Kevin told me he would get your car home. We will take you whenever you're ready. I talked to Sally. They are all in shock, of course. She said to tell you not to worry about anything and to give you their love."

I really wasn't absorbing anything she was saying.

"Will you have a little toast or something, Anne?" Harry asked. "You haven't had anything to eat in a long time."

The very thought of eating made me nauseous.

"No, but thanks," I said, trying to give him a smile. He was being so kind. "My stomach is too upset. I'm so glad you both were there for me, but I just want to go home."

It was pouring down rain when we left Melrose Street, which was comforting in some odd way. It was as if the whole world was crying for Sam. Mother insisted they both go into the house with me. It was a very strange sensation going into 333 Lincoln knowing Sam would never be there again. I wanted to call out to him, as if he might be in another room. I did feel an unfamiliar strength inside me that made me feel warm and loved. I couldn't explain it. Perhaps he was here with me. I assured Mother and Harry that they could leave and I would be fine. I needed to work out this grief in my own way and time.

"Anne, we talked to Ella last night, and we think it's a good idea for her to be in the house with you," she stated, obviously concerned. "She really wants to help in any way she can. She promised she would stay out of your way unless she was needed."

"Oh, I don't know," I said, looking absently around the room.

"Didn't you tell me that Sam said he was glad that Ella would be around to give you moral support?" Mother reminded me. "Perhaps he was thinking of the day when he might not be around. I'm sure that is one of the reasons he was okay with Ella moving in."

"Do you think he knew how serious his situation was

and didn't tell me?" I asked, my voice shaky. "He also told me we had to go on and live our lives." I broke down and let the tears flow. "Then he told me to go to the flower shop and smell the roses. Oh, Mother, this is awful! How can I go on?" I was consumed by another wave of grief. "Was Sam preparing me for the worst and I didn't realize it at the time?"

Harry, sweet Harry, watched me with tearful eyes. "God works in mysterious ways," he said stretching his arm around me.

"Okay, you're probably right," I struggled to get myself to fend off the terror that threatened to engulf me. I made myself breathe deeply and slowly. I needed to think. "Tell Ella she can move into the green room until she moves in permanently next month."

"Good," Mother said, wiping her eyes. "We'll certainly feel better knowing she is here with you."

I told them good-bye on the south porch. I glanced at Sam's gazebo across the driveway before closing the door. I walked into the kitchen where I would find Sam every morning at the kitchen table with his coffee.

"I'm home, Sam," I said aloud as if he could hear me. "I hope you can hear me and help me through this."

I looked down at the table where I saw a beautiful bouquet of white lilies. It was not there when I left my kitchen. Next to them, however, was the horrid newspaper that Sam and I had read that morning. Did the article bother him more than he let on?

"Oh, Grandmother!" I cried aloud, sitting down at the table. "What will I do without him?" I felt so hollow. "I will need all the help I can get. Please God, give me peace and strength to face this."

The lights over the kitchen sink began to flicker. She was there. She was always there, it seemed. I picked up the newspaper and threw it into the trash. Words from or about Martingale were not going to hurt us anymore! I typically pulled up my Anne Brown personality for strength, but now it was Mrs. Sam Dickson that would have to give me strength. Sam taught me so much after we were married. Sam loved 333 Lincoln, even more than I seemed to. I would have to embrace it, keep it safe, and keep it forever.

The house phone rang, which made me jump. Without thinking, I picked it up.

"Mrs. Dickson?" I tried to place the voice, but it was unfamiliar. "This is Mrs. Cameron from the hospital. We are just confirming that you want your husband to be taken to Barrister Funeral Home. Is that correct?"

"Yes, yes, that is correct," I managed to say. I hung up, knowing it was just the first of many decisions I would be making.

The knock I heard at the front door was more of a frantic banging. I went to the door and looked through the peephole to see Nancy. I let her in and we embraced, both of us overcome with sadness. I wanted her to tell me everything would be okay. I needed to hear someone say that to me.

"I wanted to be here sooner, but your mother said you needed a little time to yourself. This is so tragic, Anne, but you know Richard and I will help you in any way we can."

I nodded. "I don't know what to do next!" I told her. "He's on his way over to the funeral parlor as we speak."

She nodded, seeming like she already knew that was the case. "First of all, you can take your time with everything," she instructed. "There is no rush. You have just had a major shock, for heaven's sake. I assume Sam had a will, but if he told you about anything he wanted at a time like this, just let us know and we will take care of it."

"Yes, he did have a will," I confirmed. "However, I have no idea what's in it. Nancy, I just can't think about all of that right now."

"I know, Anne. Believe me, this is all normal," she said with a comforting voice. "It is so different, though, when it is personal. We are like family. Richard and I were so happy for the two of you! We are devastated by this."

I could tell it was hard for her to appear brave as she talked to me.

Nancy stayed another hour as she tried to assure me that each decision and day would fall into place. Sam's body was now in the hands of Richard and Nancy, which was strange for me to consider. She strongly encouraged me to eat so I could make rational decisions.

"I've had a million phone calls, Anne," Nancy shared. "Everyone's in shock and feels so badly for you."

I told her about my outburst with Scott at the hospital. I knew it wasn't his fault. I also should have been grateful that he found Sam when he did. Nancy told me she was sure he took it to be part of my reaction to everything. She said she knew Scott and that he was a fine man.

"It's already made the morning paper," Nancy warned me. "Look at it later if you like, but not now."

Having my best friend coming alongside me in this tragedy was enormously comforting. After she left, I went up to shower and change into fresh clothing.

One step at a time, I told myself.

I came out of the shower and looked at the bed Sam

and I had shared in this house. I went to his pillow and could still smell the scent of him. How could I bear this night after night? More tears and sobs welled up and spilled over. It was all too much. I grabbed the lily quilt and pulled it over my head, along with Sam's pillow. I just wish I could feel him one more time. Like my Grandmother, I held the lily quilt, weeping, as I wanted to sleep.

CHAPTER 49

By the time I awoke, it was three o'clock in the afternoon. I couldn't believe I had fallen into such a deep sleep. I splashed water on my face and put on my jeans and a T-shirt. I glanced at my bedside phone and saw there were seven messages. How could I have not heard the phone?

I came down the steps and told myself I had to pull myself together and join the living. Sam was not here and wasn't going to be coming home. As I went by the entry hall, there was a knock at the door. I checked the peephole and saw that it was Ella. I opened the door and she put down her bag to give me a big teary-eyed hug.

"I just woke up from a nap, Ella," I said, like I had to explain something. "I'm glad to see you!"

"I have some fresh chicken soup for you," she said, walking toward the kitchen. "I have other things in the car that I'll get later. I'll get this heated up for you. I'm sure you haven't had much to eat."

I was in a daze as I made my way to the kitchen table. I liked to look at the comforting bouquet of lilies. "I think I am actually hungry, Ella," I confessed. "I'll be out on the patio, so when that's ready, would you bring it out to me?"

"Yes indeed, and then I'll make myself scarce unless you need me to do anything," she agreed. "I know this is a horrible time for you, my dear." She paused. "The rain left a mighty nice drink for all the grass and flowers. I saw your Mr. Kip leaving when I drove up the hill. I guess he was doing some of his work here. Everything looks very beautiful."

I walked out to the patio. I wasn't in the mood for small talk, that was certain. I had to admit that the weather was very pleasant. The rain had cooled things off. I got a towel and started wiping off a lounge chair. Sam loved to sit here and read. I had just stretched out to think of what I had to do next when Ella came out and told me there was a man at the door to see me.

"Well who is it?"

"He said his name is Mr. Martingale, Anne," she said, hesitating. "Should I send him away or send him out here?"

I couldn't believe what she had just told me. How could this terrible man have the nerve to step foot in our home? Was he about to tell me something I needed to know concerning Sam's death at the office? I had no choice but to hear him out.

"Tell him to come out here," I instructed.

There he was in his expensive casual clothes trying to look like everything was normal. This man's greed was the reason for my husband's heart attack and death.

"Mrs. Dickson, I've come to tell you personally how

sorry I am for your loss," he began.

I stayed silent with a stern look on my face.

"I thought the world of Sam, as you know, and that's why I nurtured him to follow in my footsteps. I had no idea the seriousness of his heart condition."

I got up from my seat. "His heart didn't let him down, Mr. Martingale," I stated firmly. "You did. You, of all people, a person he looked up to. You set him up to cover for you and your corruption. You forgot that Sam was smart and bright enough to know things were not right when he took over as president. Did you really think he was the type to overlook and cover up things because of his loyalty to you? He put his heart and soul into that company and look where it got him." My anger was mounting as Mr. Martingale looked to the floor. "Your punishment will come and you will likely live through it, but Sam wasn't that lucky, was he? I hope you know there are many innocent employees that this very thing could happen to, but you don't seem to care about that. If coming here makes you feel better, then I am sorry you came. Please leave now."

He shook his head and turned to leave.

I was shaking in anger. My words were harsh, but true. I felt a sense of relief. Someone had to speak for Sam who was no longer here to speak for himself.

Ella came out with my soup. "Well done, Mrs. Dickson!" Ella said as she arranged my place setting. "Your husband would have been proud of you!"

I didn't respond to her. I wasn't so sure he would have. Sam's heart was so soft. He probably would have been moved by Mr. Martingale's apology. I calmed myself down and forced myself to have some soup and crackers. I could feel the strength it was providing.

I accepted the call from Sam's mother when it came. She had spoken with Mother, but not me. She was surprisingly calm. She had probably cried herself out like I had the day before. She said they would all be arriving as soon as a funeral date was determined. She was pleased that Mother had offered for all of them to stay with her. After I hung up, I could not even imagine what she was going through right now. Losing a child had to be twice the pain I was feeling.

I then called Mother and asked if she would go with me to the Barrister Funeral Home the next day to make plans. She was glad to see I was moving forward and was happy that I had finally eaten something.

Several bouquets were delivered. I told Ella to put them all out on the patio. I didn't want the house turning into a shrine or feeling like a funeral home. Right now, I had no interest in who had sent them. As night approached, I became less brave and more melancholy. Ella answered a phone call from Uncle Jim who wondered if he could stop by for a while after dinner or perhaps bring us something to eat. I didn't want him staying long, so I agreed that he could come by after dinner. I was anxious to see him. I knew he had lost his best friend and had to be hurting as well.

CHAPTER 50

Ella and I munched on turkey sandwiches before Uncle Jim arrived. I somewhat dreaded seeing him, but yet, I knew I would feel close to Sam in the process.

When I opened the door, he held me close as he held back his tears. I wanted to sob when I saw him. We went into the study where we both hoped to think of the right words to say to one another. Ella had gone upstairs to give us some privacy.

"I'm so glad I had that golf game with Sam," he said fondly. "We had a great time and we really spoke very little about our work."

"I know. It was wonderful for him," I said with a smile. "He came home in a great mood, so it was good for him. Thank you for that."

"For what it's worth, Anne, Sam bragged about how supportive you were with his long hours and extra stress at work. He said he was lucky to have you and how much he was looking forward to having some time alone with you for your upcoming anniversary."

"Oh my word," I gasped. "That's next week, and Sam made a reservation."

"Would you like me to cancel that for you?" Uncle Jim offered.

"Would you?" I knew it would make him feel good to do something for me and it would be an enormous relief for me to not have to make that call. "I know there are going to be so many details I'm not even aware of. It all scares me! I don't know where to start."

Uncle Jim looked so sad, not knowing the right words to say that would bring some comfort to me.

"You know, I have you and Aunt Julia to thank for bringing us together, remember?" I said, smiling as I recalled those good memories. "I'll never forget seeing that tall, handsome man! He was so nice. He always teased me and said it was love at first sight for him, but I'm not so sure about that."

Uncle Jim laughed. "I remember it like it was yesterday. He was quite smitten with you, and I thought he should slow it down a bit, but he was determined to have you! I had to admit, you were a perfect match!"

I wanted to explode with grief thinking about how wonderful it was.

"How does one half of a good thing go on in life?" I said with tears coming down again.

He gave me a moment before he responded. "You will be the strong person that he fell in love with," he stated. "You were independent and in control of your life. That was what he loved about you. You will get through this. You have many people who love you and who will help you. Julia and Sarah are devastated. Julia was the one that called me."

I couldn't think of all of them right now. All I could seem to think about was how Sam was here one minute and gone the next.

It was good to visit with Uncle Jim. He loved Sam, even though Sam had to fire him at Martingale. Uncle Jim never held it against him. I felt it best not to say anyting about Mr. Martingale's visit. I didn't want to risk Uncle Jim telling anyone about it.

After he left, I went upstairs. Everything seemed to evoke so much emotion from me. I went into my office, and for some reason, picked up my red journal and pen. I took it into our bedroom and sat on the bed to write something. I wasn't sure what. I only had one thing on my mind.

STAY WITH ME
Stay with me, Sam, for I am here alone.
Do not leave me here in our happy home.
I want to feel you here, each and every day.
I still want you in my life as I find my way.
Stay with me, Sam, I promise to really try.
It's under the lily quilt that I will only cry.

I placed the book on the bedside table and felt I should really put those words into play. Perhaps it was time to make my list for the days ahead. I knew that with God's help and the loving memory of Sam, I could do this and make a normal life for myself.

On the next page, I wanted to list the things that were

important to Sam. His dream of 333 Lincoln was huge and he succeeded. The finishing touch was the patio room, which he enjoyed immensely. He dreamed of purchasing the Brody property and developing it. Was I going to be the one to see this happen? His biggest dream was likely to have a family, and now I regretted putting him off about that. He knew I had my dreams, too, and finally supported my expansion of the flower shop because it was important to me. He was never selfish. His personal investigation would now take care of itself at Martingale's. He paved the way for truth and now we would see how it would all unfold. I closed the book.

I found it amazing that my once-important world at Brown's Botanical's was suddenly not important. It certainly was a family that I loved, but I hadn't thought about how the employees and the merchants I cared for might be feeling right now. I supposed there would be customers that would truly be concerned about me as well. I would have to contact my staff tomorrow. There was no doubt I had to thank Kevin who was there in time of my need and handled things perfectly. What if I would have been in the shop alone when they called? Despite this horrific tragedy in my life, I still knew I had much to be thankful for.

Without getting undressed, I pulled the lily quilt up around me and said my prayers. I knew I would have to convince myself that I would not have to go through all of this alone.

CHAPTER 51

I didn't have the nerve to refuse the fluffy omelet that Ella had made for me the next morning. She said I needed to eat to make good decisions and she was probably right. Before Mother picked me up at ten, I went out to the potting shed where I felt most comfortable. Kip was certainly keeping things watered and well kept, despite our hot summer coming to an end. I hated the thought of my plants in the potting shed missing my personal touch. Outside the potting shed, mums were already popping through the ground a bit early and would need deadheading or the blooms would not be there for the fall season. I studied the yard, thinking it how strange it was that nature kept on living, no matter what or who might die around it. It was a good reminder of how life is supposed to go on, even when it is painful. Sam and I were fortunate to have this little piece of heaven, as we so often referred to it, so I had every intention of keeping it maintained.

Mother told me on the way to Barrister's that Nancy and Richard would both be there to help us. That was a thoughtful gesture, but it was odd to think of them housing the body of my loving Sam.

We walked into Richard's plush office, which I had never seen before. The funeral business must be quite lucrative and Richard must possess exquisite taste.

When I told Richard right off that I wanted a small, private funeral, I could see he was a bit surprised. He was quite aware of how well known Sam was in the community. However, I was determined that Sam's funeral was not going to become a spectacle for Martingale. Sam also typically preferred that things be kept low key. Our wedding was a good example.

Without questioning my decision, they moved on to the idea of having a small luncheon in one of their social rooms following the service. That sounded very nice, and Richard and Nancy said they wanted to host that for me. Mother said she would help me make a list of those who could attend, which I appreciated. Somehow, I was shocked at how easy this seemingly difficult process had become.

When we got back in the car, Mother suggested getting some lunch. I was mentally and physically exhausted, so I insisted on going back home. I thought I would have the energy to visit the shop, but I couldn't bear the thought of it right now. I had just made arrangements for my dead husband. It was not like I had accomplished something on a "to do" list. Mother understood my emotions, she drove me home, and we parted ways.

Inside the house, Ella wanted to feed me again, but I went straight upstairs to change clothes and rest instead.

The thought of eating something made me unsettled again. How does one manage to enjoy any food at a time like this?

My cell phone rang. It was Aunt Julia. She said all the right things as she wept between sentences. If one more person told me things would be better with time, I was going to scream.

"They won't be better without Sam," I corrected her. "Things will be different, and I will just have to accept it. Have you heard how Eli is doing with his new mom and sister?" I could tell she was shocked at the change of subject.

"Remarkably well," Aunt Julia said with a smile in her voice. "I visited for a short time yesterday and it appears that Mia is warming up to the idea."

"So, when is the opening day for The Written Word?" I asked, endeavoring to avoid talking about Sam.

"I think by next weekend, we may have enough merchandise to open. I still need a couple of inspections since I made some changes, but the decorating is all done. I am very pleased."

"I am so happy for you. I should have been more helpful to you, Aunt Julia, but I was so distracted with Sam's situation at Martingale. It will be so nice having you and Sarah on Main Street."

"I will have a grand opening at some point. I've already met a lot of the street people, as you call them, and Phil came by to make sure I joined the merchants' group."

"That's great," I said, realizing that I couldn't talk about Sam without feeling overwhelmed and that I didn't care to make any more small talk. I felt tired through and through. "I need to go. I'm not good company right now, Aunt Julia."

"I understand, honey. You have to be exhausted. Get

some rest. Sue and I are there if you need us."

I hung up, realizing the world was going about its business. I guess I would too, despite a stumble or two when I would miss Sam's presence in my life. This felt more like a serious fall for me and I wasn't sure whether I would be able to get up again.

CHAPTER 52

I had another day before Sam's burial. I wanted to stay in bed all day, but I knew I had to organize my thoughts. I wondered what would be expected of me tomorrow. I had slept in my jeans and T-shirt, so I finally got up, acutely aware of the aroma of homemade bread. I brushed my teeth and went downstairs to find Ella busy in the kitchen.

"I know how much you enjoy my bread, so I also made us a few cinnamon buns," Ella said energetically.

"Oh, I don't think I can eat anything," I said, sitting down by the bouquet of lilies on the table. "I'll just have some of that coffee."

Between the strong smell of the lilies and the bread, I felt a sensory overload that was not positive. I quickly ran to the downstairs bathroom where what little was in my stomach came out of me.

This is crazy. Sam would not want this to affect my health. I am a stronger person than this.

Ella hadn't heard me, so when I returned to the kitchen, she convinced me to have a slice of toasted bread. Surprisingly, it was quite tasty, and it made Ella happy to see me eat.

"I don't think I can avoid the shop any longer. I have really deserted them. Goodness knows what is going on."

"That Sally is quite capable, Anne. I don't think you have to worry about a thing. However, getting out of this house might do you some good. Why don't you shower and pay them a short visit if you're up to it?"

"Maybe," I said, taking another swallow of coffee. "I haven't even opened my laptop. I'm afraid to think of how many emails are waiting for replies."

The front door bell rang and Ella immediately went to answer. I heard the door close quickly.

"Another beautiful bouquet for you, Anne," she said, bringing it into the kitchen. "The red roses are so striking with the white lilies. This so large that perhaps we should put this one on the round table in the entryway."

I couldn't believe how gorgeous it was. Somehow, I knew this did not come from our shop.

"Do you want me to read who this is from?" Ella asked as she smelled the roses up close. "Here's the note addressed to you." She handed me the card.

I had to admit I was very curious. I opened the card and it read: *Anne, I am stricken with the shock of this terrible news. I am so sorry because I know how much you loved him. You are in my thoughts and prayers. Ted*

I had mixed emotions as I put the card back into the envelope. I was touched by his message, but on the other hand, I questioned his honesty and sincerity. Sam had taken me away from Ted, and Ted had seemed to carry a grudge. I didn't tell

Ella who the flowers were from.

"Just put it with all the rest, Ella." Ted's flowers should not be the centerpiece in Sam's house. "I sure wish I had thought of a charity to mention. These flowers are such a waste!"

"Excuse me," Ella said with a teasing sarcasm in her voice, "am I hearing this out of the owner of Brown's Botanical Flower Shop?" She laughed at me.

"Okay, I guess that was a little extreme," I agreed, returning a smile.

"Have you thought about what to wear tomorrow?" Ella asked like she was my mother.

"No," I said, shaking my head and feeling stress my stress heighten at the very thought of it. "I guess black. I should have plenty of that in my closet."

"Did Sam have a favorite color or did he like a particular outfit of yours?" she suggested. "You might think of little things like that when you go up to your closet."

I stared into space, thinking about her words. Why should I dress up on the most horrid day of my life? However, this was not about me, as Mother so often reminded me about marriage. She was so right. Sam's life was the story I wanted everyone to remember. I was just a benefactor of his love.

I didn't hear the phone ring, but Ella handed it to me and told me this was a call I needed to take. It was Mr. Rozier, Sam's attorney. After lengthy comments of sympathy, he told me that we should meet soon to read Sam's will. I had only met Mr. Rozier once at a restaurant when Sam introduced us. I agreed to meet with him in the next week. The thought of hearing Sam's wishes were bittersweet. One day at a time, as the familiar saying goes.

CHAPTER 53

S am's funeral day was here. There was no getting around
what had to be done. Harry and Mother were picking me
up early to meet with Sam's relatives. I was told we would
meet with Pastor Hamel for a prayer and last viewing to say
good-bye before taking the casket into the chapel for the
service. Mother took my shaking hand like she had done
through many other scary moments in my life. Before we
were about to enter the room with Sam's casket, I asked
Richard and Nancy if I could have a few moments alone with
Sam before the rest of the family came in. They agreed it was
most appropriate and invited me to take as long as I liked.

My tears had been contained until I walked in to see
my Sam lying in his best suit, as if he were about to go out
for the evening. This young, ambitious man should not be in
a casket. He looked perfect, just as he always seemed to look
each day. He had just begun to live, really.

I broke into a sobs. I wanted to tell him a hundred things before his body left me forever.

"I love you so much, honey," I began as if he were listening. I took a deep breath to continue. "I will keep you in my heart forever. I will promise to fulfill your dreams and make you proud of me." I could hardly contain my crying at this point. "Please, please help me through this if you can. I will join you one day. We will be together again. We have to be together again!" I cried until I felt my heart would break in two. How could I possibly say good-bye?

Mother came in the room and I held on to her for dear life. There were no more words to say. Still staring at him, I leaned over to kiss him on the forehead, as we so often did with one another. I touched his hand and saw the wedding ring I had picked out for him. I knew it had to stay with him. We were married forever and ever. Mother remained strong, knowing I was near a breaking point.

The pastor came up behind us, gently reminding us that the service would begin soon.

"It will never be good-bye for us, Sam," I whispered to him before I turned around.

I sat in the front pew with Mother on one side and Helen on the other. I could not bear to look at Helen or anyone else in the room, but out of the corner of my eye, I saw Sally and Jean clinging to each other with teary eyes and Kevin bent over with his head in his hands. The music and words were a background blur.

Pat, Sam's sister, gave the first eulogy and it was followed by Uncle Jim. I became attentive as he spoke. The two men had shared a friendship that was not perfect, but was healthy for both of them. His words seemed to comfort me more than all the words spoken at the service thus far.

"I can remember the day like it was yesterday. It was the day that Sam said to me, just a week after meeting Anne, that he was going to marry that girl one day," Uncle Jim said, smiling. Knowing Sam like I did, I knew he meant every word. "There was no question that Anne was the joy and delight of his life."

I was shocked to hear that information for the first time. It was certainly a sign of how close the two men were. It brought a smile to my face. I knew Sam was watching.

It was over. When I turned to exit, I was surprised to see that the chapel was packed. I did not have a sense of that while the service was going on. Everyone on the list that was invited to the private service must have decided to attend! Walking down the aisle, I gazed at my shop family holding onto one another for support. This family would now become more and more important in my life. They would help see me through this because of how close we had become.

When we arrived at the cemetery, I got out and looked around to see where Sam would be buried in relation to the Taylors' tombstones. How surreal this felt. We sat in the chairs provided for the family. It reminded me of many movies I had watched with a grieving family looking on. Pastor Hamel was brief, but his telling Sam to rest in peace somehow resonated with me. Sam did need to rest in peace. He had been under so much stress for so long. I couldn't help but be proud of his determination to discover the embezzlement at Martingale. Unfortunately, Sam paid the price, even though justice would come to others. I had instructed Nancy that I wanted to leave the grounds before they lowered Sam's casket, so I got up, following others to the car. There was no looking back.

Many hugs followed at the luncheon, where I managed to have part of a chicken salad sandwich and a glass of tea. Mother never left my side and was careful and deliberate about moving people along who wanted to take too much time with me in conversation. Uncle Jim was also nearby. I hugged and thanked him for the best message of comfort that was humanly possible.

"I'll be there for you, Anne. Don't worry," Uncle Jim said as he put his arm around me. "Sam would want it that way and it will help me with my own grief."

I smiled and nodded. "I will take you up on that," I said, smiling.

I said good-bye to the Dickson family with mixed emotions. I was almost happy they were not here on a daily basis to remind me of Sam. I couldn't believe how strong Helen remained through this terrible ordeal. She, like Mother, had lost a husband. They assured me they would keep in touch and wanted to be helpful in any way possible.

I told Harry and Mother I wanted to go home. It was truly my home now and there was so much there that was a part of Sam. Ella had left the cemetery earlier and greeted us when we got to the house, offering more coffee and tea.

"I need to rest," I told them. "Thank you all for everything, but I'm exhausted."

Without hesitation, they all agreed to my plan and I walked upstairs before they even had a chance to leave.

I walked into our bedroom and sat on the bed knowing it was over. I had just seen Sam's body for the last time. I wasn't sure I could produce another tear. I grabbed Sam's pillow, which still had the last remaining pillowcase Sam had used. I buried my head in the pillow. I laid back and pulled the lily quilt up around me. It was soft and comforting. It was used to generations of tears, and just as others had done, I faded into sleep under its soft reassurance.

CHAPTER 54

The smell of coffee and that frequent ray of sunshine woke me up. Sam had made coffee downstairs. In a second, I remembered I was a widow. It was Ella's coffee brewing downstairs rather than Sam's.

I undressed from my funeral clothes that I had slept in from the night before and took a long shower. I stood, welcoming the warm water pouring over my tired body.

"Sam," I said aloud inside the echoing shower. "I feel you can hear me. Please tell God to give me the energy and guidance to get through this day."

I greeted Ella and she poured me a cup of coffee. I looked at the Colebridge newspaper laid out in front of me. It showed a photo of Sam with the headline, *Colebridge Community Leader Passes.* I was in no mood to read it. I was sure it would refer to Martingale in some way. I asked Ella to save it for me.

Grandmother's lilies still were as fresh as the first day they arrived and they continued to give me a tinge of comfort. I wish I could have kept Sam forever, like Grandmother's lilies.

"I wish you would eat a little something, Anne," Ella insisted. "It will give you a bit of energy. You look so pale. Perhaps you should rest a little more."

"No, I can't do that," I said, shaking my head. "I really must go to the shop. I have ignored them long enough. If I stay here, I will just cry all day."

Ella looked at me with pity in her expression.

When I turned on my cell phone, today's date flashed bright and clear. It was September 12, our wedding anniversary. We were supposed to be waking up at the Quarry House, not cleaning up details of a funeral. Who would have known that the Dickson marriage would be so brief? All good things do come to an end, but I never suspected our time together would be so limited.

"Anne, honey, what do you want me to do with all the flowers? The plants you will surely keep, but some of the flowers are showing their age."

"Get rid of them," I said with a sharp tone. "Be sure you save all the cards. Sam loved plants, so we'll keep them for the porch and patio. I really don't like having the flowers here as a reminder. If you can remove them while I'm gone, it would be helpful."

Ella looked at me. "What about the lilies here on the table?" she asked, testing me.

"No, please leave them."

I made myself look presentable and left 333 Lincoln to begin my new life without Sam. The fresh air actually felt great and the aroma of freshly mowed grass always made me smile. I went to the garage and saw Sam's SUV sitting there driverless. There would be decisions to deal with down the line, but not just yet. Driving to the shop, I realized it was close to lunchtime, so the girls were probably not expecting me today.

"Well, if it isn't our Miss Anne," Jean said, greeting me at the door. "How are you coming along?"

"Better, I think, since I made it here today," I answered with a smile.

"Welcome back," Sally said, coming from the back room. "It's great to see you, but you didn't have to hurry back. We did miss you, though!"

"I know, but I needed to have something else to think about," I said, looking at both of them. "I'm not sure I can muster up more tears, plus I want you all to fill me in on what's been going on. Is Kevin around?"

"He's on a run over to Barristers," Sally reported.

"He's plenty worried about you, Miss Anne," Jean said softly. "He told us straightaway he would never leave you here alone, by golly."

"I don't know what I would have done without him." Darn those tears! I couldn't seem to get them under control!

"Abbey will be here about one to help me with some wedding centerpieces," Sally said, switching the subject to business matters. "You just take your time catching up, but everything's under control. Business was booming, as you can imagine. We had to contract out some of the orders for the funeral, so I hope that was okay. There was no way we could do it, as hard as we tried."

"Of course," I said, walking to my office. "I did think

about that. When I saw a large piece from Ted Collins arrive at the house, I could tell someone else had done it. I suppose I'll start by looking at some of my mail. I don't know how long I will stay. I just feel so drained."

"Of course you do, my lady," voiced Jean. "How about I fix you a cup of tea?"

"That would be nice," I told her.

Before they both left me alone, Sally told me how the merchants had been concerned about me. They were disappointed when they heard the funeral was private because they wanted to express their condolences. Sally said the flower shop staff made a flower arrangement from all the merchants, but they each came in to express their concern.

"You have a family, not only here in the shop, but on the street, Anne. Do you realize that?" Sally mentioned, hoping to encourage me. "They all felt so badly for you."

"I do feel that," I agreed, nodding. "I am grateful and I will need my friends and family more than ever!"

Sally closed my door to give me some privacy. She knew interruptions would be likely when people recognized my car at the shop. I just couldn't turn on the computer as if it were business as usual. I took a moment to glance at Sam's photo on my desk and the drawing of 333 Lincoln I had recently put on my wall. I told myself I could do this. This was the place I needed to be right now. I began my new journey with another long, deep breath.

CHAPTER 55

I quickly breezed through the mail, sorting it into two piles. One pile was what appeared to be sympathy cards and the other looked like business mail addressed to me personally. At the moment, I had no interest in opening either pile, so I turned on my computer to see the accumulation of emails. The recent one that got my attention was from Sam's lawyer, Mr. Rozier, who reminded me about tomorrow's meeting at his office to read Sam's will. I supposed Mr. Rozier had a first name, but Sam had always referred to him as Mr. Rozier. He was about the age of what Sam's father would have been, so perhaps that's why he chose to call him that. I knew the reading of the will had to be taken care of and the sooner the better.

There were old emails from Sam that I didn't want to delete right now. Any word from him would be better than none coming my way. Once in a great while, he would pass on a "funny" as he called it. I rarely read any of those kinds of emails, but if it came from Sam, I knew it had to be good. He had one or two friends that would forward him "funnies" now and then.

Sally opened the door slightly and said Sam's secretary was on the phone for me.

"How are you doing, Mrs. Dickson?" she politely asked.

I had only met her once since she was newly hired as Sam's secretary when he became president.

"I'm doing fine," I responded.

"The reason I am calling is that I have done what I could to gather up Sam's personal things at the office, but I can only do so much, I'm afraid. Will you be coming in anytime soon?"

"No, not at all, I'm afraid," I answered rather coldly. "I will send someone to pick up his things. I know there are paintings that were special gifts, so I assume you have included them with his personal things?"

"Oh yes," she answered. "Just let us know when and who we should expect and we will have everything ready."

"I appreciate that," I said in a nicer tone. "I want to thank you for everything you have done for Sam, but I cannot go back to that office." I hung up as she wished me well.

What would be next? How does one erase such a vital and productive person from life? It was appearing that everyone was anxious to "get on," as Jean would say. I thought of Uncle Jim right away when I thought of someone who could pick up Sam's things. I picked up the phone immediately. The sooner Sam's personal items were out of the building, the better. There were many folks at Martingale who were upset with him when he exposed all the corruption, so I didn't want folks going through anything of his. I wasn't sure he had any friends left. I couldn't help but think that Mr. Martingale had to be relieved that Sam was out of his life.

"Of course I will," agreed Uncle Jim. "I will go first thing tomorrow."

"I have no idea how much there will be, but the first thing I thought of was the black and white drawing I had given him at Christmas. It is of 333 Lincoln. Be sure you especially look for that."

"I will, Anne," he said, recalling the picture. "Don't worry about a thing. I still know some people there who will be helpful if I need them."

"Thanks so much," I said, taking a deep breath of relief. Another step had been taken care of. It was progress.

There was a soft knock on the door as Kevin peeked in my office. "Good to see you back, Anne," he said with his big winning smile.

I got up to give him a hug. "I can't begin to thank you for everything, Kevin," I said, holding back the tears.

"I'm just a jack of all trades," he teased. His efforts to make me laugh were possibly so he wouldn't get emotional himself. "I was so glad you were not alone here when you got that call."

I nodded. I opted to change the subject and move the spotlight off of myself. "So, how are things with you and Abbey?"

"Pretty good, I think," he said bringing back his smile. "She should be in soon, I hear, so I was going to ask her to dinner after work."

"That's great," I said, smiling back. "She is so talented and loves the street. For all I know, she'll have her own shop one day, like Aunt Julia."

"Don't think she hasn't thought about it, Anne," Kevin commented. "All the better now that she has a handy guy to be around to help her!"

I laughed.

"Hey, has Kip had a chance to talk to you lately?"

"Not really," I responded. "We barely talked at the funeral. Why?"

"He's probably looking for the right time, but he wants you to have a heads up that he has a job offer he's considering. You know he took your offer temporarily to help us out, so I'm not surprised. I'm sure I can get us help here, but I know how much you and Sam depended on him at your home."

"Oh my, Kevin. I hate to hear that! He is so talented. We loved our patio room he built and he keeps our grounds up beautifully."

"Well, he thought fall would be the time to move on because there wouldn't be much more work at the house," Kevin explained. "It will all work out, Anne. We were lucky to have his services as long as we did." Kevin closed the door, mentioning that he had another order to deliver for the day.

What was next? There would never be another Kip. Sam really liked him and admired his talent. Sam mentioned more than once how lucky we were to have him. Hmmm…

CHAPTER 56

I walked up the steps to Mr. Rozier's office the next day to hear Sam's last wishes. I dreaded every step as if I were going to the dentist for some major procedure or about to get a doctor's diagnosis. His building was pristinely restored and fit perfectly in our town of historic Colebridge.

The receptionist greeted me warmly and offered me tea or coffee before I joined Mr. Rozier in his office. When I sat down with him at the large mahogany table, there were papers scattered across the otherwise polished surface, making it look somewhat intimidating. He assured me Sam's will was pretty simple since we had no children.

"I always liked Sam," Mr. Rozier began, trying to put me at ease. "I met him through his friend, Jim Baker. Actually, the last time I saw Sam was on the golf course with Jim recently. When I heard the news of his passing, I couldn't believe it. I knew nothing of his health history, so it was shocking to hear he died of a heart attack."

"He was under so much stress," I volunteered. "I am curious. How long ago did Sam make this will?"

"Well, let's see," he began. "I think he amended his existing will around the time you got married. You had purchased the place there on the Lincoln hill. I think that's when he knew a change had to be made. I can tell you that he had a great deal of respect for you, Anne. He admired all you had accomplished there on Main Street, but he wanted you to be secure and taken care of."

"Funny. He never shared that," I commented.

"Well, you are the sole heir of his will," he stated in a friendly manner. "Sam had significant life insurance coverage, especially one that Martingale provided him, as well as a large amount of investments. Sam was a pretty wise businessman. As you probably know, he took out a loan to buy the Brody property, and because of the parameters of the loan, that will now be paid for free and clear. He also left you with a significant sum to live on, Anne."

I paused, trying to review his words. "Seriously?" I asked in disbelief. I stared at the unbelievable figures listed as assets.

"You weren't aware of some of this? I'm sure Sam didn't feel a need to go into a lot of details. After all, I'm sure he wasn't expecting to die at such a young age."

I couldn't believe what I was hearing.

"Will you be planning to stay in your home, or is it too early to ask?"

"Yes, indeed I will," I confirmed. "I wasn't sure I could afford to, but you have certainly taken that worry away. We both loved 333 Lincoln."

"I can tell you, from all indications, it is what Sam would have wanted and you will live most comfortably." He had a friendly smile and I appreciated that he knew and liked Sam.

I signed a few papers as we made small talk and he reassured me he would be available if I had any questions or concerns after I had time to process the information he had given me.

My legs were weak as I climbed into the car. I sat there in silence, attempting to absorb all I had learned. I was overwhelmed with gratitude and my sense of relief was enormous. Sam truly loved and trusted me, which was the most special message of all. Now that I had total knowledge of my financial situation, I wanted to share Sam's generosity. My mind immediately recalled the conversations we had about Sue and her family. I thought of how often Sam told Sue that she need not worry about her children's future. He knew he could help her. One of the first things I planned to do would be to set up a trust fund for them. It would be a huge relief for Sue.

As I drove up the Lincoln hill, as Mr. Rozier described it, I realized it now all belonged to me. What I would do with it or how it would be maintained was up to me alone. It occurred to me that fall was at our doorstep. Fall was sad, unlike spring, so perhaps this season was the best one to have right now. On this property, the earliest sign of the change from summer to fall was when the tiny leaves of our black walnut tree drifted to the ground. As the season changed, I realized I would change as well. I would adjust to my new normal. What would life be like without Sam by my side?

When I parked my car next to Sam's SUV in the garage,

I was relieved to know that I could afford to keep it. It was handy for hauling larger items needed for the property. I noticed Ella's car was gone, so it was totally quiet when I walked in the door. I welcomed the solitude as I thought through the visit with Mr. Rozier and contemplated my future. Sam had trusted me to make good decisions and I wouldn't disappoint him.

The phone rang and I saw it was Mother, so I picked up.

"I'm glad I caught you, Anne," she began. "How are things going for you?"

"Fine," I answered, knowing she had something on her mind.

"I wanted to tell you that I went with Harry to the doctor today. He's had an ongoing cough for some time, and it has gotten considerably worse." She paused. "He had an x-ray today and they have already called to say they have concerns and suggested he should come in for more tests." She sounded like she was going to cry.

"Well, that's pretty much a normal procedure, Mother," I said calmly. "They want to be thorough."

"He was a smoker for many years, you know. He hasn't smoked since we've been together, but I'm scared to death that this may be serious."

She was right. I certainly understood her concern. If it were a worst case, lung cancer could be Harry's diagnosis. It was a frightening consideration. "How is he reacting to this?" I asked cautiously.

"Oh, he is playing it down, of course," she reported. "We used to take a walk almost every evening, and now he either makes an excuse or gets out of breath and we have to come back earlier."

"I'm so sorry," I said with a sigh. "Let's see what the other tests show and try not to worry."

"I shouldn't bother you with this now, Anne, but I'm worried sick at the thought of him having a serious illness."

"We are both strong women, Mother," I reminded her. "We will do what we have to do."

CHAPTER 57

Despite my efforts to be strong, I was physically weak and very tired. I told myself that it was exhausting to absorb all that Mr. Rozier had told me about Sam's investments. I walked in the house thinking about what might be refreshing to drink, but without food in my stomach, nothing really sounded good. I looked to see if there was any more funeral food that had been dropped by and discovered some ham that looked enticing. I made a small sandwich, grabbed some grapes, and poured myself a glass of Grandmother's lemonade to take out to the patio room. It was dusk and I realized our days would now be getting shorter.

As I relaxed on a lounge chair that Sam was fond of sitting in, my mind went back to Mother's concerns about Harry. Time was already moving on, and the focus was no longer about me. Other people had troubles and needed support. The two of them had such a perfect arrangement at this point in their life, but their age would now be an added concern. Thank goodness they were there for each other. Mother had taken good care of herself through the years, so hopefully she would ward off the heart disease that was so strong on her side of the family. We all had grown quite fond of Harry and certainly wanted him around for my Mother's happiness as well and just wanting good things to come his way.

When I finished my sandwich, I felt energized enough to get up and walk around this beautiful Dickson estate that had been so well taken care of by me and Kip. What would I do without him? He was so dependable, not needing a bit of guidance from anyone. Knowing Kip, he would help me find someone I could trust to take his place. I kept walking as I said good-bye to my summer plants that had provided lovely summer blooms and foliage. So much reminded me of Sam, of course. When I walked by the potting shed, I had to smile at how often he teased me about the possibility of my moving into the shed permanently! He was grateful I fell in love with it, however, or I would not have agreed to the purchase of 333 Lincoln.

Looking toward the Brody property, I knew I would have to make some decisions soon as to how it was to be maintained. The mowers were keeping it presentable, but the empty house was a disaster waiting to happen. Ignoring this prime piece of property so close to 333 Lincoln would eventually devalue my main property, so I must think of something to do to prevent that from happening.

Ella drove up and parked. When she saw me, she walked toward me with her hands full.

"What are you doing out here?" she asked, smiling. "It

looks like we'll have that full moon again!"

"Ah yes, a light unto my path," I said poetically. "Where have you been?"

"Nowhere exciting," she began to explain. "I got my oil changed, picked up some things from the drug store, and then stopped by to see an old neighbor friend of mine. Did you need me for anything? I was tickled that you went to the shop. Have you had something to eat?"

"I am just fine," I assured her. "I made a ham sandwich after I got home from seeing Mr. Rozier about Sam's will."

A look of concern came over her face as we walked toward the door of the house. "All went well, I suppose?" she asked, managing her bags from the drug store.

"Very well. Sam planned well, and for that, I am very grateful." Before Ella went up the stairs, I told her about Mother's troubling phone call.

She showed great concern. Ella was especially close to Harry and said she often talked to him about giving up smoking.

"What can I do to help, Anne? I'll be cleaning there this week."

"Until we get a firm diagnosis, all we can do is sit tight."

"I'll make his favorite pie when I go over," she said, grinning. "That will cheer him up for a bit."

"Did you say pie?" I teased. "What kind is his favorite?"

"Banana," she stated. "I have two crusts made, so while I'm at it, I just happen to know someone who likes my chocolate cream pie!"

We both had to laugh.

"Sounds like a good plan, Ella," I said, cheering up. "You are way too good to everyone."

She then bounced up the stairs, obviously happy to have a plan.

I spent the rest of the evening in my office just thinking about the events of my life recently. I stared at my notes about the Taylor House, knowing I would not be getting back to its mission for some time. There would be a lot of paperwork regarding Sam's death. How would his death impact this house's history, I wondered? I wasn't quite ready to pick up my pen again.

The longer I sat there, the more my mind cleared. There was something or someone giving me energy to address the bigger picture of 333 Lincoln. I couldn't afford to wallow in self-pity. There was work to be done and I only had one suggestion in mind to perhaps help me through it all.

That night, I slept soundly for the first time since Sam's death. My prayers helped me to feel comforted and I no longer felt afraid. My sources of strength were no doubt coming from God and those spirits I loved so dearly.

CHAPTER 58

Before I walked into my shop the next morning, I saw Aunt Julia's car parked in front of her new shop. Her grand opening was tomorrow, so I was sure she was keeping busy. She had a plastic banner that hung high on the store front, announcing the opening to the public.

She saw me approach her door and met me with a big hug. "Oh Anne, how are you doing?"

"Much better, thanks. I wondered if you want your flowers brought over today or would you prefer to wait until tomorrow?" I looked around her beautiful shop, surveying it with admiration.

"Tomorrow's fine," she said with a big smile. "I'm not sure where everything will be arranged just yet. I almost hate the thought of people coming in and messing everything up."

I understood. "Everything is absolutely gorgeous, Aunt Julia. Let me know if there's anything else I can do."

"Jim is going to be here to help us out tomorrow and my friend, Carmen, is bringing some yummy appetizers. It should be quite a party!"

"I'm impressed that Uncle Jim wants to help you and even more impressed that you are letting him!" I joked.

We both laughed.

"I am sorry to hear about Harry's condition."

"I know, me too," I said sadly. "Mother's quite upset and I'm sure flashes of father's illness and death loom in her memory while she's going through this."

"I was thinking the same thing."

"Well, I have too much to do, so I'd better get on with it," I said, walking toward the door. "I will look forward to tomorrow." Just then, I turned to her with watery eyes. "You know, Sam would be very happy for you, Aunt Julia," I said in a shaky voice.

She nodded.

"Your opening will be the first social event I will attend as a widow."

"I know, Anne, and I love that you will do that for me. I will be there for you just as you were there for me when I divorced Jim. We are a close family and we go through these things pretty much joined at the hip."

I nodded, thinking that was such a true phrase. "Well, I'm off," I assured her, getting out the door before I or anyone else said something to make me cry again.

I heard voices in the back of the shop as I walked toward my office. Sally was helping Kevin with the first delivery of the day. They both looked startled and clearly didn't expect to see me in the shop today.

"Did you get back to taking your walks?" Sally asked,

joining me in my office.

"No, but I'm sure I will. I had things on my mind today, and ever since Sam's drama at work, I am not my best in the morning. By the way, did Kevin say if Kip would be coming in today?"

"Yes, he did," she said, holding a delicate basket of baby pink roses. "He has to help Kevin deliver the Oliver wedding flowers this afternoon."

"That's a very sweet arrangement. Who is that for?"

"This is for the Ellison's daughter who is turning sweet sixteen today."

"Good heavens. I remember when she was just a little thing," I recalled. "Would you tell Kevin to let Kip know that I need to see him when he comes in?"

"I will. He wants to see you as well."

Today, the mail would have to be opened. I found that once I started the process, my mind was distracted by business as usual. An hour had gone by when I smelled something very delicious outside my door. Sally soon knocked on the door and announced that Kevin had brought a pizza back for all of us for lunch. I wasted no time in joining them. My stomach was ready for something.

Kip arrived just in time to get the last two pieces. He teased us about him always being the fifth wheel around the shop. He told me he was happy to see me back at work and we agreed to go to my office to talk.

Kip spoke first. "I guess Kevin told you that I have a good opportunity that has come my way and that I will be leaving here soon." His voice broke. "I know this is not a very good time to abandon you, Anne, but fall is here and there will be less work for me. Kevin can easily replace me temporarily by doing extra duty. I will be forever grateful to you and Sam for taking me on. I will not leave you without anyone, so don't worry about that."

"I take it that your offer from your new employer was pretty attractive?"

"Yes, it was."

"Well, Kip, I have been doing a lot of thinking since Sam passed. You know how pleased Sam and I have been with your work. The talent and creativity you applied to our patio room was amazing."

He smiled.

"I think I have a more lucrative offer for you that would be much more challenging and better suited to your talents."

He looked startled.

"Sam has left our estate in pretty good financial shape regarding its future. We both talked about what we could do with the Brody property, but then he became sidetracked with the Martingale situation and he was unable to give it more attention."

"Understandable."

"How would you like to manage the newly established Dickson Properties by building some greenhouses for Brown's Botanical Nursery and rehabbing the Brody house and barn?" I bravely asked in one sentence.

Kip was astounded by my request. He was speechless. "Anne," he finally said, "had you honestly been thinking of all of this before Sam passed away?"

"Not in detail, but in concept," I assured him.

I could tell he was shocked. "I don't know what to say."

"Well, you can begin by accepting the challenge. Plus, knowing you as I do, I think you would find it all quite fun!

I promise you a generous salary to top what's been offered you, and if you decide you want to live on the property, we can arrange that as well. There are plenty of acres."

"This is totally unbelievable!" He put his hands on his head, still quite stunned by the offer.

"You would even have my blessing to hire Kevin from the shop, if you like," I teased. "You are both way too talented to be delivery boys all your lives."

"I am flattered. What can I say?"

"You can begin with some positive remarks like yes, absolutely, and when can I start. Those would all be good things to hear!"

We laughed and stood up.

"Count me in, Anne. This is more than I would have ever dreamed."

"Count me in, too!" I smiled as I gave him a hug.

CHAPTER 59

When Kip left my office, I felt I had turned a page in my future that surprised even me. I felt more certain. I had actually used the words Dickson Properties for the first time and had referred to Brown's Botanical Nursery as if these businesses had already been in existence. Where did this confidence come from and who helped me through the conversation with Kip? I knew that with my acquaintances, I could put together a good team to make this all happen. Why did I feel I still had Sam as a partner in this venture?

I decided that I would keep this plan quiet and rather low key right now. I remember so many folks saying one should never make decisions while grieving. If the general public knew of my plan right now, they would dismiss it immediately. Mother had her hands full of worry right now with Harry, so she did not need to hear about her daughter's crazy plans.

The day seemed exceptionally long, but I was determined not to leave before the others. I couldn't believe I was so tired. Perhaps skipping my morning walk was negatively impacting my energy level. When I heard Sally and Jean say good-bye, I grabbed my sweater and purse and prepared to go home. I wanted to be rested for the next day, which was Aunt Julia's grand opening.

Ella's heavy aroma of homemade soup hit me when I walked in the door. One part of me welcomed the food and the other said it was too much to bear. When I saw Ella standing by the stove in her full apron, I felt a tinge of guilt and resentment. I should have been the one toiling away in the kitchen for Sam and me. This was my house, but it seemed like others were all playing a role in its existence. I suppose, in all fairness to me, Sam knew from the very beginning that I was not a Suzy Homemaker type.

"Hello there! I'll bet you're ready for some nourishment after your first day back at the shop!"

"Oh Ella, I'm afraid, not," I said, not wanting to go into the kitchen. "I had a big lunch today. They brought in pizza and I ate that. Please save me some for another time. I need to go up and rest. I somehow forgot how exhausting my normal workdays were. I never needed to rest like this before Sam's death. Missing him is depressing and exhausting."

"Good idea on the rest part. I'll have plenty of soup here for later," she responded. "I'll be sure to take some to Sylvia and Harry. Harry is fond of my vegetable soup."

"Great idea, Ella," I said, heading toward the stairs. "I'll take the mail up with me."

I shut the bedroom door, wanting to keep out the smell of soup, but without opening the window, I wasn't sure it could happen. I quickly changed out of my clothes and put on a comfy white T-shirt and my white cotton pants with little red polka dots which used to make me smile.

I went into my office to grab a blank notebook so I could make some notes about my plans while they were on my mind. Pen and paper were always where I started with most ideas. I was the best list maker of all time. I loved to make diagrams and columns for positives and negatives. Sometimes that dictated a decision I would have to make. I quickly glanced at my mail which included household bills that had to be paid. Sam always took care of those. Now I would have to check out his office in the study to see where he kept all our household files. I wondered if Sam happened to be watching me now. He was probably shaking his head wondering how in the world I could do all of this. There was one more sympathy card from a good customer at the shop. How long should I expect to keep getting cards in the mail? I put the mail aside to take downstairs in the morning.

I rearranged the pillows to make myself comfortable. I kept my notebook in hand. I grabbed a bottle of water on my bedside table to drink as I went over in my mind what was most important in this latest decision of mine.

First, I created a diagram of the team I would need to accomplish this kind of business. Underneath their names, I listed what I would expect them to accomplish. After the diagram, I wrote a brief description of a business plan. I started another page for the greenhouses. I knew I would want to start out with at least two of them or perhaps even three. Then I made a list of what plants I wanted to grow that would enhance my flower shop. I was always anxious to rule out the middle man. That would be easy enough. I knew just where I wanted to build them on the property. I may need to have a gravel road or path put in before the greenhouses could go up. Kip would take care of that.

I knew before going any further there were concerns and fears that wanted to pop in and out of my mind, so I put them on their own list. That list would come in handy as I interviewed workers and contractors. There was no doubt I was a visual person and now I saw it on paper. There was some kind of force driving my hand and head. Sam had provided the financial resources for me, so it was up to me to do the rest. It seemed to me that Kip was there all the time just waiting for this opportunity. Knowing his skill set, he would have the place up and running in no time, along with plans for the future.

No wonder my eyes felt heavy. I had just planned a whole new business. I fell asleep with the lights on and my notebook in hand. Tonight, there would be no tears before falling asleep. Tonight, there would be dreams about the future.

CHAPTER 60

Even though The Written Word grand opening wasn't until after lunch, the place was buzzing with people going in and out and all the parking spaces on the street were already taken. Kevin delivered a live plant for Aunt Julia's small office and also several beautiful mums which were perfect for her food table. We also filled orders for other beautiful arrangements from others who wanted to wish the new shop owners well. I forgot how well connected Aunt Julia and Uncle Jim were in the Colebridge community. I was also happy for Sarah who was able to see her mother and father working together on this enterprise. Uncle Jim was smart to embrace Aunt Julia's dream instead of giving her grief as he seemed to do when they were married.

I tried to stay in my office doing payroll, but because of the extra traffic from the opening, I was called to help Jean, Abbey, and Sally out front. I was pleased that so many had stopped asking how I was doing. Everyone's behavior toward me was like normal, whatever that was.

Sue called to tell me that she had gotten a babysitter and wondered if I would go over to Aunt Julia's with her. I liked the idea and it would give me some time to catch up with Sue. I also wanted to tell her about the trusts I was going to set up for Mia and Eli.

Kevin and Abbey went to lunch together and then they were going to stop at the reception after that. When they returned, I would go over with Sue.

"How is our Mr. Al doing?" I asked Jean when we finished up with a customer.

"I'm proud of the old chap, I must say," Jean bragged. "It's not been an easy feat for him, but he knows straightaway I'm off to England if he goes back to his old ways."

"You don't really mean that, Jean. We would never let you go. You know that." I gave her a little squeeze.

"I'm proud as punch about how you've been managing, Miss Anne," Jean said, looking down. "Even my Al gets all teary eyed when he speaks of Mr. Dickson."

I was touched. "Al was very good to Sam, Jean, and I'll never forget that."

Sue arrived in cheerful spirits and looked dynamite in what appeared to be a new outfit.

"You both look like a night on the town might be in order," Jean teased as she looked us up and down. "Go have a bit of cheer for me, if you would. I need to get on home as soon as I can."

"We'll be sure to bring you some punch and a plate full of goodies. How about that?" Sue suggested.

"I went over for a little while this morning to give Julia

a hand," Sally said. "She did a great job, but there wasn't any food out when we were there."

"Hopefully, Kevin and Abbey will be back soon," I told them.

"Not to worry," Jean said.

Just as she was finishing her statement, in came the young couple, ready to return to work.

So, off we went into a crowded, noisy room where everyone seemed to know one another. We quickly separated as we greeted others. I saw that Aunt Julia's friend, Carmen, was overwhelmed with her duties, so I offered to help pour punch so she could replenish the food.

"I'll have some that," a familiar voice said.

I looked up to see Ted.

"Hi Ted," I said, handing him a cup of punch.

"It's good to see you among friends, Anne," Ted said with a smile.

I nodded.

"I'm pretty happy for Aunt Julia and Sarah," I shared, looking at them assisting customers. "I miss Gayle from the glass shop, but who knew I would be having relatives running a shop right next door to me?"

"Life is full of surprises and disappointments. I've had both, just like everyone else."

I didn't respond.

"Take note that I am drinking punch!" He held it up like he was going to make a toast.

"It's quite good but it's not as popular as the wine bar over there," I said, smiling. "Did you notice the bartender?"

"Yeah, I was surprised to see Jim here at all!" Ted said as he took a sip of punch.

"It's nice for Sarah to have her father involved. She seems to be having a great time with all her friends. Let's see if she can convince them to buy something!"

Ted laughed. "This might not be the appropriate time to ask you, Anne, but do you plan to continue living on the Lincoln hill?"

"Oh yes, indeed I will," I answered firmly. "Sam and I had many plans for the place and I simply love it too much to leave. You're not the first one to ask, so don't feel badly. By the way, how do you like your new office expansion?"

"We like it a lot," he said, perking up. "I wish we would have gone bigger. We filled up that space rather quickly."

"I understand, believe me," I acknowledged.

Sue joined us.

"Hello, Sue," Ted greeted her. "How's that new little guy doing that you just brought home?"

"He's doing great," Sue reported. "He's such a mild mannered baby compared to Mia when I got her home. She certainly rules the roost as the big sister."

We both laughed.

"Anne, I will have to leave soon," Sue reminded me. "I have some things to take over to the shop, but you can stay longer if you like."

"Oh no, I need to leave too. Plus, I need to talk to you alone before you go home," I said, putting down the punch ladle.

"Good to see you both," Ted said graciously. "Take good care of one another!"

He said it so nicely, unlike the sarcastic tone he had used during some of our previous encounters.

We both said our good-byes to Aunt Julia, Uncle Jim,

and Sarah before we went out the door.

"Let's sit on the bench in front of my shop, Sue," I suggested.

"That's fine," she agreed. "Let me take this food into the shop first."

I sat on the bench and watched many happy people leave the party. Some were carrying packages, which was a good sign for the potential success of the new business.

"Now, what's on your mind, Anne?" Sue asked, sitting next to me.

I took a deep breath. "I went to hear Sam's will read recently and I was pleasantly surprised at how well he planned for my future."

She gave me a big smile.

"Long story short, Sue, is that Sam was always concerned about how you would be able to provide an education for your little ones. Since we don't have any children, he often said to me that we would make sure they would be provided for."

Sue looked shocked.

"I want you to know I am setting up a trust fund for them so you don't have to worry about their education."

"Oh, Anne," she said, surprised. "That isn't necessary. It's way too much to accept."

"It was his wish and it is as good as done," I stated firmly. "I want to do this!"

Sue broke into tears. "Sam was such an amazing man," she managed through her tears. "He was so good to everyone and I can't even thank him or give him a big hug."

I joined her in tears. "You can hug me," I teased. "We will tell Mia and Eli about their Uncle Sam someday.

Remember how Mia would go running to him when she saw him? He loved children."

She nodded.

I couldn't help but think that Sam was watching.

CHAPTER 61

On the way home, I realized Mother and Harry were not at Aunt Julia's reception. That was not a good sign. I reached for my cell to call them.

"Hey, you guys," I greeted them cheerfully. "I thought I'd see you tonight at Aunt Julia's open house."

"Well, we've had other things on our minds," Mother said with a serious tone. "I sent her flowers. Did she have a good turnout?"

"Yes, it was packed. Do you mind if I stop by before I go home?"

"I suppose," she said, hesitantly.

"I don't need to if this is a bad time. I just wondered if you had anything new to report on Harry's condition."

"I was going to call you tomorrow, so stop by if you like."

"I won't stay long. I promise. Will Harry mind?"

"No, of course not," she replied. "He's on the couch watching TV in the living room."

Her tone in our conversation didn't sound good. It wasn't long before I pulled into their driveway and made my way to the door. As always, Mother greeted me with a big hug when I walked in.

"I'm so glad you were there for Julia and Sarah," she said as soon as I got in the door. "Come on in the living room."

"Hey there, Anne," Harry said with a big smile. "Have a seat!"

Mother turned off the TV as I gave Harry a hug.

"So tell us about the big event." Mother lost no time in starting the conversation.

"Well, Sue and I went together and we really didn't stay that long. She had a babysitter, so she was a little anxious about being away for too long. If I knew the two of you were not coming, I would have brought you some food."

"Now that would have been a good idea!" Harry teased.

"It was beautifully done and I saw folks leaving with bags, so that's a good thing."

"Anne always says that the highest form of flattery is a purchase," Mother told Harry. He laughed and I nodded in agreement.

"Now, I want to know what's going on with you, Harry," I said, looking directly at him. There was a bit of silence. "Did you get further test results?"

"Yes we did, Anne, and one of my lungs is in pretty bad shape," Harry said very clearly as he looked at Mother.

"The worst of it is that the biopsy results were cancerous," Mother confided in a weak voice. "They seem to think it is all in just the one lung, but there are no guarantees until they go in to see."

It was devastating news, but I chose to remain strong for them. I remained silent until she finished.

"They want to remove that lung," Mother finally said.

"I told your Mother that lots of folks live perfectly fine with one lung," Harry commented.

Mother looked so sad.

"I have heard that as well," I replied, trying to comfort them. "I sure hate to hear that. Is there any urgency with the surgery?"

"Doesn't seem to be," Harry said, shaking his head. "It's been in my lungs for quite some time. The cough is gradually getting worse, which is the most aggravating part of it. I certainly have no pain. The cough gets on your Mother's nerves, I can tell you that."

"Oh, Harry, I just tease you, that's all," Mother quipped.

"So you haven't decided when to have the surgery?" I asked, looking at each of them.

"No, we're working on that," Harry said, getting off the couch. "You want some coffee, Anne?"

"No thanks, Harry," I said, looking at Mother. "Well, it sounds like they will be able to fix it," I stated, wanting to keep the conversation as positive as possible. "Is everything else okay with your health, Harry? Like your blood pressure?"

"I'm lucky there, but can't say I'm fit as a fiddle," he joked.

Mother snickered.

I stayed another half hour as they began to ask me about my adjustments in life. I tried to reassure them that Ella and I would be there to help in any way we could.

As we walked to the front door, Mother asked, "Did

you get all your thank you cards written?"

"They are still stacked on my writing desk, but I will get to them soon." I answered like a little child. "Not to worry!"

When I got in the car, I had to smile at how mothers never really change. That was so her to ask about her daughter's proper responsibilities.

Things were pretty quiet when I got home. Ella had likely been asleep for some time. Getting undressed for bed, I once again felt the horrible pang of missing Sam. It seemed like only yesterday that we had our last moments together. I wanted to keep going over and over them so I would never forget. That whole day had been good for Sam. He had a great day playing golf with Uncle Jim followed by my home-cooked meal on the patio. It was so pleasant and I don't even remember us mentioning Martingale the whole time. We then managed to reconnect romantically, a part of our lives that had been missing for some time. Little did I know it was going to be our last intimate time together. I grabbed his pillow and my lily quilt to sob myself asleep once again.

CHAPTER 62

The ringing from the landline phone on the bedside table woke me the next morning. I no longer had nature's clock to wake me now that Sam was gone. Since his death, I wanted to continue sleeping as a way of avoiding life without him.

"Are you awake?" It was Nancy.

I grunted.

"I know, I know, there's nothing worse than an early-rising new mother to call you at the crack of dawn. If I can't sleep, no one else should either!"

"Well, you must have something on your mind," I finally said.

"Aren't you Miss Sunshine!" she teased. "Are you still in bed? I thought you may be walking!"

"No, I'm still under my covers!"

"How about coming over for lunch today to catch up?"

she suggested. "I couldn't make it to Julia's opening, plus I've just been worried about how you are doing."

"Oh, I have no idea what the shop has in store today," I grumpily explained.

"My little Barrister twins here need to know who this Miss Anne is," she teased. "It's been way too long since we've talked, and besides, that's what you have Sally for at the shop. You are the boss, remember?"

"You're right," I said yawning. "I'll do my best, but don't be disappointed if I have to cancel."

"Deal," she said before we hung up.

Part of my day's plan was to get together with Kip. He was anxious to get started and we needed to get organized. I wanted to give him a key to the Brody place. We needed to look around and see if the house would be suitable for him to use as a temporary office. It could be renovated later. He would need a place to work from immediately. Having lunch over baby talk was not what I had in mind today, but I did miss Nancy and was anxious to tell her about my plans.

I was too tired to walk. I wanted to turn over and sleep for another hour or so. This just wasn't me, but many people had told me that feeling sad over Sam's death would make me tired and listless. They were so right. It was hard to think of anything exciting enough to get me out of bed. However, it was impossible to go back to sleep with the arrival of the lawn mower and weed eater outside my window.

I reluctantly got up, showered, and dressed for the day. I glanced at my notebook full of plans lying near my bed and was surprised at how many pages I filled. This had to go with me today, in case I could meet with Kip. Now I was set for coffee.

"I just don't understand these lilies, Anne," Ella complained as she poured my coffee. "They are fresh as can be! It makes me right nervous!"

"Just take them to my bedroom today, Ella," I instructed. "I think we have looked at them here long enough."

"Can I make you a pancake or two this morning, Anne?" Ella suggested. "I made myself a couple and they tasted really good."

"Oh no, Ella," I said, glancing at the newspaper's morning headlines.

There it was: *Lance Martingale Charged with Alleged Tax Evasion and Embezzlement.* Sam's worst prediction was coming true. I didn't want to read any further. I was done with Martingale.

"What do you make of that?" Ella said, looking over my shoulder.

"Sam warned me this could happen," I said, feeling nauseous. "I do hope, for the sake of other innocent employees there, that the company can survive all of this. Who cares if Mr. Martingale survives?"

"Such a shame," Ella said, turning back to the stove.

"On a much brighter note, I hope to see Nancy and the babies today at lunch."

"That will be special," Ella cheerfully said. "The little ones grow so quickly. You might want to take them a little something."

"Really, like what?" I asked innocently. "They have everything under the sun times two!"

She laughed. "You'll think of something, but it would be the proper thing to do."

Yes, I had another mother under my roof!

"Okay, I'm off," I said, taking my notebook.

"Will you be home for dinner?"

"I'm not sure," I answered. "You'd better not count on me."

Driving down Main Street was always comforting to me. It had good caring people who worked so hard for very little money. I passed Phil pulling out some of his wilted flowers and replacing them with mums. Kevin would be doing that soon with our flower boxes in front of the shop. Mums and cabbages were usually what we put in the flower boxes each fall.

Aunt Julia was sweeping her sidewalk when I pulled up in front of my shop to park. It was my habit to park in front when I had errands to run during the day.

"So, were you pretty happy with the party results?" I asked as I got out of the car.

"Oh yes, I am," she said right away. "I really didn't know what to expect, but I am actually reordering some of the items today that I sold out of that night."

"That's great! Did you have to stay very late?"

"Not really," she said. "Jim was nice enough to stay and help us clean up. Can you believe it?"

"I can believe it," I said. "Uncle Jim is a very good guy or you would not have married him in the first place!"

She blushed. "Okay, he's nice, but don't go there, Anne," she warned. "We are doing well as friends, but that's where it's going to stay."

I laughed as I made my way into my shop.

I told Sally that if she saw Kip, I wanted to talk with him. I also told him that if time allowed, I wanted to go to Nancy's for lunch.

She seemed to be happy that I was getting back to my busy self!

"You need your friends at a time like this, Anne," she said, unpacking some garden books.

"What's this?" I asked, picking up what looked like a children's book.

"Oh, it's so cute! Wait until you see this," Sally said with excitement. "It's a pick-and-smell flower book for kids. Look, it shows the flower and what it's named and then you're supposed to smell this center. It really does smell like the flower, see?"

"You've got to be kidding!" I said, reaching for the book to try it for myself. She was right!

"There are different ones that come three to a package," she described. "I thought we could sell them separately and they would fly right off the shelf here at the counter."

"This is just what I need to take to Nancy's babies. It may be a tad too old for them, but Nancy will think it's adorable!"

"Sold!" Sally shouted. "I'll bag it for you and put it on your house charge!"

CHAPTER 63

When Kevin told me Kip would not be in to help him today, I decided to call him on his cell phone. It was my goal to examine the Brody property with Kip today.

"Where are you?" I asked impatiently.

"I'm taking care of my personal business so I can get started working for Dickson Properties," he said.

How strange to hear Dickson Properties from someone else. I realized that I had a one-track-mind about moving my goals along and had neglected to consider Kip needing to turn down his previous job offer. I changed my tone to a friendlier one.

"Great. Good thinking. Do you think you can meet me at my house to check out the condition of the Brody house so we can set up something quickly for you?"

"If we can do it in the next couple of hours that would work out fine. I've got plans this afternoon, though."

"Sure, I'll just have to cancel a lunch that can wait, so I'll just meet you at the Brody house in half an hour, okay?"

"Sounds good," he agreed.

As I picked up my phone to call Nancy, Kevin knocked at my office door.

"Got a minute?" Kevin asked.

I nodded.

"Kip filled me in on your plans for him and it was a shocker. This is a pretty big deal and he's really excited."

"Yes, it is really exciting, but can you put off telling anyone just yet, Kevin?"

"No problem," he assured me. "Kip has already told me to keep it quiet. My concern is about what to do here at the shop. Kip said he is starting the new job immediately."

"Yes, I'd like him to be able to start the job now, but if you still need him here, he can stay until we find someone." I explained. "Do you have anyone in mind to replace him?"

"No, not really, but frankly, Anne, it is not much of a part-time job to offer anyone. Kip was mostly busy at your house rather than here, so I figure I can probably try to handle this all by myself again, if you'll be patient with me as I try to work it out."

"That would be wonderful, Kevin," I responded, taking a deep sigh of relief. "I will bump up your salary."

"*That* I will not object to," he teased. "Kip said that as you get set up over there, he might be able to hire me."

"I am counting on it, Kevin," I said, smiling. "There will be a need to build, rehab, and of course there will be things to grow, so I think it will be a good opportunity for both of you. I am so glad I didn't lose Kip to his other offer."

"Sam would be popping with pride at what you're doing, Anne," Kevin bragged. "You are moving forward with a dream that you both had. You won't be alone. There are folks like us who are willing to help you. You are always looking at the bigger picture, which is what I admire most about you."

"Stop trying to butter me up," I joked. "You need to start looking for a replacement for you right away. I don't think this development will be as easy as you may think."

"Right as always," he said, saluting me before closing the door.

I called Nancy and she was disappointed about my canceling our lunch. We arranged to do it the next day. She said her pasta salad and chocolate mousse would keep just fine. I checked in with Sally who was meeting with a bridal client to tell her I was leaving for part of the day. Jean said they were caught up on orders and advised me that there was no need to hurry back.

"Call me if anything breaks loose," I instructed.

When I pulled in the Brody drive from Lincoln hill, I saw Kip's pickup truck. He was walking around the property.

"It sure doesn't take long for something vacant to go downhill, does it?" Kip remarked. "I am surprised at the condition of things up here."

I got the key and opened the stuffy, empty house. It felt very strange. No one had done any cleaning after the furniture had been removed. "Sam told them to keep the water and electricity on, so I hope that's the case."

Kip went to the kitchen faucet, and after some gargling noises, water came out. He flipped on the light switch which brought to life a single bulb in the ceiling. We opened the windows, eager for fresh air. The dust was heavy on the few objects left behind.

"They lived pretty primitively," I informed Kip. "They may have had money, but nothing had ever been put back into the property for some time. To be honest, Mrs. Brody wasn't up to doing it or even caring whether it was done. I think Sam said the house was built in the 1940s and it probably has stood still in time from the 1950s if I had to guess."

"I wonder how she could've lived like this," Kip said aloud as he went to the back bedroom. "I think this room facing the back of the property would be a good place for me to set up my desk and I can hook into your Wi-Fi from next door for now. I know a couple of guys I can call to get this all cleaned up. The stuff left behind here should be trashed, would you agree?"

"I suppose, but be observant," I cautioned him as I looked into the kitchen.

I spied a soiled red and white checked apron trimmed with blue rickrack that was tied to the side towel rack off the kitchen sink. Surely this belonged to Mrs. Brody. I untied the faded apron and decided to take it home and wash it. It would be a nice remembrance of her.

Kip watched me and smiled.

For the next hour, we walked around the property. We checked out the barn. Kip seemed to be more excited about some of the things left in the barn than anything else. There was no doubt I had the right person for this job. I could see the wheels turning as he shared ideas along the way. He would treat this project as his own and that was what I needed.

There was still ample time for me to go back to work, but I was emotionally and physically drained, so I decided to go home. When I got to the house, I sat down on the south porch for a moment. I looked at Sam's gazebo across the driveway and felt I needed to talk to him.

"I took a big step today," I said aloud to Sam as if he were with me on the porch. "I am going with my heart and gut, just like you did many times. I want you to be proud of me, Sam."

ANN HAZELWOOD

Ella opened the front door.

"Oh, Anne, it's you. I thought I heard someone out here," Ella said, looking at me for an explanation. "Are you okay?"

I was silent for a moment. "Yes, I think I'm just tired from the day. I just left the Brody property next door. Kip and I went over there to check it out."

She did not move from the doorway. "You have so much on your mind, honey," she said, shaking her head in sympathy. "You just sit here for a bit. I'll get you a nice glass of iced tea."

I nodded. I did have a lot on my mind. Grieving over Sam was overwhelming and I wasn't certain when or if it would subside. It was no wonder I was tired and wanted to crawl under the covers at any given time. I went over to the wicker lounge chair and decided that a ten-minute nap wouldn't hurt a thing.

CHAPTER 64

After a good night's sleep, I told Ella I was up for my morning walk. The early fall air made it necessary for me to wear a light sweater. I decided to walk in the neighborhood on Lincoln hill because I had another purpose in mind in addition to getting some exercise. I was pleasantly surprised to find Kip's truck parked at the Brody house at such an early hour. He had two young men with him that were loading debris onto the back of his truck. It was exciting to see things happening so quickly. I waved hello and continued on down the hill to Lincoln Street. Going down the hill worked up energy and my mind moved to planning my day. I would make sure I had lunch with Nancy as planned.

Going back up was more of a challenge today. What was the matter with me? At one point, I became lightheaded and stopped to rest under one of the spindly redbud trees. I had mastered this hill many, many times. I got up to the top, took a deep breath, and continued on. I supported myself by hanging onto branches, just as I did when snow and ice made the walk more challenging last winter. Thank goodness no one was watching my unusual behavior. When I got to the house, I headed straight to the shower.

I stopped at Starbucks to get my favorite coffee and a berry muffin, which sounded appetizing for a change. I suppose I had worked up an appetite. As I nibbled and drove, I regained some energy.

There was a note to call Mother when I got to the shop as well as a reporter's name from the local Colebridge newspaper. I was done with Martingale and refused to lengthen their story by any of my comments. I went into my office and made the call to Mother.

"Harry's surgery is scheduled for next week," She began. "I thought you'd want to know. I wish I was as courageous as he is."

"I know you're worried, Mother, but the good thing is that Harry is in good physical condition," I reminded her. "I am happy to go with you if you'd like me to. Just let me know the details."

"Oh, Anne, you are too busy to take time out for this."

"I am never too busy for you, Mother. You know that," I encouraged her. "I have a feeling Ella will want to be there as well."

After we hung up, I felt like it was what she wanted to hear from me. She had no idea that I truly had become busier. I knew my plans would bring additional worry to her, so it could wait until this crisis with Harry subsided. In the back of my mind, I couldn't help but worry about the seriousness of Harry's surgery.

I helped Sally and Jean unload some merchandise that had just arrived. I missed doing the ordering for the coming seasons. It was like Christmas when we opened the boxes since things were ordered so far ahead of time. The shop was decorated for fall and Halloween, thanks to Abbey and her unique taste. Halloween was becoming a bigger holiday as each year passed, which meant we were doing arrangements for parties and home decorating. I cautioned them both not to ignore any customers as they engaged in unwrapping and preparing displays. It seemed easy for an employee to think they were busy working diligently with such duties when it was really the customer about to make a purchase that really mattered.

I found the children's flower books to take to Nancy's house and headed out the door. Nancy's house was a showstopper for anyone driving down Jefferson Street. It looked so beautiful with a multitude of mums planted around a gothic statue in the front yard. The gardens surrounding her house were also breathtaking. She obviously had someone that was taking good care of things outdoors. The castle-like structure was exquisitely decorated yet comfortable, but it was not my taste. All and all, it was a house to be admired.

Nancy greeted me at the door with Amy straddled on her hip and Andrew screaming from his high chair.

"Hey, girlfriend, good to see you!" she said with excitement. "Don't panic about the fussy babies. They are about to go down for a nap, but I wanted you to see them first."

"My goodness, they're growing so fast!" I said as Nancy passed Amy to me. She was chunky and weighed more than I thought. "You look just like your daddy!"

She smiled and put her wet hand over my mouth.

"Oh dear, they are both teething, so you're liable to get slobbered on," Nancy warned. "Come on in the kitchen and say hello to Mr. Andrew." He continued screaming, seemingly wanting out of his high chair. He paid no attention to my greeting.

Nancy took Amy from me and sat her on the floor. She pulled Andrew from his chair and placed the now-content baby beside his sister. It was only seconds before they took off crawling.

"No one is walking yet, but Amy has made some attempts to pull herself up. She will be the first one to walk, I'm sure."

"Nancy, how do you do everything with two of them?" I asked. "I'm exhausted just watching you." I found a tissue to wipe my mouth and cheek which was still wet from Amy.

"You get used to it really fast because you have to," she said with a laugh. "Every time I get frustrated, I remind myself how much and how long I waited for these cutie pies!" She grinned. "I don't have to go to the gym to work out, that's for sure. I don't know how long I can carry both of them up the stairs, especially as active as they are. Go into the living room and have a seat while I take them up for their naps.

There was reluctance from them both as Nancy expected, but they knew the routine.

I sat down on a velvet upholstered chair. The elegant furnishings were over the top for this Victorian-style house. I had to chuckle as I saw toys nestled here and there on the floor among the formal furniture. Slowly, the twins were taking over the house. I was so proud of Nancy as she took all of the changes parenthood brought in stride.

CHAPTER 65

I have everything ready for us in the dining room, Anne," Nancy announced when she came down the stairs. At the end of her long Victorian dining room table was a cozy lunch for two. She had arranged her fine china on white lace placemats. One would expect a uniformed maid to pop out at any moment to wait on us!

"I almost asked Sue to join us today, but on Tuesdays, she has a grieving group that meets," she explained. "It is on a set schedule, so she can't change it. Folks love her so much. Now that we have nursery services for our employees, she is more available for these things."

"I am so happy that is working out," I said, intrigued at the thought. "Do I belong in a grieving group?"

"Grief is a difficult thing for most people, Anne. Most of the members of this particular group are elderly widows who have no family or have limited activities in their lives. They have lost their spouses after a lifetime of being together and their children are usually not here or are not very available to them after the funeral. You have a wonderful support system of friends and family, Anne. We are all willing to help you with anything you need."

How heartbreaking for those women. It had to be so hard for them.

"So, what does Sue do for them?"

"She listens. That's number one," Nancy explained. "They know how sincerely caring she is about how they are doing and she gets them to have a little enjoyment with other folks like themselves. Sometimes they feel guilty about just enjoying life again. And, they love it when she brings in Mia and Eli to say hello. She has even gotten a couple of them to help her sew the baby funeral quilts. Sue doesn't have the extra time like she did before, especially after adding Eli to her family."

"That Eli is so adorable with those dark eyes, isn't he?" I smiled, recalling Sue's beautiful children.

"They both are," Nancy said. "We are so lucky to have her working for us. Her children are becoming friends with mine in our nursery."

"This looks delicious," I exclaimed, turning my attention to the pasta salad and turkey croissant sandwich.

As she poured iced tea in our glasses, a hint of a grin appeared when she mentioned, "I suppose you still have lots of lemonade at your house."

"Pretty funny, Nancy," I responded, a smile stretching across my face. "Yes, and lilies that have remained fresh since Sam died."

"No kidding?" she said, sitting down. "Oh, Anne, when I think about all you've been through, I can't believe it!"

The conversation had transitioned quickly. Although I had lots I could say about my feelings, I didn't want the lunch to turn into a pity party, so I told her about Harry needing surgery. After a while, I announced my plans for the Brody property. I thought she was going to fall off of her chair.

"You and Sam had discussed these plans before?" she asked in amazement.

"It was just talk, of course, but then he got so wrapped up in the Martingale investigation," I explained as my stomach started to churn. "I had my hands full just keeping Sam from getting totally stressed out over it. One heart attack surely sent a message, so it was on my mind constantly."

As she listened, Nancy's eyes filled with tears. It was comforting to me to share these details with my closest friend. She really understood.

"You never shared a lot of those details, but it certainly took a lot of courage to do what Sam did, Anne. He could have turned the other way and continued with business as usual, but Sam was too honest to do that."

"Yes, and it cost him his life!" I stated more strongly than I meant. I nearly broke into a sob, but managed to swallow what welled up inside.

"Oh dear, I really didn't mean to upset you, Anne," she said apologetically. "I wanted us to have a nice visit and provide a needed break for you. Please try the pasta salad. I tried a new recipe with some fresh herbs." She was trying her best to change the subject. "You have herbs growing in your garden, don't you?"

"Yes," I said trying to gain control. I willed myself to go with the distraction Nancy offered. "I enjoy using different mints for tea and such, but you know I was not the cook that Sam was." What was I doing? I had to bring up his name again.

I finally tasted a bit of the pasta.

"I think it's very healthy for you to talk about Sam," Nancy said as if she knew what I was thinking. "He was a great cook and you have a kitchen that every cook in the world would envy."

"Yes and at least now Ella gets to enjoy it. Maybe I'll get interested in cooking someday."

"It's working out okay with Ella?" Nancy inquired.

I nodded. "She is quite sweet and has become part of the family," I answered. "The house is big enough that I don't feel she needs my attention. She has her own quarters and likes her privacy. It has been a good solution for both of us. She has a tendency to want to mother me, which is understandable."

"So this Kip, whom I have not met, is going to take charge of the whole huge project for you?" Nancy asked, coming back to the Brody subject.

I smiled and nodded. "Yes, he's a very talented young man," I bragged. "He has worked at the shop and our place as well. He's the one who designed and built our patio room that we just finished. He will blossom with this kind of project. I'm looking for a new delivery guy so that Kip can hire Kevin to help him with some of the work."

"Kip is a single man, I take it?" she asked.

"Yes, and an attractive one at that," I added. "He sang and played his guitar at Sam's birthday barbeque one year and made all the women swoon.

We laughed.

"He has many talents, but mostly, I feel I can trust both Kip and Kevin, which means a lot going into this. My Brown's Botanical team is like family. They are all good people that I trust."

"You are amazing, Anne," Nancy said, sipping her tea. "As

an employer, you certainly have a knack when it comes to placing your employees in the jobs they can do best. Not everyone can do that. You are also lucky to have this to think about right now. It serves as a nice diversion."

"Well, you did the same by placing Sue with your grieving clients," I noted. "It's a win-win when that happens."

She nodded. "You're not eating very much," Nancy observed.

"It's very good," I said to make her feel better. I took a deep breath and took another bite.

She brought out crystal goblets of chocolate mousse topped with whipped cream and chocolate shavings on the top. How could anything look so delicious and yet be the last thing I wanted to eat? If I refused this delightful treat, Nancy will worry about me for sure.

CHAPTER 66

Y ou always said, 'If it isn't chocolate, it isn't dessert,'
right?" Nancy quoted.

I smiled in agreement.

"How is Sam's mother doing? Do you hear from her
very much?"

"I've just had one phone call from her since the funeral,"
I answered. "I should call her. Mother has called her. They
certainly get along well. I hope she, Elaine, and Pat will feel
free to visit any time."

Nancy watched as I looked at the goblet of mousse. I
wasn't taking bites like she was. I was afraid if I took a bite I
would have to excuse myself. I just didn't feel like eating.

"Is it something I said or did?" Nancy said, looking at
me strangely.

"It looks so good, Nancy, but I just can't eat another
bite," I confessed, looking at the goblet like it presented an

impossible task.

"I wasn't going to say anything, but you look like you have lost weight since the funeral," she said, concerned.

I paused. "Yes, I have," I said, not knowing whether I should tell her everything. "I just have no appetite. I had no idea Sam's death would affect me physically as well as emotionally."

She continued to listen.

"I get nauseous at times, especially when I think about him. Ella thinks I'm going to die from starvation and I'm always tired. I can hardly get through the day sometimes. The other morning, I couldn't make it up Lincoln hill without sitting down. I felt so lightheaded. I used to fly up that hill— breathing heavy, yes, but not needing to stop and rest. This has to go away. I have to get back to my normal life."

"Well, depression can certainly cause all of those symptoms," she said cautiously.

"I don't think I'm depressed, Nancy," I stated, choosing my words carefully. "I am devastated over losing Sam, but I am functioning and even planning for my future. I am sad, but I don't think I am clinically depressed."

Nancy looked me over carefully before she ventured, "You couldn't possibly be pregnant could you, Anne?"

"That's not funny, Nancy," I said, feeling frustrated with her. "My husband is dead, in case you haven't noticed." Again, my strong response surprised even me.

"Wait a minute. Don't get so testy," she said, not at all slowed by my protests. "Sam has not been gone that long. When was the last time the two of you were together? Were you still on the pill?"

I was becoming impatient with her remarks. "Well, if

you must know, I did stop taking the pill because one day I forgot to take it," I began to explain. "I kept telling Sam I would come off of it soon, anyway. Plus, there didn't seem to be any concern because Sam certainly hadn't been in the mood for any romance. I understood all the pressure he was under. Half the time, he was working late at night and he would be gone when I woke up in the morning." I couldn't believe I was sharing this all with her.

"And what about the other half of the time?" she asked, her expression serious.

Where is she going with this?

"So you were not intimate with each other in the last couple of months?"

"Not to speak of, so don't make me feel any worse than I do!" I said, wanting to get on my way.

She looked like she didn't believe me.

"You've not been pregnant, Anne, and I have," Nancy said clearly. "What you have described to me are symptoms of pregnancy. This is serious. You need to think this through. You need to see a doctor whether you're pregnant or not. This is not a healthy situation, girl! You surely can think of the last time you were together, can't you? I would think that night would have become a flashback in your mind after he died. I hate to be so blunt, Anne, but I'm your best friend and you are in the dark here!"

"I need to go, Nancy," I said, getting out of my chair. "This conversation is scaring me. I'm sorry."

"Please don't go, Anne," Nancy begged. "I'm sorry I upset you. I wanted this to be so pleasant for the two of us."

"Well, there's not much that's pleasant about my life right now." I headed toward the door. "I know you mean well, but I have to figure this all out."

"You know I'm here for you," she said, about to cry. "I love you. Please take care. Call me."

I couldn't get in my car fast enough. I couldn't believe she questioned me that way! It was painful to hear her suggest pregnancy. As I headed for home instead of to the shop, I felt myself shaking. The first thing I was going to do was check my calendar at home. I made assumptions about missing my cycle and feeling nauseous as being stress related. Why did Nancy scare me like that? She probably was right about one thing. I was going to need to see a doctor. I could not continue this unhealthy situation.

CHAPTER 67

To my relief, Ella's car was gone, leaving me alone with my thoughts. Nancy put the fear of God in me as she had all through school. She had always been outspoken and blunt. Typically, those were qualities I admired in her, but not today. Today had been painful.

I went upstairs to change out of my skirt and blouse and into my comfortable jeans and T-shirt. Feeling a tad more relaxed, I went into my office where I kept a calendar for my personal appointments and notes about when my cycle occurred. It had become less important in the last few months. The pill kept me regulated and the personal contact between Sam and me had become sporadic.

Nancy was right about one thing, however. I did vividly remember the last time Sam and I were together. Sam was his old self after he played that game of golf with Uncle Jim. The evening was so perfect that I wanted to play it over and over in my mind. I turned back the calendar a couple of months to find the date. It seemed so long ago, but it really wasn't. I could have gotten pregnant then. I hadn't even told Sam I had stopped taking the pill. It was my plan to surprise him with the news the next time he pestered me about it. Now I really did feel nauseous. The only way to settle this nightmare would be to go to the drug store and get a pregnancy test as I had done once before. I remember how relieved I was that it indicated I was not pregnant. What did I want this test to say? I grabbed my purse and headed back down the stairs.

I chose to go to Walmart right outside of Colebridge instead of the local drug store where I could easily run into someone I knew. If someone saw me purchase a pregnancy test after my husband just passed away, I would be mortified.

I couldn't find the same product I had purchased before, but I did find one that looked reliable and easy. I chose a few other health and beauty items so it made the test appear less obvious, at least to me. I chose a check-out lane that had a short line. A young man I did not know was running the cash register. So far, I didn't see a soul I knew, but I waited rather nervously anyway. Once it was my turn, I engaged him in conversation about the weather so he wouldn't notice what I was purchasing. I paid with cash so I wouldn't get caught up waiting for a charge approval. Finally, I made it out of the store and back into my car. Why did I have to be so sneaky about this? I knew the answer. I lived in a small town and I was a widow being observed. That may not have been the case in reality, but I sure did not want to take the risk of someone I knew seeing me purchase that test.

Going home, I tried to breathe deeply. Whatever the outcome, I told myself I would deal with it. When I arrived at the house, Ella's car was still gone. I ran up the stairs, taking two steps at a time. I tore the package open and quickly scanned the instructions. This was not going to turn different colors. This test would say either pregnant or not pregnant. That worked just fine for me.

Before I would look at the results, I would say a prayer. Sam was not here to help me through this, but God was always with me. I asked him to give me strength to accept the results as I went to the master bathroom and waited.

There it was. Pregnant. A secret feeling of joy wanted to explode in me, but then I decided to look over the instructions again. It told me it had a high percentage of accuracy. I sat on the floor and cried. How could this be—and why now?

"Sam, Sam, I am pregnant," I announced to the air as if he could hear. "You have to know, you have to know." I cried out loud, begging for him to hear me. I cried until there were no more tears. How many times would I cry until I thought there were no more tears?

This cannot be a horrible joke. These tests were not 100% accurate! Sam wanted children so badly and I kept putting him off until I felt the time was right. What kind of wife was I? I put my hands on my stomach and felt comfort knowing part of Sam was still alive. Alive in me! Did he know he was leaving me with this gift? Was this supposed to be punishment for denying him fatherhood when he was here? No, no, Sam's baby would be the joy of my life and I would make sure he knew all about his or her father. I got myself off the floor and moved over to my bed. I reached for the lily quilt only to begin crying all over again.

CHAPTER 68

Someone knocking at my door jarred me into the present. "Anne, Anne, are you alright?" It was Ella.

I tried to gain my senses, feeling very groggy from so much crying. Perhaps the pregnancy test was all a nightmare of some kind.

"I'm okay, Ella. I just fell asleep," I said, surprised that darkness had fallen. "I'll be down soon." I heard her leave without a reply.

I looked at the clock. It was after seven. I had been asleep for hours. No wonder she was checking on me at this odd time of the evening. I turned on the light and reviewed what had just taken place. I got out of bed to once again read the message on my test. I am pregnant. I am a pregnant widow. This would not be easy. I wouldn't tell anyone until I had it confirmed by a doctor. I certainly didn't want to be wrong about this! I didn't know an obstetrician. Nancy was the only person I knew that used one here in town and she bragged about him. Should I tell her the results of the test?

I went in to take a shower before I came down to the kitchen. I put on my robe, knowing I was heading back to bed very shortly.

Ella heard me and joined me as I came down the stairs. "Honey, are you okay?"

"Yes, I had an exhausting day and I came home to crash," I explained. "I can't believe I slept so long."

"I made that hot chicken salad you like so well. The one in the crescent rolls?" she described. "I can heat one of those up for you and make you a little salad."

"It does sound good, Ella, but forget the salad, please." I still felt so groggy.

Ella continued to tell me about her day, trying to engage me in conversation. She said she did some errands and then stopped by to see Mother and Harry. I kept nodding and smiling, but nothing was registering. As I took my first bite, I realized I could be eating for two. I had been practically starving myself in my self-pity, not knowing there was someone else to think about.

Finally, Ella left me alone in the kitchen so she could go up and watch one of her favorite TV shows. I wanted to pour myself a glass of merlot, but then I remembered Nancy saying she wasn't supposed to have alcohol while she was pregnant. Instead, I poured myself some lemonade. Were Grandmother Davis and Sam together and watching all of this play out?

The longer I sat, the more I began to realize that I could not do this alone. I was going to need Nancy's help. She brought me to face this reality and she deserved a response. I would have to trust her. She had never done anything in our past that would cause me to distrust her. She had been pregnant and knew what to do and when. She had the resources I didn't have and I wanted the best, just like she did when she came back to Colebridge. I was a strong, independent woman, but smart enough to know when things were not in my area of expertise. I had to ask for help sometimes in my business and even when running this house on Lincoln Street. Knowing Nancy, she was probably worried about how she had upset me. She never could stand it when things were not right between us and was usually the first one to apologize.

I went up to my bedroom to assure I had complete privacy and found my cell phone. I knew I would feel some sense of relief talking to someone. After several rings Richard picked up.

"Hi Richard. I'd like to talk to Nancy if she's not in the middle of something," I requested. Of course Nancy would be in the middle of something. What kind of remark was that?

"Hey, Anne. I heard you were here for lunch," he said cheerfully. "Sorry I missed you. Nancy's on the porch reading. I'll put her on the line."

"Thanks Richard," I said, not wanting to engage in conversation. Nancy had time to read? Who would have known that? It took a while for her to come to the phone. I hoped she wasn't angry with me.

"Anne, I'm glad you called," she said calmly. "Are you okay? I wanted to call you."

"I'm okay," I said in almost a whisper. "First, I want to apologize for leaving so rudely today." There was silence like she was waiting to hear more from me. "I...I...I didn't know who to call," I stuttered, wanting to cry all over again.

"Take your time. What are you trying to say, Anne?"

"You were right!"

CHAPTER 69

Nancy had the presence of mind to not say, "I told you so." She said very little. Something told me she was expecting my phone call. She remained calm about my news and suggested I get a good night's sleep. We agreed to meet in the morning. She said she would drop the twins off at the Barrister nursery and then come over to my house. I would think about how to handle Ella since I needed to have complete privacy regarding this matter. I didn't want to involve her or anyone else until I had seen a doctor. Nancy's admonition in telling me not to panic was helpful. I felt some sense of panic.

After I hung up, I think we both knew deep down that my pregnancy was certain. How could I be so naive? I rested my head on the headboard and thought about how this news would impact other people in my life.

Mother would be thrilled and yet worried about me.

She had her hands full now thinking about Harry, so my news could wait. Then there was Sam's mother, Helen. She could take this news in various ways, but in the long run, she would certainly be happy to have a grandchild from her only son. Who could not be happy with such news? My work family would burst with joy. How could we find a place to keep the little person if I brought him or her to work?

Would Ella be a possible nanny? Would she meet my standards for taking care of my baby? That was yet to be seen, but she'd be delighted to care for the baby, I felt sure. Would I be up to the job? Truly, motherhood had never been very high on my to-do list.

My thoughts were running rampant. What if the doctor said I had a virus instead of a baby? That would be a blow to accept. Viruses could be strange and might fit my symptoms. I told myself to think positively.

I was wide awake since I had slept all afternoon. I decided to make lists. That's what I did when I couldn't sleep and it would help organize my plans. I had jillions of questions I would need to know right away as far as pregnancy was concerned. How would this list affect my other pursuits like running my home, flower shop, writing a book, and developing Dickson Properties? If I could put all of this on paper, I could begin to plan my strategy. It may take a village, but I knew how to put a village together. I had pages and pages an hour or so later, all with different headings.

It seemed so cruel and sad that Sam would not be here with me through this. Sam would have been such a great father. I saw how patient and enthralled he was with cute little Mia. He would have adored a sweet little girl of his own. She would possibly have his dark hair and eyes. I could name her Samantha and call her Sammy. If Sam would have had a baby boy, he'd have burst at the seams. He would have played every sport with him! He would possibly be tall like Sam. If this baby turns out to be a boy, I could call him Samuel and still use Sammy as his nickname. This was Sam Dickson's child and I wanted everyone to know that. Well, that was easy. I guess one way or the other, I was about to have a baby named Sammy!

I couldn't fool myself into thinking that being a single mother would be easy. I knew Sue's struggle to accomplish all she needs to accomplish on a daily basis. Back to the gender—which would I prefer? Without hesitation, I would want a boy. He would best remind me of Sam. Oh, I wanted to plan it all, right here, tonight, on paper!

If Sam were watching me right now, he would laugh and make fun of me. Oh, how I wish he were here to share my tears and joy.

"I love you, Sam," I said aloud to his pillow beside me. "You must never, ever really leave me. Especially now!"

CHAPTER 70

I woke early with a lot on my mind. In the distance, I could hear that the outdoor activity had already begun. Had work on the Brody property gotten started? I felt lightheaded from jumping out of bed, but I knew it would pass. I went down to join Ella in the kitchen as she was organizing her cleaning supplies.

"You look rather chipper this morning, Anne! That's good to see!"

"I feel good," I said with a smile. "Nancy is coming over to discuss some things with me, so I thought I'd get some orange rolls out of the freezer to have on hand."

"I'd be happy to take care of that for you. I was just getting ready to clean the upstairs after you got up."

"I'll take care of the rolls, but I wonder if you could run a couple of errands for me this morning." I needed to get her out of the house.

"Just name it!" she said cheerfully.

"Since I may not be going to the shop until later today, I have some papers in the car that need to go to Sally at the shop," I explained. "On the way there, could you stop at the Brody house and give Kip a folder he is waiting for?"

"I think I can handle that," she agreed. "I can do a stop or two for myself on Main Street then."

After I put the rolls in the oven, I called Abbey to see if she could fill in for me. She was always happy to get in more hours at work and was indeed available to come in today.

It was a beautiful fall day, so I walked out to the south porch where the morning sun was shining and bright. It was a bit cool, but I thought Nancy and I could sit here more comfortably and visit.

A short time later, I was getting the rolls out of the oven when I heard Nancy drive up. I grabbed my hot cup of coffee and greeted her on the porch. She gave me a big hug.

"I guess it's too soon for us to do our happy dance?" I asked.

"I think we'd better wait a week or so, but I feel it coming on," she teased. "It's lovely out here, isn't it?"

"Yes, thought we could sit out here," I suggested. "I have hot coffee and rolls I'll bring out. Ella is out running errands."

"Great. Need help? I need that coffee desperately!"

"No, just give me a few seconds," I said, rushing into the house.

I put everything on a tray and headed to the porch. I placed the tray on the table and poured her a hot cup of coffee. I gave her a few seconds to take a couple of swallows before I began asking my list of questions. She looked at me as if she knew I had the floor.

"I really don't know where to start," I began. "The first concern is getting to see your Dr. Dietrich as soon as I can."

"I understand he is not taking any new patients, but I will call in a while after they open to see if they will agree to take you. He is so well loved by his patients and is very caring. He certainly had his hands full with me!" She smiled. I was pretty certain she was recalling the day the twins were born.

"I have to see someone soon, so could you request that?" Now that I had accepted the idea of being pregnant, I felt an enormous sense of urgency to do *something*.

"Well, aren't you the eager one!" she teased. "You've waited long enough to address your symptoms, so you'll just have to be a little more patient, Anne."

"I know, but along with being overjoyed, I am so scared, Nancy!" I said, gazing at Sam's gazebo. "I have to do this right. I've already starved the poor child by not eating."

She tried not to laugh. "What you are going through is perfectly normal. You are a healthy woman who walks every day, and once you are under a doctor's care with the proper vitamins and guidance, you'll do just fine."

We talked non-stop for another hour before she picked up the phone to call Dr. Dietrich's office. She danced around a delicate response from the receptionist, who happened to be a friend of hers. She used all her excellent communication skills and had me booked the next day due to someone's cancellation. I marveled at her ability to get what she wanted. That was Nancy, and it had been that way as long as I had known her! Needless to say, I was relieved and felt the first major thing on my list was done.

Just as she was getting ready to leave, Ella arrived. She had to have an update on the twins. Nancy was happy to report little anecdotes of their activities.

"Kip would like to you stop by as soon as you can today," Ella reported. "My goodness! Things are changing over there pretty quickly!"

I hugged Nancy good-bye and said I would call her first thing the next day. Ella told Nancy she wanted her to bring the twins during her next visit and Nancy agreed.

"I think I'll go see Kip in a little bit," I told Ella. "I'd better check on the potting shed first. I think Kip has been too busy to check on things in there."

"You need some help?" Ella offered.

"No thanks," I said, appreciative of her desire to help me. "You do such a great job keeping the house and patio plants in good shape. The least I can do is take care of my little potting shed."

She smiled.

I walked over to the shed to make sure there was room to bring in some of the smaller plants for the winter. I hated to see the summer foliage turn. Leaves were already blowing in the wind. I reminded myself that the larger green plants from Sam's funeral would have to be brought into the sunporch for the winter. Before I headed over to see Kip, I trimmed off some of the herbs, which never seemed to stop growing. Ella especially enjoyed the chocolate mint for her tea.

When I arrived at the Brody house, I saw a young man painting the ceilings of the house that was now virtually empty.

"Good morning," he said in a friendly manner. "Kip is

in the barn. Are you Mrs. Dickson?"

"I am, but call me Anne."

"Jeff Clifton. Pleased to meet you. Kip's a friend of mine."

I nodded. "You're doing a good job here!" I observed. "It's amazing what a little paint can do! I'm going to go on up to the barn to see Kip. It is so nice to meet you."

I was glad to get away from the smell of paint. It was starting to have an effect on me like potpourri always did. I found Kip in the barn covered in dirt from head to toe as he sorted out things that were left behind. He was trying to sort the items into piles. After teasing him a bit about being a frustrated farmer, he said he had to show me some things in the office that needed my approval.

Once we were in the office, he washed up a bit and showed me styles of greenhouses that could be purchased as kits. I couldn't believe it. He wanted to get them ordered as soon as possible.

"We can get these up by November so you can get seedlings planted and ready for spring!" he reported. "I'm anxious to have Kevin supervise the greenhouse's construction and later what goes in them, so I hope you get a replacement for him soon!"

I nodded and hated the thought of Kevin leaving the flower shop, even though it was my idea. We had become such a close-knit staff. Any change would be a fairly big adjustment. Well, change was inevitable and it would be a wonderful project for Kevin.

"I seriously cannot believe this is all happening so quickly!" I gasped. "I say to get going with the styles we discussed and move forward!"

"I have someone coming in to grade our road today," he continued. "We will have to make do with gravel at first. Then maybe next summer, we can add blacktop." I nodded and marveled at his enthusiasm. "Since I have your attention, another decision is whether you are still serious about using the four acres to the north for lilies."

"Oh yes!" I had almost forgotten about making the suggestion to Kip in an earlier conversation.

"Well, we will need some extra labor to clear all of that so we can get these bulbs in soon. I need your selections on varieties so that they can be ordered and are here by the time the ground is ready."

"Okay, I will do that right away," I agreed, trying to be helpful. "Do you have a catalog here?"

"Yes," he said, pulling it out of a drawer on the side of his desk. "Come next June, you will have fields of lilies!"

I immediately thought of Grandmother Davis. What a tribute to her on the Taylor property that she so coveted.

"That's all then. I need to get back to the barn. Circle your choices and I'll order them after lunch."

"Yes sir," I responded. Kip was on a roll and I was taking his orders. I loved it! After I quickly picked out dozens of lily varieties, I went back to get my car so I could make a stop at the shop. Still in my casual clothes, I drove along with a hundred things on my mind. In the last few hours, I hadn't thought a second about the fact that there might be a Dickson heir to inherit all of this.

CHAPTER 71

The staff at the shop was happy to see me when I arrived. I asked for Kevin but was told he was out on a delivery. When I expressed concern about finding a replacement for him, Sally said that she and Kevin had listed the opening on the Internet. Apparently, we had already received a few replies.

"I would like for Kevin to interview them first," I requested.

"I hope he doesn't scare them away," Abbey teased. "I am going to mention it to this nice guy in my building who just lost his job at Martingale."

I stopped in my tracks. "What did he do there? Do you know?"

"I don't think he ever told me, Anne," she replied. "They laid off a lot of folks, I'm sure you know that. Because he had less seniority than so many there, David wasn't surprised that he was included in the first cut. He thinks the whole place will fold."

That was awful news. Sam would turn over in his grave if he knew this was happening.

"Abbey, can you contact him right away for an interview?" I asked, surprising myself. "What's his last name?"

"Wainwright," she answered. "He's engaged to a really nice girl, too. I'm sure this was devastating to them since they were making wedding plans."

"Sally, when Kevin gets back, would you set up an appointment with the two of us and David?"

"Sure," she answered.

"That is so nice of you, Anne," Abbey said. "Any kind of job would be great for him right now."

I walked into my office feeling sick for the many good people that worked for Martingale that could possibly lose their jobs. Sam knew there could be a possibility of the company not surviving and it seemed to be coming true. Perhaps I could make amends by giving at least one of his employees a job.

I ignored many emails as I scrolled through them on my computer. There were still personal notes from people expressing their condolences and that was pretty touching. Most of them had never even met Sam. Sally emailed me a note that said Uncle Jim had stopped by yesterday and that I should give him a call when I had time. I picked up my phone right away.

"Sorry to be calling back so late!" I told him when he answered.

"No big deal," he said calmly. "I was next door at Julia's

hooking up a printer and decided to stop in to see how you were doing."

"Better," I said in all sincerity this time. "I wanted to contact you anyway. I'd like to tell you what I'm planning on the Brody property and would also like to get your advice on a few things. Do you mind stopping by after you get off work—about six?"

"I'd be happy to," he said. "I am pleased you are not going to let that property just sit there."

"I know. See you over at the Brody house," I said, hanging up.

I felt a real need to share my news early about the baby with Uncle Jim. I wanted him to know how much I appreciated his friendship with Sam. There was a bond with him I could not explain. I can still remember the introduction he made when he brought Sam to our Thanksgiving dinner years ago. I'm sure he had no idea then that we would become husband and wife.

For lunch, Jean brought a crockpot of chili, so I obliged her by eating a small bowl. Of course, Sally's brownies couldn't be ignored, so I took a small piece from the tray. There was never a shortage of food at the flower shop. I think everyone was always thinking of Kevin, our poor bachelor, who was always hungry.

After everyone left promptly at five, I walked around the shop feeling the need to reacquaint myself. I used to be involved in every order and request. I looked at the arrangements that were in progress and had no idea who they were for or who was working on them. I looked at some new arrangements in the cooler. Truly, the shop looked great. Oktoberfest was the next street holiday, and judging by our inventory, we were ready. I felt a sense of pride in my staff. They were all really doing such a wonderful job.

I arrived at the Brody house before Uncle Jim. It was getting dark earlier and earlier these days. Kip and his crew had already gone home, and so I walked around to see today's progress. Seeing the new road graded toward 333 Lincoln was the biggest surprise of all. Dickson Properties was on the move!

CHAPTER 72

Uncle Jim drove up in his black SUV and got out of the car with a look of pure amazement on his face. He scanned the changes taking place.

"Welcome to Dickson Properties," I said with open arms.

He laughed in disbelief and gave me a hug.

While it was still light, I suggested we take a walk around back and to the barn and I explained things as we went along. He couldn't believe the quick plan for the greenhouses and what it could mean for spring results. I bragged about Kip's abilities and innovation regarding the project.

When we walked back to the Brody house, we turned on the lights and found a lawn chair and Kip's desk chair. We settled ourselves into the sparsely-furnished office to sit down and talk.

"Sorry, but all I have to offer you is bottled water," I said politely.

"Oh, I'm fine, Anne," he said, looking around in amazement.

"I have something special to share with you, Uncle Jim," I began. He looked concerned and waited for me to continue. "I have an appointment with an obstetrician tomorrow because I think I'm pregnant!"

The look on his face was priceless. He was certainly shocked. "No way, Anne!" he responded seriously.

"I thought there was no way too, and I was in denial for a while, but then I started to figure out my calendar," I explained. "Remember the day you and Sam spent together playing golf?"

He nodded, still looking shocked. "Well, Sam enjoyed it so much. It was the first time he had been himself for some time. He had been under so much stress! It was the last time we were together and it was not that long ago."

"But Sam always complained that you were still on the pill!"

"I wanted to surprise him so I decided to go off of it after I had accidentally missed a dosage," I explained. "He was so completely consumed by work and all the stress that came with it that I never said anything to him. I feel so terrible about all that, but it was not a pleasant time for us." I started to cry, again unable to keep the tears from flowing.

"Of course I understand," Uncle Jim said, tears springing to his eyes as well. "Something tells me Sam knows and wants to help you through this. I really believe that. Martingale killed one of the best human beings I have ever known. Sam would do anything for anybody."

I nodded, blowing my nose.

"The most wonderful thing here, Anne, is that he has left you his most precious gift. You know that, don't you? Whether you are ready or not to embrace it, this is wonderful news. Way to go, Sam!" he yelled into space.

I had to laugh between my tears.

I told him that no one but Nancy knew about my appointment. He seemed to feel honored and promised complete support with anything I needed.

"When we were on the golf course, Sam did say he wasn't naive about the fact that he could have another heart attack," he revealed. "He even talked about how scary that would be for you since you had to nurse him back to health after the first one. I made light of it, but told him I'd be there for him and you should that happen. Then I made him promise to leave any Martingale discussion off the golf course. We had a great time."

"Thank you so much for that day!" I said, pulling my emotions into check. "This little Dickson is going to have to grow into quite a person to match up to his father!

"Did you say his?" he kidded.

"Well, I'm kind of hoping so," I kidded back.

We visited for another half hour about this and that. He asked about Harry and his upcoming surgery. The divorce between Uncle Jim and Aunt Julia never really severed him from our family as sometimes happens. He would always be family as far as I was concerned. I think they still love each other, but time will tell in terms of what happens between them. Ultimately, I was just glad to have this private time with him.

I hugged and kissed him good-bye, feeling so much

better. It was the closest thing to a visit with Sam that I could have right now. There was no doubt Uncle Jim would be the godfather of this dear child and, of course, I always knew Nancy would be the perfect godmother.

CHAPTER 73

After calling Sally and telling her that I wouldn't be in until noon, I headed to the office of Dr. Dan Dietrich. I drove to a newly developed area outside of Colebridge. The contemporary structure was quite sleek and attractive, unlike any kind of medical building within the quaint confines of downtown Colebridge.

Once inside, I was greeted by a receptionist who looked me over as if I were there for a job interview. I sat down in an oddly shaped orange chair and observed the beautiful paintings on the walls. It had the feel of an art gallery rather than a doctor's office. There was another woman waiting in the same area. She was buried in a magazine and not inclined to say hello or engage in small talk. Leave it Nancy to find the most elegant and expensive doctor's office on the planet. By now, I was praying that this Dr. Dietrich had some friendliness about him.

After a good twenty minutes, I was asked to go to room 3B. I was welcomed by an attractive lady of about fifty who told me to have a seat while she checked my blood pressure and collected details about my medical history. She determined my weight, added it to the record, and said the doctor would be with me shortly. There was no small talk here either. She had her job to do and that was that. I kept taking deep breaths, quietly assuring myself this would be over soon.

Dr. Dietrich blew into the room with a friendly smile and an outstretched hand. "Anne, how are you? Nancy Barrister gave me a personal call to tell me you were coming. You are lucky to have such a devoted friend."

Wow. That was so kind of Nancy. In an effort to soak in that new bit of information, all I could say was, "Oh."

"First of all, I want to extend my condolences on your husband passing away so suddenly," he said sincerely. "I actually met your husband through Richard Barrister at an event and then ran into him once or twice after that. How are you getting along with all that's happened?"

What did he mean exactly? I was feeling like there was too much to take in. I tried to slow my thoughts.

"I'm fine. I'm just anxious to know whether I am a pregnant widow."

I knew it sounded sarcastic, but suddenly it was me who wasn't interested in making small talk.

"Of course, having to deal with this right now has to be a shock for you," he said empathetically. "The record says you have done a home pregnancy test that was positive."

I nodded.

"After today's appointment, I think you'll be able to go

home with more information."

"Okay."

During the exam, he continued to chatter despite my quiet manner. He knew of my flower shop and told me how much he enjoyed going to restaurants in the historic district. I really started to like him, despite the rather cold office reception. He then told me to get dressed and to meet him in his office.

My nerves had eased by the time I entered his plush office. There were carefully placed, framed professional degrees on his walls. The beautiful décor certainly did not make this look like a medical facility. Wasn't it supposed to be a warm and fuzzy place for expectant mothers to bare their souls?

He walked into the room all smiles and confirmed that I was going to be a mother. I thought it would be the news I was hoping for, but instead, it frightened me terribly. He could tell by my reaction that I was unsettled.

"This was my husband's dream," I said softly.

"And it was not yours as well?" he asked gently.

"Not entirely," I admitted. "We had planned it for our future, but I kept putting him off because of my career and us restoring our home."

"So, now you're feeling guilty about getting to experience the pleasure he would have liked, and he's not here to share it with you, right?"

"Exactly," I said tearing up again.

"Well, that's perfectly understandable," he explained. "You will have to get used to the idea, but I promise you that the joy will consume you. This is a blessing that has occurred for a reason, and it should make you happy that you actually did fulfill his dream. I think you can expect this baby sometime between the last weeks of April to the beginning of May. We'll schedule a ultrasound, depending how soon you would like to know the sex of your child. We don't have to share the results if you choose not to know. Congratulations! Try to enjoy these special moments. You are in great shape and I think you will have a very normal pregnancy."

He made it all sound perfect as I left the building, holding my prescription for vitamins in hand. I sat in the car for several minutes trying to go over his message. I liked his positive attitude. I wanted to be happy about the news, but the thought of not sharing it with Sam was so disappointing. I wanted to cry, but held back the tears. I could just hear Mother's frequent quote that from now on, it was not just going to be about me anymore! She was right! Now it was going to be about little Sammy!

CHAPTER 74

As I stopped to get a Starbucks coffee, I had Mother on my mind. It was time I brought her into the picture. I didn't want her to find out my news from someone else. She could also use some good news by now. When I pulled into her driveway, I noticed Aunt Julia's car. Why wasn't she at her shop? Was something wrong? They were thrilled to see me and told me they were in the kitchen enjoying a cup of coffee.

"Oh, honey, this is such a nice surprise," Mother said cheerfully. "I see you have coffee, but maybe you'd like some of this coffeecake."

Harry got up to give me a kiss.

"Am I interrupting anything?" I asked.

"No, not at all," explained Aunt Julia. "Sylvia was nice enough to offer me our father's desk some time ago, and I decided that I think I can use it at the shop. It's quite old and

I've always been fond of it."

"They don't make them like that anymore," added Harry.

"Oh, I've always loved that desk too," I noted. "It will be put to good use in your shop."

"That's what I told her," chimed in Mother. "It's just collecting dust up in that spare bedroom."

"So, let me guess. Uncle Jim is going to be the one to haul it into that shop of yours!" I teased.

They all laughed.

"Not fair, Anne," Aunt Julia joked back with me. "He offered—I didn't ask him." She blushed.

"Well, since you are all here, I have some shocking news," I announced.

Mother immediately looked alarmed.

"I don't know quite how to tell you this, but before Sam died, he managed to get me pregnant." There was silence. Perhaps I told them poorly. "It's more of a miracle, really, but I just came from the doctor's office and I am going to have a baby!"

"What?" shrieked Aunt Julia.

"Oh, honey, this is a miracle," Mother said seriously. "I am going to be a grandmother!" She came over to give me a big hug. "Harry, you are going to be a grandfather!"

Harry jumped out of his seat and came over to join the group hug. I wanted to cry all over again, but there was too much joy in the room.

"You are one amazing woman, Anne," Aunt Julia beamed. "I never know how you manage to do what you do, but here you go again!" She kissed me on the cheek, her excitement obvious. "When is this baby going to arrive?"

"Well, the doctor couldn't be exact, but he said it will likely come at the end of April or the first part of May," I explained.

"A spring baby!" Mother cheered with tears in her eyes. "How do you feel?"

"Well, I think I can say that I feel normal," I reported honestly. "I had been having all these strange symptoms, but I thought it was all because of Sam's death. The doctor said it should pass soon."

"You poor thing," responded Mother. "You've had so much to deal with."

We continued the happy conversation. Now with Mother knowing, it all seemed more real to me. Before I left, we talked about who would host Thanksgiving dinner next month. I determined that 333 Lincoln remained a wonderful property that needed to have many family celebrations. I volunteered to host and assured Mother that I would be sure to invite Helen Dickson and whoever would like to attend from Sam's side of the family.

Back in the car, I did think of Helen. I needed to tell her about the baby soon. I'm sure she didn't have any hopes of having a grandchild. I headed to the flower shop knowing I had another group of people there who would be so excited to hear my news.

Jean and Sally were sharing a long submarine sandwich and inviting the UPS driver to join them. He was not cooperating and they continued to tease him.

"Top of the morning to you, Miss Anne," Jean greeted me. "Have a bite with us, why don't you?"

"I'm fine," I said, holding up my hand. "I just left Mother's house and you never leave there hungry."

"How is Harry doing?" Sally asked. It was thoughtful of her to inquire.

"He is in good spirits, but is also anxious to get his surgery over with," I reported. "Where is Kevin?"

"He's outside," Sally said between bites. "He just got back from a Barrister delivery."

"Great. You two follow me," I instructed.

They looked at me strangely. We found Kevin cleaning out the back of the van. He looked at us as if something bad just happened.

"What's up, my botanical ladies?" he asked in a silly manner.

"While there's no one in the shop and we have some privacy, I wanted to share some news with you," I began.

They waited silently for me to continue.

"We are going to add a very young person to our flower shop family," I stated. I knew they were thinking I had hired a new employee. "I just learned that I am going to have a baby in the spring!"

They didn't respond for a second.

"Bad joke, Anne," said Kevin.

"Anne, are you really serious?" asked Sally. She looked as white as a ghost.

I nodded.

"I'm at a loss!" said Jean. "This is jolly good news! A baby, by golly!"

Everyone exploded with joy.

"I'm in for a happy dance!" I finally said, laughing. We all gathered close for a hug as we danced in a circle. No one asked how in the world this happened, which made it extra joyful. We stayed outdoors for a while, forgetting about anyone that could possibly be in the shop and robbing us blind. My baby would indeed be loved by everyone at the shop. We had a bond like no other shop staff.

Kevin was anxious to call Abbey and tell her the news. Jean and Sally were already thinking of ways we could accommodate a baby somewhere in the shop. It was amazing how everyone was embracing the news. If only Sam could see all the reactions. Perhaps he *was* sharing it all with me. Hmmm…

CHAPTER 75

It was six before I returned home. I found Ella on the patio room outdoors with a blanket around her shoulders. I walked out to greet her and we commented about the beautiful weather.

"Will you join me, Anne?" she asked, so relaxed. "I was almost ready to take advantage of the pretty fire pit here, but I don't know how to use it!"

I had to laugh.

"It's perfect weather for it, don't you think?"

"It really is, and I think we should both take advantage of it. We may not have many more pleasant evenings like this. It's just like our gas fireplaces, Ella. There is a switch to turn on and that's it! It's amazing how much heat they can put out."

"Perhaps you would like me to get you a glass of merlot to help warm you up?" Ella offered sweetly.

I sat down next to her watching the flames ignite. "No, I'd better pass on that," I responded, knowing this was an optimum time to tell her about the baby. "I don't think Dr. Dietrich would approve of me drinking right now."

"Well, what does he have to do with anything?" she said without thinking. "Red wine is good for you, at least that's what I read. You and Sam love that one merlot that you have stockpiled here. What's the name of that again?"

"Wine Country Red," I answered, savoring the sweet memories. "We discovered it on our honeymoon at the Quarry House. It was from the local winery there."

"I don't know who Dr. Dietrich is, but what business is it of his to tell you not to have any wine?" she asked innocently.

"Because he is my obstetrician, Ella. I'm going to have a baby!"

She sat up and looked at me like I was crazy. "You're really not joking, are you?"

"I know it's hard to believe with Sam gone, but he left me something very precious to take care of!" I said with a smile.

"Lordy, Lordy, praise God from whom all blessings flow!" she said joyfully. "All things are possible. That's what the Lord always says!"

I laughed.

"No wonder you haven't been eating like you should."

"I know it's a blessing, Ella, but it seems so cruel not having Sam here to help share the news," I admitted. "He wanted this so badly."

"Don't worry, Anne," Ella said, trying to comfort me. "The Lord works in mysterious ways. He has a purpose for you and a purpose for that little Dickson child."

"I think so too, Ella," I said calmly.

"Well, we have to have a little celebration and I'll bet you haven't eaten," she said, getting up out of her chair. "I'll fix us a little something to snack on out here and I'll pour you a tall glass of lemonade. Dr. Dietrich will approve of that, I'm sure."

I smiled and leaned back in my chair. It did indeed feel good to relax at the end of this mentally and emotionally exhausting day.

In no time, Ella appeared with a tray of rolled-up ham, vegetables with curry dip, and some fresh strawberries. I told her about choosing the name "Sammy" for a boy or girl. She was getting so excited. We made a toast to Sammy as she drank her glass of white wine and I drank my lemonade.

I was able to sleep better now that my mysterious illness had been diagnosed and my family had been told about the baby. I was concerned I hadn't personally told Sue, but I knew she'd find out soon enough.

When I was getting dressed the next morning, I did hear from Sue as I expected.

"Oh, Anne, I heard about the baby from Aunt Julia last night," she said before I could even say hello. "I wanted to call you, but it was getting late, so I thought you'd be asleep. I just can't believe what fantastic news this is! I know to have this happening without Sam here is hard. We will all help, just like you all help me."

"I know that, Sue," I conceded. "I'm sorry I didn't have a chance to tell you personally. I knew once Aunt Julia knew, the whole town would know."

She laughed in agreement. "Mia and Eli will have a second cousin to be close to. You know, I have every piece of baby equipment available to man since I've had both a girl and a boy. You are welcome to all of it. My little family is done!"

"Thanks, Sue," I replied. I realized I had not thought very far ahead about what I would need.

"When are you going for a ultrasound?"

"I think it's a little early right now to be able to tell from what the doctor said, so I will have to wait for awhile," I told her.

"I'll be happy to go with you if you like," she suggested. "They even have little social parties for the family that goes with you. They really make a big deal about the announcement of the sex."

"No, Sue, that will not be me, and I will want to go alone," I said firmly. "I have to decide what a pregnant widow actually does, but thanks anyway."

Not surprisingly, my abrupt statement left Sue a bit speechless, so after a few more minutes, we hung up.

It was Saturday and I wanted to visit with Kip over at the Brody house to see if I could be of any help on my day off. I figured he would be working on the weekend. I would take a short walk in that direction. As I got closer, I was pleased to find Kevin there helping his buddy.

"This is really something, Anne," Kevin said when he saw me. "Kip is trying to build Rome in a day!"

As if on cue, Kip strode up to us.

"Yes, I know. That's why I thought I'd better come over and check on things," I joked. "There are changes every day! They did this road in one day!"

"Hey, Anne," Kip said enthusiastically, "I have a gas stove that I'm planning to put right here to help with the winter weather." He pointed to the center of what used to be the living room. "We don't need to replace the furnace as yet, but it's totally inadequate."

"I am not surprised," I said in agreement. "I like that you're going to place it in the center of this room so the whole staff can get warmed up around it."

"Yeah, it worked out great with the alignment of the chimney," he noted.

"Ella and I enjoyed the fire pit last night, by the way," I shared. "It's perfect weather for it."

"That's why Sam wanted it, but it also gives ambiance for that patio," he bragged.

I was glad everyone was still talking about Sam as if he were still here. I wanted everyone to do that around me. There were so many stories and contributions Sam had made and I wanted to keep them alive.

"Hey, can I do anything to help while I'm here?" I asked sincerely.

"If you're serious about that, I'd like to have these rooms swept up before Monday," he said, pointing to the broom in the corner. "Just be careful around here, Mama Anne!"

I nodded and smiled. "I'm your man!" I said, taking the broom.

We kidded around as I swept away. They teased each other while they unloaded drywall and nailed studs to the wall. It felt good to be really useful for a change. Awhile later, Kip said he was going for hamburgers and fries to bring back for lunch. It sounded great and I was hungry. Right now, I wasn't ready to be Miss Healthy. So I figured, when in Rome, do as the Romans do.

CHAPTER 76

The week began with Harry's surgery and I wanted to be there for both Harry and Mother. I planned to meet Mother at the hospital. Ella naturally wanted to come with me. I also knew that Aunt Julia would join us as soon as she dropped Sarah off at school.

By the time I found Mother, she was coming down the hall. She had just said good-bye to Harry and was struggling to keep her composure.

I hugged her tightly. "Harry is going to be just fine, just wait and see."

"We need to wait in this room. When they are finished, they will contact me by phone here." The room was filled with other families who had stressful looks on their faces.

"Would you both like some coffee?" Ella offered as she saw a counter of tea and coffee across the room. We agreed that it was a good idea.

I held Mother's hand as she described Harry's outlook this morning. She said he was in good spirits. She said Pastor Hamel had also stopped by to have a short prayer with him. Pastor Hamel told her it was time our family had some tears of joy and that we should think positively about Harry's outcome.

When Aunt Julia arrived, we already had an update that the surgery was going well. I was curious, so I asked Aunt Julia who was opening the shop for her this morning. She casually said she would just open later or not at all. I hated to hear that she approached her shop hours so casually as so many of the shop owners seemed to do. If she was going to be a serious business owner, she would have to learn to be dependable about her shop hours and arrange for help if she couldn't be there. If she continued to treat this as a hobby and worked only when she felt like working, she would soon be out of business. This was certainly not the time to even mention such a thing, so I put my opinions aside and remained silent.

We took turns taking breaks during the hours that followed. We talked about meaningless topics to pass the time as we waited for more updates on Harry's progress. Finally, Mother got a call from the doctor who told her the surgery was over and that he would meet her in another conference room to discuss the outcome. We accompanied her to hear the news, which seemed to be as good as we could expect. He cautioned us that his time in intensive care was critical to the success of the surgery. He said this would be a time to take a break and even go home for a rest, which Mother wouldn't hear of. We encouraged Mother to join us in the cafeteria for a bite to eat before any of us had to leave.

She did feel a sense of relief and we talked about what her plans would be.

After Ella took a bite of ham salad, she told Mother that she would be happy to stay with Mother and Harry until he was back on his feet. Mother would not hear of that either and insisted that the two of them would be just fine. Aunt Julia had to leave to pick up Sarah, so we promised to keep her informed regarding Harry's progress. Before Ella, Mother, and I went back to the waiting room, I called the shop to find out how things were going there. Abbey answered and it reminded me to ask her if she would consider going full time since I had taken on the greenhouse project.

"Kevin has been keeping me informed about everything, Anne, and he as much as told me I would be working more, so that is just fine with me!" she explained with excitement. "By the way, Kevin brought in David Wainwright this morning to show him off to you. He didn't know you wouldn't be here. David is very nice. He's going to come back tomorrow so he can go with Kevin on a few deliveries. I think you'll like him!"

"I'm sure I will." I had forgotten all about our scheduled meeting with David. My mind certainly had been easily distracted lately. Could I possibly handle one more thing? I did want to meet David, however, and would have to work that into the schedule.

I left Mother and Ella at the hospital and realized how fatigued I had become. Both Mother and Ella insisted I get some rest. Harry was becoming more and more alert, which Mother took as a good sign. The two were very cute as they looked longingly into each other's eyes. They were so, so lucky to have each other. With Sam gone, I no longer had that luxury.

I was so weary when I returned home. I went directly upstairs, feeling very alone in this big, quiet house. As I got undressed, I reminded myself that I was truly not alone in this house and never would be from now on. I had a little Dickson baby with me at all times.

I had been ignoring the waiting room off our master bedroom. As I stood in the doorway, I began to think about the history of this special room in our house. I had named it because it was always waiting for something to happen there. Sam and Mother thought it would be perfect for a nursery someday. I thought it was perfect for writing my Taylor book and had it nicely arranged so I could get up at night and jot down notes when I felt like it. Sam then insisted on me having a nice home office for that, so I got moved down the hall. Sam, in the meantime, found it to be quite handy as he packed for his trips. His suitcases remained there, as did many of his travel accessories, as if they were waiting for his next trip. I realized that I felt it was time to remove all of his things. Leaving everything there was a harsh reminder of Sam's passing and I needed to move forward.

As I stood there and stared at its potential, I came back to Sam's earlier comment when we first purchased the house. He had said, "It's perfect for a nursery, Anne." I remember the shudder that went through me at the very thought of it.

Now it was a different story. I would be having a little baby named Sammy within months and I would want the baby as close to me as possible. It would make a perfect nursery until he or she was at least a year old. Knowing this gave me the motivation to replace Sam's things with items that would be needed for a nursery. It also cushioned the sadness at having to go through sweet Sam's belongings. He would be so happy that this room would be used for our baby. I was certain of that.

CHAPTER 77

I eventually fell asleep after mentally planning the nursery but endured a restless night of sleep picturing Mother at Harry's bedside. I reluctantly got up to start my day. However, for the first time in a long time, I felt like eating something. I put on my sweat suit and readied myself for a chilly fall walk. In the kitchen, I started the coffee. It was nice to have Ella still asleep as I toasted an English muffin for myself. While I waited for the muffin to toast, I went out to get the morning paper. Even that simple task made me think of Sam. Despite his love of technology, he still liked to hold the newspaper in his hands.

It didn't take long to see the bold headlines when I opened up the paper. The top story was entitled, *Martingale's Founder Sentenced to Ten Years*. I really didn't want to read on, but I was curious to see if Sam's name was mentioned. As I scanned the lengthy article, it said that deceased former president Sam Dickson was the source who opened the investigation.

As I scanned further, my eyes fell on the name of Brenda Warren. She took Sam's place as vice president when he was promoted to president. It went on to say that her name was on the title of one of Mr. Martingale's many homes and that her salary was quite high compared to others in the company. Further, it stated that Mrs. Martingale was unaware of such information and had no comment on the subject. What did this mean in terms of Brenda's relationship with Mr. Martingale? She was so much younger than him. I suppose he had to hide his money in various places and this was one of them. I thought back to the time I questioned Sam about her being promoted. He just said she was qualified and what she did on her own time was not relevant. Sam couldn't have known this! Perhaps he did suspect, but maybe he never told me since I disliked her so. The relationship between Brenda and Uncle Jim destroyed his marriage. I wonder what he would have to say about all of this.

Ella came in to join me as I continued to stare at the newspaper. "You're up extra early today. Are you feeling okay?"

"Well, I was feeling pretty chipper until I saw the morning headline," I said, pushing the paper across the table.

Ella picked it up and glanced at it with interest. She shook her head as she sat down to read further.

I kept thinking about how this article would stir up the dust again for so many folks. I no longer felt like eating, so I decided to get on my way. I told Ella I was going down to Main Street to walk and I would see her later. She hardly looked up from the paper to tell me good-bye.

I was nearly to the street when Aunt Julia's name popped up on my cell phone.

"Did you see this morning's paper?" she asked, rage evident in her voice.

"I did and it makes me sick. I am shocked, to say the least, but it is what it is. Justice will eventually kick in. She may actually be innocent of the embezzling itself, but now she's connected to the money trail. Good luck to her with that!"

"Well, Jim's getting a phone call as soon as I hang up with you!" she said firmly. "I'll bet he wasn't aware of her higher ambitions. I'm so glad now he got away from there when he did, even though he was laid off. He is in a much better place."

Her words hit me hard. Was Sam in a better place now? Mixed emotions of bitterness and sadness came over me. I just didn't want to discuss it any further, so I cut our conversation short. I'm sure gossip was running rampant in the streets of Colebridge right now.

I wanted to escape by finding peace on Main Street. As I walked along, I tried to think of more pleasant things. I thought about my baby. I thought of Helen and how I hadn't called her since I told her about the baby. I'm sure Sam would like me to call her frequently and check on her. It was probably time and there was no better time than the present!

"So glad you called, Anne," answered Helen. "I was wondering how Harry made out with his surgery and if you're doing okay."

"Harry's doing fine," I reported. "He'll be in the hospital for a few more days, but I know they were going to get him up and around today already. Isn't that something? Mother is there around the clock, of course."

"Oh, that's wonderful news," she responded. "What about you?"

"Couldn't be better," I said with a smile. "I am counting on seeing you at Thanksgiving again this year. I also want to show you what's been going on with our property next door since Sam died."

"Well, Anne, I just don't know about that trip yet," she said in a worried manner. "Elaine would have to come with me and I just don't know what she can arrange."

"The whole family is welcome, so I'll send her an email to encourage her to come," I said, sincerely hoping they could come.

"I know you decided to make some changes, but you aren't doing too much are you, Anne?" she warned. "I want a full-term, healthy grandbaby."

"I will do my best, Grandma Dickson!" I teased. "I am taking my walk as we speak and the doctor said that is very good for me."

"Please give your mother and Harry my regards," she instructed. "Are you sure Thanksgiving will not be too much for you?"

"I have Ella," I reassured her. "Remember, we had a lot of cooks in the kitchen last year, so we'll be just fine!"

She laughed, recalling the memories.

"Love to you and that grandbaby," she said before hanging up.

I couldn't keep from smiling. I hoped Sam was listening. We were going about our lives without Sam, but we had the next best thing and that was his baby. Happiness would once again be in the Dickson household.

CHAPTER 78

I managed to get to the shop before anyone else and that hadn't happened in a long time. I checked the orders and decided to arrange a funeral spray we needed instead of getting sidetracked with paperwork and emails. I wanted to do something creative for a change.

When Sally arrived, humming a tune, she was surprised to see me stripping stems for the arrangement.

"Hey, you don't need to do that, Anne."

"I want to, plus I'd like you to verify the invoices on my desk before I pay them. By the way, what's making you so happy this morning?"

She grinned sheepishly.

"It must involve Tim."

"Okay, smarty pants!" she jokingly retorted. "We had a nice time last night. He asked me to dinner at his apartment. Can you believe that?"

"Wow, this is getting serious." I teasingly winked at her.

"No, I wouldn't say that, but I'm seeing a different side of him that I like a lot!" she said, beaming.

"I am so happy that you hung in there with him. I told you that sometimes friendships that take a romantic turn take longer to develop."

She nodded. "How's Harry doing?" she asked as she put her purse in the drawer.

"I assume fine, but I haven't talked to Mother yet today," I answered as I filled in the piece with coral gladiolas. "I'll call her after I finish this."

"Good morning, ladies!" Jean greeted us cheerfully with a platter in her hands.

"Yum, I smell something wonderful!" Sally exclaimed. "What did you bring today?"

"Shortbread that just came straight from the oven," she bragged. "Where's our Kevin? He made a special request for this!"

"He and Abbey are not coming in until noon," Sally answered. "We won't have anything ready for him until then."

"Voilà!" I shouted, looking at my completed arrangement. "Quite striking, if I do say so myself."

"You haven't lost your touch," Sally agreed.

We all took a moment to sample the delicious shortbread. Jean described it as an English traditional treat. We recalled having it at one of our literary club meetings. Jean said she thought Al would once again be okay with her hosting the club. She said he was embarrassed with his prior behaviors and drinking to excess. Sally encouraged her to proceed with her life and affirmed that everyone admired the fact that he was getting help from Alcoholics Anonymous.

Thankfully, the headlines of the morning paper did not come up in our conversations. I took a serving of shortbread to my office while I called to check on Mother. She said the doctor felt that Harry was doing remarkably well, primarily due to the magic touch of his beautiful, beloved wife.

I could sense her blushing over the phone.

"Did you see this morning's paper, honey?"

"Yes, it's a real shame," I responded sadly. "The story seems to just keep getting bigger and bigger. I really cannot let myself dwell on it, though."

"That's right," she consoled me. "That's what I told Harry this morning. You just stay on the bright side of things and think of your baby instead."

"Oh, I almost forgot to tell you that I talked to Helen this morning and she sends her regards to you and Harry. She still doesn't know if she'll be coming for Thanksgiving, but I sure hope so. She said it depends on who can come with her."

"Hopefully, Harry will be back to his old self by then. Are you sure you want to have everyone?"

"Absolutely!" I joyfully responded. "Remember, I have Ella! It will give us all something to look forward to." We both agreed and ended our conversation when Sally came to my door to tell me there was someone to see me. I came out to the front.

"Hello, Anne!"

I was totally surprised to see Beverly. "How are you?"

"I'm here to pick up a plant for my friend who just had a baby," she explained. "She's having a girl and I saw these little pink shoes in the window with a fern in them. It's just perfect for her!"

"I love that arrangement, too," I said, putting the flower pot on the counter. "The shoe flower pot is a vintage piece. It's likely from the 1950s. I love the charming pots from that era and it's just the thing for a nursery."

"Yes, I remembered that from when I was here last," she commented.

As I helped Beverly complete her purchase, I told her of Sam's passing. She was shocked and had questions as most people might about the death of a younger person.

"Will you continue to live at the Taylor estate?"

"Yes, I will," I said, noticing the more upbeat sound in my voice. "I have a family friend staying there with me and I'll be having a baby next spring."

The look on her face told me she wasn't sure she'd heard correctly. "Did you say you're having a baby?' she asked in shock.

I nodded, unable to keep the smile from my face. "I didn't know I was pregnant until after Sam passed away," I began to explain. I was grateful that the other staff members were working in the design room and there were no other customers in the shop.

"Anne, I don't know what to say!" She paused, truly unsure of what to say next. "I am so happy for you!"

"I'm doing just fine," I assured her. "I'd like you to visit the house again sometime. I am making some big changes there, which include building a couple of greenhouses. Sam and I had discussed it before and it is now actually happening."

"Oh my," she said, trying to comprehend it all. "That would be awesome. I always thought it would be great to work in one of those. I think I am the only one in my family that has a green thumb."

"Well, come see me in a couple of months," I encouraged her. "I might have a job for you!"

Her eyes got very large in disbelief. "Are you serious?" She seemed genuinely interested.

"I am," I nodded. "If you are available, I may contact you before then. I kept your phone number."

"Oh, I would appreciate that so much," she said, beaming. "I just have part time jobs here and there, so this would be a dream come true."

Somehow, I knew this visit from Beverly was no accident. Did Sam send her my way or did Grandmother Davis? Hmmm...

CHAPTER 79

Mother was pushing Harry down the corridor in a wheelchair when I arrived at the hospital the next day. She immediately bragged about how Harry was walking on his own before I came. It was interesting and unusual to see my mother doting over someone else besides me, her only child. They were precious together, which again reminded me how I would not grow old with Sam.

As we made ourselves comfortable in one of the hospitality rooms off the hall, Sue joined us. It didn't take long for her to begin telling cute stories about her little family when we asked about them. After a while she changed the subject to how I was feeling and then wanted to know more about what had been happening at the Brody property. Mother and Harry enjoyed the update as well. Goodness knows what Mother was thinking!

Returning to the topic of babies, Sue inquired, "Have

you thought about nursery colors or a theme for the baby's room?" Her excitement was evident.

"You mean something besides flowers?" joked Harry.

Mother laughed.

"No, but as Sam suggested early on, I am using the sitting room off the master bedroom for the nursery," I confirmed.

"Oh good. It will be so handy," Mother chimed in. "Your bedroom is all cream and white, so any color you choose will do quite nicely."

"When you find out what sex it is, your mind will go crazy with ideas," Sue shared.

"The room across the hall will be perfect as he or she grows older," I explained.

"Just so you know, I am perfectly happy to host your baby shower, but I'll probably have to fight Aunt Julia for the opportunity!" Sue claimed.

"It's way too soon to think of that, Sue," I resisted. "I haven't even gained any baby weight yet, especially since I lost weight in the beginning."

"Anne has always been so thin, so it will be interesting to see her blossom," Mother said, grinning.

"So, will you be called grandma or some other cutesy name?" teased Sue.

"I'd better be called grandma," Mother said firmly. "This will be my only shot at it!"

We laughed. It seemed quite strange to even be talking about Anne Dickson having a baby!

Mrs. Carter, Mother's next door neighbor, arrived for a visit and the chatter became louder. I used this as my opportunity to exit. A quick kiss to Mother and Harry had me on my way.

As I walked to the car, I once again felt detached from the rest of the world. Without Sam, I had a sense of aloneness that I did not feel as a single person who had never been married. I desperately wanted to talk to him. I found myself driving to the cemetery. It was the same cemetery that the Taylors were buried in. I sat in my car for a while staring at the lumps of dirt and dried flowers from a distance. I needed to select a tombstone soon and I wanted it to include a place for my name as well. I wanted him next to me just as he had been next to me in our lives together.

I got out of the car feeling grateful that no one else was around. As I got closer, I could not believe my eyes. I almost fainted when I saw fresh, beautiful lilies at the head of Sam's grave!

"Oh, Grandmother," I said aloud as I often did to her. I started to cry. "Grandmother, I miss him so much." I fell to my knees. I covered my face with my hands and sobbed until I was exhausted. My loss was incomprehensible and there was nothing left but more tears. After some time, I began to feel a sense of comfort and warmth. I stood but was not really ready to leave yet. I wanted to sit down for awhile and tell Sam so many things. As I looked around, I saw other gravesites with stone benches. Now I knew why. I made a mental note to order one when I ordered his tombstone.

"Thank you, Grandmother, for thinking of him for me," I said to the heavens. I walked away feeling much better. Besides God, who was always there to hear me, I knew there were others who understood the depths of my pain and grief.

CHAPTER 80

The next week Jean resumed the Jane Austen Literary Club meetings. I picked Mother up as usual so we could enjoy the ride together. Honestly, it felt good to be back in a routine. Everyone managed to attend the meeting. It was like a high school reunion that no one wanted to miss. Al chose to not be at home, which was probably a good thing. I'm sure there was embarrassment on his part with his addiction to alcohol. Mother told us that Harry was due to come home the next day, so it was the appropriate time for her to have a night out before having to stay at home more to assist Harry with his recovery.

Jean was extra chipper as she welcomed everyone back. This group was good for her as she continued to miss her home in England. It gave her a chance to connect with her homeland through the life of Jane Austen. Jean went all out with her delightful English treats of scones, petits fours, tea sandwiches, and the ever-loving shortbread. Since I had missed dinner, all of these offerings were welcomed treats.

After she finally got our attention between all the chatter, she nearly became overcome with tears as she welcomed us back. Aunt Julia jumped in to make a toast to Jean and all the Janeites. She said Jean would always be our English queen, which made Jean blush with pride.

"I knew straightaway this was a good idea to visit Jane once again," she stated. "I missed you all so much, as well as Jane!"

Everyone laughed in agreement.

"I trust you have been reading Jane, right so?"

That brought laughter and chatter.

"I say that tonight, each Janeite should tell what they were doing or reading during our Jane vacation," Jean instructed. "Who would like to begin?"

Sarah was the first to raise her hand. "As most of you know, my mom and I opened an English-like writing shop on Main Street, right next to Anne's flower shop," she began. "I'll bet some of you don't know we carry Jane's books and some very clever Jane Austen gifts, like a pretty white pen with Jane's name on it. We brought one for a door prize tonight. I love the stationery that has a lot of her quotes on it. You have to come see everything!"

Aunt Julia beamed with pride to see her daughter showing signs of becoming an excellent retailer. "Well done, Sarah!" Aunt Julia bragged.

"I have indeed seen the display, Sarah, and it is quite handsome," Jean interjected. "We should all give it a go the next time we are on Main Street."

"Well, I did finally finish reading *Pride and Prejudice*

in its entirety," Abbey announced boldly. "It sure was better than the other two books I tried to read of Jane's. It was so interesting to see Jane, an independent woman, come through the character of Elizabeth Bennet."

Everyone nodded in agreement.

"Has anyone else read any works of Jane's while we took our absence?" Jean asked. No one raised their hand. "Well then, Miss Abbey, you are most deserving of the Jane Austen pen giveaway tonight!"

Everyone agreed and clapped as Abbey opened the beautiful box in which the pen was stored.

"This doesn't mean that I have to start writing I hope, because I do not have the gift like Anne," Abbey teased. "Thank you so very much, Julia and Sarah. This will go on the little desk I have."

"I think everyone needs to be reminded that we have one additional guest tonight that we didn't have the last time we were together," announced Isabella.

Everyone looked around the room.

"I am talking about the delightful news of a Dickson baby who will be joining us next spring!"

Everyone clapped and cheered as they looked at me with joy on their faces.

I didn't know what to say. The announcement was unexpected and the mention of the name Dickson made me immediately think of Sam. I needed to recover quickly and think on my feet.

"I'll let you know at the next meeting whether it will be a Janeite or not!" I teased.

"I hope it shall be so!" cheered Jean.

"I also want to mention that I did receive some lovely

English reproduction fabrics at the shop in case you want to reproduce Jane's quilt or make a Jane costume," Isabella, always the salesperson, informed us. "It's too bad we didn't have this fabric when we were all making the Jane Austen quilt."

I wasn't sure Isabella should be reminding everyone about that horrific experience.

"Jolly good, Isabella," Jean responded. "It appears we will all have to do some shopping. Before everyone leaves, I want you to see the photos my friend Mary Elizabeth sent me from England. She just visited the Winchester Cathedral where Jane is buried and took some photos of her lengthy epitaph. Remember how we discussed the fact that it did not mention that she was a writer? Well, anyway, the photographs are jolly good, so pass them about."

The rest of the evening was spent visiting and enjoying the tasty food Jean had prepared. We agreed it was good to see Jean back in her element and it was fun to discuss the works of Jane once again. Mother totally enjoyed the evening. It had been some time since she had been out with anyone except Harry, and he had not felt like going out much recently. As I drove her home, I could tell she was mentally and physically exhausted. I certainly understood how she felt as I tried to continue on with my own life, sometimes gathering strength enough for only the day at hand.

CHAPTER 81

The fall season was moving along as if it was anxious to get on with winter. Oktoberfest on the street went off nicely. Nick Notto across the street chose not to open his shop so I didn't have to listen to his complaints the following Monday. He had a heart of gold, but had a negative reputation due to his nearly incessant complaining. He did agree to stay open for the children's trick or treat night on Halloween. It was a very popular time when the merchants could give back to the community. Thousands of costumed children accompanied by adults paraded to get their treats from all the businesses. It was quite the show and the shopkeepers enjoyed it as well. Sally loved to put on a costume and stand for hours at the door to hand out candy.

Along with the shape of my body, the Brody property was changing before my very eyes. Kip was pushing to get as much done as possible before freezing temperatures set in.

He had established a sizable crew that showed up each day. Kevin was now part of that crew. I told him that when the time was right, I wanted him to hire Beverly, who seemed to want to help with the greenhouses. Kevin was quite challenged by being put in charge of the greenhouses. One was up and another was slated to go up next week. I would have a good view of them from my sunporch.

Word was spreading around town about what was happening on the old Taylor hill. Instead of a ghost to talk about, they could gossip about Dickson Properties. No one could see too much from Lincoln Street and it was sometimes difficult for contractors to get their trucks and equipment up the hill. I didn't anticipate that the public would ever have free access since the greenhouses would be for my business only. I did wonder how long they would refer to it as the Taylor hill instead of the Dickson hill.

The good news of daily changes with the property kept my mind off my pregnancy. I was feeling great and energized. Ella was doing her best to see to it I was eating healthier, which I appreciated. If I were still living with Mother, she would have doted on me incessantly. Now, she had Harry to look after, and he seemed to be getting along just fine.

My next appointment with Dr. Dietrich would be the ultrasound to tell the gender of Sammy. For some reason, I always felt it would be a boy. Everyone had their opinion which they didn't hesitate to share. Sally and Jean felt it needed to be a girl so she could take over the flower shop one day. I knew Sam wouldn't have cared whether it was a boy or a girl. I often thought back to how fun it was to watch Sam with little Mia. He just loved children and noticed them all the time.

David Wainright, the new delivery guy, was trying extra hard to take Kevin's place. He was very quiet and soft-spoken. Kevin warned me that David would likely move on if he could find a better paying job. It was the nature of the business, really. The staff seemed to be content with their small increases in wages every now and then. Sally was on salary and I made sure she was well compensated. I wouldn't have much of a business today if it were not for her. The wedding business was booming even more than we anticipated and Sally deserved to be rewarded for that.

I still checked on the plants in the potting shed. It would be so nice next year to put them in a proper greenhouse instead of the tiny quarters the shed provided. I didn't want the shed to change, but it got a bit crowded through the winter as I tried to keep plants warm with my little heater. I couldn't wait to introduce my child to the wonders of the potting shed. He or she would learn about flowers and plants at an early age, of that I was certain.

The next event coming up was the Thanksgiving holiday. Elaine Dickson had emailed me and said they would do their best to be with us that day. Thanksgiving had special memories for me especially, because it was when Aunt Julia and Uncle Jim first brought Sam to dinner at my house. Since he had no family in town, they invited him to join ours. Little did anyone know he would join our family permanently. Sam and I hit it off instantly and never parted until his recent death. The upcoming holiday would be difficult, but I was determined to make it a day of giving thanks—for there was much to be thankful for.

CHAPTER 82

I called the shop to tell Sally I would be in after my visit with Dr. Dietrich. I felt that in one sense, this visit would introduce my child to me for the first time. My dreams about the baby were so jumbled—sometimes showing a baby girl and then a baby boy. At least they were only depicting one baby! Having a healthy baby was my mission, whatever the sex.

At this point, any wardrobe decisions were made solely on the issue of comfort. I was not showing yet, but I felt bigger and was bothered by any confinement around my waist. I would have to go shopping soon so I would have presentable clothes to wear to the flower shop.

When I arrived in the crowded waiting room, I looked at all the women in various stages of pregnancy. Some were looking quite uncomfortable and some were trying to manage young children with them at the same time. That was a situation that would not apply to me. This was it. This was my only shot at being a mother. Sammy would be an only child, just like me.

When my name was called, I was more than ready to leave the circus that was going on in the waiting room. It was quite a change from my first visit when the waiting room seemed so sterile and proper. Dr. Dietrich's nurse was very polite and engaged me in conversation about the flower shop and what it was like being a business owner on Main Street. She described some window displays that she was particularly fond of on our charming street and we chatted about that, which really served to put me at ease.

She remained in the room and a technician smeared a jelly-like substance on my abdomen. They informed me that the doctor would come in to explain and confirm the ultrasound's results. I watched as they moved the object around, showing the inside of my womb. At one point, they exchanged knowing glances, making me feel as if they saw something I didn't. Dr. Dietrich then came into the room and took a look at the images. He began to explain that, from all indications, I was going to have a healthy son.

"A son. Really?" I asked in delight and yet disbelief. "Are you sure?"

"Well, I have sometimes been wrong," he said in a teasing manner. "What were you hoping for?"

"A son," I said with relief. "I always felt that's what it would be."

Oh Sam, why did you leave me alone with this news, I thought to myself. *Are you watching and hearing what he just said?*

"Have you settled on a name?" the nurse asked.

"Yes," I said with certainty. "This will be—no, this is Samuel Charles Dickson. I picked Samuel, of course, because of Sam and I chose the name Charles in memory of my deceased father." They agreed that the name was a good one.

I got up to dress before meeting the doctor in his office. He reassured me that everything looked normal and well. He also knew I was struggling with Sam's death and complimented me on my bravery through this emotional time. I was glad I opted to know the gender of the baby. It made everything more personal and certainly more real to me.

When I got in the car, I could no longer keep tears from rolling down my cheeks.

"We have a boy," I finally said aloud as if Sam were right there with me. "I know he'll look just like you, honey. I will do my best to give us a healthy son!"

I took a deep breath and reminded myself of all that bravery Dr. Dietrich had mentioned just a few minutes ago. Swallowing hard, I started the car. I wanted to go by Mother's to let her know before I told anyone at the flower shop. She knew I had the appointment today so she would likely be on pins and needles.

Harry answered the door and gave me a hug. When asked, he said he felt great and told me Mother would be back soon. She had gone next door to take a pie to Mrs. Carter.

"Pie? Is that what smells so good?" I asked, feeling hungry.

He smiled and nodded as we went into the kitchen. "I happen to know there happens to be one just like it," Harry whispered as if we shared a secret. "It's strawberry and rhubarb. Do you like that kind?"

"Of course!" I responded. "She makes them every fall."

Mother returned and greeted me, an expectant expression on her face. "So Anne, how did it go?"

"It went really well. I guess we'll have to celebrate with some of this pie!"

She feigned impatience and put her hands on her hips.

"Anne, I don't think you can keep her waiting much longer," Harry teased.

"Okay, I suppose not." I paused for the appropriate amount of dramatic effect. "You're going to have a grandson!"

"Oh, honey, how wonderful!" she said, becoming emotional. "Here, have a seat and tell us all about it."

We sat down and Harry poured us some coffee. I gave her a step-by-step description of my visit and then told her the name I had chosen. She was especially touched that it included the name Charles. Harry commented about how I now have someone to take over Dickson Properties one day. I wondered if he thought a girl might not be up to the task. Mother wanted to talk about the nursery and what kind of quilt she should begin to make. She was certain it could be completed by spring. I watched the two of them come alive with the good news. They had weathered their share of concerns lately, so it was gratifying to be able to share some good news.

I finally got back to my other family at Brown's Botanicals. When I pulled up in front, Aunt Julia was talking with Nick. I motioned for her to come into the shop when she finished. Abbey and Jean were working behind the counter with sales and orders and Sally was in the consulting room with a client. David was not around, so I assumed he was on a delivery. Before I went into my office, I said hello to

Mrs. Jennings who was picking out some greeting cards. Layers of papers and unopened envelopes were patiently waiting for me as I glanced over at my desk. With no plans for the evening, I decided I'd better make a sizable dent in that work before going home.

"About time you show up for work!" Aunt Julia teased. I smiled.

"The street has been busy, so I can't stay but a bit. What's going on?"

"Well I won't keep you, but I thought you might want to know that I will be having a little boy!" I felt like I glowed just being able to say those words.

"Oh, sweetie, that is marvelous!" she exclaimed. "Wait until I tell Sarah! Were you just at the doctor's office?"

"Yes, and all is well!" I bragged. I pulled out the copy of the ultrasound to show her. "This is Samuel Charles Dickson," I announced.

She was touched and tried to keep from crying.

"I know, I feel the same way," I consoled her. "Sam would be thrilled!"

"I love the name, too. What a nice tribute to your father!"

"It's all so weird without Sam, though."

"He's with you, just like your grandmother is with you," she said warmly.

"You'd better get back to the shop," I instructed. "I'm glad I could tell you personally." We hugged before she went on her way.

As it got closer to closing time, I heard David arrive. I thought this might be a good time to gather the troops and tell them my news. When I joined them, Jean said, "Having a quiet night at home tonight, Miss Anne? It looks like we're going to get a shower."

"I'll be going in just a bit, but I wanted to share something with all of you before you go," I said, struggling to keep a smile from my face. They all stood nearby, waiting for further information. I held up the copy of the ultrasound and they still looked confused.

"This is my son, Samuel Charles Dickson," I announced.

They all stared silently before they cheered.

"I knew it! I knew it!" said Sally.

"Jolly good, Miss Anne," Jean said, reaching to give me a hug.

"Great news, Anne," said David. "We could use another man around this place!"

We laughed.

"I told Kevin you needed to have a boy!" Abbey replied. "He said he wants all boys one day."

"Oh, is this a hint of something in the future?" I teased.

"No, no, no," Abbey said, blushing.

"I think a happy dance is in order!" said Sally as she twirled around. "So does this mean we get to really celebrate?"

"You guys go right ahead. I'm afraid my merlot is currently locked up. Thank goodness I can still have chocolate!"

They all cheered.

They all hung around to share my joy, as they had so many times before. Sam's name was not mentioned, which wasn't sitting well with me.

Was everyone afraid to bring up his name because we had just buried him? Did they think it would upset me? True, I was going to be a single mother, but I was a widow and my son had a father. What was wrong with this picture?

CHAPTER 83

I left the shop feeling like I had experienced a productive day for a change. When I got home, Ella was nearly ready to go upstairs for the day.

"There's tuna casserole in the refrigerator in case you haven't eaten," Ella offered. "Would you like me to warm some up for you?"

"No, I'm fine," I said, making my way to the kitchen. "I may have some in a bit, but thanks anyway."

"Oh, by the way, Jim stopped by to see you," Ella shared. "He had been at the Brody place looking around and decided to drop by."

"I'm sorry I missed him."

"Sylvia shared the wonderful news of your ultrasound today, Anne. You must be so excited."

I nodded, smiling.

"We'll have to get busy turning that room into a

delightful little nursery."

"Yes, we will," I agreed with her and then paused. "Go on up, Ella. You don't need to wait on me. I'll be going up myself soon."

She kissed me on the cheek and up she went.

I wanted to pour myself a glass of merlot to celebrate my good news, but that was no longer allowed, so I went to the refrigerator and poured myself some of Grandmother's lemonade. I was not surprised to see the light flicker on and off. She was still with me despite how quiet she had been. I walked out to the sunporch and watched the rain splattering down all over the patio room. I immediately remembered how it started to sprinkle on Sam and me one night, and he insisted we stay out and get wet. Those little elements of surprise in his conservative personality always surprised me. I regretted that he only got to enjoy the patio for such a short time.

I went into the kitchen to warm up some casserole, convincing myself that someone was depending on my nourishment. I sat down to eat in the dim light of the porch so I could watch the rain. Someday, a little guy would be sitting here in a high chair having dinner with me. It made me smile. These were the thoughts I now had to focus on instead of thoughts of grief.

I got a call from Nancy.

"Well, the word has gotten out that you will not be having a Janeite!" Nancy teased.

I laughed.

"This is the news you were hoping for, so I am so happy for you!"

"Sorry I haven't called, Nancy. It's been a long day. I'm

just having a bite to eat now. I stayed and worked late at the shop just trying to catch up. I don't know if I can do this without a glass of wine every now and then!"

She laughed and agreed that it wasn't fair. "I hope you'll let me be the one to have your baby shower. It will be so much fun!"

"It is exciting, Nancy, but as soon as I feel happy, guilt and sadness come over me," I confessed. "Can you imagine how much I miss Sam tonight? We would be talking about the future of our son if he were here right now."

"I know," she said sympathetically. "You might consider coming to one of our grief sessions. There are other folks suffering like you and it has helped them move on without guilt. They meet in the evening, which would be perfect for you."

"I'll think about it," I said, only to put her off. "I know you mean well."

"We haven't had a good lunch and shopping spree for the longest time," Nancy stated. "I know all the cool places to get good deals on baby furniture, too."

"Sounds good, except that I'm really trying hard to get the greenhouses up and full before the first freeze comes," I told her.

"Yes, but the day away would do you good!"

"We'll see," I said before hanging up.

I went upstairs to check my emails before I showered and got ready for bed. There was one from Ted. Seeing emails from Ted always caught my attention. It read: *Just heard the big news about you becoming a mother. Since I seldom run into you now that I am sober, I thought I would congratulate you and wish you the best. If I can be helpful in any way, please let me know. All the best, Ted*

Ted was the last person I would ask to help me in any way. It was always his goal in life to get married and have children, which was why I had to move on. He was too serious, and to be honest, was rather boring at times. When I met Sam, every need of mine was met. Timing is everything, they say. One day, Ted will find that out when he meets the right girl.

I closed my laptop and prepared for bed. I looked again at the sitting room that was soon to become a nursery. For the first time, it made me smile. My Sammy would be sound asleep there one day. I crawled into bed, pulled the covers back, and reached for my lily quilt. Tonight, I would not shed tears as I held it tight. The softness was so comforting. I felt loved and happy and not alone.

CHAPTER 84

After a great night's sleep, I was ready for a brisk fall walk which would take me next door to check out the latest progress on the Brody property. Kip and three others were working away when I interrupted them.

"I think we'll have the other greenhouse up in the next couple of days if the rain stays away," Kip reported. "I will get those seedlings ordered that we talked about. We'll need some extra labor to get them planted at the same time. What do you have in mind for that?"

"I gave Kevin the number of a woman I met named Beverly and she is anxious to help," I answered. "I can plant, plus we can pull Abbey from the flower shop. I think that if all of us contribute, we can get it done."

"Yeah, Abbey's been hanging out here pretty much since Kevin is involved in the project. I think the two of them are getting pretty serious."

"Really?" It surprised me how quickly the relationship had moved forward. "I've been a little distracted lately, I guess. I'll let you all get back to work. You're doing a great job here." I continued down the hill. On the way, I got a call from Uncle Jim.

"Sorry I missed you last night," I greeted him. "What's going on?"

"I was checking on the progress of the Brody place and was astounded at how much had changed!"

"I know! It's pretty amazing, but we have to get the greenhouses up fast so we can do some planting for spring. I've got a really good crew."

"The barn is great," Uncle Jim stated. "I never noticed it before." He paused for just a short time and then asked, "Say, are you free for lunch today?"

"Well, I suppose so," I said, trying to recall the events scheduled for today. "I put some hours in last night, so I guess I can go."

"Meet me at Charley's around twelve. That will put you close to work," he suggested.

"Great. I'll see you then," I responded, a bit curious as to what this was all about.

I walked back up the hill, panting a little more than usual. When I got back in the house, Ella said she had invited Harry and Mother over for dinner and she hoped I could join them.

"I think Sylvia needs a break and I happen to know that Harry loves my beef stroganoff. I thought it was something small I could do for them."

"Oh, that sounds so good, Ella," I responded. "That was sweet of you. I feel badly that I didn't suggest it."

"You have enough on your mind, little lady," Ella teased.

When I finally arrived at the shop, Phil and Sharon were there checking to see if I had gotten to work yet.

"This visit looks suspicious!" I said.

They laughed.

"I suppose it is," Phil confessed. "The merchants' group met last night and they want to do some kind of quilt show again this winter. We're trying to put together a committee and wondered if you would help."

"Oh my! I always hate to say no, but this time I think I have to! With the baby coming and the changes on my property, I honestly have to let this opportunity pass. I just can't this time around. I hope you understand."

"We know you have a lot going on, but you were such an enormous help last year that we wanted to include you if you wanted to be involved. We certainly understand," Phil said.

"Will you display a quilt in the shop?" Sharon then asked.

"Of course I will," I said, smiling.

"We hope to have the main show in the empty shop where the Tin Cup used to be," Sharon added.

"Good idea. I'm all for it, guys," I agreed. "My plate is just too full right now."

After a few moments of conversation about news on the street, they left and I began to work. The morning seemed to go quickly, and before too long, it was time to meet Uncle Jim at Charley's.

"I'm over here, Anne," Uncle Jim indicated from a booth near the back of the room.

We hugged, and when he told me how good I looked,

I thanked him and assured him I was just happy to be over that feeling of lightheadedness and stomach sickness. After we both ordered a salad, his face took on a very serious look.

"Have you been following the saga of Martingale?" he began.

"Just enough to know it makes me sick," I confessed.

"They've been questioning me about traveling expenses and a few other things from when I used to work there," he reported.

"Well, it doesn't surprise me," I said curtly. "Your connection with Brenda certainly couldn't be helping you."

He looked down, embarrassed. "I know. And you're absolutely right."

"So you didn't know she was involved with Martingale himself?" I asked bluntly.

"Didn't have any idea until I read it in the paper," he said, shaking his head. "I knew she always had money, but I just assumed it was from her husband."

"Thank goodness she left Sam alone," I rolled my eyes. "I was furious when Sam told me she was taking his position as vice president."

"Sam was always focused, which is why Martingale wanted him as president," Uncle Jim said. "Sam was focused on getting that position and he was focused on you. No one ever questioned him about anything because he had so much integrity. Isn't it ironic that Sam turns out to be the one to question what was going on? He could have turned away from what he found, but instead, he did the right thing." He stopped to catch his breath and I think that is when he noticed that this conversation was upsetting me.

"I'm so sorry for all of it and feel I need to be there for

you with Sam gone," he confessed. "Sam had a feeling about how things would go down at Martingale the day I played golf with him. He said several things about that and talked about how worried he was about you. He was concerned about what things would be like for you when all the Martingale news became public. He didn't want anything to hurt your good reputation. I want you to know that. I also want to help you in any way I can now that Sam is unable to be with you. I want you to know that I mean that more than anything. I do, Anne."

"I understand, and I will let you know if I need your help." While I knew he was trying to encourage me, I sensed he needed to feel consoled himself. "I think we all feel like things didn't have to turn out the way they did, but we can't change that. I've gone over and over the conversations Sam and I had and wondered what I could have said to have made him feel better. I know he trusted you and it's nice of you to let me know how you feel, but I am strong, Uncle Jim. Sam knew I was strong the minute we met. I will be fine between my moments of tears. We didn't have many years together like I had hoped, but they were the happiest in my life." I knew I had to stop right there.

"Thanks, Anne," he said, taking my hand. "I just had to get this all out and let you know face to face."

"I understand," I said with a smile. "Now let's eat up!"

CHAPTER 85

I really did it! There was no backing out now. Geraniums and an assortment of spring plantings were ordered for the greenhouses. There would be nowhere to go with them if the greenhouses were not ready. Next on my list was to remind Kevin to schedule Beverly if he hadn't already. I would find any additional help. I couldn't wait to be a part of the first planting! I also couldn't believe this was really happening. I wanted to check the plant accessory catalog that was sent in the mail but that would have to wait. Mother was calling, so I answered my phone.

"I am going to Isabella's around four this evening before she closes and I really want you to come with me so we can pick out something for a baby quilt," she said, cheerfully. "I want the basement quilters to quilt it, so we need to get going on it."

I had to laugh. "Couldn't it wait a month or two?" I

suggested. "I just found out I am pregnant!"

"Oh no, sweetie! We are all just too excited to wait! Isabella said we can't take any chances by picking out something you don't approve of, so we need your opinion," she insisted.

"Okay, okay, I'll meet you there," I agreed, having to smile at her excitement. She had been through a lot of stress with Harry's surgery, and with him on the mend, she was likely eager to get back to anything that felt like normal activity.

As I turned my attention back to other things I might order, I realized my pregnancy was now the center of attention in certain people's lives. My family didn't seem to care much about the development of the Brody property. They had no idea about my future business plans, but they did know what having a baby was all about.

When I arrived at Isabella's quilt shop at four, I was greeted by Isabella and her assistant, Norma. We had started making small talk when Mother joined us.

"I know how busy you are, Anne," Isabella began. "I have pulled some fabrics that I thought you would like. You are having a boy, correct?"

"Yes, indeed," I said proudly.

"Well, I know how much you like more of a vintage look rather than the latest trendy designs. I think you would love the old-fashioned nursery rhyme characters. We were thinking of an embroidered block that different friends and family members could make. Here are the different designs." Isabella tilted a selection of adorable embroidery blocks in my direction. "We can give a block to whoever wants to participate. They can embroider the block and I will set them together before we quilt it. I know how much you enjoyed doing your redwork block, so I thought this was perfect."

"I think I've been set up," I teased. "You two had this all planned."

"These designs are precious, Anne," Mother added. "Frankly, they would be good for a boy or girl. I think it would be nice if you stitched one also."

I grinned at her. "Possibly," I said, looking at all the designs. "We could let them pick which block they like and what color to stitch it in. How about that? I like when they are done in one color."

"I do, too," Isabella agreed. "I bet you'll want to do one in red like you did in the block for the Jane Austen quilt."

"Sure. I could do the Mother Goose block since I am the mother, after all," I teased.

They laughed.

"I'll do the Little Boy Blue block and stitch him in blue," Mother said, picking up the block.

"I'm partial to the Cat and The Fiddle block, which I will stitch in yellow," Isabella said, obviously pleased that I liked their idea.

"I would like to do one for you, too, if that's okay," offered Norma. "This will be such a fun quilt. I am so glad you were a good sport to go along with these conniving women."

We laughed.

"I know when I'm outnumbered! You set it all up, Isabella, but give them a deadline so you have time to sew it together."

"I will," she said, gathering the blocks.

"It's all going on my bill, Isabella," Mother instructed

her with a smile.

"You ladies settle up, but I have to go on home," I said, going toward the door. "Mother, see you tonight for dinner. Don't forget."

CHAPTER 86

T his is so delicious!" I exclaimed. "I don't think I have had this before!"

Ella blushed with pride.

"Ella was nice enough to make this for me every now and then and bring it some on days she would clean for me," Harry explained. "I used to sometimes depend on kindhearted women like Ella and your mother."

"Oh, Harry," Mother said blushing.

"Food is the love potion for men in general, I think," I said as I passed around some dinner rolls. "Sam was the better cook, as you all know, but if I made him spaghetti or some mundane dish, he was so delighted and grateful!"

They nodded and laughed.

"It's a token of love," Harry acknowledged.

"I hope you saved room for dessert," Ella interjected. "My lemon torte cake turned out pretty well."

"I'm in," I said without hesitation. "Who would like coffee? I'll pour that, Ella."

When I came back to fill their cups, Harry wanted to hear about all the changes that were taking place on my property. I gave Kip and his crew as much credit as I could.

"Kevin hopes that by tomorrow we will be able to get the second greenhouse up, weather permitting," I announced. "It will be placed right behind the other one. If you want to watch, it's all quite fascinating. It somehow reminds me of the old-fashioned Amish barn raising. We want to get all the plants in before the first freeze. We've been very lucky so far."

"Oh, I hate the thought of that all coming," Mother said sadly. "Anne and I are not big fans of the winter season."

"That's what will be so grand about the greenhouses," I began. "You can get your garden fix all year long! I plan to move some of my own plants in there as well so I don't have to heat my little potting shed."

"You truly love all this, don't you, Anne?" Harry said fondly.

I nodded. "This project has saved me from going to Sam's grave each and every day," I admitted.

Everyone became silent.

"Did Anne tell you about the fresh lilies on Sam's grave?" Ella asked.

"Oh dear. You don't mean like they were on Albert Taylor's grave?" Mother asked with concern.

"They are just as fresh as they can be," I confirmed.

Harry was mystified.

"I'll explain later, Harry," Mother said, hoping to keep him from asking questions.

We finished dessert and Ella insisted that she would do the cleanup. Harry was tired, and frankly, I was also. I reminded Mother before she left that I would need her official guest list for Thanksgiving. I told her I was pretty sure Helen and Elaine would be coming. As they went out the door, no one said they'd see me at the rising of the greenhouse. I had to remind myself that these matters were not as exciting to others as they were to me.

The next day was cloudy with the threat of a shower, but Kevin thought everything could proceed as planned at two in the afternoon. The temperature was warm for a November day. We had been so lucky in that regard. Before I took my morning walk, I made sure to take pictures of the area before the big change. There seemed to be changes every day. I could hardly keep up with them all!

I had prearranged for the local grocery store deli to deliver some submarine sandwiches and drinks for an after party at the Brody house. I knew everyone would need some refreshments by then. This was the last big step before winter. The rest of our plans would mostly be indoors. The barn was going to get an extension on the backside to make more room for our equipment. I told Kip I didn't want to destroy the original structure of the old red barn and he felt the same.

I invited Sally, Jean, and Abbey to come by after the shop closed, which they were eager to do. Jean said Al would get a great deal of pleasure in coming as well, so I insisted she have him come along.

As Kip and Kevin watched the darkening clouds, they proceeded ahead of schedule. Kevin informed us that the second greenhouse was going to go up easier than the first.

He was in charge and they all responded to his commands as they began preparing the floor. Those of us who were not able to be of help in that phase simply cheered as each step progressed. I marveled at how excited the crew became as it came together.

When Abbey and the others arrived, Kevin lit up as if he had built it all just for Abbey. There was no doubt I was seeing love between the two of them.

There was no hesitation in getting everyone to come into Kip's office to partake of all the food and drink. As I listened to all the laughter and chatter, I knew Sam would have loved every minute of this. I wasn't sure what Mrs. Brody would have thought. Little did we know when I first paid her a visit that this would all become Dickson Properties. She had never wanted to sell to Mr. Taylor, so how would she have responded to the Dickson's takeover? One could only guess at this point, but for now, the greenhouses were completed and soon, the first planting would begin!

CHAPTER 87

I was successful at convincing Nancy to have only a small gathering for my baby shower. I wanted to wait until closer to the due date, but she wouldn't have it. Staying true to her elegant taste, she chose to host a Sunday afternoon luncheon so that my staff would be available to come. It was a perfect opportunity for Nancy to show off her entertaining and cooking skills. She brought out her antique Royal Doulton china of royal blue and gold that was fit for a queen. She said it had been in the Barrister family for many generations.

The menu began with lobster bisque followed by a beet and orange salad. Warm croissants, made from scratch and filled with cheese and ham provided the main course. Dessert stole the show when she brought out a cake with seven thin layers. The white and yellow layers of cake were separated by homemade custard that was to die for. The top of the cake had toasted meringue and coconut.

The relaxing four-hour lunch ended with a toast. Nancy offered everyone their choice of champagne or sparkling water in delicate Waterford crystal. Everyone enjoyed each and every moment, as most of us did not dine in this fashion often, if ever.

Nancy had decorated a round table in the living room to hold the gifts. Even the chandelier above the table had ribbons gracefully draping from it. This, too, carried out the theme of royal blue and gold. Nancy had meticulously attended to every detail of the event and I marveled at her ability to accomplish that while taking care of twin babies. I felt so grateful for her friendship and knew that after I had my baby, the two of us would bond in a way that would only bring us closer.

As I opened each of the gifts, it was like visiting a foreign baby planet. I was unfamiliar with so many things about babies! Nancy was nice enough to explain and comment on each one since she likely had them all! Jean, Abbey, and Sally went together to give me the Rolls Royce of baby strollers. Mother gave me a sterling place setting of a baby-sized plate, knife, fork, spoon, and cup. Mother said she would take it to be engraved when the baby arrived.

"Do babies really use these things?" I innocently asked.

They all laughed.

"Yes, they do at first, anyway," Mother said. "You have a similar bowl and cup, remember?"

The next gift I opened was a beautiful, soft cream-colored baby afghan that Ella had made.

"When did you do this?" I asked, taken completely by surprise.

"What do you think I've been doing all those nights in

my room?" she joked. "I love to knit. My next project will be a little sweater for little Sammy."

"Oh, Ella, that would be wonderful!" I was so touched that she had spent so much personal time making something for the baby. She already did so much to help me out from day to day.

Aunt Julia and Sarah had gone wild, picking out several adorable boy outfits that only a prince would wear. They seemed so tiny to me!

Sue gave me a darling baby book. It came with an elegant pen she said was perfect for a writer like me. "You should keep this in the nursery, Anne, where it's handy to write things down as soon as you can!" Sue suggested. "It's hard to keep up with the record keeping when that second one comes along."

I smiled, but did not reply. The anticipation of a second baby would not apply to me. Instead, I said, "I love that idea, Sue. I will have another book to write now!"

Isabella brought the baby quilt embroidery blocks for people to take if they wished. Isabella gave me a padded baby seat that would allow the baby to sit upright on any flat surface. It had a funny name, but Isabella quilted a cover for it and included a matching bib. It was all too cute! I honestly think this was one gift that made Nancy a bit envious. It was so creative and kind of Isabella to make such a custom gift.

Nancy then handed me another large white package with an amazing curled bow on the top. Unable to find an attached card, Nancy leaned to me and murmured, "The card must be inside."

I tore open the package and inquired about who brought it. There wasn't a response. It then hit me as it did at my bridal shower that Grandmother Davis could once again send an anonymous gift. I looked at Aunt Julia and she looked at Mother. They were all silent until I pulled out a delightful white-on-white quilted baby quilt. The admiration was immediate. Lilies were all entwined in the design. There was no doubt who the gift was from.

"Another lily quilt for me, Mother," I announced as if Mother may have been the one giving it to me.

"You still have the other lily quilt that was to go to Mary, right?" asked Aunt Julia.

"I do, and I don't think I can give it up," I admitted. "I love it so much and it's perfect in my bedroom."

Mother remained silent, as if I had made a selfish remark. I could feel her disapproval.

"Your Grandmother Davis made it?" Sally asked.

"Yes, and it had a lovely note attached to it."

"Oh, there's a note card, Anne," Nancy said, picking it up off the floor.

I was hesitant to open it, but all eyes were on me. I opened the note and read it silently to myself.

These lilies will bring many moments of joy
When you swaddle and cuddle your baby boy.
It is stitched with lots of hope and love,
And blessed by those from heaven above.

"No name, Miss Anne?" Jean finally asked.

I shook my head.

"A gift from the grandmother's spirit, am I right?"

I nodded.

"Holy cow," said Sarah. "Mom, did you get a gift from

Grandmother when I was born?"

"No, honey, Anne has always been her favorite grandchild," Aunt Julia said ruefully.

I was embarrassed and slowly folded the note, holding it between my fingers. I could tell from the looks on several people's faces that they were entirely confused, but I found the growing lump in my throat to be distracting and I knew I couldn't speak. Instead, I busied myself by gathering up remnants of wrapping paper, stray bows, and scattered ribbons. I convinced myself this kept everyone from noticing my watery eyes.

"Thank you all so much for a wonderful day and all the gifts," I said when I had gained composure. "Nancy, everything was delicious and beautiful. I think all my baby weight will come from that amazing cake."

They all laughed and clapped. It had been a most wonderful afternoon and I heard so many people begin to thank Nancy for her hospitality and generosity. Nancy told me Richard would deliver all the gifts to my house, which I appreciated. I took the lily quilt with me. That was for my hands only and I loved it dearly.

CHAPTER 88

The next week, with Ella's help, I cleaned out the waiting room to prepare for Sammy's arrival. With the cream colored walls still in good condition, it would be perfect for a boy or girl. There would be no painting required! I took Sam's things from the room and integrated them into his closet. Ella kept talking to me through the process so I wouldn't have time to think. His fashionable suits, shirts, and ties now hung neatly in place, as if they were going to be used at any moment. For now, it was comforting to have his things still around me.

When we finished, Ella and I looked over Mother's guest list for Thanksgiving. We would have fourteen adults altogether. I always checked with my staff to make sure they had a place to go on any given holiday. As in the past, Jean and Al were invited to their neighbor's house. Sally was cooking for Tim, which was making her a nervous wreck.

Abbey was taking Kevin to New York so he could meet her parents. David had plans with his family as well, so they were all taken care of. I was pleased that Mother reported William would be in town and Allen and Amanda would be joining us.

I invited Uncle Jim and he accepted, despite the rolling eyes of Aunt Julia when I broke the news to her. I told her he would always be family and explained how kind he had been to me since Sam's passing. Then I strategically threw in that he would always be Sarah's father. That analysis always worked. Frankly, I don't think she minded at all.

Ella read off her menu plan, which included a ham along with the traditional turkey. We put all the leaves in the dining room table and held our breath that we could squeeze everyone in comfortably. Mia and Eli would be in high chairs, or under the table as Ella had teasingly suggested! It was amazing how long it took to plan and execute one simple meal. I was a late bloomer in that regard. I remember years ago, all I would have to do was show up with a floral centerpiece and my duties were done!

Helen and Elaine's room was ready and made up, thanks to Ella. I arranged a vase of fresh flowers on their bedside table, without the lilies, of course. Helen made a big deal about being allergic to lilies during one of her visits with us. I'm sure that went over big with Grandmother. I looked over my bedroom and saw the baby lily quilt still looking for a permanent place to rest. It was so cuddly and soft that I could just hold it like a baby. I put it on the back of Sam's cream-colored wing back chair, which I had given him on one of his birthdays. He did love it, but I could count the times he would actually sit there for a moment, unless it was to take off his shoes.

I looked in the mirror and the girls at the shop were right. I was showing some. I hadn't told anyone, but I was certain I felt movement now and then in this tummy of mine. It made me smile. I wonder what the doctor would tell me next. Regardless of all I didn't know about prenatal changes, I did know they would all happen with or without my approval.

I was preoccupied with the seriousness of the greenhouse plant deliveries and getting everything in place before low temperatures became the norm. Supplies were arriving and Sunday was scheduled as a work day. I had asked Abbey to help and I would as well. Kip had called Beverly and some of his handymen. The weather was supposed to cooperate and I had arranged for Pete's Pizza to deliver pizzas for lunch.

An unexpected surprise was a call from Uncle Jim offering for him and Sarah to work as well. His extra help and attention was an interesting and unexpected development for me. Did he feel guilt of some kind or did he really want to be a loyal friend to Sam? I didn't want anyone hovering over me and no one knew that better than Sam. However, I have to admit that I was eager to welcome as much assistance as we could get with planting, so I eagerly took him up on the offer.

When Sunday did arrive, I was like a little kid waiting for Santa. Kevin devised a great plan outlining each person's duties. Kevin wanted me to supervise all the transplanting and placement for the two houses. One greenhouse was going to be filled with only geraniums and the other would be a mixture. Once everything was in place, watering would have to be done. There was a certain amount of confusion at first due to too many chiefs and too few Indians. However, in under an hour, everything was moving smoothly.

Since it was sunny at lunchtime, I suggested we have pizza out on our patio room, which was closer to the greenhouses. Ella made sure we had chairs and supplies. Plus, not everyone was able to take their break at one time. Poor Ella was probably wondering if she was going to be the crew chef in the future.

When everyone stopped at four, Kevin gave me a lecture of sorts. He said we were like parents to hundreds of babies that now had a new home. This was not like the flower shop where, once plants were watered, the caretaker could go about their business. He said this early incubator time would determine the rest of their lives.

I teased him about reading too many how-to books.

He laughed, knowing I was right.

"I'm going to put you in charge of that new Dickson baby when he arrives," I teased.

CHAPTER 89

Thanksgiving eve, Helen and Elaine arrived at the house after insisting they take a cab from the airport. Ella had prepared a light snack for them in case they hadn't had dinner. It was good to see them under lighter circumstances than the funeral, which was the last time they were here. They made the usual fuss over me doing too much by adding the greenhouses and not getting proper rest, despite how good they said I looked.

When I walked upstairs with Helen to show her to her room, she asked to see the nursery. I showed her the empty waiting room and she was shocked that I hadn't begun furnishing or decorating it.

"I've been pretty busy and I still have lots of time to shop," I countered.

"I will gladly pay for what you choose to buy, Anne," she offered. "Pat wants to make a baby quilt, so we're anxious to see what ideas you have for color schemes."

"That's not necessary, Helen. He's just a little baby and I'm sure many colorful things will come his way! However, it is so sweet of her to want to do that. I will get in touch with her." I paused. "Helen, perhaps you can help me with something else. Can you give me some advice regarding when to dispose of Sam's things? I can't bear to do anything. It's such a comfort to still have his things here. It's silly, but what did you do when Sam's father passed away?"

"Oh, honey, I know what you're going through," she said softly as she sat down on my bed. "I didn't move a thing for quite some time. If it comforts you for now, just leave it! A friend of mine told me that you'll know when it's time. Pat did take some of her dad's ties and has started making a really neat quilt from them. Perhaps that might be something you'd like her to do for you."

"Really?" I responded. "I don't think I have ever seen anything like that."

"There are always many charities you could donate his belongings to," she added. "But don't pressure yourself with things like that right now. You'll know when the time is right."

"Good advice," I determined, giving her a squeeze. "That makes me feel better. I miss him so much that I ache all over. Does that ever go away?"

"It never has gone away for me," she admitted. "Mr. Dickson was not always a good husband, but I loved him with all my heart."

The next morning, Ella had breakfast ready whenever anyone was ready to eat. I watched with fascination as she prepared stuffing for the biggest turkey I had ever seen.

Elaine and Helen headed to the cemetery to pay their respects to Sam. It gave Ella and I time to finish setting the table and begin preparing the side dishes. Aunt Julia was in charge of bringing desserts and she assured Ella we would have three different kinds to choose from.

Mother and Harry arrived early. They were prepared to help us in any way they could. Mother knew she had a standing job making the gravy. Harry said he would be the bartender and would offer drinks to everyone when they arrived, just like Sam used to do.

The more I looked at my elaborate table setting, the more I realized I needed place cards. I hated the commotion caused by people trying to figure out where they should sit and I wanted to make sure Aunt Julia did not get placed next to Uncle Jim. While they got along fine, I did not want to make either of them uncomfortable on such a special day. I kept moving the cards around until I got them just right. Jean had arranged the elongated floral centerpiece of reds and oranges and it was stunning. I used the wine glasses with red trim, so it picked up the color nicely.

Hours from now, the house will be filled with chatter, hugs, and hungry souls. This house was perfect for entertaining. I hoped in my heart that Sam would be watching. He would want this holiday tradition to continue. He loved sharing 333 Lincoln.

I don't know when I ever spent so much time in the kitchen! Ella had me slicing, dicing, and peeling. I just did what she told me to do. She, on the other hand, was completely at home in the kitchen and thoroughly enjoyed all the preparations.

I finally went upstairs to shower and dress for dinner.

I looked in the closet and was quite challenged as to how to look festive with my limited wardrobe right now. I settled on a white blouse and black slacks. It called for pearls, of course, which Sam had provided me through the years, starting with our engagement. It would be wonderful if my little Sammy would someday marry someone who would enjoy pearls like I do.

Helen passed by my door as I was putting the finishing touches on my outfit. "You look lovely, Anne," she said politely.

"So do you, Helen," I said as I looked at her fashionable wool suit. "That color looks so nice on you. I really need to go shopping soon," I confessed. "My wardrobe is getting very limited. Hardly anything fits!"

"I think it's supposed to happen that way, Anne," she teased. "By the way, you didn't warn me about the fresh lilies on Sam's gravesite."

"It's all pretty surreal, Helen," I explained, wondering how much to divulge. "I don't know what to say. For all I know, they may be gone the next time I go there."

"That grandmother of yours must have been quite fond of Sam. Pat said we should just smile and enjoy the beauty."

"That's right," I said, nodding. "Many things have happened that I cannot explain, but as long as it's done in love, I just accept it. I realize everyone else may not be able to do that. Grandmother knows I'm hurting and she knows Sam was such a wonderful human being, so it is what it is!"

Helen came over and put her arm around me. "Let's go down and enjoy that wonderful dinner," she suggested, leading the way. "You know I probably won't be back again until that grandson of mine is born."

Everyone seemed to arrive at once. Uncle Jim helped Harry get drinks for everyone and Sarah passed out appealing appetizers that Ella had prepared the day before.

Mia proudly shared the attention her new brother was getting from everyone who hadn't seen him. She was already playing the little mother role as she frequently watched over his needs. Sue seemed to be the picture of calmness as she took it all in. I wasn't sure I would make the drastic change to motherhood so easily. My little one had better be perfect in every way so I would survive!

CHAPTER 90

When Ella and Mother gave the word, I announced that dinner was served and that everyone should look for their place card. As we were walking to the table, Kip said, "Hey Anne, look outside. Perfect timing, I'd say!"

I went to the dining room window and saw the first snowflakes of the season. It was quickly covering the ground.

"Oh Kip, it's beautiful," I said, delighted to see the beauty of snow. "Let it snow, let it snow!"

Everyone gathered at the window and admired the perfect winter scene.

To get everyone back to the table, I tapped a spoon on my glass. "May I have everyone's attention? As your hostess on this special day, I'd like you to join me in a prayer of thanksgiving.

"Dear heavenly Father, we gather to thank you for our many blessings, despite a year of challenges and losses.

Bless those who are not here with us today. We ask that you continue to keep this family together in your care as we look forward to the blessings of the New Year. In your name we pray, amen."

Everyone echoed the amen and we paused in a rather somber silence. Knowing the lovely meal could take on a sadness I did not intend for our time together, I said, "As we enjoy dessert a bit later, I'd like everyone to share something you are particularly grateful for this year, so be thinking!"

The solemn mood was broken as several people made humorous remarks and laughter scattered throughout the room.

"Well done," Harry said, squeezing my hand as I sat down. "I'm so proud of you!"

I smiled back at him as I began my Thanksgiving feast.

Mia had new toys to occupy her in the corner of the dining room. Eli was happy in his chair nibbling on whatever Sue put on his plate. It was fun to see Kip fitting into my family. He had gotten to know most of them rather well this past year.

I was interested in catching up with Amanda, Allen, and William since I hadn't seen them for a while. William bragged about still loving his job and said he intended to remain there for some time. He said he missed his sister, but that she and Allen would be sharing a vacation with him in the near future. Amanda said she missed William as well. Aunt Julia boldly jumped in to ask if Amanda and Allen were planning to have a family anytime soon. They both laughed and said that they hoped it would be sooner rather than later. It was precious to see the two of them together. I imagined that they were going to seem like newlyweds for quite some time to come.

When time for dessert came around, I had to pass on the delicious-looking chocolate pie, lemon bars, and pumpkin pie that Aunt Julia had made. I was so full that I thought my waistband was going to pop.

After everyone had finished eating, I began, "Ella, I must say, you did an outstanding job on the meal."

Everyone clapped enthusiastically. She blushed and smiled.

"Harry, would you begin your thank-you note for the past year?" I teased.

He pushed his chair away from the table as if he were going to give a speech.

I quickly interrupted, "Oh, I guess I should have said in fifty words or less."

Everyone laughed.

"Sure will," Harry said, taking a deep breath. "I have to tell you first of all that I am very grateful to be breathing with one lung."

Mother patted him on the shoulder.

"The gift I am most grateful for is that beautiful bride that kept me very much alive!"

Most of the females at the table breathed a collective "Awww," causing us all to erupt into laughter.

I loved seeing Mother blush.

"There is no question that having Harry around is a Godsend," Mother said next. "I am very thankful for him, but then the close second is that I am grateful that I get to be a grandmother!"

More clapping followed and everyone now had their eyes on me.

"Aunt Julia, you're next," I said, wondering what she would say with Uncle Jim present.

"As you all know by now, I have become an entrepreneur and am thankful that The Written Word is now a reality. I am also grateful for the privilege of having my daughter as a partner in crime!"

This time, it was Sarah's turn to blush as the clapping began.

"Sarah, what might you be thankful for?"

"Oh boy," she began, hesitating. "I am thankful that both my mom and dad are here today with me. That's pretty cool. Secondly, I guess I have to be thankful for my friend Jake, who finally asked me out on a date!"

Everyone chuckled at the sweetness of her responses, causing Sarah to blush once again.

"Oh Sarah," Aunt Julia said as she rolled her eyes.

Now they were all looking at Kip, whose turn was next.

"Dickson Properties has been a chance of a lifetime for me," Kip said, his serious tone catching everyone's attention. "Working with Anne and Sam was amazing and now to be able to help Anne fulfill their dream has become a dream of mine. There is no question that I will always be grateful, Anne!"

I smiled and nodded, feeling a healthy sense of pride regarding what Kip shared.

Amanda's turn was next. "Oh my, this is tough," she confessed. "I will always be thankful for this extended family and I have Anne to thank for that! This husband of mine is so terrific that I thank my lucky stars every day for him!"

Oohs and aahs followed.

"Well honey, that's sweet," Allen responded. "Since

Amanda told me she wanted to be the mother of my children one day, I have thanked the Almighty ever since! We are both looking forward to that! I, too, thank you Anne for letting me enjoy this loving family. I feel very fortunate."

Everyone clapped following his response and Mother told them to let us know the minute they were expecting. People laughed, not sure whether Mother meant it to be a humorous comment or not.

"I'm glad everyone has mentioned more than one thing to be thankful for, because I have two little creatures right here that I am very thankful for!" Sue announced as she reached for Mia who was going wild. Clapping erupted and Mia joined the crowd with clapping as well. It was quite special.

Ella knew it was her turn and she shyly responded. "As you all know, I now have a new roof over my head and for this I am thankful. I am so blessed to know this wonderful family and I look forward to loving the Dickson baby as I would my own grandchild!"

I nodded with approval as everyone clapped.

"Helen, what can you share with us?" I graciously asked.

"I am thankful for my devoted daughters, Pat and Elaine, who are always there for me," explained Helen. "I have my wonderful daughter-in-law, Anne, that has been a blessing as well. I am very excited about my first grandchild this spring. I will count the days until I return for the joyous occasion!"

I joined the others in their applause. Now they all looked toward Elaine.

"This extended family of my brother's is quite an amazing gift!" began Elaine. "Anne has become like a real sister to me. I wish I could see her every day and enjoy this exciting adventure in her back yard. It is a bonus, of course, to be able to share this with my mother and I look forward to becoming an aunt!"

Happy applause followed her comments as well. The thankfulness continued.

"I am thankful for this invitation today, Anne," Uncle Jim said. "You know how much I think of this family. I hope my best friend, Sam, is listening as I tell you all once again how thankful I was to have known him. I am trying to be helpful to Anne, who is one of the sweetest persons I know. She will be a wonderful mother. There is no doubt about that!"

No clapping followed his more serious contribution. However, everyone, including Aunt Julia, had a smile on their face as they turned toward me once again.

"Thank you, Uncle Jim," I said modestly. "I have a multitude of things to be grateful for. There is a little special someone who will be named Samuel Charles Dickson. He will be a constant reminder of how grateful I should be. You'll have to ask me a year from now if I feel the same, but for now, he is a perfect little angel."

They laughed.

"On a serious note, I thank you all for sharing this special day with me. It has been a bittersweet year. I have been so grateful to have had some distractions to keep my mind going in a positive direction and you have helped immensely. I hope we can continue this Thanksgiving tradition together in the future."

Everyone clapped and repeated my sentiments.

"I think it is time to have a thank you toast for our

gracious hostess," Uncle Jim voiced as he raised his glass to me.

"Here, here!" everyone shouted.

CHAPTER 91

The crowd at the table began to disperse and engage in separate conversations throughout the house. Most of the conversations concerned the developing weather and what it would mean for their travel plans. I looked at Amanda and knew I needed to have a conversation with her before she left, so I asked her to join me for a short visit upstairs.

"Well sure, Anne," she said compliantly as she followed me up the stairs. She followed me into our master bedroom and marveled at all the changes since her last visit. She was quite complimentary of my home office. She loved the little sitting room that I explained would be Sammy's future nursery.

"Have a seat, Amanda," I offered. "I have something I want to give you."

She looked at me strangely.

I picked up the lily quilt which was draped over the

edge of my bed as always. I held it close. "This lily quilt was made by your Grandmother Davis," I began to explain. "It has lilies quilted all over it and you know how much she loved lilies."

She nodded, still understandably confused.

"There was a note attached to this quilt when Mother gave it to me. I kept it attached and it reads, *Under these lilies, I weep to sleep.* If you can, just imagine how she wept for the loss of your mother as she gave her up for adoption. I am sure she was saying she wept until she fell asleep."

Amanda remained silent.

"She was thinking of your mother when she made this quilt, I believe."

"Are you sure?" Amanda queried.

"Yes, I'm sure," I said, nodding. "Here in the curved corner it says, *For my dear Mary.*"

She leaned closer, needing to take a careful look. "Oh, Anne," she said, tears in her eyes. "How precious this is. I wish my mom would have known."

"My own mother didn't know or see this when she gave it to me," I explained. "I just loved it because it was all white and because Grandmother had made it. I selfishly used it for my own tears when Sam died. It was such an amazing comfort to me. I thought I'd never stop crying. I felt it was Grandmother comforting me in some way. She has ways of communicating with me."

Amanda said nothing but her eyes were wide as she listened to me.

"I wasn't sure I could give it up since I have used it so much, but now I feel I can," I said, pulling the baby lily quilt off of Sam's chair. "I have my own lily quilt that appeared from nowhere at my baby shower. Of course, it has Grandmother's clues all over it. It's so soft and it's for me and my baby. I love it."

Amanda took a deep breath and tried to smile.

"It's time for this lily quilt to go home where it belongs. Your mother would want you or William to have it. Grandmother never forgot her baby daughter, Mary, despite never knowing where she was."

"Thank you, Anne," she said, embracing the lily quilt herself. "I understand and I will pass on the story and the quilt to my children one day."

We hugged and I knew Grandmother was watching along with others we had loved and lost. I knew with our strong family ties, that future generations would continue with our traditions, as the Colebridge community continues.

In the final novel of the Colebridge Community Series...

Will Sammy arrive as planned?

Will Dickson Properties survive?

Will Jean go back to England?

Will Grandmother Davis move on?

Will Anne ever find love again?

YOUR NEXT FAVORITE

quilting cozy or crafty mystery series is on this page.

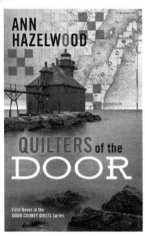

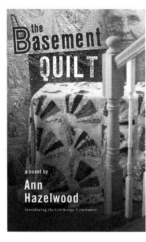

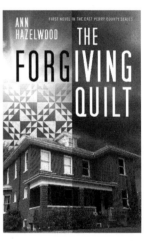

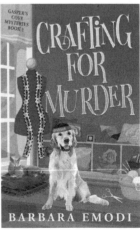

Want more? Visit us online at ctpub.com